Readers of *Amish fiction* love
Jerry Eicher's **Little Valley series…**

Ella Yoder, a young, independent Amish woman, suffered a terrible loss. But now she must pick up the pieces of her shattered life and move forward. Will her faith in God and in her community survive?

Ella and Aden's wedding and their move to their dream house is set for June. The beautiful wedding quilt is almost finished when tragedy strikes and the life they'd planned together is demolished. *Why would God take my true love home?* Ella wonders.

With Aden gone, Ella's future is uncertain. Daniel, Aden's brother, decides to finish Aden and Ella's dream house. Should Ella sell the home and land? Or will she go against tradition and move in to the home alone?

Ella Yoder has moved into her dream house. Living alone for the first time, she ponders her options. How is she to make a living? How will she live without Aden? What is to become of her?

Two would-be suitors soon make their intentions known. Ella agrees to take care of Preacher Stutzman's three motherless girls. Her heart is touched by their love for her. Could their affection be the answer for Ella's shattered heart? Does God want her to marry Ivan so she can be the mother his three children need? But there's the bishop's offer of marriage to consider…and the unusual option of staying single and living in the home Aden designed.

Ella loves the widower Ivan Stutzman's children. She is genuinely devoted to Ivan and keenly aware of his desire to propose, but her feelings stop just short of romance. Is her love for Ivan's children enough to make a marriage work?

When a handsome *Englisha* man seeks Ella out to ask about the Amish faith, Ella is wary but intrigued. She agrees to meet with him—but only with the bishop's approval. Soon Ella is torn between her devotion to Ivan and his children and her growing feelings for the *Englisha*. With dire consequences at stake, Ella must determine what her heart really wants, what God's will is for her, and whether she will stay true to her Amish heritage.

Jerry Eicher's **Hannah's Heart series** follows Hannah Byler's quest for true love within the traditions of the Amish faith. Although life in rural Montana is unfamiliar and at times dangerous, Hannah learns to thrive as she shoulders new responsibilities, deals with sudden hardships, and embraces her place in this small community of believers.

Hannah Miller's Amish faith is solid and her devotion to family and the Amish community unquestionable. Yet her young spirit longs for adventure and romance. Troubling circumstances arise that provide a good excuse to spend the summer in Montana at a relative's ranch.

Her heart awhirl with emotion, Hannah dreams about her future. Sam, the boy Hannah has known all her life, is comfortable and predictable. Peter is a wild card. And Jake is unpredictable and mysterious. Hoping for a dream come true, Hannah leaves the life she's known and sets out for the wilds of Montana.

Hannah and her husband live near a small Amish community in a rough log cabin that is far from everything Hannah holds dear. Anxious about her new role as wife and soon-to-be mother, Hannah understands she must learn to control her anxious heart if her marriage is to survive.

When her husband loses his job and answers the call to ministry, they discover hardships will either drive them apart or draw them closer together. With winter pressing in and money scarce, Hannah is determined to find hope despite the fearful conditions.

Hannah is adjusting to married life. While her husband works long days as a furniture maker and minister, she stays busy keeping their home in order. Both anticipate their baby's birth with joy.

When word of a Mennonite tent revival spreads and worry about losing church members mounts, Hannah's sister arrives and quickly catches the eye of a bachelor whose brother left the church during the last revival. And when a neighbor—an *Englisha*—announces his interest in one of the Amish widows, Hannah's husband is caught in the middle of the controversy.

Will Hannah and her husband's determination to stay faithful to God and the traditions of their church survive the turmoil?

MISSING YOUR SMILE

Jerry S. Eicher

HARVEST HOUSE PUBLISHERS
EUGENE, OREGON

Cover by Garborg Design Works, Savage, Minnesota

This is a work of fiction. Names, characters, places, and incidents are products of the author's imagination or are used fictitiously. Any resemblance to actual persons, living or dead, or to events or locales, is entirely coincidental.

MISSING YOUR SMILE
Copyright © 2012 by Jerry S. Eicher
Published by Harvest House Publishers
Eugene, Oregon 97402
www.harvesthousepublishers.com

Library of Congress Cataloging-in-Publication Data
Eicher, Jerry S.
Missing your smile / Jerry S. Eicher.
    p. cm. — (Fields of home ; bk. 1)
ISBN 978-0-7369-3943-0 (pbk.)
ISBN 978-0-7369-4244-7 (eBook)
1. Amish—Fiction. 2. Amish women—Fiction. I Title.
PS3605.I34M57 2012
813'.6—dc22

                                                    2011021196

Printed in the United States of America

12 13 14 15 16 17 18 19 20 / LB-SK / 10 9 8 7 6 5 4 3 2 1

CHAPTER ONE

✦

Susan Hostetler drew in her breath, her eyes drawn down the crowded street to the odd sight. *Why on earth would Amish people be coming to the Oyster Festival in Asbury Park?* she wondered. Hadn't she moved far enough away from Indiana and her Amish roots?

She resumed slicing the roast beef as an older man and his wife in front of the concession stand stared at her, waiting for their sandwiches.

"Sorry about that. Something just gave me a start," she said. "I'll have this ready in a minute."

The couple turned in the direction of Susan's gaze and then exchanged glances.

"I don't see anything," the woman muttered. "Unless it's those Amish folks."

The man shook his head. "They're pretty harmless. They're not murderers on the loose or anything." He laughed.

Susan kept her eyes away from them, laying pieces of roast beef on the bread before adding lettuce and tomatoes. Let them laugh, and let the two think what they wanted. Sure the Amish weren't murderers, but there was one of them back home who murdered the heart, but that likely didn't count in the *Englisha* world. The sad thing was, it hadn't counted much in the Amish world either. She should have burned her wedding dress instead of burying it in the cedar chest at home.

Her *mamm* had said, "It's each one's choice whom to marry." Well, Thomas had chosen, and she could also choose, regardless what anyone said about it.

"There," she said, wrapping the two sandwiches and shoving them across the temporary counter. "You can pay at the register."

They both raised their eyebrows and looked sideways at each other before moving toward Laura, who was working the register at the moment.

Across the street, the Amish couple was moving closer to the sandwich stand. The man was tall, his beard coming down almost to his fourth shirt button. His wife stood beside him holding a little girl. The mother was in her white *kapp* and the girl in a black bonnet—dressed just as the Amish women had done for many years. Her people would never change. But she would. And change would help the pain go away.

The crowd shifted and another young Amish couple appeared, following closely behind the first. He was round, like a short barrel, his wife skinny as a rail behind him. Neither of them carried a child. Susan caught herself hiding her face behind her hand, but then she realized how foolish it was. She no longer looked Amish without her *kapp*, and what would it matter anyway?

"We'll take two roast beef with all the toppings," a girl's voice said in front of her, bringing Susan back to the booth. "*Yah*…coming right up!" She glanced at the two girls before her and tried to smile as she began the sandwiches. *What is wrong with me? Amish talk is supposed to be out of my system by now! And here I am saying* yah *again at the mere sight of Amish people.*

"So how are you two girls doing?" Susan asked as she laid out the bread. At least she could try being *Englisha* again.

"Okay, I guess," one said with a shrug. "Just the usual stuff life gives you. Most of it stinks."

The girl beside her giggled. *They can't be out of middle school,* Susan thought. She finished wrapping the sandwiches and said, "Well, maybe these will make the day go better for you."

The girls smirked at each other and moved down to pay Laura.

Down the street, the Amish couples were coming closer. Surely they wouldn't stop at Laura's stand. Susan really didn't want to see Amish people up close right now. There were dozens of vendors lining the street. It would be the luck of the draw either way, but she was the only one selling roast beef sandwiches, and all the Amish Susan knew sure liked roast beef.

I'm trying to be Englisha *now. Even if they stop here, they won't know I used to be one of them,* Susan reminded herself.

"Are you okay?" Laura asked, walking over to stand beside her.

"Oh *yah...*yes...of course," Susan said. "Why do you ask?"

"You were a little short with the older couple. I know this festival brings a lot of business, and we're all tired. Still, it's not good manners to be abrupt, even if we won't ever see these people again."

"I'm sorry," Susan said. "I really am. I'll try to do better."

"That's okay." Laura smiled. "You did better with the two girls. I know we can't talk with everyone, especially when things get busy, but it's a nice service touch when we can."

"I know," Susan said. And she did know. Her life so far had taught her that much.

The Amish couples paused across the street, now standing close together, their heads leaning toward each other. *How like home, so natural and at ease they are.* Susan forced herself to glance away. It would do no good to think about such things. She had left all that behind. This was her new life.

In spite of herself, she looked their way again. They were talking, their lips moving and motioning with their hands. None of them looked aware of the looks they drew from curious people around them. *Insulated, that's what they are,* Susan thought. She no longer was. The world they were so guarded against, she had welcomed. At least there was comfort in the fact that they didn't know who she was, and she didn't really know who they were.

Susan brushed the strands of her long hair back over her shoulder, tucking them under her collar. There was no time to tighten the hair band, and it would make no difference anyway. A girl without a *kapp* would be *Englisha* to them, even with her Amish-looking dress. No questions would be aroused unless they thought she looked like a Mennonite girl. And what would an Amish or Mennonite girl be doing in a concession stand in Asbury Park?

The Amish were crossing the street now, coming straight toward her.

Susan clasped her hands, daring to look at them only in the last seconds before they stood in front of her.

"Hi," she said as casually as she could. "Can I help you? It's a nice day, isn't it?"

They ignored her questions as they searched the sandwich menu above her head. Quick glances between them followed, but no words.

"We'll take four roast beef sandwiches," the older man finally said. "With everything you have on them." His face was younger than she'd thought now that he had come up close. It was framed by his large beard. His eyes were a piercing blue.

Susan turned and busied herself with the bread and roast beef. She reached for the lettuce, peppers, onions, tomato, and mayonnaise. *Why did the man have blue eyes? And why did they cut so deep into her? Was he a relative of Thomas's? No, of course not. And besides, many of her people had blue eyes.*

She could tell he was watching her as she worked. She suddenly asked, "How do you want your lettuce? I can add extra pieces. And the tomatoes?" What questions. Why had she asked them?

The man didn't seem to notice anything strange. He simply replied, "*Ach*...that's plenty."

"You from around here?" the large man's wife asked with a smile.

Susan tried to keep breathing, the warning racing through her brain. *Don't be tricked into speaking their language.*

"I live in Asbury Park for now," she said. "I've been here for a few weeks."

"You do know how to make a *gut* sandwich," the portly man with the piercing eyes said. The large man next to him was silent, still eyeing the sign above him.

"I'm glad you think so." Susan slid the first sandwich across the counter and turned to wrap the others. "We also have drinks. Laura will ring you up."

"*Yah*, a Pepsi is what I want," the large man said, pushing back his hat.

"You should drink water, that's what I say," his wife said.

They all laughed.

"He's a big one," piercing eyes said, glancing at Susan again. "We don't work him hard enough on the farm."

"That would be the cabinet shop," the large one said. "We're from Lancaster County. We're spending the day visiting the ocean. Thanks for the sandwiches."

They nodded, moving on toward Laura, piercing eyes producing a well-worn billfold from his front pocket. Susan watched out of the corner of her eye. They mustn't notice her interest, but really there was no way they could even imagine the truth.

As the two couples paid and then walked away, Laura turned to Susan. "You know those people?"

"No," Susan said, her eyes still following them.

"Nice people, the Amish are," Laura said, watching Susan's face. "You look frightened."

"I'm not. Really I'm not." Susan forced a smile, pulling her eyes away from the bonnets bobbing in the distance. She had to get over this. Wasn't making a clean break from the past part of her plan?

"You wouldn't know them from Indiana?"

"No." Susan shook her head.

"I thought they might be from your home community."

"Oh," Susan laughed, "there are Amish all over the place." She turned to face an approaching older couple. "Good afternoon! Are you enjoying the festival?" she asked.

"Everything except the oysters," the man said as he ran his hand through his hair.

"He's not much for oysters," his wife explained. "Fix him a big, fat roast beef sandwich, if you would. No mustard and no pickles."

"Coming right up!" Susan said. "Wheat or white bread?"

"Make that wheat," the wife said, reaching up to run her hand over her husband's cheek. "It's better for him."

"She's just like that. A real health case of late." He laughed, his eyes on her face.

"Well…" the wife said, stroking his cheek again.

Susan sliced the roast beef, trying not to glance at them. Her mom and dad would never act like that in public.

"Have you been married long?" she asked, laying a slice of roast beef on the bread. Another dumb question that was, but it just slipped out.

A broad smile spread across the man's face. "Longer than you can imagine, dear."

"It was fifty years ago, last week," the wife said, still stroking his cheek absently. "And we just had to come back to Asbury Park to celebrate."

"Even with the oysters." He laughed again.

"We used to bring the children here for the festival," the wife said, the words flowing out of her. "They always wanted to see the ocean. All three of them did. Not for swimming mind you, but just seeing the water. That's why we never came in the summer when everyone else comes. We'd rent rooms for the day, right on the beach, and stay up most of the night listening to the waves rolling in. For farm kids, it was the highlight of their year. We'd walk the boardwalk the next day, buy sandwiches, and little things. We couldn't afford much in those days, but we did what we could. The trip was expensive enough."

"We have a farm well north of Philly," he said. "Retired now. We rent out the place, and the kids are all gone on to bigger and better things. I guess farming isn't too profitable, so I can't blame them."

"We decided to come back this year, just the two of us," the wife said. "And it's a full moon tonight. You ought to go and watch it rise yourself. There's something special about the light on the water, almost like heaven opens up its gates for just a few minutes and lets us see inside."

"We're a little religious," the man said, bobbing his head. "Hope that doesn't offend you."

"Oh, not at all," Susan said, adding tomato to the sandwich. "I'm glad you told me that. I've never watched the moon come up over the ocean before."

"Are you a farm girl?" he asked.

"*Yah*..." Susan felt the red run up her neck.

"I thought so," he said, reaching for the sandwich.

"Oh, the sandwich," Susan said, handing it to him. "I'm sorry. I was distracted for a moment."

"Thanks for listening," the wife said. "It was good to talk to you."

They nodded and moved toward Laura. The man handed the sandwich to his wife before pulling out his billfold. Susan noticed it was worn and well used, the leather scuffed and even broken in spots. His fingers trembled as he extracted the bills.

"Nice talking to you," he said, with a backward glance. Susan nodded, and they moved down the street. The woman hung onto his arm, and he slipped his hand around her waist. They disappeared into the throng.

"A nice couple," Laura said. "The salt of the earth type. You handled them well. You're a good listener. You'd make a good counselor. People warm up to you and spill their secrets."

"No," Susan said with a nervous laugh. "They probably needed someone to talk to at the moment. Besides, I couldn't be a professional counselor. I only have an eighth grade education."

Laura raised her eyebrows. "You dropped out? That's too bad. You really need to finish school if you want to make a go of things. I know you like the job at the bakery, but there's more of the world out there than what I can offer. And you need an education for it. How old are you? Twenty? I can't remember what you told me."

"A little more than that."

"Well, I know a woman doesn't like to give her age. But you do look twenty or less. It must be the farm life."

Susan took a deep breath. "I'm not a dropout. I don't want you to get the wrong impression."

"So what do you call it then? Is there an Amish word for skipping school?"

"An eighth-grade education—that's all they give us."

"Around here it's called dropping out. It's also a little more serious. Really, Susan, you ought to look into completing your schooling. You could take your GED test; study for it in your spare time. You could go from there once you passed. I might even be able to convince Robby to drive you to the community college for night classes."

"You've already been more than kind," Susan said. "But really... I don't know about more schooling. It's not well looked upon by the community."

"Oh. It's our choice, though, what each of us chooses to do with our lives," Laura said. "And you don't have to talk to me about your past or what you're running from. I'm more than willing to help you get on your feet again. I don't think the Amish community has much say in our world, do they?"

"No," Susan said, her eyes searching the mass of people on the street. "The community's eyes are hard to get away from though. It's not easy."

"I suppose not," Laura said. "But I'll do what I can to help. Someone once helped me when I was young and trying to start over."

"I appreciate it more than you know," Susan said. "I'm sure you've wondered why I'm here." It was the opening Susan felt she had to give her employer. Laura deserved to be told more than what she'd confided already. Laura didn't have to give her a job. Sure, Laura's sister had given her a recommendation, but that didn't mean Laura had to hire her…or rent her the little apartment above the bakery.

Laura smiled. "No, I don't need to know, Susan. I remember what it was like trying to get a fresh foothold. Bonnie assured me you'd be a good worker, and you have been. I don't want to pry. I'm just glad I can help."

"I was seeing a boy. For a few years…" Susan said in spite of Laura's words. "I loved him a lot."

"Yes?" Laura encouraged, her voice sympathetic.

"Then he fell head over heels for my best friend, Eunice," Susan continued, keeping her eyes on the street. "I caught them kissing each other one Sunday night when I walked out to ride home with him."

"Lord, help us all." Laura sighed. "So that's the big dark secret. Here I thought—my sister not withstanding—that you might be a murderess running from the law. Thank goodness I followed my instincts and not my fears."

"You didn't really think…?"

"Of course not, dear. It was a joke."

"I'm so sorry. It's just that, well I had to get away from the situation."

"So why Asbury Park?"

Susan shrugged. "I worked for your sister and really liked her. After the…situation…happened, I confided in her. She suggested I come here if I wanted to start over. I thought about it, and it seemed like a good idea. I couldn't stay at home anymore. I couldn't bear to see Thomas. The more Bonnie told me about Asbury Park, the more I thought the place sounded good—the city, the possibility of a job, the ocean nearby. Then Bonnie called you, and you said yes to interviewing and possibly hiring me."

"Bonnie didn't tell me all that, but I guess people make big life decisions for even lesser reasons. Sorry to hear about the boyfriend. So you were in love with him?"

"More than I wish I had been."

"Is he dating this Eunice now?"

"I don't know," Susan said.

"He won't be showing up here some dark night looking for you?"

Susan's eyes got big.

"I'm *kidding* again!" Laura laughed.

Susan smiled. "No, I doubt Thomas would ever do that."

"He must have been something," Laura said. "Really, for a girl to uproot her whole life to get away. But you shouldn't feel alone. Others have gone through the same thing and thought the same things. I'll be here to help you through this if you need me."

"I don't want to be a bother. Really I don't."

"I know you don't. And you're not, dear. Trust me on that."

"I'm not going back to Indiana anytime soon." Susan turned to meet Laura's gaze.

"Then on to your new life in Asbury Park," Laura said. "And here comes someone for a sandwich, so I think we'd best stop gabbing."

"Hello," Susan said as she turned to face a young man. "Can I help you?"

It is the right thing to do, she told herself, *the staying in Asbury Park. It's the perfect place to start over.* She had been certain since the night she arrived.

"A sandwich with all the trimmings," the young man in front of her said.

"White or wheat bread?"

"That would be white, please." He smiled. "White bread goes down easier."

"I suppose so," Susan said, returning his smile.

I really need to stop thinking about boys, Susan thought. *But how does a person do that in the* Englisha *world? Is merely talking with a nice boy okay? The rules seem scarce out here.*

She sliced the bread, feeling the boy's eyes on her face. He seemed decent, but she was obviously not a good judge of such things. She had thought the best about Thomas—and what a mistake that had been. She had believed him when he said their love was a pure one, placed in their hearts by God. He had called it a sanctified love.

Ha! She trembled to think that it was so sanctified as to be cast aside and trampled underfoot when his heart longed for someone else. How stupid she had been. What was it the preachers talked about Sunday morning in church? The stories of people who cast pearls in front of swine. Well, one thing was for sure—she would never look for love again. Not among her own people, at least. Thomas had cured her of that.

"Thank you," the boy in front of her said when she handed him the sandwich. He turned to pay Laura, pulling out his billfold. It was shiny, the leather new, and even the bills inside seemed pressed and crisp.

Like my new start in life. It will be much better this way, she thought, watching him disappear into the crowd.

"Things should wrap up soon around here," Laura said.

"The festival goes until seven, doesn't it?" Susan asked.

"Yes, but there won't be much call for sandwiches from now till closing time. People will start drifting into the restaurants for supper."

"You have to stay open though."

"But not you," Laura said with a firm look. "Robby will be here by five. We can handle things, including cleanup."

"But I can stay, really."

"Thirty more minutes and then you're gone," Laura said. "Take some time to walk the festival or whatever else you wish to do. After all, it's your first time, and Asbury Park is at its finest during the festival."

"I guess it would be nice to have some time off. Perhaps I can walk out to the ocean," Susan said.

A man approached and, after a brief look at the menu, said, "Two roast beefs." A woman, obviously his wife, came up beside him.

"White or wheat?" Susan asked. "And what would you like on it?"

"White," the man said. "And we'll take just the roast beef and salad dressing. Nothing else."

Susan watched them out of the corner of her eye, as she sliced the meat. They didn't look happy—not like the earlier couple. Was it the farm perhaps that created love between people? Were these city people? Did love perhaps not grow in the city? They did look like city people—the man's blue-checkered shirt freshly ironed, the woman in black dress slacks.

She spread the salad dressing, glancing at them as she worked.

"That's too much dressing." The man's voice was sharp. "You'll choke us to death, not to mention what will happen to our arteries."

"Lettuce helps the arteries—and the rest of the body," Susan said, forcing a smile. "Shall I put on a few pieces?"

"What are you, a dietitian? Just take most of the salad dressing off."

Susan removed most of the salad dressing, scraping it with her knife. She shook the residue into the wastebasket.

"Are you two from a farm?" she asked casually.

The man stiffened.

The woman with him laughed, punching the man in the ribs.

"There you go, Herbert. So much for incognito. The young lady sees right through your disguise."

The man snorted. "We can't even get into town for a day without someone smelling the barnyard on us."

"Oh, I didn't mean that," Susan said. "I come from a farm myself."

The woman laughed. "We're dairy farmers, dear. And thanks for popping Herbert's bubble. I told him we didn't need to spiff up, that we might as well come in our regular farm clothing."

"Right!" he snorted, reaching for the sandwiches.

Susan pushed them across the counter, and he grabbed them with both hands. Callused hands, now that she looked.

"Sorry, I asked," she said. "I meant no harm."

"Don't you worry, dear," the woman said. "It was good for him."

"You do keep life interesting," Laura said, as the couple left. "I don't think Asbury Park's had an Oyster Festival quite like this one before."

"I didn't mean to offend him," Susan said. "The question just came out."

"You're doing fine." Laura patted her on the arm.

"It's the clumsy Amish in me." Susan's voice quivered. "I intend to get rid of all my Amishness."

"Now why would you want to do something like that?" Laura asked. "It's kind of cute, if you ask me."

"I'm getting rid of it exactly for that reason." Susan clipped off the words. "I don't want to be cute anymore. I don't want to be taken advantage of and have my heart pulled out by its roots."

"That boy must have been some heartbreaker," Laura said, shaking her head. "Can't say I blame you though. But don't go trying to change too much of yourself. We need all kinds in the world, even the Amish. They are good people."

"I'm going to change!" Susan snapped. "Whatever it takes, whatever it costs. It will be worth it. And I don't want to ever see Thomas again."

"Isn't that a little violent? I thought you people were the nonviolent type? Like Martin Luther King."

"We are—except when it comes to matters of the heart. Then you can have it torn out by the roots."

"Well," Laura said, "it's not the first time a girl's heart has been broken. Take things a little easy, and don't be too hard on yourself. It could have been worse. You could have married the guy and found out all of this afterward."

Susan drew in her breath at the words.

"Now here comes Robby," Laura said. "So I guess you can go. Enjoy yourself for the rest of the afternoon. I'll see you at the bakery tomorrow at five, as usual. Bright and early."

"Even that's Amish," Susan muttered.

Her comment produced another laugh from Laura.

CHAPTER TWO

S usan took off her apron, folded it, and waited as Robby swung his legs over the side of the concession stand and stood before her, brushing loose strands of his shoulder-length hair away from his eyes. He was a tease, this boy. Almost a pest if he weren't so funny. The best approach, she had learned, was to fire back at any provocation.

"Don't tell me you're leaving already," he chided.

"Your mom said I could quit early," Susan said. "You have any objections?"

"No, of course not." Robby glanced up and down the street. "How has business been?"

"What, you think I scared people off?" Susan teased.

"What's into her?" Robby glanced at his mother. "Have you not fed her today?"

Laura laughed and said, "You two, calm down. Business has been a little slow this afternoon, but there were long lines all morning. Most of the baked goods were gone before twelve. We should have brought more, but you never know."

"Well, I'm here now," Robby said. "And the fort is under control."

"Ignore him," Laura said. "And go. We can take care of things."

Susan opened the small gate in the front of the stand and stepped out into the street.

"Don't spend all your money on candy," Robby hollered after her.

Susan ignored him and walked on. Robby's heart was in the right place, just like his *mamm's* and *daett's* hearts were. *Da Hah* had shown much grace in leading her to this *Englisha* family, there was no doubt about that. And here she was with the same *Da Hah* guiding her in the *Englisha* world who was even at this moment guiding her *mamm* and *daett* back in the community. This was not an easy thing to believe, but it was true. *Da Hah* was helping her adjust.

"What are you doing tonight?" Robby hollered louder, and Susan gave him a backward wave without turning around. She quickened her pace down Cookman Avenue. *Perhaps I'm deceived about* Da Hah's *help,* Susan thought, remembering what Deacon Ray had said so many times at church services. No doubt if he were here, he'd tell her she couldn't tell the difference between right and wrong anymore. She shivered at the thought.

Where was her coat, now that evening was coming on? She should have brought it, but it was still hanging in the closet at the apartment. Well, she would make do for now. Besides, the coat looked quite Amish. Even with Deacon Ray haunting her memory, the time had definitely arrived to change some things: including a new coat and some proper *Englisha* clothing.

But now there was supper to think of. She could have prepared a sandwich before leaving the stand, but roast beef turned her stomach after seeing and smelling it all day.

The bustle of the crowd grew thicker the further she walked. People were bumping into each other, almost pushing to get through. Susan hesitated, dashing in between people when there was a chance, standing tightly against the buildings when there wasn't. She noticed a set of concrete steps and climbed them. They didn't lead anywhere but to a small landing overlooking the street. That was enough. She had to get out of the crowd to catch her breath. Susan paused on the landing and looked up and down the street. How different the city was from home. Beautiful in its own way, painted with splashes of color from the people in the crowded street adding charm to the varied architecture of the buildings. *Is this what I really want? Can this become home?* "It's worth a try," she said out loud. She traced her steps back down to the street, turning sideways to enter the crowd between two women. Who said being Amish was the right thing anyway? Perhaps Thomas's crush on her best friend had been exactly what she needed. The push to get her thinking correctly. Otherwise she would have turned out like all the other women she knew—married with children running around her feet. Spending her days with diapers flooding the wash bucket and hanging them outdoors to flap in the wind.

But here in Asbury Park…this was a brand-new world, wide open with possibilities. Let the Amish visit Asbury Park if they wished; let them remind her of what she had left behind. She would not turn back.

Thomas is already becoming a distant memory, is he not? Susan pressed against the side of a high building, feeling the concrete stucco dig into her back. Three huge, rough-looking men with tattoos walked by, their laughs at some private joke rumbling as they disappeared into the crowd.

Susan stared after them for a moment. It was to be expected that there would be such men in the *Englisha* world, but thankfully there were others too. Men who were kind, gentle to their girlfriends, educated, mysterious, and wise in ways an Amish boy couldn't even imagine.

Susan rubbed her hand across her eyes and then reached in her pocket for a handkerchief. She would find such a kind man here in the *Englisha* world. He had to be somewhere. A man who really believed in love, who didn't say words without meaning them, who didn't dream up promises while delivering nothing. Someone unlike Thomas, with all his flowery words that had meant nothing.

Just ahead of her appeared Laura's bakery nestled on Main Street, its familiar windows beckoning. Susan dug into her pocket for the apartment key, her fingers finding nothing. Surely she hadn't accidentally thrown it out when she used the handkerchief? Laura had a spare key, but that would require a long walk back to the concession stand.

Susan searched in her other pocket, her fingers digging deep. It was high time she purchased an *Englisha* purse like other women had. Perhaps then she wouldn't lose her key. But carrying a purse would require walking around looking like…well, certainly not Amish. Yet it needed doing.

What is it about today, she wondered, *that seems like a giant leap forward? Did the two Amish couples at the stand affect me so deeply?*

Apparently. Leaving home had been such a gigantic leap off a cliff that she'd thought once she'd landed and caught her breath, nothing else would be such a big deal. But perhaps that wasn't true.

Now, though, she had to enter the apartment, and there was no key. There also was nothing to do but retrace her steps and look for it. Perhaps the crowd would be thinning by now. Perhaps the key had fallen along the sidewalk and would be lying in plain sight. *Perhaps*. She didn't like the idea of relying on such chances as "perhaps."

Susan walked back, taking her time, keeping her eyes sweeping back and forth on the sidewalk and street. It wouldn't be dark for a while. Streetlights would come on then, but they weren't as effective in searching for a key as was *Da Hah*'s sun. She came to the end of Main Street, paused, and glanced up Cookman Avenue. The crowd had not thinned as she'd hoped. Most likely a little, itty-bitty key would long ago have been cast out into the street by the shuffle of hundreds of shoes. Hoping it had somehow landed somewhere easily spotted seemed about as foolish as thinking Thomas wasn't who he obviously was. Yet there was no choice but to go up Cookman toward Laura's stand. If she didn't find the key along the way, she'd have to ask Laura for her spare.

"You lost your key?" Laura would say, smiling in sympathy. But the smile wouldn't help take away Susan's feeling of stupidity over such a thing to do. At home on the farm there were less places to look for lost things, unless they were buried in the dirt. Even then they usually turned up. Perhaps because people on the farm cared more about lost things than city folk? Susan raised her eyes, glancing at the faces sweeping past her. There were so many people, most of them laughing, talking to each other, deep into their own worlds. Why would anyone care about a lost key?

Ahead of her the concrete steps rising to the landing where she had taken refuge came into focus. Could she have dropped the key up there? She hadn't taken anything out of her pockets until later. Yet as she reached the top step, Susan saw the glitter of the late-afternoon sunlight reflecting off metal. The key lay there, balanced on the very edge of the step. She reached down for it and slipped it into her pocket, keeping her fingers wrapped around the cold metal for the walk home. There would be no more chances taken tonight with the key. *Da Hah* had come to her rescue this once, and one should not tempt *Da Hah* with a lost key twice in one day.

Finally, with the crowd behind her, she once again reached the bakery. A little door next to the baker's side door opened onto the street. Sliding the key into the lock, she opened the door and picked up her mail that had been dropped through the slot to the floor inside. There were the usual flyers, a business-looking letter, and there on the bottom, an envelope with handwriting she recognized so well. *Mamm* had written again, and on a day like this. Well, it would make no difference. As much as it hurt *Mamm* and *Daett*, she was not going back. Time would surely heal all wounds, including her parents' disappointment in her choice to leave the community.

The stairs to the apartment above the bakery were off to the side of the bakery itself. As she slowly made her way up the steps, the usual creaking that had always been comforting was, tonight, a painful reminder of the old farmhouse stairs at home.

A person didn't simply pull up stakes, leaving a life of twenty-one years behind without the heart complaining. She knew that. It wouldn't be human to not feel the loss, and she certainly was human. Thomas had proven that, even if he had accomplished nothing else.

At least she hadn't been excommunicated. That would have been a right dandy mess to deal with. At twenty-one she should have been baptized, and so should have Thomas. His actions with Eunice now revealed what the rascal had been up to. All along Thomas must have carried his doubts about her. She had wanted to be baptized two years ago, but he said it wasn't necessary, that they should wait until it was closer to their wedding date. Thomas had said one could be right with God without baptism.

Or maybe he had planned to join the Mennonites and not bothered to tell her before Eunice swept him off his feet. It had been "a moment of weakness," he had called it, but she had known better. The boy had fallen in love with her best friend a few months after Eunice's family moved into the community.

And she had been left like a cold potato for a hot one. Lovely, charming Eunice, who talked with her like they were sisters. Wonderful Eunice had dared steal Thomas's heart. Eunice was better looking, certainly smarter, and wore those short dresses that barely made it past the *Ordnung* rules. Was that what drew Thomas to her? Well, she would show him what an Amish girl could do. Not that it made any difference to Thomas now, but it certainly felt good to show him anyway.

Smart and short dresses indeed! Susan jerked her handkerchief out of her pocket and the key was sent clattering across the apartment floor. She blew her nose. It was high time she went on adapting to *Englisha* ways. Crying over spilled milk accomplished nothing. Only action could heal the pain. Wasn't that what the old people always said? Well, not exactly. They had said *work did the job,* but let them see what her fresh application of that saying proved to be. She would take up the *Englisha* life and be happy in this new world. Wasn't this what the *Englisha* called "moving on" with life?

With a flourish Susan tossed the letters on the kitchen table, sliding them far enough across so they fell off the other side and onto the floor. She ignored them and, in the late-evening light that shone in through the double-front window, looked for a match. With a flick of her wrist, she struck the match under the drawer bottom, bringing it over to the kerosene lamp. The match sputtered, caught, and sent a wide flame across the wick.

Susan replaced the glass chimney and stared at the light. *How foolish this is,* she thought. *I'm still lighting a kerosene lamp when I could be flicking an* Englisha *switch and flooding the apartment with light.*

Susan carried the kerosene lamp to the kitchen table. Setting it down, the light flickered off the apartment walls. She wondered if Laura knew she never used the electric lights in the apartment? For some reason Susan just couldn't make that small leap to electricity. But surely she would…soon.

She picked up the letter from home. She held it between her fingers, studying the well-formed, familiar handwriting. She glanced at the light switch on the wall. After a moment, she walked over to it.

She steadied her hand and reached for the little white plastic toggle. It would be so easy…just a small push and it would be over. And yet she couldn't.

"The next time I'll use the *Englisha* light," she whispered, her fingers motionless on the wall.

Long seconds she waited, listening to the dull roar of traffic on the street, before walking back to the kitchen table. Her letter was still grasped in her fingers. She buried her face in her arms and wept. The soft light of the kerosene lamp thrown out over the table played on her long hair.

CHAPTER THREE

Daylight still lingered outside of Menno and Anna Hostetler's home; the last rays of the setting sun painting great swatches of red across the western sky.

"It will be a *gut* day tomorrow for the fall plowing," Menno said, looking out the kitchen window.

"For an old man like you, don't you think it's time to turn the farm over to the younger generation?" Anna asked, sliding the loaves of fresh bread out of the oven. "With the hopes of Susan's wedding gone, couldn't you speak with Deacon Ray about finding a young man to help on the farm? What if I go out and find you fallen off the plow some morning? Or what if you're working in the back field, and the horses come home alone in the evening?"

"You worry too much," Menno said with a laugh. "I'm still young. And it does the body good to keep going. What would I do without the work on the farm to keep me busy? Nothing."

"Perhaps you could make a wood shop out in the barn and tinker around all day. That would be all the work you need. I'd feel much better about it."

"Making children's toys," Menno said. "I don't call that work. Sure they might sell well in Salem on Saturdays, but *Da Hah* didn't make a man to stay inside all day away from the sun and the rain. A man was made for the outdoors, for tilling the soil, for feeling the heat of the sun on his neck. He was made to have the sweat pouring down his back. That's how I wish to die—in the fields, close to the plowed ground."

"Who says anything about dying? I'm talking about living right until the end."

Menno studied her face for a long moment. "*Nee*, this isn't about me. It's about Susan, isn't it? You miss her."

"Well, shouldn't Susan have us worried?" she asked.

"*Yah,*" Menno agreed. "But sometimes we have to let go of the reins. We have to let the horse have its run. Only then will she settle down."

"So my youngest daughter is a horse to you? Is that how you handle the thought of her up there in the big city, playing around with all sorts of evil, getting into more trouble than you and I can even imagine, Menno? You know what I'm saying is true, and we have to do something about it."

Anna's hands trembled as she slid the last loaf of bread onto the counter. She dropped the hot pad on the floor, and as she bent over to retrieve it she groaned.

"My dear, dear, *frau!*" Menno turned to lay his hand on her shoulder. "You know I also suffer, though I can't find the ways to speak them at times. Our daughter is like a fine filly, high-spirited and full of zip. No matter how it grieves us or how much we miss seeing her face, we must let her run, keeping our hands off the reins. *Da Hah* has not forgotten her or our prayers. Do we not pray for her as we have for all our children? She will come back if it is His will. Of this I am more than confident."

"You speak words that have no meaning, Menno. Words like the *Englisha* speak. Words about caring when they place no action behind them. Take me to the big city. I want to go, Menno. I have the address where I send the letters, and that Bonnie woman Susan worked for will give us good directions. I know Susan will come home if we both speak to her. She will see how foolish this all is."

Menno pulled her trembling body close to his, kissing her on the forehead. His bent fingers brushed her cheek. "You know I would, dear, if it would do any *gut*. But we could make things worse, much worse than they already are. If we go up there and cry our tears all over the street, it will not change anything. Susan had her heart broken by young Thomas, and only *Da Hah* can be putting the pieces back together."

"But we could try, couldn't we? Doesn't *Da Hah* bless those who try?"

"The things of the heart should only be handled with tender hands," he said. "Man's hands are made from the clay of the ground, and they break things easily."

"What if Susan learns the *Englisha* ways and never comes back to us? You know how hard it is to turn back the tide once it's gone out. She will be exposed to so much, Menno. To so much evil in the world."

"I know." Menno pulled her tight. "But we still have each other to care for. Should we not be thankful for that?"

"I am." Anna pushed him away. "And I can start by getting you supper."

"*Yah*, you will, though I wasn't worried about that. And why are you making bread this time of the night?"

"I guess because I'm all *fahuttled* on the inside. I can't even think straight."

"Have you written to Susan lately?"

"A few days ago. She should have the letter by now."

"Has Susan written since her first letter, the one telling us she arrived safely?"

Anna nodded. "But the letters don't say much. Nothing about how she's feeling, just little things about the bakery and how nice Laura is. It's not like Susan at all."

"You must let go, Anna. Life still must go on. Come, sit with me, and we can pray. That will do more *gut* than all our worry and talk will ever do."

"What if she finds the love she's looking for out there? Oh, Menno, I can't stand the thought of it. Can't you go over and talk to Thomas about this, see what problems the two of them ran into. Things had been going so well, then *boom* it was all over."

"You know that will do no good," Menno said, tugging on her arm. "Anyway, I don't want to go traveling to the big city. It's not right somehow. Come, we must pray to *Da Hah* about this. He is the only one who can help us."

"How can you be so certain, Menno? Really, Susan might find what she's looking for out there. Some of our young people already have, and Susan could be one of them. Surely you don't doubt that?"

"I know," Menno said, guiding Anna by the arm. "And I know she might find something she likes better than what we have to offer. This weighs heavy on my heart as it does yours. But we can only pray."

"Oh, my Susan, my baby girl!" Anna cried. "What if she's lost to us forever, Menno? Even the Mennonites would have been better than this."

"Come…" Menno helped Anna kneel beside the couch.

"Oh…" Anna groaned. "How can I stand this any longer?"

Menno stroked her arm and prayed. "Our dear *Gott im Himmel*. You are the one who made the stars, the heavens, and the earth, fashioning them with the fingers of Your hand. Draw near tonight and hear the cry of our hearts for our youngest daughter, Susan. We confess our many sins to You. We know the many times we have failed You in raising our children. Yet you say in Your Book that You are a God of mercy and compassion. Have mercy tonight. See the pain in our hearts and look after Susan. Protect her from danger, keep her from the perils of the city while she lives there, and guard her against the temptations in the *Englisha* world. If it be Your will, bring her back to us someday. Amen."

Anna paused and then slowly got up. She walked to the bedroom and returned with a clean handkerchief. She wiped her eyes. "I'd better get you some supper now," she said.

"I'll help," Menno said, rummaging around in the cupboards. He took down two plates and then got silverware from the drawer. He set the items on the table before stepping out into the utility room. Soft noises broke the silence as he filled the gas lantern with air. Thoughts raced through his mind. Had he given Anna the correct advice? Perhaps they should be traveling up to Asbury Park with a hired *Englisha* driver. Or on the bus and train. But no, he *had* made the best decision.

He lit a match, turning the lantern's handle just a little, listening for the hiss of the gas before he pushed the flame close to the white mantle. The lantern lit with a soft *poof*, burning brighter and brighter in evergrowing spurts of light. He wiped the back of his hand across his eyes. Not that long ago Susan had been a little girl, brought into the world by the old midwife Martha Stoll.

The midwife was gone now, and Susan was no longer a babe. So quickly she had become a toddler who grew spoiled from all the attention from her eight older sisters. Perhaps that had been part of their problem with raising Susan. The youngest child always got spoiled a little. *Yah*, perhaps this was true, and a brother in the house to grow up with might have helped. But he couldn't do anything about what *Da Hah* chose not to give.

School had been an easy thing for Susan, her grades always high. She got along well with whoever the teacher was, always willing to learn. Did an easy schooling sow the seeds for what was growing now? The *Englisha's* education could be that way. It carried so many dangers. The mind was a strange thing, quick to think highly of itself and disregard the ways of the fathers.

Anna hadn't said much when Susan started running with the young people, more and more the vision of a lovely woman each day. One didn't speak of such things, though it had worried him often. That was when he first started praying for Susan, praying hard that she would find the right man for marriage. Anna had also been praying, he was sure. So much could go wrong with such a high-strung personality.

Thomas had seemed to be the answer. From their school days, Thomas hadn't wasted any time getting his word in for Susan. Had the boy misjudged his own abilities? Or was he simply unable to keep the girl? From the sounds of it, Thomas had rejected Susan, which was strange indeed.

Perhaps he should have interceded with Thomas and Susan when the problem first came up a month or so ago. But it had seemed best not to. Young people needed to work out their own problems, especially when it came to things of the heart. If older people intervened, it often made things worse. Even Anna hadn't disagreed with him on that point. It was just later, when things had gone so badly, that she had her doubts.

Swinging the lantern, Menno went into the kitchen, squinting his eyes. How he did miss Susan's cheery smile around the place! He held the lantern aloft, searching for the hook driven into the ceiling. Finding it, he flipped the loop over it and let the weight of the lantern move out of his hands.

"Supper's ready," Anna said.

"That was quick," Menno said, sitting down and pulling his chair forward.

"There's not much to eat—just leftovers."

"I'm not complaining." Menno patted his stomach. It wasn't overly rolling, but perhaps some humor would help. He glanced up at her face. It was nice to see Anna smile, even if faintly.

They bowed their heads in silence, and when they raised them again, Anna dished the food out for him. She didn't have to serve him tonight, but Menno allowed it, sensing that it helped her now that she had no children to mother.

"Thank you," Menno said, when she was done. "You always know exactly how much I want."

"If it makes you feel better, perhaps you can care for me someday." Anna turned back to her own plate.

"Cheer up." Menno reached over to tickle her chin. "We have many more years together, and so many family members still to be thankful for."

She nodded, trying to smile.

"Are there any family gatherings planned soon?" he asked. "We need to have more of them."

"Perhaps some of the girls will come over Sunday evening. I don't know. Would that help?"

"It would do us both good," Menno agreed, watching her face.

She tried to smile again, losing the attempt.

"If our youngest just hadn't turned out so badly," she said. "What did we do wrong, Menno? And Susan was the best of the bunch."

"We'll make it," Menno said getting up and rubbing her back. "We will…with *Da Hah*'s help. And Susan will come home again."

Anna didn't meet his eyes as he returned to his place and sat down. Silence settled over the table as they ate.

When Menno stood, Anna said, "We have to butcher soon. I think several of the girls will go together with us. We can take the hog over to John and Betsy's place since they have plenty of room."

Menno nodded, his eyes focused on the blank wall. He imagined the big city. What was the place like where Susan lived?

Chapter Four

Susan stirred, raising her head from the table and noting the light of the kerosene lamp. She picked up the envelope from home and held it so the light fell across the front. For a long moment, she studied the letters before opening the end with a quick twist of her hand. A single piece of paper came out. At least it wasn't a long letter. The pressure from home wouldn't be too bad.

My dearest daughter Susan,

Greetings in the name of Da Hah. *I am sitting here tonight, trying to write you something, but what can I write? I imagine you understand how it goes. We all miss you quite terribly. Your smile is no longer here to brighten our day. I hear a noise in the house and I look up expecting to see your face, but you are not here.*

How are you doing? I hope well. Bonnie's sister surely must be taking good care of you.

Betsy and Miriam stopped by last week, and Ada's children are up once in a while. All the sisters said to tell you hi when I write next. I offered them your address, but they aren't the greatest letter writers. I think the real reason is they don't know how to write you, now that you have gone Englisha. *Have you considered returning yet? We so wish you would.*

Are you really going the Englisha *way, Susan? It's so hard for me to believe you would. I keep thinking there is some mistake*

*somewhere. Did you or didn't you say when you left that your
stay in New Jersey would be only until the winter or perhaps
spring? The words seem so long ago, lost somewhere in the pain
of my heart, and I can't remember.*

*I know I shouldn't be taking this so hard, as you no doubt have
your reasons for your actions, but I can't help myself. I can't
help asking again and again, was there really no way you could
have patched things up with Thomas, whatever your quarrel was? He looked so sorrowful in church the other Sunday. I
never heard a word from him on what the problem was, so I
guess you can be thankful for that. Some boys feel a need to run
down their old girlfriends' reputations until they are ruined.*

*The fall weddings are beginning. Pete and Rose had theirs
announced on Sunday. I expect there will be several more. Your
daett is well along with his fall plowing, and the silo-filling
crew was here last week. Somehow your daett still makes his
rounds with the crew. I think it's time he asked Deacon Ray if
he doesn't know of some young boy who can help us on the farm
next year. I doubt if your father will agree to such a thing. He
is stubborn like you are.*

*I guess I had better close before I get the paper wet with tears. I
really hope you come home soon, Susan. There has to be some
way to work your problems out with Thomas. If not, there's still
no reason to run away from all of us. Your room still awaits you
upstairs. I have left it just as it was when you left.*

Your mamm, *Anna Hostetler*

"*Mamm,*" Susan whispered in the silent apartment, folding the
piece of paper, "please don't make this any harder than it already is.
And of course Thomas is acting like a saint. He thinks he is one. Just
wait until you discover he's dating Eunice, and you'll find out what
he's really like."

Standing up, Susan forced her thoughts to focus. *Right now I have
to fix supper. Think on that. And afterward, I need something—perhaps
a walk to the beach. I could watch the moon rise over the water, which*

might be exactly what I need to lift my spirits. You can make it, Susan. You can make the city your home. I know you can. Keep that chin up now, and you'll be okay.

She walked over to the gas stove, turned on the burner, and reached for the frying pan. Thank *Da Hah* Laura had a gas stove. The microwave always seemed to glare at Susan from its place over the stove, its red blinking light showing the time. That was another barrier she had yet to cross. What must it be like to heat food with invisible rays from the *Englisha* world? Dangerous and scary, to say the least.

Susan took the meatloaf out of the refrigerator, sliced two pieces, and added a chunk of butter to the pan. She dropped the meatloaf slices into the pan, leaving them to warm while she retrieved the bread and jam from the pantry. Setting the items on the table, she stood beside the stove, listening to the sizzle. When the pieces were browned on one side, she flipped them over.

It was a meager supper by Amish standards, but good enough for tonight. When the meat was ready, Susan transferred it to the table and sat down. She closed her eyes to pray. One must pray over meals even in *Englisha* land. Perhaps especially in *Englisha* land.

Outside, the day was ebbing. The streetlights would soon be turning on. What time did the moon rise over the ocean? The man hadn't said, and she might well be too late already. But it didn't matter, really. Even a risen moon over the water would fit her mood better than a lonely apartment.

When she was finished, Susan dumped the plate and utensils into the kitchen sink and grabbed her coat from the closet. Was the key in her pocket? *Yah*, and this time she wouldn't lose it. Was the sky clear? It was hard to tell with the streetlights on, but earlier there hadn't been a cloud in the sky.

Closing the door behind her, Susan walked down Main Street, turning the corner at Cookman. The crowds had thinned out some, and the people were walking slower now. It might be a good idea to stop in at the concession stand and tell Laura where she was going. Not that she was back at the farm anymore or even a teenager who needed to report on her actions, but old habits die hard.

"So what are you doing out?" Laura asked when Susan walked up. "I thought I let you off for the night."

"She couldn't sleep," Robby said with a laugh.

Susan didn't look at him. He deserved to be ignored.

"I decided to take a walk to the ocean," she said. "There's supposed to be a full moon tonight."

"That would be nice," Laura said. "I wish I could go along, but we have to close up the stand."

"Then I should help," Susan offered.

Laura shook her head. "Robbie, your dad just called and said he was coming after all, so there's no need for you to stay. Why not go ahead and enjoy a walk with Susan?"

"But I don't need…" Susan started to say.

"I'll go with her," Robby interrupted, swinging out over the side of the stand.

"No, you won't!" Susan glared at him. "You need to help your mom close up."

"Can I, Mom?" he turned to look over his shoulder, a mischievous look on his face.

"We'll manage," Laura said. "So run along, unless Susan objects for some reason."

"See!" Robby gave Susan a sweet smile. "I'm a good boy. Can I come along, please?"

"If you don't tease too much—and don't talk."

"I'm as *mum* as a clam." He clamped his fingers over his mouth, his next words mere mumbles. "See, not a sound comes out."

"Okay," Susan said unable to conceal a laugh. "But don't forget."

Robby followed closely behind as she led the way. He was a funny boy, almost like a brother, Susan thought. But what was a brother like? When one had eight sisters, it was hard to tell.

They walked in silence through the ever-thinning crowd. People seemed to have moved back toward the main part of town…or perhaps out to the boardwalk. Robby was keeping his vow of silence—too much so.

"Talk," she ordered, and he laughed.

"It's closer down this side street," Robby motioned with his head.

Susan glanced down the dimly lit street. It didn't look any scarier than the barn at home or any number of other dark places on the farm. The feeling was different here though—in ways that were hard to explain.

"Do you think we should?"

"Sure, why not?"

"The street is dark."

"So? Does it never get dark where you grew up?"

"I told you no teasing, remember?" she said, though she had to smile. So this was what having a brother is like.

"So do you want to?" he asked again.

"Sure, why not!"

"Don't be scared," he said when they were halfway down the street. "Do you have bogeymen on the farm back home…like we do here?"

Susan looked around. The light barely reached her, the shadows dark on the concrete sidewalls. Little squeaks came from somewhere, sounding like rats in the barn loft. But why would there be rats here in Asbury Park? "No bogeymen. Just witches and warlocks," she said.

"That's really cute," he said. "Miss Hostetler just made a joke."

"Who says it's a joke? It might be true."

"So you have Amish brooms, and you ride them through the dark Amish cornfields?"

"The fresh corn patches work best," she said. "When the corn's about knee high. Otherwise the tall stalks gets tangled up in the broom handle."

Robby laughed out loud as they approached an open lot with spooky wooden posts standing tall in the shifting light of the streetlamps.

"Howdy there!" Robby hollered to one of them.

"Shhh…," she said. "You're making a lot of racket."

"Who cares? No one can hear us with all that racket back on Main Street."

"That's what you think. What was that squeaking back there? I hear it again now."

"I don't know. I didn't hear anything," he said. "Lots of creatures could be crawling around here. But the bridge is just ahead, so don't worry. This is Asbury Park after all, and I grew up around here. It's as safe to me as your barnyard was to you, I promise."

"And what do you know about my barnyard?" She looked over to him in the light of the streetlamps. "You think I'm a country girl, ignorant and stupid, don't you? You probably think I grew up barefoot and shoveling manure from horse stalls."

He laughed.

"Well, isn't that the truth?"

"Far from it, Miss Hostetler," he said. "I see you as the paragon of beauty and virtue, sun kissed, your brow untouched by the sorrow and sweat of common man. You are a lady from the bounty land brought up to know splendor and glory undreamed of by such a commoner as myself."

"You are such a liar," she teased back. "And a great big fat one. So shut your sugary mouth and tell me what you really think about me."

"I kind of like you, you know. I've never had a sister."

"That's better. Now stop talking again. I want to watch the water while we're crossing this bridge and listen to the ocean ahead of us."

"It sounds the same as it always does," he said, not slowing down.

"You sure aren't much of a romantic type, considering your recent outburst. I would have thought better of you."

"Remember, I grew up around here," he said. "It's not romantic to me."

"That's not an excuse to ignore such music as this. It will never grow old to me. Listen." Susan paused. In the distance they could hear the gentle roll of waves coming in to meet the shore.

"You are correct, as always," he said, standing still, his hand on the steel railing. He tilted his head skyward. "Do you think we should listen here all night?"

"Not if you're going to keep talking." She let go of the rail and barged past him.

"Girls don't like me, just like you don't," he said, catching up with her.

"What has that got to do with anything?" She turned to face him.

"Of course they do. Or at least one certain girl will. There's someone out there for everyone."

"Really?" He snorted.

"Don't you believe in true love?"

"No."

"Well, I do!" she declared.

"Is that more of your farm wisdom? Perhaps the lore you learned riding through the cornfields?"

"That's not funny anymore."

"Okay, we'll leave that point. I hate to disappoint you, but love is the product of the imagination, the trick of the gods to lure us into actions we would never do in our wildest dreams."

"You are a sad, sick human being, Robby. Do you know that?"

"Strong words, young lady. Very strong words."

"Well, they're true."

"So how has love worked out for you so far?" he asked, coming up beside her.

She turned her face away from him.

He went on. "Has it led you down the fairy path, promising you great things, whispering of the nectar of the gods, and then dashing the dream to pieces about the time you were ready to touch glory?"

"You ought to be a poet," she said.

"You didn't answer my question, young lady."

She took a deep breath. "God made love, and it's good, and that's the end of the question. You just have to find the right person."

"Merry hunting, my darling. Prepare to be disappointed."

"The heart that stops looking is the heart that dies. Mine isn't dead yet," she snapped.

"Whee!" he said. "Please tell me the girl didn't get all this from the farm."

"It comes from riding a broomstick above the tall cornfields," she said.

He laughed, his face turned toward the water. "I thought that subject was forbidden."

"Only until I bring it up again. That's how it works, don't you know?"

"Quite," he said. "Well, we still have the ocean before us, don't we? It at least is true and faithful."

"So it is," she whispered.

"Come," he said, taking her hand to lead her across the wooden boardwalk. He motioned with the other, making a broad sweep across the sky. "Behold, great princess from the farm, the mighty ocean at night."

CHAPTER FIVE

The breeze blew in from the ocean, soft on their faces. Dim lights from passing ships shone in the distance like pinpricks on the dark waters. A soft murmur rose from the sand as the waves rolled in.

"You're funny, Robby. You know that?"

"Is that all you have to say?" he asked. "After all that effort I put in? I was trying to be good."

Susan let go of his hand, stepping forward. "Oh, but this is beautiful! I've never been out here at nighttime. Thanks so much for bringing me."

"You were coming yourself, and I just tagged along," he corrected, looking out over the sandy stretch of beach. "But I'll take the compliment. Let's run on the sand."

"Just a minute!" Susan paused. With one hand she removed her shoes and held them loosely by her side.

"You should have brought your bathing suit," Robby said.

"It's too cold. And besides, I haven't got one," she said.

"Oh that's right. You have something against bathing suits, don't you?"

"Only when I'm wearing such things where the whole world can see."

"I bet you've never had one on in your whole life," he said.

"No, I haven't," she admitted, pausing to wiggle her toes. "The sand feels so different at night."

Robby held out his hand and said, "Come with me."

She took it, pulling back as he pulled forward, propelling herself with the momentum, feeling the soft footing shift under her feet.

"Run," he said, approaching the edge of the waves. "Run like you've never run before!" He let go of her hand and sprinted forward, becoming a dim shadow ahead of her.

Susan hesitated. Should she give in to this feeling of abandoning one's self? The world was somehow much larger out here. Ahead of her the horizon was shrouded in darkness, stretching on and on into nothingness. Underneath her feet the sand moved.

"I'm coming!" she shouted. "Wait for me."

"Run!" he shouted back, his voice distant.

She ran, her strides hesitant at first. *There's a certain trick to this,* she thought. *A way of planting my feet for the next push forward.* These were lessons not learned on the farm. But this was a *gut* thing. Susan propelled herself forward, lifting her dress high. Who could see anyway in the falling darkness?

The wind brushed against her cheeks. Her eyes searched ahead. Robby's form was a dim blob ahead of her. Boys ran fast, but she had grown up on a farm. The time spent running to and from the back fields had not been wasted. With a burst of effort, she increased her speed. Robby's form came into view and then seconds later, she passed him.

"Whew!" he said, slowing down. "You did grow up on a farm."

"That was fun," she said, gasping for air as she slowed to his pace.

"Just good old city fun." He flopped down on the sand. "I guess one has to know where it's found."

"Are there many more of these hidden pleasures around?"

"Not many. Shhh…the moon is coming up."

She lowered herself onto the sand and looked up to the moon, its first dim glow bubbling up on the horizon.

"It's coming," he said.

Susan watched as the light increased. How *vundabah* this was. The minutes seemed to hang on each other like molasses running out of a barrel. The emerging form of the moon cast its light across the waters. The bubble loomed larger, soon becoming a simmering halo on the horizon.

"You've seen this before," she whispered.

He nodded. "It's almost enough to make a person believe in God."

"Don't you?"

"I do in moments like this…"

She watched the light expand until the whole ball was visible, save for a tiny sliver missing from the top.

"It's not quite a full moon anymore," he said. "That was a few nights ago."

"Did you come down here then?"

"No, I haven't been here in a long time."

"Then why now?"

"You, I guess." He turned on his elbow. "You and that touch of the farm you bring with you."

"And to think I was trying to lose that mark."

"I didn't mean that in a bad way," he said, turning his head, his face half lit by the light off the water. "But then perhaps it's more than that. You think God lives out in the country?"

"*Yah,* but He surely lives here too. I hope He does."

"God is everywhere. That's what they used to tell us in Sunday school."

"You don't go to church anymore, do you?"

"Not for a long time."

"Your mom took me to her church last Sunday. We'd have gone again today if it weren't for the festival. You should come with us sometime. It would do you good."

"I didn't know you were full of missionary zeal. I thought farm folks were more laid back, less in your face. That's what I liked about you."

"Well, I didn't mean to offend you. It was just a suggestion. If you have problems, maybe you can find answers there."

"You think I have problems?"

"I think we all have problems. I know I do. And plenty of them."

"Nothing that church won't cure, I'm sure."

"I hope so. I know I sure wouldn't want to stay home on Sundays. Even if I'm going to a church where my parents would disapprove…or even think sinful."

"Going to church sinful?" He looked at her. "How is that?"

"You must not know much about Amish people."

"No, not much," he said, tracing lines in the sand, darker shadows appearing where his finger had been. "Other than things like plowing their fields with horses, one-day barn raisings, lots of pie eating...and nice girls."

"Really!" She laughed. "I'm sure that was before you met me."

"You're okay," he said, his finger pausing. "So why would they object to mom's church?"

"Are you sure you want to know?" she asked.

When he nodded, she took a deep breath and began. "Church attendance has to stay—shall we say—in the family. And according to the family, that could be Old Order Amish, New Order Amish, Black buggy Amish, Yellow buggy Amish, Schwartzentruber Amish, Beachy Amish, and who knows how many more. Then there are the Mennonites—liberal, conservative, Black Bumper....well, you get the idea. But the Baptist church where your mom goes is....well, just not acceptable."

"You sound a little bitter," he said.

"I think that's just an echo of your own voice you're hearing," Susan said. "As for me, I've accepted things the way they are. Who can change them?"

"But you're changing yourself?"

"That's something I *can* change. But even when I do, who knows if it will be any better."

"Is that what you want to find out?"

"Perhaps."

"Well, let me know when you do."

"While I'm finding that out, why don't you go to church with your mom? Or somewhere else if you don't like her church."

"You *are* a little missionary. Who would have thought it? A real live Amish missionary."

"That's not nice," she said, looking down at the sand. "And you really should go to church. You will have to face God someday, you know."

"Okay, Missionary Hostetler," he said, getting to his feet. "Let's go. I'm not quite the savage you think me to be, even if I don't attend church."

"I didn't say you were one," she said, following him across the sand.

"I know you didn't," he said, giving her fingers a quick squeeze in the darkness. "All is forgiven, even if I don't go to church. You want to take another run?"

"Not tonight. I'm tired. And it's been a long day." She looked out across the water.

The moon was now well above the horizon, casting white light on the waves.

"The moon is still beautiful," he said, following her gaze. "Even when it's risen. Sometime I'll have to take you sailing at night. There's nothing quite like it, drifting along under the light of the full moon."

"Another of the secret pleasures of city life?"

"I like to think so," he said. "At least city life for those of us who live near an ocean."

They had reached the boardwalk again and paused.

"So, you really do know how to sail?" she asked. "I didn't know you had a boat."

"Oh," he laughed. "I rent one. I'm not a Kennedy you know. Only a poor boy whose dad took him out on the water when he was a youngster. We rent boats down at the marina."

"So your dad taught you? How nice."

"He doesn't like sailing much, but he took me when I wanted to learn. Now I'm old enough to go by myself."

"So are you serious about taking me out on a boat at night?"

"You'd really go?"

"Of course. We never did anything like that on the farm. I'll even help pay for it—if it's not too expensive, that is."

"I'll take you, and you won't have to pay for it. I'll have to reserve the boat in advance though. And we'll have to watch the weather. I don't go out when there's a storm."

"No, I suppose I'd not want to go in a storm either."

"Then it's settled," Robby said.

"By the way, I want you to know how thankful I am for all your family is doing for me," she said. "It was nice of your mom to give me a place to stay. She didn't have to."

"Mom's a nice woman—and a nice mother," he grunted.

"*Yah*, so is mine. And *Daett* is a good father."

He smiled at her choice of words. "So if the farm was so great and if your parents are so nice, why are you off wandering around in the city by yourself?"

"I'm not really," she said. "*Da Hah*—the Lord—is with me. I guess I'm following my heart."

Robby didn't say anything until they had crossed the footbridge again and were back on Cookman.

"Thanks for coming along," he said. "I enjoyed it."

"Me too, but I thought it was my idea to go."

"Oh yeah, I guess it was," he said, turning toward her, the street-light shining on his face. "I just tagged along. Can you find your way from here?"

"I think so. Thanks again."

"It was a pleasure." He nodded at her and walked away.

She watched him for a few moments and then caught herself. What if he turned and saw her staring at him? It had been a nice night, and he had turned out to be much less of a teaser than he'd pretended to be. Robby even had a deep side to him. He seemed like the brother she never had, but what a strange way to feel about an *Englisha* boy. Could she ever be attracted to an *Englisha* man? It was nice that Robby didn't make her feel nervous like she did around other *Englisha* males.

Susan reached the door to the apartment, digging into her pocket for the key. She unlocked the door, entered, and locked it again. The stairs squeaked on the way up, and Susan took her time on each step. It was a pleasant sound, a reminder of home and a good ending to the evening.

CHAPTER SIX

✤

Susan clicked off the alarm, the gray light from the city seeping in through the window shade. At four o'clock in the morning, the darkness would have been deep at home as the fields waited for the sun. Here no one waited for the sun. It was as if mankind could get along fine without the things God had to give.

Susan pushed back the covers and made her way to the dresser where she struck a match, transferred the flame to the kerosene lamp, and replaced the glass mantle. This hang-up about not using electric lights had to stop. She was no longer home on the farm. Some morning soon she would cross the threshold into *Englisha* lighting. That day, she knew, would mark another big step for her.

Yah, she told herself as she dressed by the flickering light, why could this not be the morning? Waiting longer wouldn't make it any easier. Taking a deep breath, she whispered, "Goodbye." Looking back at the kerosene lamp she said, "I will always keep you in my memory."

She reached over and gently placed her finger on the wall switch. Could she do it? With a breath and a quick count to three, she flipped the switch. Instantly the room was flooded with light. She blinked and rubbed her eyes. So that was it. Not so very hard after all. She *was* moving on, as the *Englisha* would say. Still, this would take some getting used to at four in the morning. She walked over and blew out the kerosene lamp.

Faint noises rose from downstairs. Laura must have arrived for the Monday morning baking, and Susan needed to be downstairs. Breakfast could wait. She was used to that. You did the chores first on the farm, and then you ate.

Flipping the light switch to off, Susan went down to the bakery.

"Good morning!" she called as she considered announcing her triumph of the morning. *I finally turned on the electric lights!*

"Good morning, dear," Laura answered as Susan made her way to the back of the bakery. "My, you're cheery for a Monday morning."

"No late nights for me," Susan said with a grin. "And don't forget, I'm used to early mornings."

"That's my girl," Laura said. "And I'm glad you're ready to work. We'll likely have part of the after-festival crowd show up this morning. Seems the visitors stay around for Monday morning—at least enough of them to make for a busy day."

"I wonder if the older couple got to see the moon rise over the ocean," Susan said, measuring out flour.

"I was thinking about Robby," Laura said. "He said he enjoyed himself, but he wouldn't tell me more. Like usual."

"I gather from what he said he used to go to the ocean more often," Susan offered.

"He did," Laura said. "But things have changed for him—and not for the best. I wish he'd get things right with the Lord."

Susan poured milk into the mixer and turned it on. "He seems to have a tender heart."

"Yes, he's always been that way." Laura brushed the back of her hand across her eyes.

"You left flour on your face," Susan said.

"Oh great. That would look funny to the customers," Laura said with a laugh as she wiped her face with a dishtowel.

"*Mamm* used to end up with flour on her face every time she set foot in the kitchen," Susan said. "Somehow it made the food taste better. At least that's what *Daett* always said. Perhaps we just grew up believing it because he said so."

"Someday I'm going to have to visit your folks. They sound like nice people."

"They are," Susan agreed as she reached to turn on the oven.

"I'll be right back," Laura said, stepping out of the kitchen to service the now empty display cases. Moments later she returned carrying the empty trays, dumping them into the sink.

Susan pulled the first batch of rolls from the oven and slid them onto the counter to cool.

"What cookies are we offering today?" Susan asked. "I can get those started."

"I think peanut butter, Tollhouse, gingersnaps, and macaroons," Laura said.

Moments later Laura left for the front again to start filling the urns of coffee so they'd be ready to turn on just before the bakery opened. Susan began the gingersnaps, stopping only to take the finished sweet rolls from the oven.

She drew in a long breath over them. These did smell *gut. Perhaps this morning is special? A day of new beginnings? But then perhaps I'm imagining things. Perhaps turning on electric lights for the first time could do strange things to a person.*

Laura returned. They worked together in silence, rushing at the last minute to finish filling the display cases before the first customer walked through the door. Susan pulled on a freshly washed white apron a few minutes before six. A quick glance in Laura's direction brought a smile of encouragement.

"I'll get cleaned up myself," Laura said. "We've done really well this morning."

Laura walked over to the coffee urns lined up on the counter, throwing the switches before disappearing into the back office.

"You look dreamy this morning," Laura said, returning in a few minutes with a fresh apron on.

"I think today I shall buy a purse!" Susan announced with a laugh.

Laura smiled. "That's right. I don't think I noticed you don't own one. You might find some nice ones in the local stores, but the better buys are at the mall. If you like, we can go tonight. My evening is free."

Susan's face brightened. "That would be wonderful. Thank you!" She pulled open the front door and set the doorstop. She turned to face a tall young man who walked in with a smile on his face.

"Good morning," he said in a chipper voice.

Susan felt a flush spread up her neck. He was *gut* looking and even more. She guessed he could almost have been raised on a farm. She could even picture him in Amish clothing. But she shouldn't be thinking about such things. She hardly knew him, and he might even be married. How could she think such worldly thoughts?

Susan made her way behind the cases where the man was surveying the rolls. "I think," he said, slowly, "I'll have a bear claw and an apple fritter. Oh, and coffee—black—please."

Susan used metal tongs to put the bear claw and apple fritter onto a plate. She grabbed a paper cup and drew his cup of coffee.

At the register she said, "That'll be four seventy-five."

As he paid, he noticed Laura, nodded to her, took his change, and made his way to a table where he settled with a newspaper.

The front door opened again, and two more people came in, followed by an older couple and then another single man. Quickly a line was formed. Susan and Laura were kept busy.

Busy as she was, Susan stole an occasional glance at the man with his newspaper. Why was she thinking about men so much this morning? She really wasn't interested, even in light of her bold words to Robby on the beach. Had she actually said she would keep her heart open? Well, it wasn't going to be taken on Monday morning by an *Englisha* man in Laura's shop. That was for sure.

The newspaper truck went by the window, and a paper banged against the front window. Laura liked the paper brought in right away since footprints on the headlines didn't make for easy reading.

"Excuse me," she said to the two ladies in front of her. They were taking their time deciding, looking and whispering to each other as if world peace depended on their choices that morning.

Susan retrieved the paper from the sidewalk and made her way back to the display cases.

"The headlines aren't good," the bear claw and apple fritter man said as she went by.

Of course they aren't, Susan thought. *Since when are headlines good?* Hesitating, she stopped by the man's table. Hadn't Laura always said to present a friendly demeanor to customers? This was being friendly, even if he was *gut* looking.

"Headlines are seldom good," she said without looking directly at him.

"Yes, but they're particularly bad this morning," he said. "I just thought I'd warn you. I suppose everyone will be taking precautions for a while."

Susan unfolded the paper. The front-page letters seemed blacker and larger than usual, jumping out at her, grabbing her attention. When she gasped, the man said, "I'm sorry. I didn't mean to startle you. Obviously you hadn't heard."

"No." She drew her breath in. "Do women disappear every day off the streets here?"

"I take it you're not from around here," he said. "Asbury Park is usually a nice city, but like all big cities…" His voice drifted off, the final words unsaid.

"No, I'm new," Susan said. She stopped. Should she have said that much to a stranger? With local women disappearing, shouldn't she be careful?

"I thought you were new. I know Laura pretty well," he said. "Though I haven't been here that much lately."

"I started here a couple of weeks ago."

"Like I said, I don't come in that often these days."

Susan lingered a second and then said, "Well, I have to get back to work."

The two older women were turned toward her, displeased looks on their faces.

"Have you decided?" she asked the ladies as she made her way behind the display case.

"One small cinnamon roll for me," one of the ladies said. "And a lemon twist for my sister. Two coffees."

"Well, the rolls are all about the same size and price," Susan said. "But I can pick out the smallest one, if you'd like."

"That will be fine," the woman said, waiting as Susan made the selections and placed them on plates.

"Who ever heard of such a thing?" the other whispered as they moved away. "Why wouldn't you have small rolls for people who want them? And charge less for them?"

The women moved toward a table as the man Susan had been

speaking to got up and left. *Not even a backward glance,* Susan noted. *But why should I care? Perhaps he is the kidnapper mentioned on the front page of the paper.* That would make perfect sense given the success she had with men.

Laura and Susan waited on more customers. During a lull, Susan asked, "Who was that man who came in first this morning? He said he knew you."

"Duane Moran. He works down the street at H&R Block. He handles our taxes. I think he was away at a seminar last week—IRS updates on tax law, that sort of thing."

"Oh," Susan said.

What exactly is a tax person? she wondered. *At least he wasn't a kidnapper.*

"Duane's a really nice fellow," Laura said.

"He did mention the headlines with what happened over the weekend. He seemed concerned about us."

"What happened?" Laura asked. She reached for the paper. As she read, she sighed. "This is absolutely awful. And the missing girl was last seen on Cookman Avenue the first night of the festival."

"I hadn't read that," Susan said. "But perhaps they'll find her soon." So much for Robby's assurances on how safe Asbury Park was.

"Perhaps," Laura was saying. "One thing for sure. You will need to take precautions for a while. We all will."

"That's what Mister…Mister whatever you said his name was said."

"Duane. Yes. He would say something like that. And it is a good warning."

Susan nodded. "I hope they find the woman. As for me, I think God will protect me even in the big city. That's what our people believe."

Laura was silent for a moment, but then she said, "Yes, but there's no sense in taking chances, Susan. So don't take any."

"I'll be careful," Susan said. "But I'm not going to be scared home this easily. I need to stay."

"I didn't mean anything about going home, but perhaps you could move in with us for a while if being alone here scares you."

Susan shook her head. "Thanks, but I like it here. I even like living alone. So unless it gets really dangerous, I would like to stay in the apartment."

"Okay," Laura said. "Suit yourself, but do be careful."

Susan nodded and turned to greet a teenage girl entering the front door. "Can I help you?"

"A small coffee, please, ma'am."

Susan poured the coffee and said, "Laura will take your money."

"Okay."

As the girl turned toward the register counter, Susan noticed that she was obviously pregnant. And quite well along. She also noticed the girl's dress was wrinkled and dirty. Susan glanced away. This really wasn't her business.

The girl looked back to Susan and smiled as she handed Laura the money, dropping a quarter in the process.

"Oh, I'm sorry!" The girl bent over to chase the coin underneath the counter. She was breathing hard when she stood up.

"I'll help you with your coffee." Susan stepped out from behind the counter.

"That would be very nice of you, ma'am," the girl said. "I am a little heavy, as you can see."

"*Yah*, I do see," Susan said. "Is your baby coming soon?"

"I think so," the girl said, sounding uncertain.

Susan almost asked her another question but thought better of it. The girl was trying to smile, but she looked very uncomfortable. Susan noticed the girl's eyes had grown moist as she took a table facing the counter. Susan felt the girl's eyes on her the whole time she worked. *Is something wrong?* Susan wondered. *What is it about me that's captured her attention?*

When the girl finished, she walked over to where Susan was standing behind the counter.

"I thank you very much," the girl said. "That was good."

"Maybe we'll see some more of you," Susan said. "You're always welcome back."

"That's very kind of you," the girl said, her eyes moist again. "I think I will be back." With that, the girl smiled, ducked her head, and left.

Chapter Seven

Thomas Stoll stood looking out the tall windows of his father's cabinet shop, his eyes sweeping over the fertile farmland. Southern Indiana was that way. An Amish farmer here could make a *gut* living at most anything he tried his hand at. It was cabinet work that was hard to make a good living at, removed as they were from the big cities.

The little town of Salem thought well of itself but produced few new homes or remodeling jobs. *Daett* refused to advertise widely, placing only a small sign out by the side of the gravel road and an even smaller one out on Highway 337, as if that made any sense. He wouldn't even put "Amish" above the name. They just read "Cabinet shop," as if that alone would attract interest.

When would this ever end? Was his life to be spent from grade school to the grave toiling in his father's cabinet shop, keeping the business open, sending cabinets out the door one after another? Sure the work kept a little money in the bank, but working inside was nothing compared to the feeling of working his own land—land like so many others in the community had. Thomas surveyed the open fields, allowing the fantasy of his own farm to flow through his mind.

With a farm there would be fields of corn in the summer. Corn which gave enough to fill a towering silo. There would be waves of golden wheat in the fall growing next to green pasture grass. There would be cows—a herd of twenty or so, hanging around the barn, their udders sagging with milk. There would be a hay wagon to drive down the dirt roads. And all the while, the glorious feeling of being closer to the earth, to *Da Hah,* to life itself.

In his fantasy, Thomas could see himself able to afford a *gut* horse at the sale barn. A driving horse who could pass buggies coming home on Sunday nights from the hymn singing. Instead he had to drive Freddy, his slow gelding around and watch as other buggies passed him, pulled by fast horses purchased with farm money.

Sure, Freddy was okay, and he shouldn't be complaining. *Daett* would be horrified at his unthankfulness. *Daett* always said *Da Hah* gave and *Da Hah* took, and one did not ask questions. Freddy was a decent horse and not that old. He never shied on the road or jumped fences in the barnyard, but a good trot was the limit of his preferable speed.

Thomas's thoughts turned to Susan. He remembered how she had never complained about Freddy's slowness the many times he'd taken her home on Sunday nights. Thomas sighed as he ran sandpaper over the grainy walnut wood. He was twenty-one now and on his own. He was old enough to buy what he wanted, but a fast horse wouldn't be a wise investment on the limited income from the cabinet shop. Especially if he hoped to marry soon. Sure, he could put his money into the purchase of a farm, but farming was difficult work to learn if a person hadn't been raised on one. He needed someone to teach him.

Was that why he was drawn to Susan? The thought turned inside him, but he pushed it away. It was not a fair question. Since grade school he had loved Susan, and there had been no thought of a farm back then. Only lately had it dawned on him what would happen after their marriage. He would be moving onto her family farm. If there had been any doubt about the matter, Susan's father, Menno, had alluded to the fact last Thanksgiving over the noon meal.

"We are hoping you'll be up to taking the farm over soon. After the wedding of course," Menno had said. They had all laughed at the hurried reference to the wedding.

Susan had looked at him, happiness written on her face.

"It's a nice farm," Susan whispered in his ear later. They had held hands that night on the couch and talked far into the night after the others were in bed.

"I don't know anything about farming. I'm a cabinetmaker," he said.

"You can learn. Don't you want to be a farmer, Thomas?"

"Of course I do. I've just never had the chance."

"Then the chance will be coming your way soon," she said, her fingers tracing his face. "I know you'll make a *gut* farmer. As good as what *Daett* is himself."

But that was then. Where is Susan now? Living somewhere in New Jersey. That was the word passed around in the community. He didn't dare ask Menno or Anna. They might be on Susan's side after his foolish actions. The thing with Susan had gone badly enough, and he wouldn't risk more by seeming to use them to pressure their daughter.

What in the world had come over him anyway? A few minutes of talking outside in the shadows of Emery Yoder's house, and he had given in to the sudden urge to kiss Eunice. And Susan had caught him in the act! Their future life together was over. He sighed again.

Yah, what Susan blamed him for had happened, but it wasn't as bad as Susan claimed. *Yah,* Susan's friend Eunice was impressive, and he had fallen hard for her. But it was not supposed to mean anything. Certainly it was not meant to break off the relationship he had with Susan. Even if Eunice liked him in return.

Thomas laughed. According to Susan's version of things, he ought to be seeing Eunice now. But what a joke that was. He wasn't in love with the girl. Impressed? *Yah.* Taken by her? *Yah.* But not in love. And Susan hadn't helped things with all the praise she had heaped on Eunice when she and her family first arrived.

"Eunice is just the funniest girl I've ever met," Susan had said. "She and I can share almost anything. Eunice has some of the best pearls of wisdom to give. She knows so much about life."

Not that he had given it much thought at the time, but looking back, the praise certainly hadn't helped. His interest had been stirred before he ever met Eunice in person. Now what was he to do? Write a letter to Susan? Thomas laughed again. Now that would really kill off the relationship. What kind of foolish letter could he write to New Jersey?

Dear Susan,

Thomas imagined the words looking awkward on the page.

I'm sorry for what happened between us, and I consider the matter to be mainly my fault. Please forgive me, which I don't think you will. So now that our relationship is over, I've been thinking the last few months about also doing something crazy with my life. Something like leaving the Amish for the Mennonites. What do you think about that?

I know I never thought I would take such a step before, but I wanted to let you know how things are turning out. I've just been thinking that perhaps if I'd take such a step it would make it easier for you to return. Would you consider this, please?

I know you were happy on the farm, and I don't want to be the reason for your departure from the Amish. So maybe I should leave, getting my tail out of the community for your sake. Would that help you with coming back?

I'm very sorry for what happened. I hope things are going well with you. Best wishes. Hopefully I will hear from you soon.

> *As one who will always love you,*
> *Thomas*

He laughed again. There would be no such letter. And he had no plans to join the Mennonites, Susan or no Susan. Nor did he plan to leave the community, even with how horribly things had turned out. Susan had refused to speak to him or see him after she caught him in the conversation and kiss with Eunice. Even when he visited her house later during the week, she sent her *mamm* to the door. She'd left the hymn singings by herself or with her cousin Duane.

But leaving for the *Englisha* world? Now Susan was taking things pretty far. Apparently he had totally misjudged her. Did she have a wild side all this time, and his interest in Eunice gave her the chance to do what she'd wanted to do all along? Susan was deliciously sweet but obviously a little dangerous. But that only added to her charm. She was still Amish at heart, and once Amish a person was always Amish. Is that not what Deacon Ray always said? Susan would surely be manageable if he could win her back. *But how do I do that?* he wondered.

Thomas jumped and looked up as his *daett* came through the paint room door.

"Phew, it's rough in there!" his *daett* muttered, taking off his face mask.

"I'll take my turn," Thomas offered, lifting his mask off the wall.

"Take it easy in there," his *daett* said as Thomas slid on the face mask and fastened the straps under his chin.

Thomas nodded and disappeared, closing the door behind him.

He glanced around, trying to see with the amount of light coming in from the windows. Gas lanterns couldn't be used in the paint room, and there were no electric lights, of course. Even a small portable generator was out of the question. Deacon Ray would be down here the first Saturday night if he heard such news. No excuses would be accepted. What a shame that was. On cloudy days like this, even the large windows all along the outer wall let in insufficient light for running the air sprayers.

The quality didn't suffer, but it sure strained the eyes and slowed the work. Why must life be so hard to maintain the traditions of the fathers? But he shouldn't be questioning his life right now. Still, that was apparently what happened to a man's thinking when a girl sent him packing. Leave it to a girl to muddle it all up until he couldn't tell which side of the world was up or down. She had even provoked him to think about leaving for the Mennonites. That was too awful an idea to even think about.

Thomas grabbed the stain gun and began, running a thin spray up and down where his *daett* had left off. As he worked, he couldn't stop his thoughts. *Perhaps I should take Eunice home some Sunday night?* The idea jolted him. *What an awful thing to consider. And what if Susan found out? But Susan is in Asbury Park.* He smiled, running the sprayer up and down the cabinet doors. What would it be like to have Eunice with him in the buggy? No girl had ever sat there but Susan or his sisters. Was Eunice really as much fun as Susan said she was? That conversation outside Emery Yoder's house had been interesting enough.

He could sneak Eunice out some Sunday evening without anyone knowing. *That is, if my sisters could keep their mouths shut. And they would if they knew what was good for them.* His hand paused, the sprayer light in his fingers, his heart racing at the thought.

CHAPTER EIGHT

✦

Thomas sat at the supper table, staring out of the kitchen window. Thoughts raced through his mind, the last splash of color on the western horizon unnoticed. *Tonight would be a* gut *night to pay a visit to Eunice,* he thought. *Why should I wait any longer when my mind is made up?*

"Thomas, do you want a piece of pie?"

His *mamm's* voice jerked him out of his daze.

"He's thinking about Susan so far away and gone." His oldest sister, Lizzie, smirked. "He's mourning the *gut* thing he's lost."

"No, I'm not. And don't bring up Susan," Thomas said. "I was thinking of better things."

"*Hah!* Like there are any," Lizzie said.

"You wouldn't know." Thomas tried to look calm as he finished the last bite on his plate. "And, *yah,* I'll take some of your pie, *Mamm.*"

"Well, it sure wouldn't be like you, passing up pie," *Mamm* said. "I hope you're feeling okay. Speaking of Susan, I'm sure you two can work out whatever your differences are. But I don't see how it can be with her gone to that *Englisha* city. Of course, if that's even true."

"It is true," Lizzie said. Two of the other sisters nodded as Lizzie continued, "And she'll be getting herself into all kinds of trouble, if you ask me. You should have kept the girl under control while you had her, Thomas. Shame on you."

"I tried to patch things up, but it didn't work," Thomas said in his defense.

"Then I take it you have broken up for good?" *Daett* said.

"I'm not sure," Thomas said. "But, *yah,* I guess it could be. It just sort of happened."

"I'm sorry to hear that," *Daett* said. "You made a nice couple."

"Don't go saying that," *Mamm* said. "Thomas probably feels bad enough already."

"Did she dump you?" *Daett* asked, cutting into his pie.

"*Daett!*" *Mamm* said. "Don't be asking such things."

Lizzie made a choking sound from her corner of the table.

Thomas glared in her direction. There was nothing more he had to say about the matter. He supposed all this was mostly his fault.

"You don't have to talk about it," *Mamm* was saying. "It's always hard—these things are. But they do happen."

"That's right." *Daett* chewed on his pie. "Sometimes something will happen that takes two people in different directions."

"Have you tried contacting Susan?" *Mamm* asked. "Perhaps you could write her a letter."

Thomas laughed. "She'd probably tear the paper to pieces as soon as she saw the return address."

Daett smiled. "Women do cool off over time, so don't be so sure about that."

"Well, *I* wouldn't write him back," Lizzie announced. "I'd make any boy suffer if he did to me what Thomas did to Susan."

"Now, now," *Mamm* said. "We all make mistakes. But you didn't do anything inappropriate, did you, Thomas?"

"No, of course not."

"He was sneaking around with her best friend, Eunice," Lizzie said.

Thomas kept his mouth shut. Let Lizzie have her say. It was better to get this over with than to have it fester in everyone's mind.

"You shouldn't be accusing your brother," *Mamm* said.

"Well, he did," Lizzie said. "I heard it straight from a good source."

"I didn't realize what I was doing was that serious," Thomas admitted. He finished the last piece of his pie. "*Yah,* I did speak with Eunice after hymn singing one night, and Susan didn't like that. Now it's over between us."

"I think Thomas should visit Susan, wherever she's at," Margaret, the twelve-year-old, offered.

"Me? Go visit her?" Thomas said. "I don't think so."

"You never know what an apology given face-to-face might do," *Mamm* said.

"Is the girl worth that much?" *Daett* asked.

"*Daett!*" *Mamm* said again. "Don't push the boy too far."

"She's worth a whole lot," Thomas said. "I just don't think it would work. Plus, I've never been out of Indiana. Besides, it might not be that simple anyway. Susan might have someone else by now. Perhaps an *Englisha* man. I mean, she's out in the world. Not that I think she'd do anything wrong, but I figure there are plenty of men who would be interested in her."

"You shouldn't be so down on yourself," *Daett* said, getting up and patting Thomas on the shoulder. "Never let your thinking of yourself stand in the way of speaking to a woman, son. Look at me and the charming woman I got. Why, every boy in the community was clamoring to take her home after the singings. Well, I walked in, spoke to her, and that was all there was to it!"

"You did not!" *Mamm's* cheeks were red.

"Come on now," *Daett* teased.

Mamm offered a small smile. "You were something, I have to admit."

"See!" *Daett* said. "I'm an expert in such matters. Be a man and go after the woman, Thomas!"

"But not to the *Englisha* city!" *Mamm* gasped. "I don't think that's a good idea. It could be dangerous."

"Perhaps you're right," *Daett* agreed. "That is not the way of our people. And now I think we've pestered poor Thomas with enough advice for one evening. Don't you agree?"

"We're so sorry that things didn't turn out well, Thomas," *Mamm* said.

Thomas nodded as *Daett* bowed his head for the closing supper prayer. After *Daett* finished, Thomas went up to his room and changed into a clean shirt and pants. If Susan had suspected the worst about him and Eunice, and if it was all over between them, then why not consider seeing Eunice? He had nothing more to lose.

Leaving his room, he passed Lizzie in the stair hallway.

"You changed your clothes. Where are you going?" Lizzie asked.

"Out!" he said, not slowing his pace. "And keep your mouth shut about it."

"*Mamm* and *Daett* will see you," she said.

He didn't answer as he closed the stair door behind him. Of course they would see him, but that wasn't the problem. It would be seeing Eunice that was the problem, and so he wouldn't tell them. It was that simple.

"I'll be back before long," he said to *Mamm* in the kitchen. *Daett* hadn't looked up in the living room, thankfully. *Mamm* could pass on the information if *Daett* asked. Likely *Daett* wouldn't care as long as he wasn't sleepy tomorrow morning for work.

"You're not up to something you shouldn't be doing are you?" *Mamm* asked, concern on her face.

"No," he said, because he wasn't. Not in the way she meant anyway.

"Don't stay out too late," *Mamm* said, as he shut the washroom door. Thomas grabbed his good coat from one of the top hooks, grabbed a lantern from the shelf, and lit it. Walking out to the barn, he paused to glance at the sky. Faint clouds driven by high winds scurried across the moon. It didn't look like rain was on the way. Not that it made any difference working in the cabinet shop, but the local farmers needed rain.

He pushed open the barn door and called for Freddy. A sharp neigh came from the barnyard. Stepping outside he snapped on the tie rope, leading Freddy back inside. Placing the lantern on a shelf, he threw the harness on and fastened the straps. He blew out the lantern, led Freddy outside, shut the barn door, and hitched his horse to the buggy. They rattled out the driveway. Hopefully the Amish houses he passed would think he was on a late-night errand for his *daett*.

Thomas drove north, then east for two roads, and then north again. Pulling into the small farm of Eunice's *daett*, Jonas Troyer, he left his horse standing by the barn with the reins hanging limp on his bridle. Freddy would go nowhere until he came back. He might not be a fast horse, but he was a *gut* horse who knew when to stay put.

Thomas knocked on the front door and waited. Surely Eunice was

home at this time of the evening. Supper ought to be over, so there
would be no embarrassment from walking in uninvited. Hopefully
Eunice would be willing to step outside on the porch for a few minutes, and they could make their plans quickly.

Steps could be heard from inside, and the door opened.

"Good evening," the deep voice of Eunice's *daett* said, his eyes
searching the darkness in front of him.

"Good evening." Thomas shifted on his feet. *There is no reason to fear,*
he told himself. *I have a perfect right to be here now that Susan is gone.*

"Who is it?" Jonas asked and stepped closer.

"Thomas Stoll."

"Oh, one of the Stoll boys."

"*Yah*, Thomas Stoll," he repeated. "Would Eunice be in by any
chance?"

"*Yah*, she's upstairs."

"Could I speak with her?"

"Oh…well, let me ask." Jonas stepped back into the house.

Thomas cleared his throat, shifting again on his feet.

"*Ach*, you can step inside if you wish." Jonas opened the door wider.
He studied Thomas when he stepped inside holding his hat in his hand.

This is not going well, Thomas thought. *Perhaps I should have waited
until some Sunday night. But then others might see me talking with Eunice
and guess my intentions. Family can keep secrets—but trusting others is
risky.*

"I hope I'm not bothering your evening," Thomas said as faces
appeared in the kitchen opening. Eunice's *mamm,* Martha, a round
woman, jolly on most occasions, came out, sober-faced.

"Did I hear you ask for Eunice?" she asked.

"*Yah*," Thomas said, relaxing. A mother would know how to handle this situation.

"She's upstairs," Martha said. "I'll go and speak with her."

Thomas nodded, staying by the door as her steps sounded on the
stairs and then faded. The faces in the kitchen doorway disappeared.

"*Ach*," Jonas said, "you can have a seat."

Thomas attempted a smile and cleared his throat as he sat down.

Hearing footsteps coming down the stairs, he jumped to his feet, his hat still clutched in his hand. Surely Eunice would invite him outside somewhere, and he wouldn't have to make conversation in front of everyone.

But it was Martha who appeared at the bottom on the stairs, and Thomas's fingers dug into the rim of his hat. Had he been rejected without even a word?

"Eunice will see you upstairs," Martha said with a sweet smile. "She's in her room, the one on the end of the hall. Just knock."

Thomas took a deep breath, glancing at Jonas who gave him a quick nod. Apparently they knew of his honorable reputation and trusted him.

"I won't be long," Thomas said, opening the stair door. He found his way up the unfamiliar steps. A low light was burning somewhere in the hallway above him. The light became stronger until a kerosene lamp set on a shelf on the wall appeared. He quickened his steps. Knocking on the last door, he waited.

"Come in!" Eunice's clear, light voice said. He turned the doorknob with a soft click and stepped inside. She was lying on the bed reading, her head propped in one hand, her eyebrows raised sharply, her *kapp* still on her head.

"Well, Thomas. What are you doing here?" she asked with a wide smile.

"I thought I'd come by, and…well…ask you something."

"Anything important?" she said, still smiling. "Do sit down and make yourself comfortable."

He sat on the edge of the bed. "I can't stay long, but your *mamm* said to come on up."

"Oh, *Mamm* knows I'm still decent this hour of the night, so I don't know why she even had to come up and check. *Mamm* should have sent you right up." After an awkward silence, Eunice asked, "So how is Susan doing?"

Why should Eunice ask about Susan? Thomas wondered. *I didn't come to talk to Eunice about Susan.* "I wouldn't know," he finally said.

"She hasn't written to me, either." Eunice sat up on the bed, laying her book down beside her.

Thomas cut to the chase. "I was wondering if I could bring you home some Sunday night."

"Really? Well, that would be nice. So it's true what they're saying? It's really over between you and Susan?"

"I suppose it is."

"I'm so sorry."

He looked at the floor. "Things change, I guess."

"So when will it be?" Her face lit up. "This will be quite the occasion, I must say. Me going home with the handsome Thomas Stoll. I'm still the new girl around here, you know."

"Well, it's just me." Thomas felt heat spreading up his neck. He wasn't used to such gushiness.

"I must say, I never thought the day would come. Not that I hoped you and Susan would break up. Even if we gave in to temptation and kissed each other. She was a really wonderful friend, but this is really something for me. I'm so glad you came over tonight!"

"Well, it was nice talking to you after the singing that night."

Her face clouded for a moment. "That's been a while ago. There's been plenty of times since then when you had a chance to speak with me. Surely you knew I would have loved that."

"Ah, I wasn't certain." He shifted on the edge of the bed. "Susan and I had been seeing each other for a long time."

Her smile dimmed. "Oh, I can understand that. Susan is a very wonderful person, and I'm sorry it didn't work out. Your asking me is so nice. Can we make a big deal out of it? Maybe bang some plates and throw the rice?"

"Um, not really." He stared at her. "We don't do things like that around here."

"You don't bang plates and throw rice at weddings?"

"No."

"Oh, but of course I wasn't really serious. I know this isn't a wedding. I'm just happy, that's all."

"I would rather not make a big deal out of it."

"Oh." Her face clouded but she looked ready to move closer to him.

Thomas stood up. "I think I'd better be going. So in a couple of weeks, maybe?"

"Not this Sunday? You know I can't wait that long."

Thomas's neck grew hot again. "We'll make it soon, okay. And don't make a fuss, please."

"I won't." She stood, going to open the door for him. Holding the knob, she leaned against the frame, the light of the kerosene lamp playing on her face. "Goodnight now."

"Goodnight," Thomas said. He sidestepped through the door and turned to walk down the hall. The girl was *gut* looking, there was no doubt about that. At least as *gut* as Susan. But he had best be forgetting Susan.

"See you, Thomas!" Eunice said, her light voice lingering in the narrow hallway.

He hadn't kissed her even though she had clearly wanted him to. *That has to wait. Perhaps till I take her home—or perhaps even longer.* The pain of Susan's leaving still bothered him way too much.

CHAPTER NINE

Laura maneuvered her Volkswagen bug into the parking space at the Monmouth Mall. "I think this is as close as we're going to get to the doors. It's crowded tonight, as usual."

"That's okay. I can use the exercise," Susan said. "The bakery keeps me on my feet all day, but there's nothing like brisk walking to get the blood flowing."

"So true," Laura agreed.

As the two women climbed out of the bug, Susan paused, her eyes sweeping over the grandeur of the mall front. "Wow! There's nothing like this in Salem, Indiana."

As they headed toward the mall entrance, Laura cleared her throat. "Susan, there's something I need to tell you."

"Oh?" Susan turned to face her.

"Mr. Moran called me today at the bakery."

Susan looked puzzled.

"You know—Duane. The customer from this morning you asked me about."

"Oh, *yah*...uh, I mean yes." Susan laughed. "Him."

"He asked about you," Laura said.

"Me?" Susan stopped short, and a car horn honked behind them.

Laura took her hand, leading her a few steps out of the way. "I didn't mean to startle you, but I want you to know about his interest. He's a really nice man. I think it's almost an honor that he called to ask about you."

"An honor? He's an *Englisha* man."

"Susan, most of the men around here are. We don't have many Amish people here."

Susan glanced away. Duane being a nice man was fine, but what should that matter to her? "Laura, I might be honored, but really, Duane shouldn't be asking about me. I'm just a plain Amish girl fresh from the farm. I'm sure if you told him that, he'd be gone so fast he wouldn't even leave any dust behind."

Laura laughed. "I *did* tell him, dear. And I hope I wasn't too forward, but like I said earlier, I've known Duane for years."

"You told him I was Amish?"

"*Used* to be Amish" Laura corrected. "He didn't seem to mind. In fact, I think the fact piqued his interest even more."

"So are you the community matchmaker?" Susan asked as the automatic doors opened for them, ushering them into the hall lined with stores on both sides.

"No, silly!" Laura said. "He's the one who called me."

Susan's mind whirled. *What would it be like to date an* Englisha *tax person? Perhaps eating supper with him in a fancy restaurant? What would it be like to talk at length with someone who has that much money? And he must have gobs and gobs of it. Thomas's bank account would look the size of a pea compared to this man's. Not that such things matter, but still…*

"The reason I'm telling you this now is that I mentioned our shopping trip tonight, and he said he might stop by the mall and perhaps run into us," Laura said. "I thought I should warn you."

"Okay, thanks." Susan glanced down the long walkway in front of them. The place was so crowded with shoppers there wasn't much chance they'd see him. She wouldn't worry about it.

"So do they still have matchmakers among the Amish?" Laura asked, steering Susan to the right. "They should have some nice purses down this way, and there are a few things I need to get too."

"No, there are no Amish matchmakers," Susan replied.

Laura smiled. "Robby finally told me about your night out on the beach. He said you're good with a laugh, and that you both had a good time."

"It was wonderful," Susan admitted. "Robby's a lot of fun. Almost as *gut* as an Amish boy. In fact he seems kind of Amish. In some ways, at least."

"I'm not sure he'd take that as a compliment," Laura said, slowing down. "The purses I want you to look at are here in Penney's."

The two women walked into the store, Laura leading the way to the purse racks. Susan looked but couldn't shake the feeling that her *mamm* was watching her. The very idea of carrying a purse in public made her throat tighten. The colors seemed gaudy to her, and the few she thought she might like had prices that shocked her. She could never afford one of these.

"Do you see anything you like?" Laura asked, running her hand over a dark leather offering, its outline trimmed in gold. "How about this one?"

Susan turned the sales tag over. "Laura, I certainly can't afford this." Not that she would dare buy the purse if she could. Her instinct against such a fancy item was still strong, even though she knew these Amish hang-ups of hers would have to cease.

"This one's nice." Laura lifted a white purse and turned it sideways. "White, but not too white."

Susan studied the purse. It was less fancy than the others and white would be a *gut* choice. Black would have been better, but white was passable. She knew she needed to be *sure* of the choice so she wouldn't worry later, wondering if the purchase had been a sin or not. Finally she looked at Laura and said, "I'll take this one."

"Are you sure? Some of these red-and-blue ones are a bit cheaper." Laura turned the tags over for Susan to see.

"No, this is the one." Susan's voice was firm. "It's white." A clear conscience was worth a little extra money.

Taking the purse from the rack, Susan paid at the register, leaving the purse in the bag as they walked out into the rush of people again.

"You can start to use it," Laura said. "It's purchased now."

Susan shook her head. "I'll take it home first."

Truth was, she needed a little more time to get used to this. Carrying the purse around in the bag might help.

"I need to go to the other end of the mall," Laura said. "You can come along or you can check out one of the other stores. I have to come back this way. We can meet here, if you want."

Susan scanned the store signs around her. Locking on one store's logo, she said, "I think I'll browse through that bookstore over there," she said.

"Perfect," Laura said. "Will you go anywhere else?"

"No, just the bookstore."

"Okay. I'll meet you here in fifteen or twenty minutes." Laura quickly moved away and blended into the crowd.

Susan watched until she had disappeared before walking toward the bookstore. She felt somewhat alone with Laura gone, but taking a deep breath, Susan entered the bookstore and perused the shelves. That there were so many books in the world amazed her. Books she had no idea existed.

One rack had a sign that said "*New York Times* Bestsellers." *What are* New York Times *Bestsellers?*" she wondered. Susan picked up one of the books and read the back cover. It sounded good, so she opened the pages and read a few paragraphs. Quickly she blushed and stepped back. She replaced the book on the shelf. How did people write using such language, let alone *read* it? *Even married people didn't talk to each other with such words…did they? But how would I know?*

Susan looked around to see if someone had seen her reading the book. No one seemed interested in her. Several people were reading from books on the shelves, so it must be okay. Susan took another deep breath and tried a different title.

She read a paragraph in the first chapter, scanned further, and then replaced the book. The storyline was too spooky, and how did anyone know about such things? The idea was completely unbelievable. Deacon Ray would stroke his beard and look really sober at the very idea. How could someone come back from the grave and watch his relatives live their lives?

This is discouraging and strange, she thought. *Are there no* Englisha *books worth reading?* Her eye caught a display deeper into the store, and she caught her breath. *What? Amish people on the covers of books? Rather, they looked somewhat Amish. But how is this possible? No Amish person would stand still for such a picture—especially this close to their faces.*

Picking up a book, she paged through it, reading here and there. It wasn't that bad, the storyline following an Amish girl's travails with her boyfriend. Well, they should talk to *her* about travails with boyfriends. Now *that* would be a story. But no one would be interested in her life. Apparently though, the *Englisha* were interested in Amish life—but she sure wasn't. She had lived it.

Turning back to the *New York Times* Bestseller list books, Susan tried again. There had to be something here she could read. She took another book off the shelf. Flipping through the pages, she read here and there, laughed and continued reading. Now this was something a person could read. She read on, skimming through a chapter. It was interesting. Deacon Ray wouldn't like this either, but it was a *gut* storyline. A man traveling back and forth in time, ending up somewhere in a strange land without his clothing. Susan laughed again. She checked the price on the back of the cover. It was expensive, but she would buy it.

Susan walked to the register and paid for the book. This was something to read, at least.

"Sixteen dollars and fifteen cents," the man said. Susan jumped. The price had been marked clearly, but it was still a lot of money when said right out loud like that.

Paying with a twenty, Susan placed the change into her pocket. Soon she would use a purse like the women did, but not tonight. Now, she might as well find a place to sit and read until Laura returned. Her search located a bench in the middle of the press of people, looking like an island in the middle of the sea. Surely Laura would be able to find her here.

She sat down and opened the book, beginning on the first page this time.

"Excuse me," a man's voice said a few minutes later. "Do you mind if I sit down?"

"No." Susan replied, not looking up. She continued to read.

He cleared his throat, and she looked at him. She stood up. "Mr. Moran! It's you."

"Oh, so you do remember?" He smiled. "Do you still not mind if I sit down?"

"Of course. I mean, of course not. Why no…I don't," she said, the words falling over each other.

Oh, please, where is Laura! Her mind raced. *What am I supposed to say to this man? And what will people think when they see me talking with such a* gut-*looking* Englisha *man?*

Chapter Ten

The crowd of people in the mall moved past Susan, ebbing and flowing like the waves of the ocean. Beside her sat Mr. Moran, the *Englisha* man. Susan couldn't help but be concerned about who might be watching. But this was not Amish country, and no one knew her. Susan took a deep breath and edged away from him. Hopefully he wouldn't notice the small movement.

"So," Duane said, smiling, "I hear you're new to Asbury Park. Are you adjusting okay?"

"Okay, *yah*. Really *gut*," Susan said. What a bumbling, mumbling mess she was making of this. Why had she ever thought an Amish girl could make a go of it in the *Englisha* world? At least Thomas had been one of her own people—an equal. This man was way up there in the world, almost too high for her to speak with.

"I guess I should have introduced myself better. I'm Duane Moran," he said. "And I work in town at H&R Block."

Susan nodded. "Laura told me."

"Oh," Duane said. "But I guess I'm not surprised. Did Laura tell you I called today?"

"She did." Susan kept her eyes on her shopping bag.

"I know Laura from way back," he said. "I'm not surprised she mentioned my call. I guess I should have spoken with you myself this morning. It seemed easier this way."

"It doesn't matter," she said. *Whatever that means,* she thought. Now she was having a hard time breathing with him so close and smelling of

70

leathery cologne. The light scent hung in the air. Thomas wore cologne at times, but he never smelled like this.

"You come from Indiana, Laura said."

"Out in the country." Susan caught her breath. "We live close to Salem. That's our only nearby town. We go there for grocery shopping and some of the small things."

"There's nothing wrong with living in the country," he said. "I was raised in the city, but the country's great. I don't get out of town often enough to suit me."

"Really?" she glanced at his face.

"Sure," he said. "The country's where the hardworking people live. Do your folks still live in Indiana?"

Susan laughed. "Yes, and they always will, believe me."

"Sort of have their roots down, then."

"You could say so."

He sure didn't know much about Amish people. They put down roots while still in their mothers' wombs. And woe to the man or woman who tried to pull them up.

"Salt of the earth types then, working hard all their lives." He rubbed his hands together.

Did she dare ask him a question? Yes, she'd venture it. "Do you ever work outdoors?"

"Me?" he looked at her and chuckled.

She glanced away. "I just wondered, that's all. I know it's none of my business."

"No, I'm afraid not. I do most of my work sitting at a desk."

"Oh," Susan looked at the floor this time.

"Do you like the book?" He motioned with his chin toward the book she had lain on the bench.

"So far it's a little strange but interesting. Expensive, that's for sure."

He laughed. "Certainly not country prices at this mall."

"No," was all she could think to say.

After a silent pause, he stood up and said, "Well, I have to get going. It was good to run into you. I hope you enjoy the book. I certainly did. Tell Laura hello for me."

"I will." Susan stood.

He smiled and disappeared into the flow of the people. She caught a glimpse of him going past the bookstore before she sat down again. Laura would be back soon, and being caught staring after an *Englisha* man would have looked quite ridiculous.

Susan opened the book, but the words were a blur as her mind ran over the encounter again and again. How had she handled herself? He hadn't spoken to her as if she were a country hick. He said he liked the country, but that could mean anything. What had he thought of her? That was a horrible thing to even consider. She shouldn't be concerned about what an *Englisha* man thought of her.

Susan stood again and paced the floor in front of the bench. Thoughts of Duane kept running through her mind. What a clean face he had. He looked like he lived a healthy, wholesome life. Thomas had looked wholesome too, but what *gut* did that do?

"Oh!" Susan exclaimed and jumped when Laura appeared out of the crowd in front of her.

"Sorry it took so long." Laura said, looking flustered. "But I see you found something to read."

"*Yah,* I bought a book. And I think I'll like it."

"Let's go then. It's going to be late enough by the time we get back." Laura led the way toward the mall entrance.

Susan followed, trying to keep up. Laura seemed in a hurry, taking huge steps. *Shouldn't I say something about Duane,* Susan wondered. *If I don't now, it will be harder later.* But the words were sticking to her throat. "Mr. Moran stopped by for a few minutes while I was waiting for you. He said to say hi," she finally got out.

A faint smile formed on Laura's face. "I thought he might. Well, he's a good man, let me assure you of that."

They reached the car. Laura unlocked the door with a burp of the key fob and climbed in. "I'm glad Duane stopped by to speak with you," Laura said as Susan climbed in and Laura pulled out of the parking lot.

Susan smiled. What else was there to do? Smiling covered most of the bases in Amish country.

"I don't know about your prospects at home," Laura was saying, "but a girl like you surely had plenty of chances. I can't imagine the Amish boys leaving you alone. So you might not be looking for a new relationship, but if you are, don't throw Duane's interest away too quickly. Maybe he's a shock to you, since you haven't been around our kind much, but Duane's a nice man."

"I…I didn't know he was interested in me."

"Oh!" Laura said with a short laugh. "I didn't mean to imply that exactly, but I'm a woman, and, well—a mother. And I just sort of have a feeling about things like this."

"I think I'd be a little below his world," Susan said.

"You're on his level, don't worry about that. But like I said, I don't profess to be a matchmaker. But I want to help out where I can."

Susan cleared her throat. "I think we'll just forget about Mr. Moran for now. But what can you tell me about schooling? I'm thinking I should look into getting—what did you call it?"

"Oh, of course," Laura said. "Your G-E-D. That's what people get when they haven't completed high school and are too old to go back."

"That would be me."

"I didn't mean to make you sound old," Laura said.

"I am old!" Susan laughed. *Old enough to be cast aside, forgotten, broken to pieces, counted unworthy of love, and all sorts of things like that. All of which came from Thomas, the heartbreaker who is probably smiling into Eunice's eyes right now.*

"Are you okay?" Laura glanced at Susan's face for a brief moment. "I didn't mean anything by that remark."

"I know." Susan forced a smile. "I was just thinking, that's all."

"You are a very beautiful girl, Susan. Remember that. No matter what anyone says."

"You don't have to be so nice." Susan pulled out her handkerchief. Now why did she have to go crying all of a sudden?

"Don't worry about Duane. I'll take you up to the community college sometime soon," Laura said, reaching over to pat her hand. "They have practice test papers you can get to help you prepare for the GED. You'll find out what lessons you're weak on, and you can study those. What do you say to that?"

"I think that would be a *gut* idea." Susan put her handkerchief away. Crying time was over now. They were almost back at the apartment, and life moved on. *Isn't that what everyone says?*

Laura slowed the car and pulled up to the curb. Susan grabbed her two bags and stepped out. "Thanks for taking me. It means a lot."

"I enjoyed it," Laura said. "Now, remember to lock up extra careful. Are you using the deadbolt and the chain?"

"Yes," Susan said, her hand on the car door. "But *Da Hah* will watch over me."

"I'm sure He will, dear, but lock the doors anyway. Okay?"

"Okay." Susan stepped back from the curb and watched Laura take off down Main Street.

She found her key, unlocked the apartment door, entered, and carefully relocked the door on the inside. She went slowly up the creaky steps, their soft sounds soothing her spirit. *What are* Mamm *and* Daett *doing tonight? Probably still sitting on their rockers in the living room. I really should write them a letter.* Not everything she was doing could be said of course, but enough so they might not worry as much.

At the top of the stairs Susan reached for the light switch. With a flip of her wrist she flooded the room in light and a smile crossed her face. This was much better than a kerosene lamp. One could see everything as clear as daylight. She was moving into the *Englisha* world.

Glancing at the clock, Susan walked over to the desk. It was time for bed, but there was still time to write a letter if she hurried. Opening the drawer she found paper and pen and sat down at the kitchen table.

"Dear *Mamm* and *Daett*," she began, the pen moving firmly across the page. Then the thoughts stopped. *Something is wrong.* She stopped writing and looked around the room, pondering what it could be. With a sigh, she got to her feet and retrieved the kerosene lamp from the bedroom. She found a match and lit the wick. Leaving the lamp on the kitchen table she walked over and turned off the electric light. *That ought to be better*, she thought, sitting down again. The room glowed in the soft, flickering light of the kerosene lamp. Becoming *Englisha* would have to wait.

She picked up the pen and continued.

> *I'm doing as well as can be expected. The bakery is really busy even as winter approaches. I think winter comes a little earlier here than in Indiana—at least from how the air feels. The Oyster Festival the city has each year is over, and I got to meet some Amish people. Can you believe that? I don't know who they were, and I didn't introduce myself. It would have taken too much explaining.*
>
> *I'm so sorry for the hurt my move has probably caused you. I didn't intend to hurt anyone at all, and I hope you understand. Mamm, you have always been so good about understanding things, as has Daett.*
>
> *Laura and I made a trip to the mall tonight. I purchased a purse and a book. I think I'll like both of them. I'm planning some other things also—small little moves I can make to get settled in here.*
>
> *Well, it's past my bedtime, and I must get my sleep. Take care all of you.*
>
> *Tell everyone hi for me, and I haven't forgotten about any of you.*
>
> *Laura is a very sweet lady and is taking good care of me.*
>
> *Yours truly, Susan*

She folded the paper and left it on the kitchen table. There would be time to address an envelope and seal it tomorrow. For now, she needed sleep. She checked down the stairs one last time to make sure things were the way Laura wanted them to be. The door was securely locked. Beyond that all she needed to do was pray, which would help more than anything else.

She knelt beside her bed and prayed softly,

> *Dear* Da Hah, *I'm so sorry for all my sins and faults. I know* Mamm *and* Daett *are very disappointed in me, and I am*

*often disappointed in myself. Please help me, and I will trust
that You understand.*

*You know how I feel about Thomas, and that I am still bitter.
Please keep me safe in this big city. And thank You for Laura
and Robby. They are very wonderful people. In Jesus's name I
pray. Amen.*

Susan changed into her bedclothes, climbed into bed, and blew out
the kerosene lamp. The apartment settled into darkness, only the glow
of the streetlamps visible behind the shades. It wasn't quiet in the city
like the farm, but she had almost gotten used to the sounds. Thankfully
Da Hah was taking care of her, just as He took care of the community
at home. She had to believe that or all was lost.

CHAPTER ELEVEN

The morning was starting slow. Susan waited behind the counter, having served only two customers since the bakery had opened fifteen minutes earlier. She was just about to check the cinnamon bread baking in the back when the door opened quietly and a familiar young girl walked in. *Where have I seen this young woman before?* Susan wondered. "Good morning," she said.

"Morning," the woman mumbled, opening her coat and reaching inside.

Recognition crossed Susan's face. This was the pregnant girl who had studied her so carefully a few days ago.

"I'll take a small coffee," the girl said, pulling a handful of change from her pocket.

Hadn't she ordered a small coffee the time before? Would she sit around today and watch me again? Not that it bothers me, but the girl does look troubled.

Laura was in the back office, so Susan rang up the purchase. "Can I help you with the coffee to the table?" Susan asked.

"No, I'm fine," the girl said, her eyes sad. And then she added, "Are you Amish, ma'am?"

"Oh!" Susan jumped. *Do I still look so Amish?* "I used to be. I left the Amish recently."

"I see," the girl said. "The Amish are nice people."

"We try to be." Susan offered her a smile. "How is the baby coming along?"

The girl's faced darkened, and Susan wished she hadn't asked.

"I'm having many troubled thoughts about the baby," the girl said. "It's hard, you know."

"I can imagine," Susan said. She wasn't quite sure what the girl meant, but carrying a baby had to be difficult. It was hard sometimes even at home when the women were surrounded by the community. How much harder would it be in the *Englisha* world?

"I'm trying to find someone to take the baby," the girl said. "I can't care for him myself. My mom doesn't think I know what I'm doing."

"Oh!" Susan gasped. "That would be hard. Have you found someone yet?"

"No." The girl shook her head. Then she looked up at Susan with a wide-eyed stare. "I'm still praying hard about it."

"That's *gut*," Susan agreed. *At least the girl believes in Da Hah.*

"Well, thank you again," the girl said. She gave Susan a weak smile before turning to walk out the door.

So today she isn't staying to watch me. That's just as well. But there is something about that girl. What is it? Susan watched the girl's form go past the window. Seeing the girl again made Susan wonder if today might be the day Mr. Moran would visit the bakery again. She had watched for him the past few days, expecting he would come in. But he hadn't. *Is he like the rest of them? Like Thomas? A charming fellow who tempts girls with his attention and then disappears like the morning mist off a pond? Those kinds of boys are like ducks who take to the air, leaving only water droplets falling from the sky. Painful droplets that turn into tears.*

"Seems kind of slack around here," Laura said, poking her head out of her office. "If too many people show up at once, let me know." She smiled and disappeared again.

Susan stared at the empty tables and chairs. What would her *mamm* and *daett* be doing today? *Daett* still worked all day in the fields. This morning he would be outside doing the fall plowing. He really shouldn't be doing the heavy work anymore. He was way too old—well past the age when even Amish men were supposed to slow down.

Maybe if she had pushed Thomas to be married this year instead of next this breakup wouldn't have happened. But then if the kiss had still happened, how awful that would have been.

"It wasn't my fault!" she said out loud. She turned to look behind her. *What if Laura heard me? She'd think I'm crazy for sure.*

The front door opened and an older woman walked in.

"Can I help you?" Susan asked and added, "It's a really fine morning, isn't it?"

"As fine a morning as can be expected," the lady said. "You certainly sound cheerful this morning."

"Well, I try to be. Can I get something for you?"

"I'll take a strawberry turnover and a small coffee."

Susan placed the turnover on a plate and moved to the cash register. "That will be two ninety-nine," she said.

The lady handed Susan a five-dollar bill, collecting the change with a trembling hand. Susan came around the side of the counter and picked out a plastic cup. "I'll help you with the coffee. Is that okay?"

"Well, you are sweet, darling. Of course it's okay."

"Which kind do you want? We have several selections."

"Oh, my goodness! Just the regular, old-fashioned kind. I never can get used to these newfangled flavors."

"Cream? Sugar?"

"A little cream, dear, but no sugar."

Susan prepared the coffee for the woman and set it on the table where the woman had seated herself.

"You have a good day now," Susan said. "And I hope you like the turnover."

"I'm sure I will." The lady smiled. "I think I'll come back here more often."

"I hope you do!" Susan said, hearing the door open behind her. As she turned to head back to the counter, she heard a familiar voice.

"Good morning, Miss Hostetler." It was Mr. Moran.

Susan continued her way behind the counter where she felt more comfortable.

"Good morning." Susan tried to sound natural. "What can I do for you?"

"I was expecting the usual," he said, a twinkle in his eye.

"It's been a while," Susan said. "I think I've forgotten."

"True," he said. "I like the apple fritters. I'll take one of those and a large coffee. Is Laura in this morning?"

"She's in the office. I can call her, if you wish."

Susan noticed then that Mr. Moran had a stern look on his face—as if something was wrong. *What can it be?* she wondered.

"No, don't bother her," he said. "I'm just concerned. There's been another missing woman from around here. Have you seen the paper this morning?"

"No! I haven't opened the paper. Surely not here in Asbury Park again?" she gasped. "That's awful. Who could be doing this horrible thing?"

"I'm sure the police wish they knew, not to mention the young woman's parents."

Susan forced herself to reach for his apple fritter, her hand shaking. She knew she must trust *Da Hah,* but this was not *gut* news at all.

"Was it close by?" she asked, nearly dropping the fritter.

"At Monmouth Mall. That's where the woman was seen last. I'm sorry to bring you the news, but I'm quite concerned."

"We must pray for the family," Susan said, handing him his order.

"Yes, that would be a good idea. And for yourself. You are careful, I hope?"

"*Yah.* Laura reminds me often."

"It's bad when things like this start to happen. Often they aren't over with for quite some time."

He handed her a ten. Taking his change, he still looked distracted. Suddenly he asked, "Are you busy over the lunch hour?"

"I don't know," Susan said. "We usually are."

"I could come by and take you over to the diner to eat. I don't have much time, but it would give you a break from here."

"You…take me out to eat? I…I…I've never done that before."

"What? You don't always eat at home on the farm, do you?" he asked with a laugh.

"That's not what I meant…I meant…"

He laughed again. "Yes, I know what you meant. I'm sorry, I was just teasing you. How about if I stop by a few minutes after one? If you can get away, we'll walk over to the diner. I can have you back in no time. Surely Laura can handle things for a little while."

He is asking me out to eat? What does that mean in the Englisha *world? Is it something friendly? Obviously…but how friendly? Friendly as in a smile at a hymn singing, or friendly as in taking a girl home in a buggy, or friendly as in a goodnight kiss? Certainly not that!* she decided. "I don't know," Susan replied. "We're usually busy over the lunch hour. I'd better stay here. But thank you." Her neck felt warm…burning, the sensation spreading fast. This was awful, absolutely *awful.*

"Maybe some other time then." He started to turn but hesitated. "Let me know if you change your mind. I'm working outside the office at a client's place until eleven. But between then and say quarter to twelve you could call me at the office. Laura has the number. Oh, and do pray for the family of the missing women. I will too." With that, he turned and was gone.

"That was a nice man," the older lady said, getting up from the table. "Is he your boyfriend?"

"No!" Susan said quickly. *An* Englisha *boyfriend? Why, the world would stop turning if an Amish girl ever had an* Englisha *boyfriend.* But hadn't she come here to look for love? *Yah,* but not this. *Then what am I looking for?* Thoughts raced through her head. It was so confusing and mixed up. *If only Thomas hadn't gone and messed everything up!*

"You have a good day," the lady was saying. "And I will also pray about that kidnapper that's loose on our streets. Heaven knows he won't bother old ladies like me, but I can still pray."

"Thank you," Susan whispered as the lady left. It was *gut* that people were praying. That at least felt a little bit like home.

"Not busy yet?" Laura asked, coming out of the back and surveying the empty shop. "Did I hear Duane's voice?"

Susan kept her eyes on the window. "He was here. He told me there's another woman missing. This time from the Monmouth Mall, where we were the other night."

Laura opened the newspaper and read the story while Susan silently struggled with her thoughts. Why did she feel like she was missing something regarding the lunch invitation? How could so many conflicting emotions be racing around inside her at the same time?

"God help us all," Laura said, as she read. "I sure hope the police find this man soon."

Susan cleared her throat. "What an awful experience for the woman and her family to go through."

"Yes, it is," Laura said. "I wonder if it's safe for you to stay alone at the apartment anymore. I couldn't live with myself if something happened to you while you're here. How would I explain it to Bonnie, let alone your parents?"

"I'm fine," Susan said. "I can't afford any other place. I come from the country. I'm strong and resourceful."

"You could stay at our place until this blows over. We have a spare bedroom upstairs."

"But I'm not family. And I couldn't. Really, I couldn't."

"Don't look so distressed," Laura said. "You're almost family."

"Oh, that's a sweet thing for you to say," Susan said as tears formed in her eyes. The door opened behind her, and she covered her face. She couldn't be caught crying in front of customers.

Laura squeezed her hand under the counter.

"He asked me to lunch," Susan whispered, keeping her eyes focused on the kitchen.

"Who?"

"Mr. Moran."

"Duane?"

"*Yah.* I told him I couldn't. That I had to help in the shop because I really do, and I don't mind."

"We'll see about that," Laura whispered back.

Susan dried her eyes and turned to greet the young man who had walked up. "Good morning. Can I help you?"

Behind him the door had opened again, and two others came in. Clearly the morning rush was starting.

CHAPTER TWELVE

Two customers remained in the bakery, a woman and a man separated by two tables and lost in their own worlds. Outside the street traffic had slowed down, and the bell over the door had been silent for ten minutes.

"So let's have this out about Duane," Laura said, pinning Susan in her place behind the counter with a sharp look.

"I don't want to go," Susan said, her face resolute.

"What exactly did Duane ask? Perhaps we should start there."

Susan was silent for a moment, thinking back over those few moments. "Well, he said that if I could leave over the lunch hour, he'd take me to the diner across the street. And that it wouldn't take very long."

"And you said what?"

"That we're usually busy over the lunch hour, and that I couldn't go."

"Is that all?"

Susan shrugged before continuing, "He said if I changed my mind I should call him between eleven and twelve. That you know his phone number."

"Yes, I do. And I think you should call him and go," Laura said. "That is, unless you really don't want to. I don't want to force you into something you don't want to do."

Susan's eyes grew wide. "What does it mean in the *Englisha* world when a man asks you out to the diner over the lunch hour?" she asked. "How serious is that?"

"You poor thing." Laura patted Susan on the hand. "I guess you wouldn't know. It's not serious at all. Just indicates an interest—a start perhaps, but nothing really. You don't have to worry. And Duane is an outstanding young man. He doesn't come to our church, but he does go. I can't remember where. I'm sure that's important to you."

"It is," Susan said. "I suppose he has the bishop's approval on his life."

Laura looked startled for a moment and then burst out laughing. "You do have a sense of humor. It's kind of sudden at times, but it's there nonetheless."

Susan looked puzzled but continued the conversation. "I just don't know. Mr. Moran is kind of nice, but it's so sudden."

"That's understandable, dear. But don't expect Duane to give up easily—not if I know him."

Susan took a deep breath and said, "Okay, I'll go then." *Is this a mistake?* she wondered. She did want to go, but she also didn't want to go. What a mess to be in. And it was so strange. That was the problem, no doubt. The strangeness of everything. Surely life would get easier, when things weren't so odd. And she simply couldn't stay cooped up in the apartment for the rest of her life. Thomas was in the past, and life must move on. This must be part of moving on.

Laura had a big smile on her face. "I think that's the right choice, dear. You just take it slow and easy. I know Duane won't push things. If he does, you come tell me, and I'll have a talk with him."

"You sound so serious," Susan said. "Like a lot of things are going to happen between us."

"I guess I do." Laura shook her head. "And that's really wrong of me. I'm sorry, I didn't mean to push."

"It's okay," Susan said. She glanced at the clock on the far wall. "Mr. Moran said to call between eleven and twelve. Will you do that for me? See if he still wants to...to take me out?"

"I could, but why don't you call him, dear? It would give you practice with our world. If the man invites you to lunch and told you to call him at his office, then you have the right to. Remember now, you don't have to feel intimidated at all."

"*Me* call *him*? He's a tax person. And the building he works in—it's all glittery and glitzy."

Laura laughed. "He's also a man, Susan. Just remember that. A man—and a good one. Don't be afraid of our *Englisha* ways."

The door opened, and Susan glanced again at the clock. Could she really do this? Call Mr. Moran? The thought was freezing her throat like homemade ice cream did when swallowed too quickly. Even the sweetness of the thought didn't take away the fear.

Susan busied herself with the customer, but kept an eye on the clock, noting the time advancing. With each tick her stomach twisted into a larger and larger knot. There was still time to back out. She didn't have to make the call. But she wanted to. That was the problem. Hopefully another customer would come through the door soon and keep her attention off the clock. But really, she was making way too big a deal out of this. It was nothing, really. It was like a smile between a girl and boy back at the Amish Sunday night hymn singing. They could be friends or just like each other's company.

The door opened and she waited on the young couple who entered, watching them as they chose a table. They laughed softly over the murmur of each other's words. Perhaps he had asked her out today, to meet him at Laura's bakery for a few quick moments. If he had, it seemed to be working fine. Susan glanced at the clock again. It was past eleven. She took a deep breath and walked back to Laura's office.

"Will you give me Mr. Moran's phone number?" Susan asked, trying to keep her breathing even. *Why is this so hard? I've used the phone in the phone shack at home many times. But this is like…well, this is totally something else. I've never called a tax person who wanted to take me out to eat.*

"Right here," Laura said, showing her the number. "Take your time. I'll take care of the shop."

Susan waited until Laura left and closed the door before she dialed. She listened to the ringing of the phone in her ear.

"H&R Block, Mandy speaking," a woman's voice said. "How may I help you?"

"Ah…" Susan cleared her throat. "I need to speak with Mr. Moran." Apparently he didn't answer his own phone. But of course he wouldn't. He was a tax person. There were secretaries who worked for tax people.

"Just a moment," Mandy said. The phone clicked.

Susan clutched the receiver and waited.

Suddenly he was there. "This is Duane Moran."

"Ah, Mr. Moran," she managed.

He laughed. "Hello, Susan. Duane is fine. Have you changed your mind about lunch, I hope?"

"If you still want to take me. Laura said she would take care of the shop."

"Always a darling, Laura is," he said. "How about twelve sharp? Will that work for you?"

"Yes, certainly. At the diner? Shall I meet you there?"

"I'll save a booth by the window, okay? And, Susan…"

"Yes."

"I'm glad you can come."

"Yes. Well, thanks. I'll see you then."

"Goodbye," he said.

"Goodbye." She pressed the receiver against her chest, feeling the redness move all the way up to her cheeks. She had made the call! Who would have thought such a thing possible just a few months ago? She, Susan Hostetler, had just called a *gut*-looking *Englisha* tax person to accept a lunch invitation. That was enough to make even the cows standing in the fields at home blink in astonishment!

Susan cracked open the door and glanced out. The line was lengthy in front of the counter. There was nothing like work to soothe jittery nerves! Stepping up beside Laura, she waited on customers.

"What time?" Laura whispered as she got an order together.

"Twelve sharp," Susan answered as she continued working, the line becoming even longer.

"I shouldn't be going," Susan whispered. "We're getting really busy."

Is there still time to call Duane and explain? raced through her mind.

Laura didn't answer but kept working, moving deftly between the pastries and the cash register. Finally at five minutes before twelve, Laura said, "You better go now."

"But the line?" Susan said, almost moaning.

"Go!" Laura's voice was firm. "I've been busy before. This is not new to me."

Susan wiped her hands and took off her apron as customers glanced at her. She walked past them, ignoring their looks.

Yah, she thought about saying out loud. *I'm going to see an* Englisha *man for lunch. Just stare at me. As if I don't feel bad enough already—and guilty.*

Outside, the noise of the noonday traffic swept over her. As she made her way down one block to cross at the light, she broke out in a nervous smile as she once again thought that here she was, Susan Hostetler, going to have lunch with an *Englisha* man.

A few people were standing at the light. She got in line, looking with them across the street to the traffic signal. Finally the little white man in the black box signaled *Walk*. The waiting pedestrians surged forward, Susan moving too. In the rush and the crowd, Susan suddenly lurched as something caught at her foot, wrenching her shoe and sending her in a forward fall. Her hands went out to break the spill, the impact solid on the palms of her hands, the pain stinging all the way up to her shoulders. A groan escaped in protest against the pain before she stifled the cry, clamping her lips together. A woman stopped and asked if she was okay. She quickly nodded, embarrassed by the fall. She stood up and, with an upward glance, saw the little man in the traffic box turning red and holding out his hand. The signal had changed, and soon automobiles would come crashing her way.

But her left shoe! It had come off and now lay five feet away, tipped over, the low heel broken off. The waiting cars, their fierce-looking grills staring at her, were ready to claim their rightful place in the intersection. She'd have to leave the shoe and move to the curb. It was ruined anyway. As she reached the curb, she turned to see the cars were already moving through the crosswalk. A large blue van ran directly over her abandoned shoe, squashing it into a flat piece of black in the middle of the street.

Susan took a step forward on the sidewalk, feeling the up and down motion of her hips. At least she could walk, and she didn't have far to go. *Great!* What would Mr. Moran think when she came limping into the diner, one foot wearing only a sock. A true country hick, no doubt. One who couldn't even walk from the bakery to the diner without losing her shoe. "He'll have to think what he wants. He's the one who asked me to come," she said aloud. She continued to walk, trying to minimize the up-and-down motion. Thankfully, nobody around her seemed to care.

So where is that diner! Yah, *right over there, a block ahead.* One thing was for sure, that tumble had cleared her head. It felt as clean as a cloudless sky in the middle of a summer hayfield.

CHAPTER THIRTEEN

Susan approached the diner, trying to see through the front glass window. What a sight she must make, one foot shoeless. She still walked down the middle of the sidewalk. Already the concrete bit into the sole of her foot, pressing odd objects against her skin, no matter how carefully she stepped. She could feel something running slowly down from her skinned knees—probably blood, but at least it was hidden by her dress.

Susan pushed open the diner door, standing aside to hold the door for a customer coming out. *Where is Mr. Moran?* Yah, *there he is.* Had he seen her approach? No, he couldn't have. He was just turning around.

"Susan!" He greeted her with a smile, standing as she approached the table. "It's so good to see you. And my thanks to Laura for letting you off over your lunch hour."

"The shop was busy," Susan said, taking a seat. Had he noticed her shoeless foot? Apparently not.

He was ready to sit down but he stopped and asked, "Did I just see what I think I saw?"

"What did you see?" she asked. Now that was a stupid thing to ask, but perhaps he was asking about something other than her shoeless foot.

"You walked in with only one shoe on. What happened?"

"The shoe—*yah*. It fell off when I stumbled crossing the street. Now it's flat as a pancake and still in the middle of the street."

"Susan!"

"It's nothing, really," she interrupted. "Other than wearing my sock

out, but that's not a big loss." Duane still looked at her, which was fast
becoming embarrassing. Surely he wasn't going to make a big fuss over
this.

"You said you fell."

"Yes, but I'm okay."

"You fell in the middle of the street?"

"*Yah.* I was crossing at the light. There were other people with me,
and I stumbled for some reason. The shoe stayed there, and the light
changed, and *bam...*"

"You could have gotten hurt. *Are* you hurt?"

"No, I don't think so." *Am I? Come to think of it, my knees do burn a
bit. And I can still feel moisture on my left leg.*

"A person just doesn't fall on the pavement without some scrapes
happening. Are you sure you're okay?"

What was she supposed to do? Pull up her dress and look? Right
in the middle of the diner? With him watching? Not a chance in the
world. Not even on the farm. Thomas had never seen her legs, and she
sure wasn't going to show them to an *Englisha* man.

"You're sure you're not hurt?" Duane repeated, his voice unbeliev-
ing. He was still standing over her.

What should she say? She now felt the blood on her left leg dripping close to her dress hem. It would soon be visible.

"I do feel some blood trickling down my leg," she said, not able to
look him in the face.

"Susan, you have to have it looked after."

He sounded concerned, but maybe that was his tax person voice.
It sounded strong, manly, like he could make things happen just by
speaking.

"How?" she asked. "I'm in a restaurant."

"Are you ready to order?" a woman's voice said behind them. They
both turned around. The waitress stood there, pad and pen ready.

"Just a moment," he said. "We have a problem, I think. Do you happen to have a first aid kit?"

"Sure, in the back. Did someone get hurt?" the young woman asked,
concern in her voice.

"Susan skinned her knees outside. I think she needs them looked after."

"Oh, sure," the waitress said, sticking her pad and pen in her apron pocket. "Let's have a look and then I can see what I need to bring back."

Susan clutched the edge of her dress. What was she supposed to do? Thomas would have understood and left the room, but Duane was still standing there. She pulled the dress up, inches at a time, until the hemline was past her knees. She could see blood trickling down her left leg in long, red streams.

"Oh, that's bad," the girl said. "You'd better come back to the restroom and wash up first."

Susan felt the hot flush of red creeping up her neck. Had Duane looked? She stood up, daring a quick glance sideways at him. He had been looking, but his face only revealed worry. But then, he saw women's legs every day, didn't he? *Englisha* girls showed their legs all the time. And hers were nothing out of the ordinary.

"I'll take you to the doctor, if you need to go," he offered.

"I'll be okay." She moved away from the table, trying to smile. "This is nothing that hasn't happened before. I skinned my knees often growing up." Now that sounded stupid, like she fell down on the farm every day.

"Sorry it had to happen today," he said. "I'll wait for you here."

"Oh," Susan paused, remembering the time. "You're on your lunch break. Why don't you order and start eating? You don't have to wait on me."

"I'm sure my boss will understand," he said, finally sitting down.

The waitress headed to the restroom, calling to one of the other waitresses to watch her tables for a minute. When Susan arrived at the ladies room, the waitress held the door for her. "You did take a nasty spill," the woman said, wrinkling up her face in a grimace. She pulled down a bench from an overhead shelf. "Now sit here. We use this for little children, but it's clean."

Susan lowered herself, holding her dress away from her legs, hoping the blood hadn't stained it already.

"We'll have this cleaned up in no time," the waitress said, running warm water over a paper towel in the sink. "Here," she said, handing the wet towel to Susan. "I'll get the first aid kit while you're cleaning up. I'll be right back."

Susan pulled her dress up higher and wiped the blood off. The wound was ugly. Obviously, concrete was much harder than the dirt of Amish schoolyard playgrounds.

The waitress quickly appeared again with the first aid kit. She opened it, selected a tube of salve, and handed it to Susan. Susan squeezed some of the paste on her leg.

"Now this," the girl said, ripping the paper off two large bandages. She pulled the covering off the bandages, placed the gauze pad over the injuries, and pressed down, leaving the bandages tightly fastened.

"Thanks," Susan said. "That's better already."

"I'm glad to be of help. Now, back to work!"

"Thanks so much for your help with this," Susan repeated.

As Susan and the waitress approached the table again, Duane jumped up and glanced down at Susan's knees.

Anticipating his question, Susan said, "I'm fine now."

"May I take your order?" the waitress asked. "I'll try to hurry the food—put it in as a rush."

Susan picked up the menu and glanced through it. "How about a hamburger and fries? And a small Coke."

The waitress turned toward Duane. "And you?"

"I'll have the steak sandwich—and coffee."

"Coming right up," the young woman said. She disappeared in the direction of the kitchen.

"I'm so sorry about making you late," Susan said. "Really, you didn't have to wait."

"Don't worry. It gives me an excuse to be away from the office. I'm just glad you didn't get hurt worse than you did. You know you shouldn't be falling down in the middle of the street. Asbury Park isn't like the farm. Here the cattle will run over you."

"They do that at home too," Susan said with a laugh.

He laughed too and then turned serious. "Speaking of danger, I sure hope you're being careful at night. You shouldn't be walking around outside alone in the evenings."

"Are the two women still missing?"

"No." He shook his head and stared out the window. "I'll spare you the details, but they were killed. It's a crazy city sometimes. Not at all like what you're used to."

Susan shivered. He wasn't telling her everything, which was fine. She really didn't want to know more.

Within a few minutes the waitress returned, balancing plates with their sandwiches on one hand. "Now wasn't that fast?" she asked.

"Yes, very fast!" Duane said. "Thank you."

"Enjoy the meal," the waitress said. She sped on to the next table.

Duane paused and Susan wondered if he might offer to pray before they ate. And what should she do if he didn't? Meals needed to be prayed over, especially in Asbury Park.

"Do you pray?" he asked, sensing her hesitation.

"*Yah,*" Susan said, closing her eyes and bowing her head. Would he pray out loud? It would sound *gut* to hear a man pray over food again. It seemed like years since she'd heard her *daett's* voice rumble prayers in the old farmhouse.

Quiet moments followed. She glanced up. He still had his head bowed and his eyes closed. He must be praying silently. Well, she couldn't expect too much. This was, after all, Asbury Park.

"Done?" he asked as he lifted his head. He smiled.

She nodded, meeting his eyes. They looked kind, as they had since she'd arrived at the diner. He must be a *gut* man indeed, just like Laura said.

They ate in silence. It was pleasant enough, with no tension between them, which was also *gut*. Time with Thomas used to be that way. But why was she thinking of Thomas?

"Do you have any plans for your next few evenings?" he asked.

"Not really. I usually stay in the apartment," she said. *Is that what he wanted to know? He looks pensive.*

"There's a really nice restaurant uptown. I could take you there sometime. When you're feeling up to it."

"I think I'll feel fine really soon," she responded.

"So," he said, smiling, "you want to go sooner rather than later?"

"Oh, no!" She gasped. "That's not what I meant. I mean…"

He smiled again. "Then it's a yes?"

"A yes? For what?"

"For a meal at a restaurant uptown."

Susan listened to the sound of her own breathing, not able to look at him. Did she want to go out with him to a restaurant? For dinner? What did such an invitation mean to the *Englisha*? She'd struggled with this lunch date. Making up her mind, the words slid out. "Sure, I can go. Sometime, that is."

"Good!" he said, finishing his last bite. "Then it's a date." He stood up. "And now, I really do need to get back to the office. Will you be okay getting back to the bakery?"

"I'll be fine," Susan said. "And thank you for lunch. I enjoyed it."

"I enjoyed it too" he said. "See you later, then. And remember, your meal is paid for." He picked up the check and headed for the cash register.

Susan quickly finished her meal, wondering how Laura was doing with the bakery crowd. As she stepped out onto the street, she wondered *What just happened in there? Did I really accept an invitation to a fancy uptown restaurant with an* Englisha *man? Yes, I did! Surely there is nothing wrong with that.*

Chapter Fourteen

Menno Hostetler lifted his face toward the Indiana sky, the dark barn behind him as he watched the first rays of the sun breaking the horizon. "Dear *Hah im Himmel*," he prayed. "Protect Susan, wherever she is. We've never had a child who's strayed so far from home." *Where is Susan?* It was so hard to imagine her anywhere but upstairs in her bedroom or even beside him right now, walking out to help with the chores. How had she become so interested in the *Englisha* world? So sudden it had seemed. But such things didn't happen that fast. A person didn't plant a seed and harvest it the next day. He had not always lived a perfect life himself, so he knew the temptations of the world. Had a seed dropped into Susan's heart years ago and then sprouted in due time? When had this happened? Had he been asleep and not noticed? Had he been too busy with the work on the farm? Only *Da Hah* knew the answer to those questions. And He often kept His secrets hidden from the hearts of men.

He pushed his straw hat back on his head. Already the air was brisk for this time of the year, moving lightly across the open fields. Winter was not far away, and it could well be a hard one. His bones ached—if that was any sign of what was coming. But they might be aching no matter the coming weather. Old people's bones often ached, did they not?

Menno turned to walk to the barn, finding his way across the yard in the ebbing darkness with practiced ease. The lantern in the washroom could have been lit and brought along, but he wanted to see the sky this morning. He could light the lantern in the barn once he arrived there.

Pushing open the barn door with its creaky hinges, Menno stepped inside. This was his barn, his place where he performed his work on the farm. It was a place of comfort and peace. Since his marriage to Anna so many long years ago, he had lived here. And he would die here. Not likely anytime soon, but all men died in due course. Since Adam ate the apple offered to him by his helpmeet, Eve, it had been *Da Hah's* just punishment on mankind.

One of the horses neighed from the stall, and soon another added its high-pitched whinny. *Gut* horses they all were, worthy of trust and capable of hard work. They likely expected to work in the fields today, finishing the fall plowing, but that wouldn't happen. Tomorrow perhaps, with an early start.

Today would be a long and exhausting day of butchering at John and Betsy's place. Four of his girls would be there, pooling their skills and energies. They would all return home tonight with meat to stock their freezers for winter. He really needed to hurry instead of thinking sad thoughts about Susan. Anna had already started breakfast when he'd left the house.

Menno found the lantern on the dark shelf, blew off the dust, and forced the air pressure higher. The matches should be on the same shelf, and he searched for them. He found one, striking it on the rough wood. It lit, flickering as he brought the flame up to the mantle. Menno twisted the gas knob with his fingers at the same time. With a satisfying *pop*, light flooded his face. He turned his eyes away, shaking the match once before tossing it aside.

Hanging the light on a nail, he glanced over at the double row of milking stalls. Only a few months ago the cows were still being milked. Now dust was gathering. He needed to clean again, but each cleaning wouldn't last long. And it could wear a man out, this upkeep without purpose.

Would anyone ever milk cows in the barn again? He had everything here—the equipment, the stalls, the fields outside to keep the cows. The only thing lacking were the cows and the people who milked and cared for the stock.

Menno sighed. Thomas and Susan were to have been those people.

But he mustn't think of that now. The horses needed to be fed whether they worked today or not. And the driving horse needed to be harnessed for the trip to John and Betsy's place. He approached the horse stalls, picking up the hay fork on the way. The hay was in the loft, and throwing it down was becoming harder, seemingly by the day—but perhaps he was only imagining it so. Chores always looked worse when a great sorrow was on a person's heart.

One of the draft horses, his neck bulging with muscles, tossed his head and whinnied loudly.

"What's up, old boy?" Menno stepped up to run his hand over the massive face.

The horse jerked his head away, his nostrils flared, rearing up in his stall, then landing and slamming his back hooves against the boards.

Menno laughed. "Are you that anxious to work? Well, I'd be glad to take you out and whip the last of the fall plowing. But I've got other things to take care of today. We've got to butcher and get ready for the winter."

The horse reared again, his eyes wide, striking his front feet hard against the stall.

"You don't understand now, do you? Calm down. We can work out all your wild oats tomorrow."

The horse stood still, his head fixed in one direction. Menno could suddenly see the faint flicker of moving light playing in the horse's staring eyes.

"Oh, *Gott in Himmel!*" Menno whirled about, his hay fork flying across the barn floor. Small flames were rising from the loose hay just inside the door, reaching for the wooden boards and crackling with heat.

"Oh no!" Menno shouted. "What have I done!"

He tried to run toward the flames, but slipped, sliding down on both knees. *Was it the match? But I shook it out! I must not have succeeded.* He'd acted old and careless by tossing it onto the floor with only a quick shake of the hand. *How could I have done something so foolish?* The fire must be put out. He needed water and a bucket. The horse trough was outside, but it would take too long running back and forth. The old milking buckets were in the milk house, and there was water at the spigot. Menno ran, banging open stall doors as he went, not bothering to slow down as they whacked against the wall.

He found the buckets, grabbing one off the wall. He lifted the handle on the spigot, his heart pounding as the first bucket filled. He filled the second one. On the run back, he moved slower. Every drop of water was worth its weight in gold.

Menno stood back from the small flames and tossed his buckets of water. The water sizzled on contact, the flames sputtering in anger as they died. Menno stood, breathing in the heavy smoke. He had put out the fire. He was an old man perhaps, but an old man still capable of saving his barn.

Turning a bucket upside down, Menno sat down to catch his breath. *Da Hah* had been *gut* to him this morning. He had been helped. Taking off his hat, Menno ran his hand over his forehead. Little drops of sweat moistened his fingers. He smiled. It was *gut* to sweat again, even on a cold morning.

Menno saw a small turn of flame, followed by a crackle of fire again. Jumping to his feet, he ran over to the straw and beat it with his hat. The wind from the blows drove the sparks in deeper. Menno stamped with his feet, but it was too late. The straw was deeper here, and behind that lay more bales ready for bedding the horses this evening.

Water! He needed more water—and he needed help. He could run into the fields and call down to Ada's place, but help would never arrive in time.

Menno jerked the barn door open, his blackened straw hat flying into the yard.

"Anna!" he yelled. "Anna! The barn is on fire!"

She will hear! he thought. *Surely she will hear!* He left his hat on the ground and raced for the water in the milk house, grabbing two more buckets. Trembling, he waited while they both filled.

There was no sound from Anna. But then…*yah*…there she came, her soft footsteps running across the yard.

With a great cry of alarm Anna burst into the barn. "Menno, where are you?"

"Here! I'm in the milk house. There are more buckets, and you can fill them with water."

He heard nothing from her, only silence. Grabbing the two buckets he ran, letting the water splash wildly. She was still at the barn door, her eyes wide.

"Menno, are you okay?" she asked, her arms full of quilts.

"I'm fine," he said, getting ready to toss the first bucket on the flames.

The fire was hungry, seeking more fuel. If it reached the hay mow above, all would be lost. Once there they would never be able to stop the fire.

"Throw your water!" she said.

"We need more water—and quick!" he gasped. "The buckets are in the old milk house."

"Menno!" Her voice was sharp. "Throw your water—both of the buckets."

What is the woman's problem? he thought. Then he saw what she planned to do. She had her quilts ready—some of her best ones, obviously just grabbed from the cedar chest.

"But…" He stood there, looking at the fire.

"Throw, Menno! Throw your water. Now!"

He bent over and threw. One bucket right after the other. She dropped the stack of quilts on the floor, grabbing one, flaring it out with both hands, bringing the whole quilt over the sizzling fire. Without hesitation she followed with another one and then another.

His hands shook as he watched.

"Throw one on!" She ordered as she bent over to grab another quilt.

He placed his hand on her arm. "It's out, Anna. The fire is out. Don't damage another of your quilts."

"The fire is out?" She paused.

"Those were your best quilts." He walked over, lifting them off the smoking straw and laying them aside. He ran his shoe through the black ash, searching for sparks.

"We had to save the barn," Anna said. "It's Susan and Thomas's barn."

"You smothered the fire with your quilts." He pointed at the blackened pile.

Anna looked at him. "Well, you threw the water on. I think that helped as much as anything. How did the fire start?"

He hung his head, his hair in his eyes. "I guess I'm getting old. I wasn't careful enough putting the match out." He ran his fingers through his hair.

She touched his hand, "It could happen to anyone, old or not. Don't give me a scare like this again, okay? I thought something had happened to you."

He drew her tight into his embrace. Releasing her he said, "Let me go get some more water. I'll make sure the fire is out."

"It's out," she said. "But I'll watch it until you get back."

He walked to the milk house, coming back slower, two buckets of water in his hands. Empting them where the fire had been, he stirred the ashes with his shoe again. For good measure he retrieved his hay fork, and dug around in the straw.

Menno helped Anna carry the damaged quilts out to the front lawn. They spread them out on the grass, where the first rays of the sun streaking across the lawn could reach them.

"I hope that's not a sign of what lies ahead for the day," Menno said.

Anna shrugged. "I'll have your breakfast warm when you're ready. I imagine we'll be late now."

Menno nodded and turned to walk back toward the barn. It was hard growing old. He'd nearly burned down his own barn! His mind quickly turned to his even graver concern. But it was worse having a daughter he loved living out in the *Englisha* world.

Chapter Fifteen

The smell of breakfast filled the room. Anna was bending over the stove, bringing out the biscuits she'd been keeping warm.

"Now we'll be late for sure," Menno said, sitting down at the kitchen table. "And I still have the hog to load onto the spring wagon."

"At least the barn didn't burn down," Anna said. "Be thankful for that." She placed the biscuits on the table and then sat down.

"*Yah*," Menno said, bowing his head.

They prayed silently until Menno raised his head. Silence was the easiest way to pray now with Susan gone. It seemed like so much of their lives had grown silent with her departure.

Menno piled the eggs and bacon onto his plate. "Do you think a whole hog will be too much meat for us this year?" he asked.

"I'd rather not cut back," Anna said.

"Susan might come home" is what she really means, Menno thought, but he was unwilling to say it aloud. He couldn't say the words either, even though he was the one who usually said, "Susan will be coming back." Instead, Menno said, "Meat's always an easy item to get rid of." He poured milk into his granola.

Anna made the best granola in the community, baked fresh every few months—or more often if needed. She hadn't needed to since Susan left.

When Menno finished, Anna asked, "Can we pray right away? I need to get the utensils ready."

Menno nodded, laying down his spoon and bowing his head. After they were done, Anna left the table. Menno got up and took his bowl and plate to the counter. He usually left them on the table, but his wife deserved the kind gesture. She had, after all, saved the barn for him.

"I'll be out soon to help you load the hog," Anna called from the washroom.

"I can do it myself!" Menno hollered back. "Since when can't I load hogs by myself?"

"Since you're old," she said. "And since Susan is gone."

"I'm going to try," he said, going toward the door.

"You better wait for me!" she called after him.

He ignored her. *The Hostetler women do have a way with hogs,* he had to admit. Anna usually got them loaded much quicker than he could. Butchering days brought her out to the barnyard—usually her and one of the girls, when they had still been at home. Together the two could load a hog in no time. When he tried, the hogs turned into squealing monsters, refusing to go anywhere...except where he didn't want them to. He could plow all day or walk behind a disk till dusk, but there were some things on the farm he couldn't do very efficiently. Hog loading was one of them.

But he was going to try! The fire had injured his dignity, and perhaps hog loading would go differently this morning. It was worth a try and would certainly impress Anna. This morning he could use something going right. Menno pulled the spring wagon up to the chute behind the barn and loaded the crate. He aligned the door of the crate with the opening where the animal would run up. *A lot of good this will do,* he thought darkly. *With a squeal and a toss of the hog's nose all my planning can be undone. But I'm going to try!*

Now, which one had Anna said was to go? *Yah,* the mean one. She was also the fattest one who had never borne a litter. Menno found a stick and beat on the side of the pen, stirring up the trio by adding a simultaneous "Woof." They looked at him as if he had just landed from another planet. Taking one more look at him, they ran around the enclosure before settling down again in the mud.

"Get going there," he hollered, jumping inside the pen and attempting to guide the mean sow with his stick.

She grunted and headed in the right direction.

So far so gut*!*

At the bottom of the chute the hog stopped, studying the landscape around her. When Menno hollered at her, she lunged sideways toward Menno, nearly upending him into the mud. She turned around to stare at him before rejoining the others.

All three of them now stood looking at him, their snouts in the air.

"Now who's the boss?" Menno was sure he heard one of them ask. He pushed the thought away. The morning had been stressful enough. He didn't need to hear hogs talking to him.

"Now, get going!" Menno hollered again, prodding the sow with his stick. The hog moved one step at a time, taking her time before arriving at the bottom of the chute again. This time she went up a few steps before making a mad dash back to the others. Menno stayed out of her way. *This is not going well,* he decided. *And here comes Anna, catching me in the middle of my feeble effort.*

"I told you to wait for me, Menno," Anna said as she laughed. "Before long they'll throw you in the mud and totally ruin your clothing. You remember that happened a few years ago?"

"That was a long time ago." Menno scowled.

Anna entered the pen, patting the sow on the back and scratching her ears. "Now, right up there we go, big girl. And don't even be thinking of doing anything else."

With a push on its behind, the sow moved, grunting as she went. She stopped to sniff around at the bottom of the chute.

"Keep moving!" Anna continued to push.

Menno swung his legs over the fence. The least he could do was guard the door to the crate. Perhaps a quick whack on the ears might persuade the sow to not charge sideways.

"You stay away, Menno!" Anna called. "You'll scare her."

He stopped short, waiting. The sow marched up the chute, stopping for a few sniffs at the door before going in. Anna pushed the door shut and clicked the latch.

"She must have been tired from all the chasing I did," Menno hedged.

"Just get the horse," Anna told him. "There are some things you aren't *gut* at. And hog loading is one of them."

Menno mumbled as he left, bringing back the harnessed horse a few minutes later.

Anna helped him hitch, climbing into the open seat and holding the lines as Menno hopped up.

"Get-up!" Menno said after taking the reins. He slapped the lines against the horse's back.

They drove down the blacktop in the spring wagon, the hog crate secure behind them. Every once in a while the hog smell crept up to the front seat when the wind changed. Anna's bowls and knives clattered under the seat when Menno turned onto the gravel road, swerving to avoid a rut in the road but hitting two more.

The hog grunted.

She seems satisfied enough with herself, Menno thought. *Even with her precarious future, clueless of what lies ahead.*

Turning into John and Betsy's driveway, Menno stopped by the sidewalk.

Anna climbed down from the open buggy. She dug her bowls and knives out from under the seat.

"Do you think you can get the sow off without my help?" Anna teased.

"John's here," Menno shot back.

But Anna was already heading up the sidewalk, both hands wrapped around her utensils.

Menno pulled in front of the barn and left the hog grunting in the crate. *Let her contemplate her fate in peace,* Menno thought. *Likely the sow had it figured out by now.*

Other buggies were pulling in, and Menno went over to help unhitch.

"*Gut* morning," he said with a fatherly smile.

Miriam climbed down first, reaching back to bring the baby out. Her husband, Joe, was already out on the other side, pulling off the tugs.

"It's a beautiful morning," Miriam said. "I see you still have your hog on the wagon. Is that the mean one?"

Menno laughed. "Your *mamm* made sure that one came!"

That Anna had also loaded the sow wasn't worth mentioning, although from the twinkle in her eye Miriam looked like she probably knew.

"We brought ours over yesterday," Joe said. "I think everyone else did too."

"Now go and play," Miriam said to her two youngest sons. "Go out in the barn, but stay away from the sow in grandpa's spring wagon. Okay?"

They both nodded solemnly and took off running.

Joe led his horse forward as Menno held the shafts to keep them from slamming into the ground.

Menno put them down and turned to help Esther and her husband who had just driven in. "*Gut* morning," he said again, nodding to the children as they tumbled out. Esther had five children, all well behaved. His daughters except one were all doing fine. That made it even harder to accept that Susan was acting the way she was. She had always been his favorite, which might explain her actions. Wasn't that how children became spoiled?

"*Gut* morning," Esther replied, the last one out of the buggy. Her husband nodded to him, not saying anything. Henry was a *gut* man for Esther, he just didn't talk much.

"Anyone else coming?" Menno asked.

"It's just the five families," Esther said. "I think everyone's here."

"I've only helped unhitch two buggies," Menno commented.

"Edna and Jacob's buggy is out by the barn," Esther said, motioning.

"So it is," Menno replied after turning to look.

As Henry led the horse forward, the banging of metal on metal in the yard drew Menno's attention. John was getting the water trough ready to heat in the yard. He had the trough turned upside down, dumping out the dried debris he had knocked loose. He set the trough back up, this time on supporting metal I-beams. The beams held the trough off the ground, the wood for a fire piled near the old oak tree. John shook the trough into place, dropping the water hose in as Menno walked up.

"*Gut* morning," Menno said. "Looks like you're ready to go."

"Just about." John shouted toward the barn, "Turn on the hose!"

Water suddenly spurted, jerking the hose in the trough. John fed more hose inside and then grabbed some wood. He stacked it underneath, ready to light.

"I see you still have your hog on the wagon," John said.

"She can stay there for a while," Menno said. "At least until we're ready for her."

"Then we'll do the other three first," John said. "We should get started soon." John lit a match, stuck it under the kindling, and moments later a crackling fire was going.

"Do you need more wood?" Menno asked.

"The boys can get more with the wheelbarrow if we run out," John said. "Let's get this fire good and hot for now. The sooner the better."

It's confession time, and now is as gut *a time as any,* Menno thought. John might not laugh quite as hard as some of his sons-in-law. "We had a fire at the barn this morning."

John jerked his head up. "A fire? In the barn?"

"*Yah,* but we got it out. Actually Anna did. She brought her quilts out and used them to smoother the flames."

John doesn't look satisfied, Menno thought. *I was dreaming to think I'd get off easy.*

"Was it an accident?" John asked. "The lantern perhaps? They can be tricky sometimes. A cow kicked one out of my hands when I was a youngster, but that ended up on the concrete floor. Thank *Da Hah* it didn't explode."

John was a nice man. He was trying to make things easier. "I didn't shake the match out well enough. It landed in the straw," Menno said.

"It could happen to any of us," John said.

"There are still no excuses," Menno said. "We teach our young boys better than that."

Just then a shout rose behind them, coming from the direction of Menno's spring wagon. It was followed by the piercing screams of a young child.

"Oh no!" John yelled, the first to turn around. His hat flew to the ground as he took off running.

Menno tried to keep up with John, straining to run, his blood running like ice in his veins. Someone must have opened the crate! Now there were boys standing around, beating the sides of the crate with their hands.

Miriam and Joe's oldest boy, Jonas, was next to the crate, his arm between the bars. The sow had the boy's hand in her teeth and was jerking up and down. Slobber and blood were flying right and left.

Chapter Sixteen

As Menno hurried toward the spring wagon, he saw Jonas's body. His head was thrown back and his face was contorted.

"He's caught! He's caught!" one of the cousins was shouting, jumping up and down beside the wagon.

"What were you trying to do?" John shouted, not waiting for an answer. He slid to a stop and grabbed Jonas from behind.

"Don't pull!" Menno ordered, bracing his hands on the side of the crate. "Just hold the boy until she lets go."

Jonas whimpered, tears streaming down his face

A stick! We need a stick! Menno thought. *Where is the stick I used as a prod this morning? Didn't I put it in the wagon?* Yah*, here it is!* He grabbed it from the bed of the spring wagon and poked it through the crate slats, jabbing it hard into the sow's stomach, shoving as hard as he could. He yelled at the top of his lungs, "*Yah heee!* Let him go!"

The sow gave a great snort and released the boy's arm. She jumped to the far side of the crate. John held the sobbing Jonas as the sow contemplated them with beady eyes.

"What where you doing here?" John demanded.

"We were just trying to unload the sow," one of the cousins said, his voice trembling. "We wanted to help."

"You were told to stay away!" John lowered Jonas to the grassy lawn, cradling his head in his arms.

Menno heard running feet behind them and then gasps as the women approached. They formed a circle around John and Jonas, a few running back toward the house, their skirts pulled up nearly to their knees. They would be going for water and soap. Hog bites needed to be cleaned quickly.

Miriam pushed through the line, taking over for John, murmuring and stroking Jonas's forehead. The others backed off. Menno pushed in close enough to see the puncture wounds in the boy's arm—long lines of jagged teeth marks where the sow had crunched down and pulled. One of the boy's fingers went off in a crazy angle, and there was white slobber all over his hand and arm.

Menno glanced up as movement came from the house. Esther and Betsy, John's wife, were returning with two plastic water buckets, washcloths, and towels. They ran across the lawn, their faces red from the rush and the weight of the buckets. Setting the water down, they knelt on either side of Miriam. She held Jonas's arm as they dipped the washcloths into the soapy water and squeezed the liquid over the boy's injured arm.

"Will it hurt more?" Jonas asked between moans.

"No worse than it already does," Miriam said. "We have to clean the cuts."

"We'd better do something about this finger first." Esther held Jonas's hand by the wrist. "It's going to hurt worse if we don't."

"Is it broken?" John asked.

"I don't know," Esther said, holding her hands over Jonas's eyes and whispering to the others. "It's definitely not right." She stroked Jonas's hair.

"Should we leave that for the doctor?" Betsy asked.

That is a good point, Menno thought, looking around the group. *Someone needs to call a driver, and the sooner the better.* Esther's husband, Henry, caught his glance and nodded. Without a word he ran to the barn. He'd take care of it. Few men were better at getting things done than Henry.

"Cleaning is the problem," Miriam was saying. "But you'd better straighten the finger, even if it's broken."

Jonas whimpered, burying his head in his *mamm's* chest.

"Just do it." Miriam whispered as she held her hand over Jonas's eyes this time.

"The men had better do this." Esther stood up. Betsy stayed down, holding Jonas's arm.

John grasped the boy's palm.

Jonas seemed to have stopped breathing.

John jerked the boy's finger hard.

Jonas screamed, digging his face deeper into his *mamm's* chest.

"There now. It's done," John said, releasing the hand.

Betsy continued to hold the arm, lifting it for the others to see the straightened finger.

"It wasn't broken, I think," John said. "Just out of joint."

Henry's wagon rattled down the driveway past them. His hand on his hat, Henry clutched the lines with his right hand. He was likely heading for the nearest phone shack and would be back with a driver soon.

"Okay, here we go." Esther knelt down again, dipping one of the washcloths in water and gently moving it over the punctured skin. Betsy did the same on the other side of the hand.

Jonas had his eyes open now as Miriam stroked his forehead. The two women worked, allowing the soapy water to run into the wounds and working the blood and slobber off. At times Jonas flinched, and they would pause, continuing with the task when his whimpers died down.

"We need fresh water," Esther announced, looking around the circle.

Two of the older teenage girls took off running toward the house.

Menno fidgeted. There must be something he could do. He looked at the sow still in the crate. She was grunting, her nose in the air, seemingly satisfied with herself.

"You won't live long now!" Menno vowed with a glare. Several of the boys smiled but sobered when Jonas screamed again.

"That bite is pretty deep…and the one over here," Betsy whispered. "I hope the driver gets here soon."

"Henry will find one," John said.

Betsy nodded.

Across the lawn the two girls came running back with fresh water, soap suds rolling over the top of the buckets. Menno smiled at the sight in spite of Jonas's continued whimpering. The girls must have dumped in extra soap in their haste, but that was better than not enough.

On the ground, Betsy and Esther exchanged the water buckets, and the cleansing continued.

A pickup truck soon rattled into the driveway. Old Mr. Davis, a neighbor from down the road, was driving. Mr. Davis jumped out of the truck and ran over to the circle.

They all turned to look at him.

"Henry found me in the field, and told me what happened. Where are we taking the boy?"

"You'd better take him to Louisville, to the children's hospital," Miriam said. "He looks like he doesn't need more than stitches and cleaning up, but I don't know. These are hog bites. I'd feel better if we took him someplace other than Scott Memorial in Salem."

Heads nodded.

The men lifted Jonas and carried him over to the truck. Miriam and her husband, Joe, spoke in whispers for a few minutes. Apparently the decision of who should go was made between them. Miriam walked with Joe to the truck. She climbed into the passenger's side and pulled Jonas tightly against her shoulder. Joe shut the door and said something before stepping back as Mr. Davis took off.

"Okay!" John shouted as the truck turned onto the main road. "Everyone back to what they were doing. We have a long day ahead of us. And boys, keep away from the hogs—even if they look harmless!"

Most of the boys hung their heads, their hats tipped low over their faces.

"Now," John turned back to Menno, "it looks like you get to butcher your hog first."

"*Yah!*" Menno said. He had no problem with that. Someone handed him the twenty-two rifle, and they all backed away. Walking up to the crate, he pushed the barrel close to the sow's head and fired. Vengeance of sorts—the kind that didn't belong to *Da Hah*, he figured as he handed the gun back to Edna's oldest boy.

"The water's hot," John hollered from the water trough.

"Come!" Menno said, picking up the spring wagon shafts. He steered while the boys pushed, backing up to within a foot of the steaming water. They attached ropes and pulled the sow out, lowering her into the trough. In one side and out the other she went, the scalding water splashing as the trough nearly tipped over.

They heaved the sow up onto a wooden picnic table that creaked under the weight. Starting on each end with knives held on edge, they peeled the hair off. The day's real work had begun.

"Come on! We're already late!" John hollered, as more picnic tables were brought over.

The women came with their kettles and then separated the meat into piles. A grinder was brought out, the gasoline engine attached to a belt. Two boys fed the meat in while Betsy watched.

"Keep your fingers away from the auger!" Betsy repeated the words in a chant. "We don't want fingers lost today," she added at times. "One accident today is enough."

John stoked the fire as more hogs were brought and drug through the scalding water. Intestines were taken out and turned inside out on the grassy lawn. Scrubbers were assigned, and they went to work on a picnic table, brushing down the future sausage tubes.

"I can help here," Menno offered, approaching the red-faced boys working on the intestines. Grateful hands offered him their scrub brushes.

Betsy intervened. "Nothing doing!" she ordered from her place at the head of the meat grinder. "If *Grandpap* wants to help, there's another brush over there in the grass."

Menno laughed as the boys groaned.

"I'm never eating sausage again. Not ever in my lifetime," one of them muttered, taking his brush up again.

"Hah! Come winter," Menno said, "you boys will be eating with the rest of us. This memory will be long gone."

"I suppose so," the boy said. "But it sure looks awful now. Pig guts... *phew!*"

"Surely you knew where sausage came from?" one of the others said with a laugh.

"Knowing and seeing are two different things," the boy said. "Do you ever get used to this when you're older, *Grandpap*?"

"I suppose so." Menno shrugged. "I don't think about it anymore. I just bite into Anna's delicious sausage on cold winter mornings and I think, 'My, this couldn't be better!'"

They all laughed and scrubbed away.

By lunchtime the lawn lay littered with meat, blood, hair, and sausages in various stages. They all washed their hands in a basin set outside by the washroom door and then filled their plates with the prepared lunch fixings. They ate under the shade of the oak trees.

"I'm going down to call Miriam," Joe said, getting to this feet. "She should have been back by now."

"I'm sure Jonas is okay," John assured him.

But we would all do the same had it been one of our children, Menno thought. He watched Joe leave moments later, his shoulders squared as he drove his buggy out the driveway. *Da Hah* had given him *gut* sons-in-law—all of them. Only Susan remained single, but that was best not to think about right now.

When lunch was finished, the work resumed while the younger girls took the remaining lunch food back into the house.

Joe returned, and he unhitched his buggy by the barn.

"What's up?" John hollered to him.

Joe didn't answer until he had the horse in the barn and approached the group. They all turned to listen when he cleared his throat. "The doctors have worked on Jonas, Miriam said, cleaning up things. Sounds like the danger of infection will be the biggest problem. They want to keep him overnight so they can keep tabs on his wounds and make sure there's no infection."

"Do you need to leave?" John asked. "We can bring your share of the meat over this evening."

Joe shook his head. "Miriam will stay with him for the night, and Mr. Davis is back home already. He offered to take me down tonight after the chores."

"Not really bad news, but still bad enough," John said.

"I know," Joe said. "We can be thankful it wasn't worse. Now, where can I help?"

John waved toward the meat grinder. "You could give the boys a break. They've been hard at it."

Smiles covered the faces of the boys.

"Aw, it's not that bad," Joe teased. "Let me see what I can do."

They stepped aside and threw themselves onto the grass, flailing their arms in gestures of mock exhaustion.

Betsy laughed, but let them be. She turned and walked toward the house, taking a bowl of ground meat with her. "I'll be back in a little while," she said over her shoulder. "You boys aren't going to lay on the grass all afternoon, right?"

They all groaned their reply but were happy to be relieved even for a short time.

By four o'clock everything was done, the meat divided, and the area cleaned up. They all had home chores ahead of them, except for Menno. Sure, he had to feed the horses, but that didn't keep a person's mind occupied for very long.

Menno sighed as he took the hog crate off the spring wagon and washed out the bottom with the garden hose. He helped Anna load the tubs of meat, and they readied to leave. *We will eat well this winter,* he thought, holding the horse while Anna climbed in.

He pulled himself onto the wagon bench seat, took the reins from Anna, and hollered, "Get-up." The horse set out at a brisk pace.

"It's been quite a day," Anna said as they went out the driveway.

"*Yah.* Too bad Jonas had to get hurt."

"We need to write Susan and tell her what happened."

"You can do that," Menno said with a shrug.

"She might come home," Anna said.

Menno looked at her and shook his head. "No, I forbid it. Jonas will be fine. You won't go making things sound worse to Susan than they are. That's not right."

"But Jonas could get a bad infection," Anna insisted. "You heard Joe say so yourself."

"He's in the hospital, under a doctor's care. You will not ask Susan to come home unless there is good reason for it. As of now, there is no reason."

"But she's our daughter!" Anna said, her fingers clutching the side rail of the buggy seat as the horse and wagon turned a corner.

"I know," Menno said. "But nothing *gut* comes out of tricks like that. Susan would figure it out once she got back. I say that if Susan comes home, it will be by her own free will."

After a silence, Anna agreed, teary-eyed. "You're right. I know you are."

"*Yah*," Menno said. He was crying too—only on the inside.

Chapter Seventeen

✦

Susan stood at the front window of the apartment, the early morning racket from the street a dull roar below her. There was so much to do! Did she dare move so quickly? Making all these big changes? *Yah!* she thought, these were big changes, but life was taking her in this direction. If she held back, her chance might never come again.

Laura had been kind enough to allow her the day off, so she ought to be thankful and enjoy it instead of spending it worrying. Yet how did a person keep from worrying with so many *verbotten* things she planned to do. There was getting a driver's license and working for a GED certificate—both of which were forbidden by the church *Ordnung*. But the church *Ordnung* was now far from her. She needn't be worried about the church rules anymore...but she was. The letter from her *mamm* hadn't helped.

"I'm not exactly Amish anymore," she said to the window glass. "It's just that Amish doesn't go away so easily." Susan turned away from the street with a sigh. She would get ready for this day off. There were questions to ask at the college about taking the GED test. That might even be fun. Robby would be driving her around. He had also picked up the state's driver's manual earlier in the week for her. Nothing had looked too difficult as Susan studied it the last few evenings. All this help was likely Laura's doing, even though she made the plans sound accidental. Like Robby just *happened* to have time to drive her around today.

She also needed to shop for a new dress. The special night with Duane was tomorrow night. The thought made her catch her breath.

She *could* wear one of her current dresses, but *nee,* that wouldn't work. They all looked, well, Amish. They wouldn't do for an evening with Mr. Moran…Duane.

Duane…He wasn't at all like Thomas. He'd stopped by the bakery a few times since their lunch together. But he never said anything more about the dinner invitation. In the few minutes while waiting on him, he would smile and make conversation like usual. He acted as if he had forgotten his own suggestion.

The tension the man caused was enough to make goose bumps burst out all the way down her arms. She had been ready to tell him when she saw him again that *nee,* she couldn't go after all. She had expected him to bring the subject up the first morning she saw him after the diner outing, but he hadn't said a word. And when he *did* finally bring it up, she had agreed to go. *It's perfectly understandable,* she decided, *considering all that charm he exuded.*

Thomas wasn't like Duane at all. He blurted out words and let the sticks fall where they would. Did that come from being Amish? Perhaps. Or maybe Thomas was just plain clumsy? Or maybe just pushy. Forcing his way around like he owned the world. Well, it didn't matter. Thomas was in love with Eunice. He could have her! She wanted nothing more to do with the man or her former best friend. Let them both go fly a kite.

Pulling her thoughts back into the present, Susan looked around. Now what to do about the letter from home lying on the table? She had read through it again last night. The news was troubling, to say the least. Susan walked over and picked the envelope up again. She took the letter out and unfolded the paper. Her eyes scanned the words. What was *Mamm* saying? She never quite knew with her—or maybe it was this way with all Amish people. They said something, but a person couldn't be sure if the words were to be taken at face value.

Dear Susan,

Greetings in the name of Da Hah. I hope as always this finds you well and happy. I wish you would come home, but your daett and I are trying to understand. Laura must be a sweet lady. Please thank her for us—that she is taking such good care of you.

Yesterday we had our day of butchering at John and Betsy's place. We came home with the spring wagon loaded, and now we have plenty of meat for the winter. Your daett *is worried we have too much, but meat is an easy thing to get rid of.*

The day contained quite a bit of excitement. Menno tried to burn down the barn while he was doing morning chores. Not that he really did, but he forgot to properly put out the match. He's getting old, I guess. He tossed it on the barn floor near some straw. His first attempts at putting the fire out only drove the flames deeper into the pile. I came out at his call for help, bringing some of my quilts along, and helped him smother the fire. Don't worry, we can make more quilts. Much easier than building a new barn!

We got to John and Betsy's place with that mean sow—you remember her, I think, since you helped raise the piglet. She always had the nastiest temper. Anyway, Menno left her sitting in the crate on the back of the spring wagon. One of Miriam's boys, Jonas, got his arm bit pretty badly when the boys took it upon themselves to unload her. Jonas had to stay in the hospital overnight. We haven't heard anything more. I suppose he'll be okay, as the doctor didn't say otherwise.

Please be thinking of us often, as we are of you. And may Da Hah *keep you safe. We are praying.*

With much love, your mamm

"Well," Susan said out loud, "obviously *Mamm* wants me to come home." Of course, she knew that already, but *Mamm* was thinking of something a little more permanent than a quick visit. *Should I go home for a visit? No, not yet. Too much is going on right now. And it would be hard to get back into moving forward later.*

She needed to write back…or better yet, call just in case Jonas had taken a turn for the worse. Hog bites could be quite serious. She could try the phone shack at Edna and Jacob's place and see if anyone answered.

A loud knock came from the door downstairs and interrupted her thoughts. Susan jumped. Robby! And she wasn't quite ready. Well, he could wait, but not down there. She raced down the steps and jerked open the front door.

"Hi, Miss Sunshine," he said.

He stood there, his shoulder against the doorframe, a look of great patience on his face. "Your buggy awaits you, oh great Amish princess."

"Footman," she said, drawing out the word, teasing him. "You must wait while I finish preparing for the journey."

"You look ready to me," he said.

"Well, I'm not, so come upstairs and wait."

"I thought Mom told you the time to expect me," he grumbled, following her up the stairs.

"I thought you grew up with sisters, Robby. So don't you know not to push?"

"Three of them," he muttered, pulling a chair out at the kitchen table and sitting down with a sigh.

"Your face is tired," she said. "You should have gone to bed earlier."

"I had a long night." He flicked his hair over his shoulders. "And it didn't turn out so well. And don't look at me that way."

"Troubles, have we? Perhaps the princess can help?"

"It's because of you that I'm in trouble," he said. "Why would I want the one with the shovel to dig deeper?"

"You shouldn't blame other people for your troubles. You have to take responsibility."

"Are you always this full of wisdom?"

"Filled to the brim and bubbling over!" She stepped into the bedroom to retrieve her new purse from the dresser. She counted out money from her small hidden stash and shoved the bills into the purse.

"Hey, I could use some money," he said, leaning his chair back to peer around the bedroom door. "You shouldn't keep that much cash in the house."

"Be quiet!" she ordered. "I'm thinking," she said.

He laughed.

She ran through the day's list in her head. First, the papers she needed were already in the inside pocket of her purse. And, *yah,* she already knew that money shouldn't be kept in apartments, especially in big cities. But habits were hard to break. She came out, flashed him a smile, and asked, "Okay, so what did I do or say that led my dear footman astray?"

He grunted. "It was all that stuff you told me at the beach about love and looking for it that got to me. It made me stupid enough to try again."

"Well, good for you! Who is she?"

"You wouldn't know her. Just a girl."

"See, that's your first problem. It shouldn't be 'just a girl.' She has to be special."

"Like any of them are. They smile and say sweet things, and then they're gone after the meal. All you have left is precious money spent and nothing gained."

"You *could* try a haircut." She gave him a looking over. "I think that would help."

"Any other suggestions, Miss Wisdom?"

"You could start by treating her nicely, regardless of what happens."

"Even when I lose money and waste my time?"

"*Yah,* because if you develop anger waves against females, they know it. The next one you met will run into all that anger coming from your brain and *bam!* she'll be gone. Females don't like anger waves. It turns us off."

"Ha!" he said. "Let me see one first who is worth the sweetness, and then I will be sweet back to her."

"You met me, didn't you? And am I not the image of a sweet girl? Fresh off the farm, filled with goodness and virtue? Why, my smile ought to give you the pleasant brain waves you need for weeks to come."

"You are so full of yourself!"

"I'm just joking. Can't you take a joke? Remember, I had an Amish boyfriend who gave me all that sweet talk. Now look at me. I'm out on the streets of Asbury Park with an *Englisha* man."

"I think you exaggerate," he said. "You probably dumped him to run out to the world. Isn't that what Amish babes do?"

"*Babe* yourself!" she snapped. "And I didn't dump him, but I should have. Just goes to show how blind I was. And now you should learn like I did. You pick up the pieces and go on."

"Is that farm wisdom?"

"I don't know," she said. "It's some kind of wisdom, I guess."

"All I want to do is find one decent girl," he said, looking forlorn.

"Do you want to join the Amish?" she asked.

"Hey!" he said. "That might not be a bad idea. Have they got more babes like you? Nicer ones, of course—but a little like you?"

"What makes you think I'm such a saint? And quit saying 'babe,'" she said. "It doesn't sound nice. And, *yah,* there are lots of good girls. If you can get to them before they're spoken for. Of course, you would have to be Amish, which is another matter entirely. I certainly don't see that happening."

"I'd have to cut my hair, right?"

"A whole lot more than that. I'm sorry, but you're not even close to being Amish."

He looked cheerful. "It can't be too hard. I mean, driving a horse and buggy."

"You'd better stay in your own world," she said. "Believe me, it's not that easy. And we have our own troubles." She motioned toward the letter on the table.

He raised his eyebrows. "May I read it?"

"*Yah.*"

He opened the letter and read silently. "Sounds like someone wants you to come home," he said when he was done.

"That's what I thought."

"Are you going?"

"No, but I probably should call home about Jonas. I'll run down to the bakery and use your mom's phone."

"Maybe you *should* go for a visit. It sounds like they love and miss you."

"Someone else doesn't, so forget it!" she snapped.

"Ah, the princess is bitter." A smile played on his face. "You've made me feel so much better." He jumped up. "Are you ready to go then?"

"I have to make the phone call first."

"You can use my cell while we're driving."

"Thanks."

"Welcome," he said as he started down the stairs.

"How did I make you feel better?" she asked, following him.

"You said you're not a saint."

"How does that make *you* feel better?"

"Believe me." He held open the street door. "Halos hanging around a girl's head is not good. It gets to be a little too much."

"Do I have a halo?"

"Not right now, you don't."

"That's very mean. You know that, don't you?"

He grinned, showing all his teeth.

She glared at him. "Where is the buggy?" she asked, when they reached the street.

"Over here, princess! Ready and waiting." He waved his hand toward his car parked at the curb.

CHAPTER EIGHTEEN

The light was red at Main and Cookman. Robby gunned his engine while waiting.

"Would you behave yourself? I'm trying to figure out how to use your phone," Susan said.

He laughed. "Just dial the area code for Indiana and then the number."

Susan punched in the numbers and listened as loud beeps followed each number she pushed. "What now?" she asked.

"Push the send button," he said, taking off when the light turned green.

"That's not funny!" she said, trying to glare at him as she grabbed the door handle to hang on. "Oh, it's ringing now." *Likely no one will answer,* she thought. *The phone shack is a long way from the house, and it's the middle of the morning back home. Folks would be busy with the day's work, although someone might be walking by if it is time to pick up the mail.*

There was a click and little voice said, "Hello."

"Hello, hello!" Susan replied. "Is this Vernon?" she said, taking a guess. It was often hard to tell voices over the phone.

"No, it's Andrew. Who are you?"

"Susan," she said. "I'm calling about Jonas. Do you know how he is?"

"Oh," he said. "Susan."

"*Yah.* How is Jonas?"

123

"He's home from the hospital, that's all I know. Do you want to speak with *Mamm*?"

"*Yah*." She clutched the phone. *Do I really want to speak with Edna? Will she lecture me? Likely. But I need information about Jonas…*

"*Mamm!*" Andrew hollered.

Susan jerked the phone away from her ear. There was nothing like a farm boy's voice to stretch a person's eardrums. Susan rubbed her ear and glanced at Robby.

"He's calling his mother," she explained.

She heard Andrew shout again, the phone further away from his mouth this time. "It's Susan from that faraway city."

Finally Edna's voice came on. "Hello. Is this Susan?"

"*Yah*," Susan said, relaxing. Even if Edna pressed her about coming home, it was good to hear her sister's voice. "I'm calling about Jonas. I received *Mamm's* letter last night. Is he doing okay?"

"As well as can be, considering his arm was all chewed up from hog bites. You know how infectious those can get."

"He won't lose his arm, will he?"

Robby jerked to a stop at another stoplight.

The roar of car engines coming from the vehicles crossing the intersection made it hard for Susan to hear. She held her hand over her free ear to block the noise.

"No," Edna was saying. "Where are you, Susan?"

Oh no! Here come the questions. What can I say? I'm driving around with an Englisha boy, going to get my GED and take my driver's test. No! "I'm living in an apartment in Asbury Park, New Jersey," she finally managed.

"Is that a big city?" Edna asked.

"I don't know. I guess so. It looks big…at least to me."

"Are you behaving yourself, Susan?"

"You know I am," she whispered, lest Robby hear.

"When are you coming home? We all miss you an awful lot."

"I wish you wouldn't say that, Edna. This is hard enough already."

"Then why don't you patch things up with Thomas? Surely whatever your problems are with him they can be worked out."

"How do you know I haven't been trying?"

"Well, of course I don't know for sure. But whatever you're doing doesn't seem to be working."

"I can't make it work with Thomas," Susan said. "That's why I'm here and not there. Tell me, is Thomas dating Eunice?"

"Not that I know of," Edna replied. "Why do you ask?"

"Then he's keeping away from her to make me look bad," Susan responded. "I found them together after a hymn sing one night."

"Ah, now I see. But you shouldn't be so bitter, Susan," Edna said, her voice patient. "It could be making you do things you wouldn't do otherwise."

Susan took a deep breath. "He betrayed my heart," she whispered. She didn't want this to go any further. "I've got to go, Edna. I'm using someone's phone."

"Okay, but don't forget us now, Susan. Remember!" Edna said.

"I won't. Please tell *Mamm* I called."

"I will," Edna said. "Goodbye."

"Goodbye." Susan closed the phone and handed it back to Robby.

"I take it that didn't go too well," he said.

"Jonas is doing okay. That's the important thing," she said.

"I suppose so." He accelerated as another light turned green and nearly ran into the car in front of him.

"That was close!" he muttered, slowing down, allowing ample distance between the two vehicles.

"So enough of my troubles," Susan said. "Tell me about this girl you were talking about earlier."

"Why should I tell you? And if I do, will you tell me your secrets?"

"No," Susan said. "But I want to know your girl troubles anyway. Tell me about her. Please."

"Well, I met her at a bar last week…"

"You go to bars?" She gasped. "But you're Laura's boy!"

"So what? A lot of guys with nice moms go to bars," he said with a laugh. "Look, Susan, I'm not interested in Mom's religion anymore, not with church and all. And besides, what has my going to a bar have to do with Mom?"

"It's not right, Robby. That's what it has to do with."

"Oh, so you don't want to hear the story after all?"

Susan met his look. "Of course I do. But you shouldn't be in bars. So go ahead. I'm listening."

Robby sighed. "It's not like I'm a bad person just because I go to bars for a quick drink. I don't get drunk or do drugs or sleep around, if that's what you're thinking."

"I should hope not!" she exclaimed. "Amish boys aren't saints either. Well, *some* of them aren't. Thomas was never wild, but some of the others are. But they straighten up eventually. I suppose that can happen to you too."

"Well, that's a novel way of looking at it," he said with a shrug. "But, hey, I'm not wild just because I go to bars occasionally. Look at me! Do I look wild to you?"

Did she dare say the truth? "To be honest, you do look a *little* wild."

He laughed out loud. "I suppose it's my long hair. Okay, so I may look a little wild to an Amish girl. But I don't *act* wild."

"No, I've never seen you act wild," she agreed.

"Well, that settles it then."

"*Yah.* So we agree. You go to bars, which you shouldn't. But you don't act wild."

Robby laughed. "Back to the story. I had never met this girl before. Well, maybe once in passing a few weeks before, but she was with someone else. That night she was alone, so I walked up and talked to her."

"Just like that?"

"Of course. How else would I do it?"

"Perhaps a woman wants to know who you are. I mean, you could be anyone."

"That's why I told her, first thing. 'I'm Robby and I grew up around here,' I said."

"How does she know that? You could be lying. You're in a bar, which is not exactly the best place to be."

"I know," he said. "Sin, degradation, evil, wickedness, and all that."

"*Yah.* And especially in a place like that, a girl wants to know who you are before she becomes friends with you."

"Do you want to hear the story or not?"

"*Yah,* go on."

"I asked her if she wanted to go across the street for a burger, and she said yes. We had a nice chat over our meal, and I thought everything was going great."

"So what's the problem?"

"The problem is that when we parted, I asked her if I could see her again next week. She said no! I don't get it. Why did she accept my invitation for a burger when she obviously wasn't as interested in me as I was in her? I don't get women!"

"You shouldn't take it personally, Robby. There could be any number of reasons. Maybe she's seeing someone else."

"Of course I take it personally! That's what it's all about."

"Have you thought about meeting the right kind of girl in…say… church?"

Robby let out a long sigh. "I'll take your advice under consideration." He wrinkled his face into a fake smile as he turned left and pulled into a triple-story parking garage. Squeezing the car into a parking slot he said, "This is the closest parking to the college—our first stop of the day. Does the princess need an escort inside?"

"You might as well come," she said. "That way I won't feel pressured about hurrying—worrying about you being bored in the car all alone. You might even find a self-help book in their library on how to win girlfriends."

"Cute, really cute."

Robby led the way to the college administration building, pausing to point out the tall pillars in front that reached all the way to the second-story roof.

"That's nice," she said. "It's certainly nothing like the little buildings they have in Salem, Indiana."

"They built the pillars to impress country girls who come to visit," he said with a grin.

As they stepped inside, Robby said, "Over there is the information desk, the place to start your journey. As for me, I think I'll go see about a girlfriend book."

"What do I ask for?" she whispered.

"Just explain what you need," he said, not pausing. "They'll be helpful."

Susan watched Robby walk away and then took a deep breath. The place was huge, even larger than it had appeared from the outside. She never felt more like a little Amish girl far away from home.

CHAPTER NINETEEN

Susan approached the desk and glanced around, hoping the well-dressed lady would look up and notice her.

"Excuse me," Susan finally said softly.

"Yes, may I help you?" the lady asked.

At least she seemed friendly. She was much younger than she had appeared from a distance. Susan relaxed, managing a smile. "I need help finding materials on how to prepare for your GED exam," Susan said.

"You didn't finish high school?" the lady asked.

"I…no…I didn't finish," Susan said.

Should she explain that she was Amish? Better not. An Amish girl living in Asbury Park who only completed the eighth grade? That was an unlikely story.

"Well, you've come to the right place! We are more than glad to help," the lady said.

Robby's head appeared from behind a nearby aisle of books behind a wall of glass. He waved and smiled.

"There are two ways to study that I recommend," the lady continued. "Either you can take our night classes or you can study online. Here is the web address and the hours the college gives the classes."

Susan glanced at the papers the lady handed to her.

"May I take this home with me and decide what I want to do?" she asked.

"Of course," the lady said with a smile. "Whatever way works for you is fine."

"Where is the exam taken?" Susan asked.

"Here at the college. But you should study first. Each exam has a fee attached, and you will have to repeat the entire exam if you fail any section. I advise a full complement of studies before you attempt the test."

"Okay," Susan said, turning to go.

She found Robby in the library across the hall, his nose stuck in a book. She got his attention by whispering, "I'm ready to go."

"Oh!" he jumped and slammed the book shut.

She looked at the title as he slid the book back on the shelf. "*The Five Love Languages,*" Susan read aloud. "Hmm."

Robby's face turned a bit red.

"You don't have to be embarrassed about the book," Susan said, leading the way outside and down the steps. "It sounds pretty good. Maybe I need to read it too."

"Yeah, I think maybe we both do," Robby agreed.

"Now, where do I get my driver's license?" Susan asked.

"Wow! You're really moving ahead quickly, aren't you?" Robbie asked.

"Do you think I'm moving too quickly, Robby? I'm just trying to make a new life here in the *Englisha* world."

"No, you're fine." He didn't hesitate. "You've never struck me as lacking in the intelligence department. I was just kidding. And what did the college tell you?"

"I can either come here for night classes or study online," she told him. "Which one do you think I should do?"

He shrugged. "Mom has a computer at the bakery. Do you think you could learn to use a computer?"

"I don't know," she said. "Is it hard?"

"Nah, a piece of cake." He laughed.

"Robby, did you finish high school?" she asked, as they climbed into the car.

"Yes," he said, starting the engine.

"Isn't college the place where most *Englisha* young people go after high school?"

"Yes, I guess."

"Did you go to college?" she asked after he paid the parking fee.

He was busy looking up and down the street, but he turned to answer her with a quick, "Yes."

"I feel so stupid," Susan said. "You must really think so too. Everyone here has a high school diploma and most likely some college. With just an eighth-grade education, I feel so...so *dumb*."

"Quit beating yourself up," he said. "You're doing just fine. And most people admire you for trying to catch up, whatever your reasons were for not completing high school."

"I wonder if Mr. Moran thinks so. He's a good example of what I mean. He's so smart. I have no business being with him. At least I don't have cow manure still stuck on my shoes."

Robby laughed. "Hey, it's a free world. Anyone can go out with anyone. And he must like you. Don't worry about it—just enjoy it. I think if anyone is stupid or dumb, it's that Amish boyfriend of yours."

Susan was hardly listening. "Mr. Moran probably has college learning coming out his ears."

"He probably does," Robby agreed. "But I wouldn't worry. There's more to life then college. You'll do okay."

"You're just saying so to make me feel better."

"Hey, I've got a college education, so I should know. Now isn't that true, Miss Hostetler?"

"It is true," she said, grateful for the compliment. Robby did have cute logic. "But it doesn't feel true inside. I still feel like a duck out of water."

"A nice-looking duck out of water," Robbie corrected. "Here we are at the DMV. Time for your first test."

They got out and walked to the building. Robby held the door for her and motioned her toward a cubicle that didn't have a line. She walked up, uncertain what to do.

"You give them your information, and they give you a number and the test material," Robby whispered in her ear.

"May I help you, ma'am?" a woman at the window asked.

"I...uh, I need to apply for my learner's permit." *Is that the correct wording? Hadn't Laura used those words?*

The woman nodded. "I'll need your birth certificate."

Susan dug the paper out of her purse and handed it over the counter.

There was a clicking of keys. The woman pointed to a bank of computers. You take the test there. Your number is 305. When you're done, wait until your number is called. If you pass you'll take a quick eye exam and we'll give you your permits.

Susan stood there, frozen.

"Is there anything else?" the woman asked.

"I don't know how to use a computer," Susan finally got out.

"Oh, then you'll want to take the test manually." She brought out a sheaf of papers, selected one and handed it to Susan, along with a pencil. "You can take the test at one of those desks over there," she said, pointing to several desks in the corner. "When you're done, bring the test back to this window."

Susan forced herself to move.

Robby met her halfway to the desks. "Calm down," he said. "This is not the jail house. You can do this! Concentrate and work on your questions. I'll wait for you over there," he said, pointing.

She glared at him but then settled down to take the test. She read the multiple-choice questions. They seemed easy enough, most of them following the material she'd studied in the apartment. She began filling in the circles by her answers. When she was done, she handed the paper in and found a seat by Robby.

"What happens next?" she whispered to Robby.

"I don't remember," he whispered back. "It's been a long time. But I think they do an eye exam and take your picture."

"My picture?" Susan gasped.

"Yes. How else can they make sure your driver's license belongs to you?"

"I know that. It's just, well…I've never had my picture taken before. It's a great evil back home!"

"Really?" He was staring at her. "You're joking, of course?"

"No, I'm not. You sure don't know much about the Amish."

Robby was incredulous. "Taking a picture is a sin? Wow! No

wonder I'm a sinner. I was born with a camera flashing in my eye. Mom couldn't stop taking pictures when I was a baby."

"It's not really a sin," she said.

"I am so relieved!" he said in mock relief, sliding deeper into his chair. "I hope they hurry. I'm getting hungry."

It isn't a sin, is it? People get their pictures taken all the time in the Englisha *world.* Susan's mind raced. *I'm really stepping into the* Englisha *world now. I need to get over these guilt feelings.*

Robbie reached over and rattled her chair. "Your number is up on the board!" he said.

Susan jumped up and walked to the counter. The lady looked her over before smiling. Susan wondered if it was just her imagination or did the lady know she was dealing with another ignorant girl getting her license after crawling off the farm?

"Step over here," the lady directed, still smiling. She motioned toward a chair with a long, white machine standing in front of it. There was a camera perched on a tripod...like a glass eye staring at her.

Susan hoped no one could hear her heart pounding. She was surprised when the woman stopped at a different machine.

The clerk motioned for her to look into this machine. When she placed her eyes on the peepholes she saw various sizes and shapes of letters inside. The woman asked Susan to read off what she was seeing, altering the formations inside the box after each answer.

"All done. No problems at all," the woman said moments later. "Stand over here, and we'll take your picture."

Susan stood in front of the machine with the glassy eye. She wanted to close her eyes so she wouldn't have to look, but the woman wasn't likely to take her picture with her eyes closed.

The woman adjusted the lens and a light flashed.

"Your learner's permit will be ready in a minute," the clerk said. "You can go back to your seat for now."

This is all there is to it? Susan wondered. *Just a flash and my picture was taken?* She'd always figured picture taking involved a little more, considering how evil it was supposed to be.

"I'm hungry," Robby repeated when Susan sat down. "I hope they hurry."

Susan concentrated on calming herself, ignoring Robby. Boys were always hungry. At least her sisters always said so, and they had young boys to back up their opinion.

"What are the plans for this afternoon?" Robby asked, rattling her chair again.

"I need to shop at the mall," she said without thinking.

"The mall!" Robby exclaimed. "I hope you don't expect me to help with shopping."

Susan smiled. "Of course not. You can sit on the bench and count the people going by."

He glared at her. "I think I'm taking you straight back to the bakery."

"I think we both need food," she said. "I'm feeling a bit weak, but at least I'm not *grouchy*."

"I'm behaving quite nicely," he said. "And if you'd stop saying nasty things about me, I'll tell you what I was about to suggest."

Susan gave him a sweet smile.

"That's better," he said.

"So what were you going to say?" she asked.

He waited, obviously teasing her before answering. "I was going to suggest that since you need practice driving, which I assume you've never done before, we could do that this afternoon."

"Oh! You're being nice," she said. "But I…really…I've…It's just that I've never driven before."

"That's what I just said."

"But your car. It's so big! And I could wreck it." Susan felt the horror of the thought spreading over her face.

"I'm not going to let you wreck my car, believe me," he said confidently.

"But *me*! Driving a car!" she protested, half rising from her chair. "I don't think I can."

"Then why are you getting a learner's permit?"

"To drive a car."

"See!" He threw up his hands. "Women make such perfect sense."

"We always do," she said. "It's just that you men don't understand us."

He took a deep breath.

She laughed.

"Number 305, your permit is ready," the clerk called from the counter. She held up a plastic card.

Susan stood and took tiny steps forward.

"Your permit! Congratulations! In three months you can take the driver exam if you're ready."

"Thank you," Susan said, turning to go,

She stopped by the chairs and studied the picture. It looked like the mirror did in the bathroom, only smaller. She looked a bit scared though, as if she had just committed a crime or something. Her pony tail had worked loose, and strands of hair hung around her face. Why hadn't she thought to get things tucked in first? But it was too late now.

Robby was on his feet, looking over her shoulder, laughing.

"You can smile," he said, "It's not a criminal record. It's your passport to freedom!"

"Freedom?" she croaked.

"Driving around," he said. "Your own wheels and all that. Being able to go where you want to go when you want to go!"

"I think I need food," she said. "Right now before I pass out!"

"That's the best thing I've heard all morning," Robby said, holding the door for her.

Chapter Twenty

✦

Robby and Susan sat at a picnic table, the rolling hills of the park behind them. Robby had said he was starved, but he had insisted they bring their meal here to eat even though it took an extra half hour to get here. He sat across from Susan, serenely eating his sandwich.

"Eat slowly," Susan said.

"I'm hungry." He was staring off into the distance. "It's nice here. I like it."

"I'm nervous and you're making me rush. Slow down."

"Take all the time you want," he said, finishing his last bite and standing up. "I'm going to look around."

"Don't forget I still want some time to shop."

"I'll teach you to drive in ten minutes," he said without looking back over his shoulder.

Confident male, Susan thought. How did he expect her to slide behind the wheel of a car and learn to drive in ten minutes? *Yah? In ten minutes?* Well, at least the park looked nice and open, with plenty of grassy lawns. If things went wrong, they could go bouncing off the blacktop and across the fields until the vehicle stopped. Perhaps that was what Robby planned. But there were also trees—lots of them in the distance. And trees weren't *gut.*

Positive thoughts, Susan decided. *That's what I need. Things like happiness and thoughts of easy sailing down the road, the car wheels humming under me. Picture your hands safely guiding the automobile,* she told herself. *But there are ditches on both sides of the road, aren't there? Ditches had always looked perfectly harmless before. But now they are lying in wait, hoping I will crash so they can take me into their arms.* She shuddered. *What does it feel like when a car runs into a ditch? Awful,* she thought. *There's no doubt about that.* She shook her head. This was all Robby's doing—him and his inflated ego. Rushing her into driving before she had time to adjust to the thought.

"Come back here!" she hollered at him, shoving the rest of her sandwich into the bag. She couldn't get another bite down. "We're going to get this over with—like *right now!*"

"What's wrong?" he asked, not turning around. "This is beautiful. Come and look at the view."

"I want to drive now!"

He turned slightly and cupped his hand over his ear. He shook his head.

Susan repeated the words and walked toward him.

"I heard you the first time!" he exclaimed when she walked up. "I just wanted you to see the view."

"Really!" she said, forgetting to glare at him. She had to admit it was beautiful looking across the fields.

"Look!" He swept his hand outward. "Over there is where the reenactment of the Battle of Monmouth is performed every year. Soldiers dress up in period uniforms and march and shoot at each other. It's a glorious event."

Susan looked across the open field in the direction Robby pointed. At least there were no trees there. But they probably don't allow cars to drive on the open fields.

"See over there? That's the Craig farmhouse," Robby said, pointing. "It's dated from 1745 and fully restored. It's almost Amish looking, don't you think?"

It does look sort of Amish, Susan thought. *But that isn't possible. The Amish don't shoot and march in wars.*

"Beyond those woods are the orchards," Robby continued, "with apple, cherry, peaches, and nectarines. We can stop and see if anything is still in season. That is, after you've learned how to drive."

"Maybe we should start then," Susan said. "We don't have all afternoon."

"Well, maybe we should," he agreed. "This will be as easy as stitching."

"Let's just get it over with, okay?"

"You sound like you're going to the dentist." He made a buzzing sound between his teeth.

"Worse!" she said. "But you've never been Amish."

"I guess there are advantages to my world." He smiled, leading her back to the car.

"What do I do?" she asked, standing by the hood.

"Get in," he said, opening the driver's door.

Susan slid in, feeling the cold touch of the steering wheel under her hand. She tried to get comfortable.

"Don't do anything yet," he said, walking around to the other side to get in. "Okay, first your seat belt," he said, snapping his into place.

"*Yah,* that much I know," she said.

"The rest is just as easy," he said.

"That's because you already know how to drive."

He ignored the comment. "First thing, the pedal on your left is the brake. That makes the car stop. The one on the right is the gas or the accelerator. Now you name them, and step hard on the pedals while you do."

"Brake. Gas. Brake. Gas." Susan moved her foot back and forth.

"Faster!" he said.

"Brake. Gas. Brake. Gas." She repeated the words, moving her foot as fast as she could.

"Okay. That's enough. Hit the brakes hard!"

Susan did, pressing until her foot hurt.

"Easy does it. Don't break the pedal."

"Now what?" she asked, lifting her foot and catching her breath.

"Press on the brake pedal again and turn the key."

Susan pressed the pedal down hard and turned the key. The rumble of the engine made her jump. She jerked her hand away from the steering wheel.

"That was good," he said. "You didn't hold the key too long. If you do, that will grind the ignition."

"I didn't know that," she said.

At the moment, grinding the side of the car against a tree seems a more likely occurrence, she thought. *What if Thomas could see me now?* Susan shuddered at the thought. *He wouldn't like it, and he'd probably pray that I would repent of my sins.*

Robby continued. "Now, leave your foot on the brake as you're preparing to go. Always remember—if you panic or if there's any trouble, go for the brake. Think brake. 'Brake. Brake. Stomp. Stomp. Stomp.'"

"Okay, now what?" Susan asked.

"Release the emergency brake. That's this," he said as he demonstrated. "Then move the gearshift—that's this one—from 'P' for 'park' to 'D' for 'drive'."

"What will happen then?"

"You will drive…once you let off the brakes."

"Okay." Susan forced herself to breathe again.

"Slowly now, slowly," he said, his voice tense.

"I thought you said this was easy."

"It is easy. Now let out on the brakes, but stomp on it if you panic."

The car moved forward a few inches and increased speed. *I'm driving! Me, the Amish girl Susan Hostetler, is actually driving! The world is moving slowly past the window.*

"Turn left here," Robby hollered. "And there's someone coming. Brake! Brake!"

"I'm turning," she said, not slowing down as the car went by.

"Stop sign. Brake. Brake!"

She stomped hard and the tires squealed.

"Sorry."

"That's better than running a stop sign," he said. "Now turn left."

She went left, and then left again, rounding the circle a few times, stopping at the stop sign each time. Susan felt her breathing become easier.

"It is easy," she said out loud.

"You're learning. Remember that," he said. "Don't be too confident. Let's turn right at the stop sign this time."

Susan turned, following the blacktop. The trees were closer by the road here, but she could do trees now. One simply had to stay on the road.

"There's a hill coming up," he said. "Remember the brake."

The car was going by itself, and she let it. This was fun! The blacktop hummed under the tires. This must be what it felt like to be a real *Englisha* person sitting behind the wheel of a car.

"Slow down. Brake. Brake."

"This is fun!" she said.

"There's a turn coming up," he warned.

Susan turned the wheel, the tires squealing as they angled around the corner.

"You're going to kill us," Robby shouted. "Stop right now! There's someone coming again."

"*Yah.*" She stomped for the brake. They *were* going a little fast. She gasped as the car shot forward in a burst of speed instead of stopping.

"You're on the gas," Robby screamed. "*Brake! Now!*"

The car in the other lane was getting closer. Where is the brake? She stomped again. Robby's hands went flying against the dashboard. Her seat belt bit into her neck, and the tires squealed loudly.

"Heaven have mercy on us!" Robby said as the car settled and Susan shifted the gear into park. "This woman is going to kill me for sure."

Susan put her head on the steering wheel, shaking with laughter. "You were so right! This is fun!"

"You are insane, woman! Get out of the car this instant!"

"No, I won't. I'm just getting the hang of this."

"I can't take this anymore," he said, looking pale.

She pulled the lever down to "D," took her foot off the brake, and pressed the gas. The car jerked forward.

"She is going to kill me!" Robby muttered. "And I am my mother's only son."

"What do I do next?" she asked, jerking to another stop at an intersection.

"Get out of the car and let me drive."

"Come on, Robby. This was your idea!"

He sighed. "Okay. You need to use your turn signals. They're on the left-hand side. Pull down for left and push up for right. Practice it a few times."

Susan kept her foot on the brake. "Up goes right, down goes left," she said, pushing and pulling, listening to the sound of the clicks.

"Stop it," he said. "I can't bear the sound anymore. Just use them from now on when you turn."

"You're a good teacher." She turned to smile at him. He looked pale.

"Don't look at me," he said. "Your eyes are measuring me for my coffin."

Her shoulders shook with laughter, but her hands stayed on the wheel.

He glared at her.

"If Thomas could see me now!" she said. "Wouldn't that teach him a *gut* lesson!"

"So now we have the ghosts of old boyfriends haunting us?"

"Don't worry. He doesn't bite. He's a pacifist ghost."

"Does he know how to drive?" Robby asked.

"Of course he doesn't. Now, where do I go?"

"Around and around the merry old bush, I guess. How long do I have to endure this?"

"We've got all afternoon!" She gave him a sweet smile, accelerating with a jerk.

He lay his head back on the headrest, waving his arm. "Just go."

"No more instructions then?"

"You can practice what I've told you. You need *lots* of practice. Just stay here in the park area. You're not ready for city streets."

"Okay," she said reluctantly.

A minute later, they passed the picnic table. Her sandwich bag was still lying there.

"Remind me to stop next time." She motioned toward the table and the car weaved.

"Someone else will take it to the trash," he said. "Just keep me alive. I'm too weak to walk. Just keep going. Blinking. Turning. Stomping."

On the third pass, Susan pulled over and the car bounced off the curb.

Robby smiled hopefully. "Does this mean you're surrendering the wheel?"

"The bag," she said. "It needs to go into the trash can."

"Oh, the bag." He got out and headed toward the picnic table. He picked up the bag and walked to the trash. Hesitating after he dropped it in, he came back to the car, opened the door, slid in, and buckled the seat belt.

"Thanks," she said. "I'm ready to go to the mall now."

"To the mall. Thank God! I'm going to live after all." He undid his seat belt and opened his door.

"No, no!" she said. "I'm driving. I need the practice."

"You are not," he said, not moving. "It's four lanes on the way to the mall."

"Well, I guess that would be a bit much," she agreed. "But up till then."

"Oh, no!" he moaned, snapping his seat belt back on. "I can't believe I'm doing this."

As they pulled out of the park, Susan turned onto the main road, the back wheel bouncing over the curb.

Robby moaned again as Susan accelerated and clutched the wheel. The cars seemed to be going much faster than they usually were. One driver honked his horn at her.

"They're going so fast," she said, looking sideways at Robby. He was looking straight ahead, not moving.

"They're not moving any faster. It's you," he said moments later. "But you can stop anytime."

"Tell me what to do," she hollered as another car horn blasted.

"The light ahead," he whispered. "It's yellow. Slow down gently, but don't hit the guy in front of you. Easy on the brake now."

They came to a stop, and Susan let go of the steering wheel, wiping the sweat off her palms.

"You'd better do this," she said. "Can we change drivers now?"

He shook his head. "Not here. It's not safe. But keep going once the light turns green."

"It is green," she said, pushing the gas pedal only a touch. The car still jerked forward.

Robby groaned. "Keep going," he said. "And turn on your right turn signal to get in the slower lane."

She flinched at the clicking sound and looked back to see the traffic behind her.

"You can get over now," Robby said. "There's no one there."

Susan turned the wheel and the car eased over into the curbside lane.

"Now what?" she asked.

"In there," he said. "Turn into this car lot."

She turned and they bounced to a stop. Robby had his hands braced on the dashboard.

"Thank You, Lord," he said, not moving for a long time. "We're safe! The woman's actually got me praying."

"That's *gut!*" She tried to laugh.

"Just let me behind the wheel," Robby said, getting out. "I declare I will never teach an Amish woman to drive again. Never in all my life."

✦

CHAPTER TWENTY-ONE

Cars in the four lanes drifted past as Robby drove silently back toward Asbury Park.

"Is something wrong?" Susan asked.

"No." He didn't look up. "Nothing at all. But my whole life keeps floating in front of my eyes."

"Was it that bad?" she asked between giggles.

"You have a really nasty side, you know that?" he said.

"Hey, you just passed the exit for the mall," she said, not answering his comment. He could think of her however he wanted. It had been his idea to teach her to drive.

"So?" he said, not looking at her.

"I wanted to stop in, remember?"

"I remember, but we're not stopping in."

"So you're that mad?" she asked. "You know that's a little childish."

"I'm not mad," he said. "I'm just frazzled to the bone, my nerves are shot, and my blood is still frozen from fright. And you did it on purpose." He glared at her. "You took all your frustrations out on me."

"Maybe I did," she said, "but it was fun."

"Is that like 'Amish fun'?"

"I guess it is," she said. "I hadn't thought about that. Still, that's no reason not to take me to the mall."

"I've had my adventure for the day."

"So you expect your mom to take me?"

"I'm sure she will," he said.

"I can't ask her," Susan said. "She's already done so much for me."

"Then I'll ask her," he said.

Susan considered. Maybe he was right. This late in the day, Laura wouldn't mind if Robby watched the bakery.

Finally Robby relaxed. "See? This is how you drive." He had sped up and was now moving deftly in and out of the lanes.

"Are you trying to get even?" she asked, hanging on to the shoulder harness of the seat belt.

He grinned, showing all his teeth.

She turned in her seat. "I guess I should tell you there's a police car with flashing lights behind you."

Robby mashed on the brakes and swerved into the slow lane, eyeing the rearview mirror.

"I don't see anything," he said quickly looking into the rearview mirror, his voice shaking.

"I was stretching the truth," Susan said with a grin. "But it did get you to slow down."

"Please, God," Robby muttered. "Help me get through this day with this woman."

"God's probably teaching you patience—and using me to do it," she said.

"I didn't know I needed any," he said. "I just need patience with you."

"You sure do!" she agreed.

"Let's see," he said. "Didn't I promise to take you out on the ocean sometime?"

"You did and I'm holding you to it."

"Then no more nasty tricks for at least ten minutes," he said.

"Okay," she agreed. "No more tricks. Hear that brain? Go to sleep."

He took the next exit and came to a stop at the first light.

"You were a very bad example today," he said.

"I'm very sorry," she said, not looking very sorry at all.

"That's what I thought," he retorted, turning left toward the bakery. Moments later he declared, "Here we are! I'll have Mom out in a jiffy."

"I'm coming in."

They both got out.

As they walked into the bakery, Laura looked up from the rack she was filling. "Back already? I don't see any shopping bags."

"She almost killed me, Mom!" Robby exclaimed. "I'm not taking her shopping!"

Laura's smile got bigger. "Then I should have been there to help her."

"Nothing like women sticking together," Robby grumbled. "Anyway, let me take care of the shop and *you* can take her shopping. She's got her driver's permit, some driving lessons from me, and her information for the GED. That's enough for one day."

"He's just kidding," Laura said in Susan's direction.

"I know. And he has been wonderful today. You should have seen what all he did for me!"

"Let's see now," Laura said. "You're talking about my son, Robby, right? Or was someone else with you today?"

The front door opened, interrupting them. Two customers walked in.

"Get going," Robby whispered. "I'll take care of things."

"Let me get my purse." Laura disappeared into the office.

"Thanks for everything today," Susan told Robby. "It was very nice of you."

"Welcome," he grunted, a smile playing on his face.

Laura appeared again and Susan followed her out to her car, glancing at Robby's vehicle as they passed. It wasn't quite a horse and buggy, but she was going to have pleasant memories of the first car she'd ever driven for a long time. Yes, it was a horrible thing for an Amish girl to enjoy, but shivers of delight were going up and down her spine. She had driven an automobile! A worldly *Englisha* automobile.

"Did Robby behave himself?" Laura asked as they got into the car.

Susan had to laugh. "I think I'm the one who misbehaved. I gave him a rough time when he took it upon himself to teach me how to drive."

"I'm sure he deserved it. You do him a lot of good."

"You really think so? If anything, I'd like to help him get past this bitterness he seems to have toward God."

"The good Lord will have to take care of that, dear," Laura said.

"Robby was a little spoiled growing up, I'm afraid. His big sisters doted on him all the time."

"It does happen," Susan agreed. "We never had a younger brother to spoil. Maybe that's why they spoiled me."

"It's not quite like a younger brother," Laura said. "And I doubt you were spoiled."

"Thanks, but I'm sure I'm a little spoiled. I know Thomas thought so."

"We'll leave Thomas in his own world," Laura said. "So what about Duane? Is he still taking you out tomorrow night?"

"*Yah*," Susan said, looking out the car window.

"Do you think you can fit into our world?" Laura asked.

"I'm trying," Susan replied. "That's what my shopping trip is about. I need new clothes. Will you help me? I have no idea what to buy. I've never even worn a dress that is printed. We're only allowed to wear solid colors. But they still need to be modest."

"I guess it's a good idea Robby brought you back."

"I didn't want to bother you, but *yah*, this is much better."

Laura looked her over for a long moment, "We'll have to see what we can do for you."

"Do I look that terrible?" Susan glanced down at her dress. "I imagine I do, but I guess I'm used to it."

"You look fine, but let's see if we can dazzle Duane tomorrow night."

"I've never dazzled anybody in my life!" Susan exclaimed.

What would that be like? she wondered. *Even Thomas had never been dazzled. Unless by Eunice…but that's a thought best not dwelled upon.*

Laura took the Monmouth Mall exit off the four lane, and Susan felt herself tense at the task ahead of her. When would she be an *Englisha* girl with all her Amish ways behind her? And did she want to leave all of them behind? Her situation was so very confusing.

After Laura parked, Susan followed her across the lot to the mall entrance.

"It's busy today," Laura commented.

"I hope the shoppers haven't purchased all the good dresses," Susan said.

"This is a mall, dear. Don't worry—they have lots of dresses. Now, let's see." Laura paused. "Shall I take you to Lord & Taylor or J.C. Penney?"

"J.C. Penney," Susan said. "I think that's more my style."

"Normally, yes. But you're going out with Duane." Laura scrutinized Susan's dress again.

"But I'm just an Amish girl. I can't move too fast or I'll get dizzier than I already am."

"Hmmm…well…Let's try our faithful J.C. Penney then."

"Besides," Susan said, "Lord & Taylor looks expensive."

"We'll see what Penney's has to offer."

They entered the store, and Susan glanced up and down the aisles. She rubbed both hands over her face. "You're going to have to help me, Laura. I have no idea where to start."

"What colors do you like? Let's start with that."

"Dark, black, solids."

When Laura stayed silent, Susan went on. "Those are Amish colors."

"Let's just forget about that for tonight, okay?"

"I'll try," Susan said, stopping at a rack. "Hey, this looks safe." Susan took a beige dress off the rack. "It's a little Amish with a little *Englisha* added in with these ruffles."

"Is it your size?"

"Yes, I think so."

"Okay, go try the dress on. The dressing rooms are over there."

"Change? Over there? In the store?"

"Don't worry, it's private," Laura assured her.

"Okay. I'm also taking this with me." Susan held up a light-gray dress with white polka dots trimmed in white lace.

"Okay," Laura said.

Moments later Susan came out of the dressing room wearing the beige dress.

"It's beautiful!" Laura said. "Do you like it?"

"Yes," Susan said. "And to think I'm really buying an *Englisha* dress."

"Turn around," Laura said.

Susan did a slow turn.

"Looks even better," Laura said. "Do you want to try on the gray dress?"

"Yes. I'll be right back."

Susan had the beige dress with her when she reappeared wearing the gray.

Laura laughed. "Susan, dear, in that dress you still look too much like a fresh-off-the-farm girl. You certainly can't wear that one tomorrow night."

"But I love it," Susan said. "I can wear it in the bakery, can't I?"

"Yes, the bakery would be fine. Now let's pick out something else I'm not quite satisfied about tomorrow night."

"The beige dress is okay."

"If you think so," Laura said. "I don't want to push you into anything."

Susan's face brightened. "I want to see what you would pick. My guess is it would be really beautiful."

Laura laughed. "I'm afraid you have too much faith me, but let's see if you agree with my taste."

Laura moved to another rack and then another before pulling out a dark purple blouse with a black leaf pattern. "How about this? It would look great with black slacks."

"Pants?" Susan's hand flew to her mouth. "You want me to wear *pants*?"

"What's wrong with pants?"

"Nothing, I guess!" Susan gasped. "It's just that…I think it's too soon. Maybe later…but the top is really nice. Can a skirt go with it instead? A skirt I can do."

"A skirt it will be then." Laura continued looking through the racks, finding what she wanted. She held the two items side by side. "No sense in pushing things. Try these on."

Susan returned a few minutes later wearing the skirt and blouse.

"Now *that* is what I call splendid!" Laura said. "Do you like it?"

"I do," Susan said. "But I feel guilty."

"You'll buy it anyway, won't you?" Laura encouraged.

Susan nodded. This bridge needed to be crossed sometime. Why not now?

She carried the items to the checkout counter and paid for them. She watched as the clerk bagged the clothes.

"They're mine!" she whispered to Laura, who was standing close to her. "And they are so *Englisha*."

Laura squeezed her hand. "I'm glad I could share in your special moment. I do declare you're becoming like a daughter to me."

"Thank you." Susan picked up the bags and followed Laura out to the car.

On the way back Susan said, "I wanted to ask you about how I should prepare for my GED test. The lady at the college said I could either study online or take night classes. Either way has its drawbacks, I suppose."

"What do you want to do?" Laura asked. "Would you be more comfortable taking the night classes?"

"Maybe. But someone would have to drive me there and back. Would it be too much of a bother to use your computer in the bakery? That is, if I can learn how. Robby said it would be easy."

"Don't believe everything Robby tells you." Laura laughed. "But you are welcome to use the computer. We have a good internet connection."

"Then that's what I'll do," Susan decided just as they arrived at the bakery.

Laura parked the car. As they got out, she asked, "Susan, you're still being careful at night, aren't you?"

"Yes. Is there still danger? They found those women, didn't they?"

"They did, but not alive, I'm sorry to say. And they haven't caught the person who hurt them yet," Laura said.

Susan shivered. "I'll be careful, and I'll pray really hard."

"If there are any more attacks, you are coming to live at our place—no questions asked."

"Let's hope there won't be," Susan said. "Goodnight—and thank you again!" She closed the car door, and Laura took off. Finding the key in her purse, she opened the apartment door, making sure the lock was turned in place behind her. The city could be a scary place with all the streetlights and noise. Yet it was hard to imagine anything happening here in her safe haven.

Susan waited to throw the switch at the top of the stairs, pausing to look around as light flooded the room. There would be no kerosene lamps tonight—and perhaps never again. Before long she would be using the computer in Laura's office. She was moving into the *Englisha* world, and that was as it should be.

Opening her closet she hung up the new clothes, stepping back to admire them. *What will it be like wearing one in public? Will people stare? Probably not. They wouldn't know that underneath all that finery is a hard-beating Amish girl's heart.* Susan sighed, closed the closet door, and walked into the kitchen to prepare supper. It had been an exhausting day, and sleep would be very sweet tonight. Almost as sweet as sleeping upstairs in the old farmhouse with the windows open to the field breezes.

Stop it! she ordered. *You are becoming an* Englisha *girl now.*

Chapter Twenty-two

⁂

Thomas held his horse by the reins as the two buggies beside him took off from Deacon Ray's dark barnyard.

Where is Eunice? The singing had been over for ten minutes, and his instructions had been plain. *Come out right away. I'll be parked next to your brother's buggy.* Eunice's brother was gone now, and still the girl hadn't come. Soon there would be questions asked about why he was sitting here waiting. His sisters would usually be picked up at the end of the walk, so that wouldn't suffice as an explanation.

Freddy shook his head, for once pulling against the reins. He might be slow on the road, but standing still while the other horses took off was apparently a humiliation even he was unable to bear.

Across the dark open space beside him another dim buggy light came on. A boy, his features shadowed by his hat, held up his buggy shafts. He swung his horse under them with a quick movement of his hands.

Thomas sighed. *Does Eunice plan to make me drive to the front walks? Perhaps forcing me to show my hand for all to see? Coming from her this is entirely possible,* he thought. *Susan would never do this, but Eunice obviously isn't Susan.*

A woman's form dashed out of the shadows, a hand clutching bonnet strings. His dim buggy lights caught the color of her dress—a light, dusty blue. *How like Eunice,* he thought. *She would wear a flashy dress on the night I'm taking her home. Come to think of it, Eunice usually wears flashy dresses. At least all she could fit into the Ordnung.*

Thomas turned his buggy wheels to the right. The least he could do was be polite. It would be a pleasant evening spending time with Eunice. That is, if his expectations were correct.

"Good evening!" Eunice said, pulling herself up the buggy steps. She sat down beside him, her dress brushing against his legs. "Sorry I'm late. Barbara and I got to talking, and time slipped away."

"That's okay," he said, letting out the reins. Freddy took off with a jerk, pulling the front buggy wheels sideways on the gravel.

"Wow!" Eunice said, her voice rising. "What a horse. I didn't know you had such a go-getter."

"He's nothing special," Thomas said. The girl might as well get her thinking straight from the first. "He just got a little anxious waiting while the other horses took off."

"Now, Thomas, you don't have to be modest around me," Eunice said. "Really. I just saw what I saw with my own eyes. My guess is your horse can pass most of the ones on the road."

Thomas didn't say anything for a long moment. He finally managed to get some words out. "I'm afraid not. Freddy is quite a slowpoke."

"Oh, no," she said, groaning. "I thought I was going to get a fast ride tonight. My brother Nelson's horse can barely lift its feet most nights going home from the singing."

"I'm afraid my horse is no faster than your brother's," Thomas said, not looking at her.

"You're still teasing me, aren't you?" Eunice asked. "Didn't someone say you had the fastest horse in the community?"

"No. I don't know anyone who would say something like that," Thomas asserted. "Deacon Ray's boy—James. He has a fast horse."

"Well, I sure thought I heard you did. But it doesn't matter," Eunice assured him. "Don't worry. Someday I'm going to ride in a buggy with a really fast horse pulling it. We'll pass everyone on the road and then some. But I'm sure you know all about that. You probably had a fast horse before this one."

"I didn't ever have a fast horse." Thomas slapped the reins.

"Oh," Eunice said. "I'm sorry. I was sure you did."

"It's okay," Thomas said. "Our family is not the best situated when it comes to money."

Eunice sighed and leaned against his shoulder. "Nor is our family, with all the moving around we do. I told *Daett* we have to stop it sometime or he won't even be able to afford our weddings."

"I thought this was the first community you'd moved to," Thomas said.

"*Acht* no!" she exclaimed. "*Daett* moved twice while I was still in school. But I guess we made it all right. At least I think we're still normal."

Thomas laughed. "You look normal enough to me."

"That's *gut*," she said. "I'm glad you think I'm normal."

She had her head turned now and was smiling up at him.

He slapped the reins again, but it was a hopeless cause. Freddy had no speed, even for a few steps. They lumbered through the darkness, the minutes passing.

Eunice ignored Freddy's slow progress. She told Thomas about the past week's happenings on their farm. He didn't say much until he reached her *daett's* driveway, pulling to a stop by the barn.

"I think I'll tie up instead of unhitching the buggy," he said.

"But you're staying for a while, surely?" she asked, obviously alarmed.

"*Yah*, if you want me to," he said, climbing down.

"Of course I do." She climbed down and waited in the shadows as he tied the horse.

Taking his arm, they walked to the house.

It's nice the way Eunice is hanging on my arm. Susan never did this, Thomas thought. *Certainly not on her first time home with me. But that was a long time ago.* Pausing, Thomas tilted his hat back to look at the sky. The stars were out in all their glory, with no sign of the moon anywhere. His sudden pause caused Eunice to trip, falling forward, breaking her fall by putting her free hand on the ground.

"I'm so sorry!" Thomas said, giving her a hand up. "I should have warned you I was stopping."

"That's okay," she said. "Do you often look up unexpectedly?"

"Sometimes." He laughed. "It seems like there's more time to look up at the stars on Sunday nights."

"That's funny," she said. "There's the same amount of time on Sunday as on every other day."

He resumed his walk. *Why can't the girl be quiet for even two seconds? Susan wouldn't ask questions like this or make a strange comment. And she wouldn't be surprised by my stopping to look at the stars on a Sunday night.*

Eunice took his arm again and looked up at his face. "You're quite the romantic, aren't you? Looking at the stars on Sunday nights. Is that the real you? Or is that just for show?" She held open the front door for him, while he stepped inside and took off his hat.

"I'm not sure," he finally answered.

She held up her finger. "Hush now," she whispered. "*Mamm* and *Daett* are already in bed, and we have the living room to ourselves. Isn't that wonderful?"

"*Yah,* I guess," he said, sitting on the couch.

"I'll be back in a minute." She disappeared into the kitchen. He stared at the walls. Things looked different tonight in the low light of the kerosene lamp. Unfamiliar…almost as if he'd never been here. He pushed thoughts of Susan from his mind. He would soon become used to this place, just as he had Menno and Anna's home.

Minutes later Eunice bustled out of the kitchen bringing a plate of cookies. Setting them on the floor in front of the couch, she nestled up against him.

"What kind are they?" he asked, leaning forward to take one.

"Chocolate chip. Do you like chocolate chip?"

"*Yah,* I can eat them well enough," he said.

"What kind did Susan make for you on Sunday nights?" she asked.

"Perhaps we shouldn't speak of Susan," he suggested.

"I don't think she'd mind, really," she said. "Isn't it over between the two of you?"

"*Yah,* I guess so," he said. "She's not here anyway."

Eunice shrugged. "Then let's talk about *us,* shall we? If you don't like conversation about Susan. Tell me about what you do. Doesn't your *daett* have a shop of some kind?"

"We have a cabinet shop," he said.

"You don't sound too excited about your work."

"I'm not," he said. "Most of our people are farmers, are they not?"

"That doesn't mean you have to be. I think a cabinetmaker is perfectly wonderful. You're probably very *gut* at it, aren't you?"

"*Daett* thinks so," he said. "But we only work for the local people."

"Then see, there you go. Your *daett* knows what you're *gut* at, and you make enough for a decent living."

"We could make more if we worked for people in the big cities," he said. "But *Daett* won't go after that business. I don't understand why. I think Amish cabinets would sell well in Louisville or even Indianapolis."

"Whoa...you do have your eyes set on the stars," she said, leaning forward to take a cookie from the plate and then passing it to him. "Here, you haven't had your second one yet. Is there something wrong with my cookies? I made them especially for you. It took an awful lot of doing to keep the boys away from them—not to mention the girls. You ought to feel really special."

"I like your cookies," he said, taking a bite. "But back to what we were saying. I'd still be making cabinets—even if we'd just sell to Indianapolis."

"I'm sure you would," she said. "So do you really like my cookies?"

"There's nothing wrong with your cookies, really. They are perfect. As *gut* as *Mamm's*. I was talking about making cabinets though."

"I'm sure you're a *gut* cabinetmaker, even if I've never seen any you've made. You look like one to me, so I'm perfectly happy with what you are."

"I guess I ought to be happy with the ways things are." He looked out the window at the dark sky with its bright sweep of stars.

"*Yah*, I think we ought to be happy with the way we're made," she offered. "Isn't that what our people believe? Look at us as an example. I never thought the day would come when you would ask to bring me home. But for whatever reason, the day arrived! Should we not be happy with that?"

She moved closer, leaning toward him.

Getting up to walk over to the window, he didn't answer.

Moments later soft footsteps followed him on the hardwood floor. Her hand took his arm again. Her face brushed his.

"Did I say something wrong, Thomas? I'm sorry if I did. And I'm sorry about Susan. But we can't change that, can we?"

"I don't know," he said.

"She gone, Thomas. No one goes out to the *Englisha* world like she has and comes back. You know that, don't you?"

He said nothing, tracing the heavens with his eyes.

"It's true, Thomas," she insisted. "And you should stop dreaming about it. And what if Susan does come back? Can you imagine the trouble she will bring with her?"

"Do you know something I don't?" He turned to face her.

"*Nee,* but I'm not stupid, Thomas. I know what goes on out there in the world. It's hard enough to live a life of holiness here without going somewhere without any rules to live by."

"How do you know Susan is living a wild life?" he demanded.

"You don't have to think too hard to know that," she said. "But you should stop thinking about *her.* I'm here now, and I'm very happy to be with you."

"What if I can't?" he asked.

She stroked his face, the touch of her fingers soft on his skin. "I was afraid your mind was still troubled. The memory of her might not go away quickly. You were together for so long."

"I know." He turned back to the window.

"You and Susan weren't meant to be, Thomas. Can't you see that?"

"I thought we were meant to be," he said.

"But she obviously didn't, Thomas. Now come back to the couch. I'm tired of standing by this window."

"I think it's time for me to go," he said. "We have a full day's work ahead of us tomorrow. And *Daett* is pushing with an extra order of cabinets he wants to get out."

"You will come back soon?" Her fingers traced his face again.

"I really don't know, Eunice. It's very confusing right now."

"Then I won't hold it against you, Thomas. Perhaps you need more time to heal."

"I really need to go," he said, opening the front door.

"I'll see you later then." She followed him out onto the porch.

"I don't think so, Eunice," he said. "We shouldn't make any more plans."

"Susan's not coming back, Thomas." Her voice lingered in the night air as he crossed the lawn. "I'll be waiting for you."

He untied Freddy and climbed into the buggy. He didn't turn on his buggy lights until he reached the main road.

✦

Chapter Twenty-three

Susan held the gray polka dot dress up to the light. *Yah*, she would wear the dress today. Her first time to actually wear an *Englisha* dress, and there would be *no* guilt feelings allowed. Was not *Da Hah* smiling on her, letting her know the guilt had been foolishness all along…those thoughts of *Englisha* this, and *Englisha* that? *Mamm* and *Daett* were wise people, but perhaps they weren't right about everything. And Thomas, well, he was obviously wrong about a lot of things.

Tonight she would go on her date with Mr. Moran at the Italian Restaurant on Asbury Avenue. *What does an Italian restaurant look like?* she wondered. *Fancy, no doubt, and I, Susan Hostetler, am going to eat there! Who would have thought such a thing possible only a short time ago? Certainly not Thomas. But what does he know? He was swept off his feet by Eunice.*

Susan glanced at the study booklets on the kitchen table. She had begun her studies last night after the bakery had closed. So far so good. She could do this. She turned off the apartment light and made her way down the creaky stairs. Outside, she locked the apartment door behind her, ducking under the awning over the bakery door. The lights were already on, so Laura had to have risen even earlier than the Amish did, considering her thirty-minute commute into town.

"Good morning," Susan said as she entered and closed the door behind her.

"Good morning!" Laura turned around to look at her, raising her eyebrows at the sight of Susan in her new dress. "My, aren't we looking sharp this morning! Turn this way—under the light. Yes, you did make a good choice. It's a nice fit for your figure."

"Don't say that." Susan laughed. "Dresses aren't supposed to show your figure."

"Within limits, I'd agree," Laura said. "But you're not Amish anymore."

"I hope it's not sinful," Susan said. *There are those awful guilt feelings trying to make me miserable again.*

"I wouldn't worry about it, dear," Laura said. "If it's out of line, I'll be the first to tell you. I'd say you have a long way to go before that time. Your dress is very beautiful. Now cover it with a big, long apron so it stays clean."

"Thanks." Susan took a deep breath. Laura liked her dress!

The two women worked side by side, baking rolls and cookies and serving the first customers long before the streetlights blinked off outside. In the break after the first rush, Laura grabbed a cup of coffee and motioned for Susan to do the same. "Take a quick breather," Laura said, "before someone else comes in."

Susan filled a small cup, keeping her eye on the front door. Someone always had a way of showing up when they tried to take a break. They would then place an order and nestle down for a long stay at the tables. She didn't feel comfortable sitting again until the customer had gone, and her coffee was usually cold by then. Laura could sit when customers were inside, chatting away—but then she owned the bakery.

Susan added cream and a dash of sugar. Not too much, just enough to take the bite off the taste of the coffee. Too much sugar, her *daett* often said, and you couldn't taste the coffee. "Why drink it then?" he would ask and smile at the power of his own logic. *It's funny that this morning thoughts of* Daett *are coming,* she thought. But they were here, and she allowed them to come. *Would* Daett *approve of the new dress? Not likely.*

But she would never wear it around him. Her Amish dresses would stay stashed upstairs in the apartment closet. The dresses would be there for when she visited home. There would be no sense in causing her *mamm* and *daett* undue sorrow if she did return.

The door opened behind her. Likely a couple of older ladies who would dawdle for an hour while ice crystals gathered on her coffee. Forcing a smile she turned to greet whoever it was, catching the eye of the same young woman who had been in twice before. Today she was wrapped in a thick coat that failed to hide her advancing pregnancy.

"Good morning," Susan said, setting her coffee out of sight behind some canisters. "What can I get for you?"

For some reason, the girl seemed frightened…confused. She said nothing.

Susan remembered that before the girl had taken only a small cup of coffee, staying to chat only briefly before leaving.

"Do you want the usual?" Susan smiled. "A small cup of coffee, right?"

The girl was trembling, but managed to say, "I can't buy coffee this morning, but I need to speak with you. Right bad, ma'am."

"You want to speak with *me*?" Susan asked. *What could this pregnant girl possibly want with me?* she wondered.

"How can I help you?" Laura asked, getting up. "Susan only works here, but if there is a problem with our service, you can speak with me."

The girl glanced between the two women. She looked ready to run. One hand was draped over her swollen stomach, the other grasped the edge of the counter.

Susan gasped as one of coffee canisters teetered. She jumped forward, grabbing it before it crashed to the ground.

"Are you hungry?" Laura asked. "If you don't have any money, I'll give you rolls and coffee. Would you like that?"

The girl ignored Laura, her eyes focused on Susan's face.

"Please ma'am," she said, speaking to Susan. "I beg of you. Will you help me? I have no one else I can turn to. You have been so nice to me the other times I was in here."

"Come, darling." Laura took the girl's hand, trying to lead her toward a table. "What's your name, dear?"

"I don't want to give my name. I want that lady's help." The girl was clinging to the counter.

"No one can help you if we don't have your name," Laura said, trying again.

The girl stayed by the counter.

"I have to have help!" she moaned. "I love the child too much."

Susan moved closer. *Perhaps I can help the girl—but how?* "I'll talk to her," Susan said to Laura. She took the young woman's hand just as the door opened behind them.

"I'll take care of the customer then," Laura whispered. "Take her to a table."

The girl went willingly, walking ahead of Susan but keeping a grip on her hand. Waiting while the girl took her coat off, Susan draped it over a chair. She placed her hand on the girl's shoulder while she slid into a chair.

Taking a seat across the table, Susan offered the girl a smile.

The young woman's troubled gaze went around the room, but she was breathing easier now.

"So, what is your name?" Susan asked. "I'm sure it's pretty."

The girl laughed for the first time, but the sound was harsh.

"There's not much left of it, ma'am, pretty or not," the girl said.

Susan waited and then touched the woman's arm. "Is it the baby? Are you still having trouble with the baby?"

The girl leaned in closer, ignoring the question, a slight smile on her face. "It's Teresa Long, ma'am."

"Teresa," Susan repeated. "That's such a nice name."

"As you can see, I'm with child," Teresa said.

"Your husband, does he know you are here?" Susan asked.

Teresa looked up and grabbed Susan's arm with both hands.

"I have no husband. But I know you can help me because you're Amish, aren't you? You said so when I was here before."

Susan nodded. "*Yah,* I am. But what can I do for you?"

"I know how holy the Amish people are," Teresa said slowly. "So please don't throw me out until you hear what I have to say."

"We won't throw you out, Teresa. Do you need help with the birth?" Susan asked, stroking the woman's hands that clutched her arm. "I'm not a midwife, but perhaps Laura knows someone who can help... with the cost and all. I could give some—a little money, but not much."

Her bank account was almost empty, depleted by last night's purchases. Susan started to get up. Her purse was in the back office.

"Please don't leave!" Fright flashed across Teresa's face. "I know I am a bad girl in the eyes of the Amish, but it's of my child I'm thinking."

Nothing Teresa was saying made sense, but Susan sat down again. Laura was almost done with her customer. Perhaps she would understand what Teresa wanted. "Where do you live, Teresa? Do you have enough food?"

"It's not that, ma'am." Teresa's eyes fixed on the street outside. "Charlie says I have to get an abortion. That there's still time, even now. He says he can find someone."

So that's the problem! The young woman is faced with the choice of killing her child, pressured into a choice she didn't want. She needs help to find a way out. "You don't have to kill your baby," Susan told her. "I'm sure we can help. Laura will be done soon, and we can talk to her."

Teresa shook her head. The bakery door opened, and a man walked in holding a small girl's hand. Teresa's eyes turned to look, but quickly returned to Susan. "If I do what Charlie wants, they will kill the child. God knows I couldn't take that."

"You don't have to!" Susan said. "Really, you don't."

"Charlie has left me—until I get an abortion."

"God doesn't want you killing your child, Teresa. You don't have to listen to Charlie."

Across the room the man was selecting the pastries he wanted, allowing the little girl to pick her own. It would be a few moments at least before Laura could come over.

Susan caught a glimpse of her coffee behind the canisters. It would be cold by now.

"That's what I want," Teresa said as she tapped Susan on the arm and pointed with her chin toward the man and girl.

"What?" Susan turned to look.

"The life they have," Teresa said. "Look how he loves her! But that's not usually found in my world. And it never will be. I need someone to take my child. To raise him in a godly home."

Susan let out a deep breath. "God is able to do miracles for anyone!"

"He can?" Teresa's eyes lit up.

Susan nodded. This young woman was living far from any life she knew, but Susan knew the girl's heart must yearn for God. They were different people, and yet the same in ways that were hard to understand.

"Then you will do it?" Teresa asked.

Susan felt the woman's fingers digging into her arm. "Do what, Teresa?" she asked.

"Take my baby as your own! Take him to be raised in Amish country. Where he doesn't have to grow up to be the kind of person I am."

CHAPTER TWENTY-FOUR

Susan looked out at the street through Laura's big glass window, the roar of the automobiles loud in her ears. *What had Teresa just said? That she wants to give me the baby? Wants me to take it back to the community? That's not possible! And I can't take care of a baby! Besides, I barely know this woman.*

"Please!" Teresa said, her voice seeming to come from far off.

"But you don't even know me!" Susan exclaimed, looking into Teresa's eyes. "And, Teresa, I came here to get away from my Amish community. I'm not really Amish anymore."

The tears now running down Teresa's cheeks were shimmering rivers that caused Susan to grasp Teresa's hand even tighter. *Where is Laura?* she thought desperately.

"I want my child to have a chance in life," Teresa was saying. "There are no chances around here. There is no hope in my life—nor will there be in his if he stays here."

"But there is always hope," Susan said. "We have to believe in God and do what's right. Even I have to move ahead with hope. Right now I'm working on my GED."

Teresa shook her head. "You don't understand. You and me, we're not in the same world. The things you hope for are not the things I can hope for...here."

"There must be some other way I can help you," Susan said. "I'm a good listener. Would that help? I live in the apartment above the bakery.

You could come by and we could talk. I can do that." Even as she said it, Susan knew how lame such an offer must sound to Teresa.

"You're more than kind, ma'am, as I expected you would be. But it's my child I have to think about. I have to make plans for him *before* he comes. And it can't be that long now."

"Have you seen a doctor?" Susan asked.

Teresa laughed. "I've been to the few doctor's visits the state helps out with. I don't have any money for a doctor myself. And my mom barely brings in enough food for us to eat. I lost my job at the gas station since I'm showing big now."

Susan stroked Teresa's arm. What else could she say? The mountain this girl had to climb was certainly larger than any she had ever experienced.

"You will help me with the child then?" Teresa asked.

Hasn't the girl been listening? "Are you talking about adoption?" Susan asked.

"Yes, adoption," Teresa said. "I will sign any papers you want. I never need to see the child again. Whatever it takes I'll do, but he has to be in good hands."

"Maybe Laura will know how to handle this," Susan said.

Teresa shook her head.

Susan caught Laura's attention when the customer left and motioned with her eyes to come.

Laura moved toward them.

"Surely there are good-hearted people around here who want to adopt children," Susan said.

"No." Teresa leaned forward. "It has to be an Amish home. If you can't take him, perhaps you know someone who can from your community. I don't know any other Amish, so you are my only chance. They said on TV that the Amish are closed communities. Nobody can get in from the outside, but you're already in, ma'am. And the chance that I should meet you, right when I needed it the most—now that's a miracle from God. Didn't you say God works miracles?"

"Yes, He does!" Susan whispered. *But how am I supposed to take an* Englisha *child and expect an Amish couple to adopt him? And what about the government red tape and expense? And who among my family would want the child? None of my sisters had problems conceiving. All their children were considered blessings, but more would be too much.*

"Are the two of you having a nice chat?" Laura asked, laying her hand on the young woman's shoulder.

Teresa smiled and nodded.

"I need to talk to you, Laura." Susan got up. "Will you wait here, Teresa?"

"Yes, ma'am," Teresa said.

"So the girl's name is Teresa," Laura said as they walked back to the office.

"Yes, and she's in a lot of trouble." Susan closed the door behind them. "She wants someone to adopt her baby. Well, really, she asked if I or an Amish couple would take the child. Apparently she has a high opinion of Amish people and doesn't want the child to grow up to live like she does."

"The poor girl," Laura said. "At least she's making some good choices. Abortion would have been an easy option for her, I'm sure. The government goes out of its way to see to that."

"So what do we do?" Susan asked. "It's too much for me alone, but we can't just send her back out on the street, can we?"

"No, we can't," Laura agreed. "Do you think she'd be willing to visit the Crisis Pregnancy Center? I don't have close ties to the one run by the Catholic diocese, but our church supports it."

"I don't know, but I'll ask. That sounds better than Teresa's idea. I mean, Indiana is a long way from here."

"She'll need care either way," Laura said. "Did she say whether she's had medical attention yet?"

"She's been to a doctor a few times. What the state supplies, she said."

"That's at least something," Laura said. "I guess you're getting to see the underside of Asbury Park. First, the murders and now this."

"I'll ask her about the Crisis Pregnancy Center then," Susan said. "I think I heard a customer come in."

"This girl may be delusional," Laura said as they walked back. "I'm not sure how seriously you should take what she says."

"She's been in here before," Susan said. "And she seemed to be looking for something then too."

"Susan, I think it would be a good idea if you walked her home. See where she lives. Look into what the conditions are. Make friends with her, and we'll take it from there. Okay? She can't live far if she walked."

"Go with her? Right now?" Susan asked.

"Yes, now."

"There is the bell again," Susan said. "What about the bakery? You'll be here by yourself and customers are coming in."

"Sometimes life calls with greater duties, dear. The customers can form a line if they want to. I'm sure you can make it back before the lunch rush."

"I'll hurry," Susan said, opening the office door. Two people were waiting at the counter. Laura went out and greeted them immediately, while Susan slipped back to the table, this time sliding into the chair next to Teresa.

"Teresa, what you're asking isn't easy. There are a lot of things that must be done. And thinking of your baby's care is the first thing. Would you like me to come home with you right now? You can show me where you live. We can take you to a doctor later for a checkup. That's very important you know."

"I can show you where I live," Teresa said. "It's just across the tracks."

"Don't you know the name of the street?" Susan asked.

Teresa didn't answer right away. Finally she said, "We're not really supposed to be living there, so we have to be careful."

Susan stood. "We can talk more on the way."

"I guess so," Teresa said, sliding out from the table and getting to her feet.

Susan held the door open for her and guided her outside.

"This way," Teresa said, motioning to the west.

They crossed at the stoplight, passing the diner where Duane had treated Susan to lunch. That seemed like another world at the moment.

Teresa held one hand on her stomach and hung on to Susan's arm with the other. "He just kicked real hard!" Teresa said with a big smile. "I think he likes you. That will help a lot, won't it! Make things much easier. I hope he remembers a little bit about me though. Do you think he will? Even when I give him away? He's still part of me, isn't he?"

"He's very much a part of you," Susan agreed. "And perhaps you don't have to give him up. Perhaps we can talk with the father and persuade him to take care of the two of you."

Teresa laughed. "If you take my baby boy to Amish country, that will be enough of a miracle for me."

"How do you know the baby's a boy?" Susan asked. "You keep referring to him as 'he'."

"I'm his mother...duh," Teresa said.

"I didn't know mothers could tell," Susan said. "I've never had a child."

"They might not all know, but I know it's a boy," Teresa assured her. "If I'm wrong, I'll be really surprised."

"I have eight married sisters with children. I wonder if they knew," Susan said. "They never mentioned anything."

They turned another corner, moving further away from the main streets of Asbury Park. They were approaching the railroad tracks.

"Eight sisters did you say? And all of them married?" Teresa asked.

"*Yah,*" Susan said. What did it matter if *yah* slipped out now? Teresa would like the touch of Amish.

"I knew you were a holy people," Teresa said. "Just like I've seen on TV. I want my son to grow up like that. It's much better than how I'm living."

"I'm sure God can make things right for you," Susan said as they crossed the railroad tracks. The quality of the buildings ahead of them was decreasing compared to the buildings downtown.

"God is taking care of me," Teresa said. "Even though I sinned. Whoever would have thought I'd meet an Amish woman in Asbury Park? And one who will take care of my son. I know my boy will grow up to be a great man of God. Perhaps he'll come and visit me once he's older and has a beautiful wife. Wouldn't that be something?"

"It would be," Susan agreed. "But you have to think of other things right now. Like seeing a doctor and taking care of yourself during the pregnancy."

"Here we are." Teresa stopped and pointed toward a rundown, wooden, two-story house. The front yard was strewn with debris. "There's supposed to be nobody living here, so we don't lock up. Not that there's any danger. Mom and I have nothing to steal, and we're not good-looking enough to attract attention."

"Twenty thirty-one— two zero three one," Susan read aloud.

"Please don't tell anyone," Teresa said. "This is all we have."

"I won't," Susan said. "And you are pretty! Don't let anybody tell you otherwise." *Teresa is good-looking enough,* Susan thought. *Sure, she looks worn and weary, but that is understandable considering her circumstances.*

Teresa smiled. "That's nice of you to say, but like I said, you're not from my world." She led the way across the yard and pushed open the rickety front door. A set of stairs led upward, and Teresa took them one step at a time.

The stairs didn't squeak much, considering how ratty there were. Wood pieces were broken out of the steps and the edges were worn thin by years of use.

Arriving at the top of the steps, Susan paused to take in her surroundings. Everything was fairly clean, but the furniture was old. What passed for a kitchen area was a single sink with a dripping faucet. The refrigerator front was rusty with great slabs of paint pulled off the door. A hall led out of the room, and she could see curtains covering two doorways. One was probably a bathroom.

"You really live here?" Susan asked. *Why did I ask such a mean question?* Susan thought belatedly. *I sound so harsh.*

"Thankfully we have power and water," Teresa said, not seeming to be offended. "That's a lot to be thankful for! Charlie got things hooked up somehow from the place below. Back when he was still being nice to me. Don't ask me how though. He just did it. Mom pays a little to the landlord, and we try to keep things toned down. We don't turn on the lights much—just these dim lamps Mom got at Goodwill. Nobody else wanted them, I guess."

"Lamps?" Susan asked as she walked over to the kitchen table. Around the edges of the table the veneer had worn off. *No self-respecting Amish would have anything like this anywhere near their house. Perhaps in*

*the barn, but not inside the house. But Teresa can't help it, and she would
feel worse if she knew my thoughts,* Susan decided.

"The lamps?" Teresa had a puzzled look on her face.

"Oh." Susan refocused. "*Yah,* well, these look a little like Amish
lamps. I have one in my apartment."

"You do?" Teresa was beaming.

Susan nodded. It was *gut* to see joy filling Teresa's face.

"Then God has already been working in my life," Teresa said. "We
have Amish lamps in the house, and I didn't even know it. I'm so
thrilled."

"I'm glad you like them," Susan said.

Teresa glanced down the stairs when a door slammed below them.
Susan jumped.

"It's Mom," Teresa whispered, "She's home."

"Are you sure?" Susan asked. The footsteps coming up the stairs
sounded awfully heavy for a woman. But when she glanced down she
saw a middle-aged woman appear carrying a single grocery bag.

"Hello," the woman said warily when she reached the top of the
stairs.

Susan nodded as Teresa said, "Mom, this is Susan. Susan, please
met my mom, Maurice."

"Hello, Maurice," Susan said.

"Susan is Amish," Teresa said. "She's the woman I've been telling
you about. And Susan's going to take my baby to Amish country. Just
think about it, Mom! He's going to grow up to be a real honest Amish
man. And I might even get to see him someday—when he's big and
all grown up."

"Teresa always has her head in the clouds," Maurice said to Susan.

"Mom, I really *want* this for my baby!" Teresa exclaimed.

Maurice set the bag on the table. "Whew! That bag doesn't have
much in it, but it's heavy after the walk from the store."

"We don't have much money for groceries," Teresa explained.

"And food stamps don't go as far as you think," Maurice said.

"Does the government help out with this place?" Susan asked.

"Yes, but you can see what it gets us. The landlord manages to keep the inspector away somehow. If this place was up to code, we couldn't afford it."

"That's why I have to get a better life for my child," Teresa said.

"Her boyfriend, Charlie, wants the child gone," Maurice said. "But Teresa won't do that."

"Abortion is murder," Susan said. "Teresa understands that."

"Those words don't go over well in this part of town," Maurice said. "Look at us, at where we live. The law says abortion is a woman's choice. That's good enough for me. Besides, I'm not the one who went and got pregnant."

"Mom!" Teresa said. "Don't talk like that. You had *me*."

"I know, dear. And I'm not sorry I kept you! That was a good choice I made. One of the few."

"We'd like to help in some way," Susan said. "My boss, Laura, and I. That's why I came over…to see what we could do to help Teresa."

Maurice laughed. "So you really are an Amish woman? I don't know that I ever met one before. Not in *this* neighborhood!"

"I *was* Amish. I'm joining the *Englisha* world right now."

"She has contact yet with her folks back home though," Teresa said. "She can find an Amish couple for me."

"Is this true?" Maurice asked. "That you still have contact. I mean, don't they *shun* you if you leave? Isn't that the word the TV used—'shun'?"

"No, I'm not in the *ban*."

"Well, then," Maurice said, a smile spreading across her face. "I must say I'm surprised by my daughter. I never really thought she'd find an Amish person to take her child. I'm sure not going to raise another child in this place—or in any other place. And Teresa doesn't want the government's Child and Family Services involved, so that left us in a bit of a pickle."

"Mom," Teresa said, "I've been telling Susan all about me."

Maurice ignored her. "Ever since Teresa saw the thing they did on TV about the Amish, she can't get enough about the Amish. She'll stay up all hours of the night for a chance to watch that movie…what's it called? Oh yes—*Witness*. And what was the other one? *For Richer or*

Poorer. Oh, I did get all misty at the end of that Harrison Ford one. How they all gathered around at the end to protect each other. Yes, that did make me cry a little."

"But…" Susan took a deep breath. "I can't promise anything. I know what Teresa asked me to do, but I can't take the child myself. I don't know about adoption. The Amish don't adopt many children. They usually have plenty of their own."

"Why are you here if you're not taking the child?" Maurice asked.

"Trust me, Mom," Teresa said. "Susan is going to find my boy a home."

Susan cleared her throat. She needed to speak up now. If she didn't, this moment would come back to haunt her. Teresa obviously wouldn't listen to her denials, but Maurice likely would. Things would have to be made clear.

Facing both women, Susan said, "As I said, Laura and I want to help. But adoption is beyond my ability to promise. I can't say that will happen. I'm sorry."

"Did you hear that, Teresa?" Maurice looked at her daughter.

"Mom, please! She *is* going to help me!" Teresa insisted.

Maurice softened her voice and said, "Listen, honey. I don't want to see you hurt and disappointed again. You have to face facts. You can't live on false hopes like this. That's what you did with Charlie. You thought he'd marry you, and you and he would be happy ever after. But it just doesn't happen that way in real life. That's something I know a bit about. The fact you have to face is that I cannot and will not raise your child. I've humored you about this because I've never seen you want something so bad. But if this Amish woman can't promise an Amish home for your child, then you're going straight down to that pregnancy center to see if they will help you arrange an adoption here."

"Mom, I *can't*. Please! He is my child, and I can't do that to him. I don't want him growing up in the world I live in."

"He won't be in your world, child," Maurice said. "They can find a nice, upright home. Or you can still let Charlie arrange the…"

"No!" Teresa said. "I will not kill my son!"

"Listen to me. With your child gone, Charlie will come back to you. Think what that would be like. He'd hold you in his arms again and love you. We'd have a real man in the house again. And maybe you could marry him someday, Teresa."

"He wants to kill our boy," Teresa screamed. "How can I love such a man?"

"By coming to your senses, that's how!" Maurice said. "Jerk yourself out of that dream world of yours! Either arrange for an adoption or end the pregnancy. There are no other choices. And you need to decide now. I know you. Once that baby pops out, I know you won't want to give him up. So you're either going to let Charlie handle this or you're going to put this child up for adoption locally. This Amish thing is a pipe dream of yours that's obviously not going to happen."

Teresa collapsed into a chair, her arms spread across the table. She sobbed onto the dirty tabletop.

Susan tried to move, but everything felt frozen in place. She shouldn't even be here. She had absolutely no business being in this place. So how had this happened? How in the world could she ever do what Teresa wanted her to do? That was expecting way too much.

Seeing her daughter's pain, Maurice went over and wrapped her arms around Teresa. "You're such a dreamer, my little darling. You know I love you, but this has gone on long enough. The world is what it is, and we can't make it anything else. All this talk about God and how He helps people. It's good talk. I've played along with you because I hoped too, I guess. I hoped that maybe God would hear you and give you what you really want. But, sweetheart, it's not happening. It's just not."

Both women were in tears, and Susan found herself also unable to hold her emotions in check. Through her own tears, she heard herself say, "I'll do it."

Maurice went silent, turning to study her.

Teresa didn't move.

"You will take the child?" Maurice asked.

"I will write home," Susan said. "I will tell them Teresa's story, and they will ask around. That's all I can promise."

"So what do you think, Teresa?" Maurice asked. "Is that good enough for you?"

Teresa's shoulders shook, but she made no sound.

"That's good enough for now," Maurice said moments later. "The baby isn't due yet. Why don't you see if God will answer my little girl's request? If the way she prays is any indication, that letter will be answered right back with good news."

"Okay." Susan swallowed hard, feeling the burden of her promise. The whole situation now lay on her shoulders, heavier than a hamper full of wash. Why had she ever thought herself capable of coming here to help? It had seemed so simple, so right, back at the bakery. And now she had promised to write a letter home with a very strange request.

"Is that okay with you, honey?" Maurice asked, running her fingers through Teresa's hair.

Teresa nodded, her head still buried in her arms.

"Do you need any other help with the care of the child?" Susan asked, taking a deep breath. "That is why I came over in the first place. Teresa needs to see a doctor again, I'm sure, and Laura is willing to arrange it and pay for it. Is that okay?"

"Is that okay, honey?" Maurice asked.

Teresa's head moved up and down again.

"Anytime then," Maurice said, answering before Susan asked. "God knows we're not going anywhere."

"I'll go now," Susan said. "I'll let you know what Laura can arrange."

She left quietly as both mother and daughter embraced. The stairs were silent on the way down. Susan paused outside to make sure she could find this place again. She whispered the number above the door under her breath and then found her way back to the bakery.

Chapter Twenty-five

✦

S usan entered the bakery to find the lunch line forming.

"It took longer than I expected," Susan whispered, slipping behind the counter.

"Don't forget your apron," Laura said.

"Right. I almost forgot." Susan looked down at the still unusual sight of polka dots down the front of her dress. She grabbed an apron and thoroughly washed and dried her hands before returning to the counter.

The next two hours both women worked steadily as customers came in for a simple lunch snack of their favorite pastries and coffee. As soon as one party left, Laura or Susan had to hurry out to bus the table for the next set of customers wanting a table.

Finally, just after two thirty, the rush died down.

Susan sat catching her breath as Laura poured two cups of coffee.

"We need a break!" Laura announced. "And we'd better take it while we can. Besides, I'm anxious to hear about your visit to Teresa's."

"The place they live in is awful," Susan said. "I've never seen anything like it before. Of course, how would I? I've lived on the farm in the country all my life."

"I imagine the country has its dumps too," Laura said. "But they might not be near an Amish community. Now tell me, how are we to help Teresa?"

"I met her mother, Maurice. She's still skeptical of any way this can work out well. I think she wanted Teresa to take up the baby's father's offer to abort the child, but Teresa knows better. As to how we can help, I'm afraid Teresa really wants me to find an Amish couple to take the baby. To my own shock, I agreed to at least write *Mamm* and *Daett* and have them ask around."

"Do you think someone will step forward and take the child?"

"I really don't. But how could I tell Teresa that? It would break her already hurting heart. But I had to offer to try. Everything went by so fast. Both Teresa and her mother were in tears. I just couldn't walk out with the girl's heart broken. She's apparently seen stories about the Amish on TV and thinks that would give her child the perfect life she never had."

"So the mother and daughter played on your emotions?"

Susan shrugged. "They got to my emotions all right, but I don't know about playing. It seemed pretty genuine."

"You do have to be careful, dear. We *Englisha* have our characters," Laura said. "And I wouldn't put much past people if they get their minds set on something."

Susan wondered if perhaps she was being hoodwinked—acting like a country bumpkin who couldn't see through the scam. She decided to trust Teresa's story.

"I'm still going to write home," Susan said, "and see if they know anybody from the community who wants to adopt. It's a long shot because it's not like everyone has a lack of children. The children are all wanted among the Amish—but wanted as *Da Hah* gives them. And that's not usually through adoption."

"I imagine that would be a good attitude to have if a person didn't believe in birth control."

Susan smiled at Laura's bold words. The *Englisha* just came right out and said things.

"So Teresa and her mom will accept our help?"

"Yes." Susan sipped her coffee. "I told Teresa's mom about your offer to arrange and pay for a doctor's visit for Teresa. She said we can stop in anytime and pick up Teresa for the appointment. They aren't gone much, I guess."

"I'll make some calls and see what can be arranged. The sooner the better, I suppose. I didn't get that good a look at the young woman, but I'd say she's pretty far along."

Susan nodded. "From how my sisters all looked, I'd say so too."

"All the more reason to get her to a doctor right away. If Teresa wants to give the child up for adoption, the paperwork should be started. And there are plenty of people lined up to adopt. Finding a good, decent couple shouldn't be hard at all."

"She has her heart set on an Amish couple," Susan reminded, turning to glance outside at the bustling traffic. *How did such a dream as Teresa's get planted in her head with this big city all around her? Perhaps the city made country life look so much better? Teresa made one giant leap and landed squarely in my life!* Daett *would say* Da Hah *was in such things. But is He?* Yah, *I will write the best letter I can, even believing the answer will probably be no. Surely no harm can come out of an attempt to help Teresa,* she decided. Mamm *and* Daett *won't think ill of my helping an unwed mother.* Nee, *there is something else troubling, in the back of my mind but I can't quite put my finger on it.*

"I think the girl will come around eventually," Laura was saying. "Once we get her to the clinic and she gets into the flow of things, she'll see the reality of the situation. Especially when she hears about all the local couples waiting for babies. Dreams tend to fit reality at the end. I wouldn't worry about it, if I were you."

"Still, I have to write the letter," Susan said. "I promised."

"You do that." Laura patted Susan on the arm and got up from the table. "Here comes Robby. I just saw him go past the window."

"Robby?"

"He told me not to tell you," Laura whispered. "He's coming by to take you on another driving lesson."

"You're kidding! After what happened last time?"

"I don't know about that," Laura said. "I never heard the details. But whatever it was you put him through, he's willing to take you out again."

"But where?" Susan asked.

The door opened.

Laura said, "I don't know. Why don't you ask him?"

Susan stood and stared at Robby. "You're taking me driving?" she asked.

"I have evaluated my life," he said, bowing low and sweeping his arm across his knees. "And I have decided the princess is worthy of my dedication and loyalty. Even unto *death*. Which, under the circumstances, may be the case."

Laura laughed. "You two are the limit! Now scram before anyone sees your antics."

Susan was suddenly cold all over. The traffic going past the window looked like missiles coming toward her, ready to crash into her.

"You ready?" Robby asked. "Let's go!"

"You're kidding me, aren't you?" Susan asked, as they went out the door. "We'll look at the car, and then you'll back out and tell me it's a joke."

"It's no joke. Really. I'm up for this."

"So will it be in that park again?" Susan asked. "Because I don't have the time to go all the way up there. I have a dinner date with Duane."

"Then you'll drive here in the city," Robby said.

"I'll kill you for sure."

"I'm not worried."

Susan thought about it. *I can do this. I can do this!* she repeated, hoping it would give her confidence. Driving was a great privilege, and she did want to learn. It really wasn't that hard. It likely was mind over matter. After all, she could drive horses from on top of a wagon-load of hay and live to tell about it. Why was an *Englisha* automobile such a fearful thing?

Robby unlocked the door and motioned her inside. "Behind the wheel you go."

Susan climbed in, now muttering softly, "I can do this. I can do this. Think horses. Think horses. Think horses."

"Saying your prayers?" Robby asked as he climbed into the passenger side.

"Very funny," she said.

"Actually, we might need prayer," he said.

"Your seat belt," she said, taking charge and snapping on her own. She would show him!

"Done," he said. "Remember, it's brake left. Gas right."

"Shhh…" She put the vehicle into drive, her foot on the brake. "I'm thinking buggies and hay wagons right now. Leather reins and wind blowing across the fields with the hay-loaded wagon swaying under me."

With that, Susan saw a space in the traffic and eased out, her fingers tight around the wheel. "Here we go!" she said hopefully. *Think farm. Think farm and pulling left and pulling right. No backward jerks, just stomping the brakes, gently, and gas for forward. Think lines out and lines in. Feet not hands.*

"There's a light coming up," Robby warned. "And it's red."

"I know…and I'm stopping." Susan pressed the brake, seeing past the red light to the glare of the advancing sun toward the west.

How many times had she squinted into the sun to steer the horses at home, pulling into the exact position for the grain elevators? She had stopped many times with only inches separating the sides of the wagons.

"That was a nice, smooth stop," Robby said. "You're doing okay."

"Thank you!"

"The light has turned green," Robby said.

"I know." Susan kept her eyes on the car in front of her and eased on the gas. It was a little like letting out the lines, only with a car you pushed them.

"Keep going straight," Robby said. "Thankfully, the traffic isn't too bad today."

"Like that helps. It only takes one other car for me to have an accident."

"Now turn left at the next light. You need the practice."

Susan pushed the turn signal down as she slowed down.

"The light's green," she said, making the turn in one smooth motion.

There was a pothole ahead—like a groundhog hole the horses could get their hooves caught in, which wasn't *gut*. She steered slightly to the left, missing the bump. She glanced at Robby. He was looking in the side mirror.

"You should have gone through the hole," he said. "If we'd been on a four lane, swerving might throw you into the car beside you."

"The horses could have caught their hooves," she said, slowing for another light.

"*Horses?* What has that got to do with driving a car?"

"Tires. Horse hooves. Aren't they about the same?"

"No, Susan! No."

"Horse hooves break and car tires blow," Susan continued, pressing her point.

"Just *drive!*" he commanded. "And you can fix tires. You can't fix horse hooves. Remember that. Turn again."

"*Yah*," she agreed. "Horses have to be put down if they break a leg."

"Enough with the horses already, okay? This is a *car*. Remember that."

"It helps me drive," Susan said, as a car horn blew behind her. She jumped.

"Slow down," Robby said. "There's another light ahead. And don't worry, the honking horn wasn't about you."

"It's green now," she said, rattled. "What if it turns red?"

"The light turns yellow before it turns red."

"It's yellow now."

"I know that, but you have time. Keep going."

Susan saw the light disappearing over the top of the windshield glass, the color still yellow.

"You're doing okay," Robby said. "But that was cutting things a little close."

From a distance behind them they heard the squeal of brakes followed by a dull thud of metal crashing.

"Oh no! Did I do that? Did I cause a wreck?" Susan gasped, stomping on the brakes, thrusting Robby forward as his body strained against the shoulder harness. "What did I do? I was driving carefully!" Susan asked, the words coming out in a rush.

"You didn't do anything," Robby said. "It wasn't us. It was the guy behind us. He must have tried to make it through the light and got hit."

Susan glanced in the rearview mirror and saw a car behind them, steam rolling out from under its hood. It had been knocked in the side by another vehicle coming from the cross street. An angry man was getting out the driver's side of the car, his muffled shouting filling the street.

"It wasn't us, and we didn't see the accident," Robby said. "You don't really want to be involved in city accidents."

"But we saw it happen. Perhaps the police will want to hear our story?"

"We saw it *after* it happened," Robby said. "Even I wasn't looking in the side-view mirror when they hit."

"The light was still yellow when we went underneath," she said. "I remember that much."

"So you want to tell the officer that? Who says it was or wasn't yellow for the other guy? See, you'd better leave those things to the people who can figure them out. You didn't see him drive under the yellow light, so you really didn't see anything. Besides, both drivers are out of their cars. No one was hurt."

"Well, okay…I guess," Susan said, removing her foot from the brake, preparing to move on.

"Wait! I'll drive back," Robby said. "This has been enough practicing for one day."

"But we hardly started," Susan complained.

"Even so, we're finished for today," Robby said.

Chapter Twenty-six

S usan let out a short gasp, but Duane didn't seem to notice. The restaurant was breathtaking. Never had she seen anything like it. The walls were a pale cream, the carpet a matching flowery spread. From where she stood, the tables looked huge—even the ones set for just two people. The tall, brown plush chairs with their high backs looked elegant. *What am I doing here?* she wondered. *And is my purple blouse and skirt gut enough for a place like this? Is it gut enough to be seen with Duane, who is looking so handsome in his sharp black suit?*

"Seating for two for the Moran party," Duane said to the nodding maître d', who was dressed in a black suit, a little black matching bow tie up by his throat, accented against his white shirt.

"Yes, sir," the man said, pulling a little book from his pocket and flipping through it. Apparently he found what he was looking for. He smiled. "We are rather full tonight. This way, please."

Duane turned and motioned Susan forward.

Are people staring at me? Susan wondered. She tried to walk straight as she followed the man's bobbing back. Duane kept close to her, walking right at her elbow. The maître d' stopped at a table in a cozy corner of the room near the back, a huge painting with an Italian theme hanging next to it.

"Please be seated, ma'am," the maître d' said, pulling out a chair for Susan. As she sat down and he gently pushed the chair toward the table, he said, "Your server will be with you shortly."

"Thank you," Duane said.

The man disappeared, heading back to where he came from. The soft hum of conversation rose around them as Duane pulled out a chair and sat across from Susan.

"You shouldn't have brought me here," Susan whispered. "I'm not dressed right."

"Your outfit is lovely," he said. "I just hadn't gotten around to saying so."

"You're teasing me."

"No, I'm not. It's perfect for you. It brings out the country color in your face. Quite proper, I say. Did Laura help you choose?"

"Laura? Yes, she did."

He smiled knowingly.

"Laura has far better taste about these things than I do," Susan said.

"Oh, I imagine you could have made the choice yourself," Duane said. "You'd be good at such things. I know you would."

Susan felt a warm glow at his praise. Thomas never talked about her dress selections or how she made them. But this was a different world, and she would enjoy getting used to this.

As the server approached, Susan tried not to stare. She was dressed in a sharp-looking, dark-gray pants suit that was trimmed in white. She wore long, dangling earrings that sparkled in the light.

"Good evening," she said. "My name is Tanya, and I'll be serving you this evening." She placed two fancy menus in front of them.

Susan couldn't take her eyes off the woman. Young, beautiful, exquisitely dressed, and so perfect and confident. So unlike she was.

"Would you like to begin with an appetizer?" the waitress asked. "Perhaps drinks?"

"Sure. Let's have the anchovy appetizer. Just one," Duane said. "As for drinks, sparkling water for me."

"And for you, ma'am?" The server turned to Susan.

"Water...water will be fine," she said, hoping her voice hadn't squeaked.

The woman smiled, nodded to Duane, and then disappeared. Susan thought they seemed to know each other. *Duane likely comes in here often,* she decided.

"I'm sorry for not asking you about the appetizer," he said quietly. "I wanted you to sample the anchovies. You can order whatever you want for your entree."

"You do think I'm a country hick, don't you?"

He smiled. "No, but you *are* country, which I like. I'm guessing you've never had anchovies. Am I right?"

"What are they?" she asked.

Duane smiled. "There! Just like I thought. Take it from me, they're very good."

"You haven't told me what they are."

"They'll be here before long. Then you'll see."

"What if I don't like them?"

He laughed now, obviously enjoying himself.

"You're tormenting me for your own pleasure," she accused.

"Perhaps," he said. "But it's in fun."

"You know that's not nice. Taking people places they don't belong so you can enjoy yourself at their expense."

"You judge me too harshly," he said.

"Do I?"

He shrugged. "I'll leave you to determine that, but you have nothing to be ashamed of. You are smart, poised, possessed of common sense, and...beautiful."

She couldn't look at him, especially if he was going to say things like that. Perhaps she was judging him too harshly. He had brought her here for a nice dinner, after all. "I forgive you then!" she said.

He laughed, and the sound seemed to wrap around the table. Duane had an infectious laugh, and she liked it.

"Your appetizer," the server said from behind her. A platter of anchovies arranged beautifully with colorful garnishes was set on the table. "Enjoy!"

"Those are anchovies?" Susan asked. "They look like little fish."

He laughed again. "They *are* little fish."

He would have to stop laughing soon, she hoped. She was enjoying the sound way too much.

"You eat them with the skin on, just as they are. They're served with roasted peppers and mozzarella cheese." He placed some on his appetizer plate and then demonstrated how to eat them, a look of sheer ecstasy on his face.

"Try one," he encouraged. "Find out what food in *our* world tastes like."

"The *Englisha* world," she said, her fork poised. "Do I dare? What if I don't like it?"

"Just try one."

Susan lifted a bite of one of the shimmering little fish to her mouth, sliding it onto her tongue, expecting the worst. The fish had looked almost raw. *Are they raw?* She chewed. To her surprise the taste was actually pleasant.

"Now the peppers and cheese," he said, watching her face.

She added them, and the taste became even better. A broad smile spread over her face.

Duane looked like he wanted to jump out of his chair with pride.

"Half and half." He divided the appetizer down the middle. "I should have ordered two servings, I guess. But I didn't want to spoil our dinner."

Susan slid her share onto her appetizer plate and ate, taking her time, enjoying each bite. "Each bite seems better than the last," she said. "Not quite the same as meat and potatoes."

"I'm glad you like it. Our server is coming back, and we haven't looked at the menu yet."

Susan quickly picked up her menu.

Tanya arrived. "Are you ready to order or do you need more time?"

"If you could give us a moment," Duane requested.

He likely knew what he wanted, but is asking so I can have more time, Susan figured. "Please go ahead and order," Susan said. "I'll decide quickly."

"Well then," he said, "I'll take the boneless chicken breast."

So he did know what he wanted without looking, Susan noted.

"And on your salad?"

"Honey mustard on the side," he said. "And I'll have it with my meal, please."

Now they were waiting for her.

Susan's eyes had already caught a word on the menu she knew she liked. At least she knew what it was—and it wasn't chicken or steak. Those were too common back home. But once in a blue moon, her sister Betsy made this and Susan always loved it.

"The cheese ravioli, please." Susan rolled it off her tongue with a confident smile. *There!* She knew how to say the word—an Italian word, at that.

"That's a great choice," the waitress said. "Would you like a salad with that?"

"I think I'll pass, thank you," Susan said.

When the server left, Duane leaned forward on his elbows. "So what have you been doing with yourself?" he asked.

Susan sat straighter. "That's a long story. Are you sure you want to hear it?"

"You can start," he said. "I'm sure it's interesting."

"I'm studying for my GED on Laura's computer, practicing driving so I can take the driving test, and today an unwed young pregnant woman came into the bakery looking for help. Laura is going to take her to see a doctor, and we'll help her from there."

"Wow!" he said with a low whistle. "You have been busy! It doesn't sound like there's a moment left to catch your breath."

"It does seem that way, but it helps the days go by faster. I'm trying hard to fit into the *Englisha* world."

"Still lonesome for home?" he asked.

"More than I want to admit sometimes," Susan confessed. She was surprised at the admission. She hadn't even told Laura that.

"It's to be expected," he said. "But you're doing really well adjusting. Some women would be scared to attempt all the things you're doing and to make all the changes you're making."

There he went, saying the nice words she liked hearing. He was much better at it than Thomas had been.

"By the way," he said, "how are your knees?"

Oh, he had to go and remember that. She'd almost forgotten about it. She dared a glance at his face as she felt blood rushing to her head.

"That's an embarrassing subject," she whispered.

"It's nothing to be embarrassed about," he said. "I've taken many a spill myself."

Apparently he hadn't remembered seeing her legs, which was *gut*.

"I don't wear the shoes you women do. I imagine I'd trip a lot more in women's shoes."

"That does make a difference."

"By the way, what happened to the shoe that came off? You said you left it in the middle of the street. Did you retrieve it?"

Susan shrugged. "It was gone by the time I walked back after lunch. I limped back to the bakery the best I could and threw away the survivor. Thankfully I had another pair."

A plate appeared silently next to her head and Susan jumped.

"Excuse me," their server said. "I didn't mean to startle you."

Duane leaned back and the server placed his plate in front of him. She placed the other plate in front of Susan then disappeared again.

"We can pray before she gets back," Duane said, bowing his head.

Susan followed him, startled by the suddenness.

Just as he finished his short prayer, the server returned with his salad.

Susan watched out of the corner of her eye to see every move Duane made so she could do likewise. She noticed how he held his fork. When he cut his chicken, she cut her ravioli. She moved slowly lest with a simple slip of the knife ravioli would be down the front of her blouse and skirt and all over her lap.

"Do you like the ravioli?" Duane asked.

Susan nodded.

"This is the best Italian restaurant around," he said. "That's what they say in their advertisement, anyway."

"Is it true? It sounds a little prideful," Susan said, thinking it felt good to talk about a fault that wasn't her own for a moment.

"It has nothing to with pride. It's just a little slogan used to attract customers."

"'The best Italian restaurant around'? That's their slogan?"

"Yes."

"Well, this place sure seems nice—and fancy too. Even this picture on the wall must have cost a fortune."

Duane turned to look at the picture.

"I think that's actually a Mexican scene," he said. "And I don't think it's very expensive. They try to create a certain mood here. It's not really about being rich. Asbury Park doesn't have that many rich people."

Susan was surprised. *He doesn't think he's rich? Thomas certainly couldn't afford the prices she'd seen on the menu. Neither could her daett or anyone she knew back home.*

Susan finished before Duane did. She sat patiently, soaking everything in. When the check came, Duane gave the waitress a credit card. Moments later she returned with a piece of paper for him to sign. Susan had seen this done before—buying something without having the cash in hand. It still amazed her. *Why not just pay with cash?* she wondered.

"Ready to go?" he asked, getting up and moving around behind her to help pull her chair back.

Susan felt dazzled and light-headed as they walked through the restaurant and out the door. Duane opened the car door for her, waited until she slid in, and then closed it.

After walking to the driver's side, he got in and started the car. "I enjoyed our meal together," he said as he drove to her apartment.

"*Yah,* it was delightful," she agreed, looking up at him. "I mean, *yes,* it was. Thank you so very much. I can't tell you how much I enjoyed it...even if I felt out of place."

"Perhaps we can do it again sometime," he suggested.

"I'd like that," she said.

He quickly got out and came around to open her car door. He walked with her to the apartment door and waited as she unlocked it. Duane watched her go inside and heard the dead bolt click.

He waited until I was inside and had the door locked. That's how he is, Susan thought. *Caring but never definite about the future. Saying "sometime" we could do it again. The best way, likely.* Love, if it did come, would not be easy, especially if it came in the form of an *Englisha* man— and such a good-looking one, at that.

CHAPTER TWENTY-SEVEN

S usan stood in the early morning chill and dropped her letter into the blue mailbox on the corner. Traffic was still thin. The part of the sky she could see above the buildings was a dusty gray, shrouded with a layer of light from the street lamps.

What would it be like to once again see stars unhindered by the city's attempt to light the world? she wondered. Why was she thinking such thoughts this morning? Likely because of the letter she'd just dropped into the mailbox. She'd kept her promise to Teresa. The chance that someone would respond to the letter and offer Teresa's baby a home was slim. Still, who could blame Teresa for wanting such a dream? The young woman was indeed more outstanding than she had appeared to be at first. Yes, Teresa had made some bad choices, but the city was full of people who had made bad choices. At least Teresa wanted more for her baby than city life, which seemed to be a mass of contradictions to Susan. It could mess with anyone's mind, especially people raised in the country.

There were nice restaurants along Main Street, but none were across the tracks where Teresa lived. There were nice people like Laura, Robby, and Duane in the city, but somewhere beyond that a kidnapper and murderer stalked women. There had been no new kidnappings or deaths in the newspapers or news of late. Perhaps the police had caught the criminal. But how could such opposites live so close together? The good and the bad? The beautiful and the ugly? Life was so much simpler under the open skies at the farm.

Mamm *and* Daett *will sure be surprised when the mail arrives with my strange request,* Susan decided. She had tried to be as hopeful as possible, casting Teresa and her situation in as good a light as she could. Still, Amish people didn't quickly make up their minds about most things. Not even when the subject was a minor affair, let alone the adoption of a child.

One thought had been bothering Susan all night. *Does* Da Hah *want me to take the child?* The idea seemed impossible. How could she raise a child without a *daett* to help? And Teresa wanted an Amish family—and she wasn't Amish anymore. No, taking the child was simply out of the question. Teresa had said the parents must be Amish, and Susan wasn't ready to return let alone with a child.

Susan glanced up at the skyline, thinking again of the home place. *Is* Daett *out in the barn by now? He doesn't milk anymore, but he's probably up doing something.* Daett *and* Mamm *both wanted someone to take over the farm so they could move to a* dawdy haus *on the place. Well, that wasn't going to happen—and it was Thomas's fault!*

She shook her head and walked back toward the bakery. She was an *Englisha* girl now. Duane had been so amazing last night. So manly, so smooth, so at home in that fancy restaurant. He hadn't said much about it afterward, but he didn't have to. He clearly belonged in the world she aspired to. Anyone could see that. He belonged here just as she had belonged on the farm. *Can Duane really be interested in me? In a country girl? In a bumpkin who obviously doesn't know anything about big city ways?*

Again she wondered if Duane was playing with her like the cats played with the mice they caught in the barn. Having a good time before they ate them. *Duane doesn't look like he would eat girls!* Susan laughed. She had to stop being silly. Duane was a nice man. Just because Thomas turned out to be a bad apple didn't mean all men were like that.

Suddenly Susan shuddered and came to a complete standstill. What she'd been worried about abruptly came into focus and ran through her heart like cold water. Would *Mamm* and *Daett* think the child she had written about was hers? Hers and Thomas's? *Ach, and what should I do about that?* Taking a deep breath, Susan turned and looked at the mailbox.

The letter was already mailed. *Is there some way of getting it back? No. Surely my family wouldn't think such a thing.* Mamm *and* Daett *know me better than that! But hearing of a baby, that is likely going to be the thought that crosses everyone's mind back home. They will think it explains why I left so abruptly…and hadn't returned. Why didn't I think this through? Why didn't this occur to me before?*

This would offer a ready explanation for the split between Thomas and her, which she had never fully explained to anyone. People would believe this to be the real explanation for why she had fled into the *Englisha* world and refused to make up with Thomas. She had gone away from the eyes of the community to have a baby. The Amish community would think her letter about adoption was an excellent cover story. They might assume it would give her guilty conscience relief to make sure the child was raised by an Amish couple instead of being raised in the *Englisha* world. And it would make sense because if she ever chose to return, she would be close to the child. *This is what everyone will think!* Her m*amm* and *daett* would never pass on her request because they would assume her reason for the request was obvious.

Susan shivered. How could someone get into such a mess simply by trying to help a young woman with her troubles? Now the world darkened. Above her head even the streetlights looked menacing and the building beside her looked ready to crush her with its weight.

She must gain control of herself. *The letter!* Yah, *it must be gotten out of the mailbox. But how? Perhaps there is someone at the post office who can help. But what about my promise to Teresa? Should I go back on my word just to save my reputation?* Susan ran back to the mailbox and opened the lid and checked the top tray of the mailbox. She reached inside. Perhaps by a miracle the letter could be retrieved.

Her fingers came up empty. The face of Teresa sobbing at the kitchen table rose in Susan's memory. *Is this feeling in my chest a little taste of what Teresa felt when she first realized she was with child? This shame, this fear, this torment along with the questions of "What if…" and "Why?"*

Could Susan turn away from such a plea for help when Teresa had no one else with faith in *Da Hah* to go to? Surely she could explain so the people at home would believe her when she told them the child wasn't Thomas and hers. She had to take the chance. She'd given Teresa her word. Susan turned again and headed back to the bakery, her steps firm. A promise was a promise! Teresa had come to her for help, and a person was not to turn away those who asked. Did not the preachers say so often in their sermons?

But what about *Mamm* and her shock when she first reads the letter? What about her thoughts of her youngest daughter being defiled by her boyfriend? Would *Mamm* believe she'd been swept up by the years of courtship and allowed things to go too far? *Possibly,* Susan admitted. *But* Daett *would surely know better!* That's where her hopes lay. *Daett* would say, "Susan and Thomas wouldn't do something like that. We can trust her. We can believe she's telling us the truth."

Susan quickened her steps. She saw Laura's car slowing down and turning into the alley for the usual parking spot. Another day in the city had begun. She had duties, even if she was laden with worries. In this way the city and the farm weren't that far apart.

Laura was already inside when Susan walked in.

"Good morning!" Laura said. Without missing a beat, she continued, "So what happened last night with Duane? Did you have a nice time?"

"Oh, *yah!* It was great." Susan decided she wouldn't explain how out of place she'd felt.

"Tell me more," Laura encouraged. "I want details!"

"There really isn't much more. We had a good time. I'm so new at this. I hope I didn't make a fool of myself!"

"I'm sure you didn't," Laura said. "So is Duane making any progress?"

"Progress?"

"You know what I mean. Now, don't act dumb," Laura teased.

Susan forced herself to laugh.

"He moves kind of slow," she said. "Which is good, I guess."

"I bet you still have that Amish fellow on your mind," Laura said. "With perhaps some hopes of getting back with him?"

"No, that won't happen. Especially after he hears about my request to *Mamm* and *Daett.*"

"Teresa's adoption request?" Laura asked.

"Yes," Susan said.

"That could make trouble with him?" Laura looked puzzled. "Is it taboo to bring an outside child into the community?"

"No," Susan said, debating whether she should reveal the reason for her fear. Letting out a breath, she said, "Laura, I had no sooner dropped the letter in the mailbox this morning when I realized that some people in the community might get the wrong impression. They might think the baby is Thomas's and mine! That I left the community to have the baby here."

"Really?" Laura said, pausing to look at Susan. "They would think that?"

"Yes, I'm afraid some might," Susan said. She readied the batter for cupcakes. "I can't believe I didn't think about that before I promised Teresa I'd ask about the adoption. I knew something was worrying me, I just couldn't get it out. People will think it's my child, and that I'm covering up my pregnancy by pretending it belongs to someone else."

Laura raised her eyebrows. "But look at you—you're not pregnant."

"I know that—but they don't. And I'm here, so that provides an explanation of our breakup."

"So your ex-boyfriend will have his reputation besmirched?" Laura asked.

"He will, along with me. I wish I hadn't mailed that letter. I even tried to get it back, but it was too late."

Laura worked silently on doughnut batter. "Hey, wait a minute! The simple solution just came to me. You can make a trip home in the next few weeks and show everyone that you're not…well…swollen with child. Maybe you can go after Thanksgiving— which, by the way, you're to spend with us."

Susan laughed. "A trip home for that reason? Yuck. As for Thanksgiving, I'd love to come. But a trip home? I don't think I'm ready."

"Yes, it might be hard," Laura agreed. "It looks like your helping Teresa is going to involve more than you thought."

"You're also helping," Susan reminded her.

"True," Laura said. "That reminds me. I did call the clinic and explain the situation. They're willing to see her this afternoon. I thought I'd take her while you watch the shop. Is that okay?"

"Sure," Susan said. "Talking about home, have you heard from your sister lately?"

"No, not recently. Not since you arrived, in fact."

"I've wondered how Bonnie's children are doing," Susan said. "They were such dears. I miss babysitting for them sometimes."

"There's another good reason to take a trip home." Laura smiled.

Susan thought about it as she worked. She had two reasons now for a trip home. But there were oh so many reasons *not* to go. The trip would bring up a lot of unwanted things. Pleas for her to stay. Facing her parents' dismay when she left again. *Is there another way to establish my innocence? Maybe* Mamm *and* Daett *won't even make a fuss. Maybe I'm worring over nothing.*

"Robby's coming by after work today," Laura said, interrupting her thoughts. "He wanted me to tell you."

"Driving lessons again," Susan said. "That man is a glutton for punishment."

"Oh, he teases you, I know, but he told me you're doing quite well."

"I've been imagining I was driving the horses on the farm," Susan said. "And it helped. I went left, right. I let out and then pulled back on the reins."

"I'd say you're doing quite well then." Laura dropped the first of the doughnuts into the sizzling oil.

Chapter Twenty-eight

※

Susan removed most of the coffee pots as the evening approached, carrying them to the sink for cleaning. She left two on the counter. The customers were few in number at this time of day, and Robby would arrive soon for her driving lesson. He did have a certain bravado around him...or was it courage? Whichever, she was learning how to drive—and in the city at that!

Out of the corner of her eye, Susan watched the cars going by on the street. Robby would likely be early. Well, he would have to wait until she finished cleaning up. Laura had left a little before two thirty to take Teresa to the doctor. She should be back soon. Susan had given her directions to Teresa's house, so hopefully Laura had been able to find it okay. Susan heard the door open and turned from the sink to see Duane enter. She hadn't expected to see him. He'd never been by in the evening.

"Did I catch you by yourself?" Duane said. "No customers this time of the day?"

"Not usually," she said. "Laura went to take the young woman I told you about to the clinic."

"Laura's practicing her good deeds then."

"Teresa needs good deeds, believe me. She said the father will leave her if she doesn't get rid of the child in some way. Can you imagine?"

"Some men are like that, I guess. Hey, what about tonight?" Duane asked. "Are you up to going out somewhere?"

"Another fancy restaurant? I don't know if I'm ready for that just yet, even though it was very wonderful," she said, her eyes wide at the thought.

"I was thinking of something a little simpler. Maybe we could go out to the mall. We could eat at the food court there, and if you had some shopping you want to do, I can go with you."

"That's nice of you," she said. "And really thoughtful to think of shopping. But I don't have anything I need—or can afford right now. Besides, I really should study for my GED."

"Come on!" he said. "Women always have shopping to do."

His smile was just too charming to resist. "Well, I guess I could *look*," she said.

"There you go!" he said with a laugh. "How about I pick you up at six-thirty?"

"Six-thirty," she repeated. Would that give her enough time to finish her driving lesson with Robby? "Yes, six- thirty will work," she said.

"It's a date then," he said, turning to leave.

Susan watched him go. He was more than *gut* looking, he was also thoughtful. Not at all like Thomas, who had his own schedule planned and she was to fit into his life. But that was the Amish way. The man made his plans, and the woman followed.

Duane doesn't seem to be like that at all. So nice, he is. Could she imagine marrying someone like Duane? She had often easily envisioned being married to Thomas. But with Duane it was harder to picture. A shiver ran up her back. Marrying an *Englisha* man would be so daring, so different. She should at least consider the possibility. And there was plenty of time to decide. Duane wasn't pressing for a serious relationship. He seemed quite relaxed about such things. Another *gut* quality.

Susan glanced at the clock. The time to close was arriving. She cleaned the coffee canisters and stacked them on the counter to dry. The few leftover doughnuts and rolls went into plastic canisters. Laura usually took those home or dropped them off at a homeless shelter.

The door opened again, and this time Robby walked in.

"Hi," he said, sliding into a chair.

"Are you taking the extra rolls and doughnuts to the homeless shelter?" she asked.

"Mom didn't say," he said. "How many are there?"

"Just one container."

"I can eat those myself," he said with a grin. "I'll take them."

"Didn't your mother teach you to share?" she teased.

"Nope! And no manners either. I'm a rough, uncultured male, so give me one of those doughnuts! I'm starved."

"You should eat them with vegetables." She handed him the container.

"Yes, *mother*," he said, taking a doughnut in each hand and stuffing a bite into his mouth.

"That's disgusting," she said. "I ought to take you back to the farm and put you out with the horses in the barn."

He swallowed and then finished off the first doughnut. "I'd like that. I'm tired of the city."

"I wasn't serious."

"Well, I am." He eyed the second pastry and took a bite. "Hey, by the way, you led me astray with your advice the other day. I did what you said and got exactly nowhere."

"Oh, no!" Susan groaned. "Not girl troubles again."

"No, not again," he corrected. "They never stopped."

"So what happened this time?"

"I did exactly like you said. This time it was Tom's sister, one of the guys I play basketball with at the YMCA. Last night she tagged along, and after our game I asked her out to eat. I asked really nicely if she wanted to go out for ice cream—something very innocent. She said, 'No way! Nothing doing.'"

"Maybe she's already seeing someone?"

"She's not." He gulped down the last of the doughnut.

"Then maybe you should try again. Don't you *Englisha* have something called 'playing hard to get'?"

"I think I'm quitting the *Englisha* team and joining the Amish," he said, getting to his feet. "Come on, let's go. I have stuff to do. I can't babysit you all evening."

"You know I didn't ask you to do this," Susan said, following him out. "What if I wreck and kill you tonight?"

"Then my ghost will haunt you for the rest of your life."

"*Whoa...*" Susan said. "Spooky, are we?"

"So will you drive good tonight?" he asked, sliding in on the passenger's side.

"Better." She smiled, snapping her seat belt on before starting the engine. "I'll think horses and buggies and pulling left and right."

"Whatever works," he said. "Just go."

Susan carefully pulled out onto the street and headed down Main.

"So you would join the Amish?" she teased. "You wouldn't like it, believe me."

"Turn left here," he said and she obeyed.

"Let me choose the route tonight, Robby."

"I guess it will be all right. Just don't get us killed."

She drove along quietly for a minute and then said again, "So *would* you really consider joining the Amish?"

"I don't know." He wasn't looking at her. "I need to do something different."

"You're sure blue tonight over this girl thing. But joining the Amish isn't the answer, believe me. I'm leaving the Amish, so I should know."

"I'm not serious," he said. "But Mom says this girl Teresa is."

"So you know about her?" Susan braked for a red light.

"Mom told me about her. By the way, I'm supposed to tell you everything is going fine."

"The appointment? It went well?" Susan turned to look at him.

"Watch the road," he ordered.

"I am watching, but tell me what your mom said."

"Mom said Teresa went to the doctor and there were no problems. Her mother went along too."

"They live together."

"Teresa was very concerned about you, asking whether you had written to the Amish people. Mom told her you had. And Mom said there were tears when the ultrasound showed the baby would be a boy."

"I imagine there were," Susan said. "So Teresa guessed correctly. She's been saying it is a boy. Amazing!"

"Are you going to cry too?" Robby asked. "If so, I want to drive."

"I'm not crying."

"They have another appointment next week," Robby went on. "And the baby is due in December. Teresa didn't know her dates for sure, which is, of course, more information than I wanted to know. But Mom said to pass it on."

"You're a sweet boy," Susan said, turning at the light.

"Do you have any idea where you're going?" Robby asked.

"No, but I was depending on you to know."

"That's what I figured. So turn left here, and we can make our way back."

"So when are we going out on the ocean?" Susan asked. "Remember? You promised."

"I haven't forgotten."

"To be honest, I had kind of forgotten it until just now. There's been so much going on. My GED studies, the driving, and now Teresa. There's no hurry, I guess."

"It's good of you to be so understanding," he said, bitterness clouding his voice. "It's a shame there aren't more of you."

"Robby, now come on. You have to keep trying. There are nice girls out there! You'll find the one for you. Besides, you won't think me so nice if I turn green and throw up all over your boat."

"You probably won't even get seasick," he said.

"I wouldn't count on it."

"You've never been out on the ocean before?"

"No, but don't rub it in. Remember, I'm from inland country. We don't have an ocean in Indiana." She let out a sigh and added, "The ocean was so beautiful that night of the almost-full moon. Remember?"

"Yes, I remember. Turn right at the light."

"Almost as beautiful as the moon rising over the fields at home."

"Where do you see that from?" he asked.

"From my bedroom window," she said, recognizing the street they were on. The bakery lay just ahead.

"That would be an experience," he said with a sad smile. "Well, we're back—and all in one piece. I would say the country girl is doing very well. A few more times, and you should be ready."

"Thanks for taking me," she said. "And so often."

"I'm glad to," he said as they both climbed out.

He waited until she'd unlocked her apartment door before he took off.

It must be a thing with men in the city, she thought. Thomas never waited until she was inside the house. Rather, she stood and watched him go out the driveway on Sunday nights, until his buggy lights disappeared into the distance. But that was part of the past and best forgotten.

CHAPTER TWENTY-NINE

Susan stood in front of the closet, running her fingers over the dresses. Which *Englisha* dress would it be tonight? Duane hadn't seen the beige one yet. Would he think she was wearing new dresses to impress him? That decided it. She pushed the beige dress aside. She would wear Amish tonight. Her past was Amish, and she was still dealing with Amish things right now. Duane might as well be reminded of that fact. The nice, light-blue dress would be just the thing. At least it didn't scream Amish at first sight like several of her other dresses.

After she changed, Susan sat down to study the GED lessons she'd printed out. She wanted to spend every available minute studying. There was no sense standing at the window watching for Duane. No decent girl hung around windows watching for her date to arrive. At home Thomas's buggy wheels would have rattled in the driveway, but here one roar of a car engine couldn't be distinguished from another. Duane would have to knock.

The math numbers swam in front of her eyes, and Susan shook her head, wiping her eyes with her finger. She wasn't crying, was she? It had to be her imagination! Her mind left the math problems and turned toward home. *No, I can't be homesick! Why should I be? Things are going well, aren't they? Yes!* The thought that *Mamm* and *Daett* might get the wrong idea when they got her letter troubled her. But there was Laura's solution of a trip home. Could she do it? Should she?

Yah, *in some ways a trip home would be* gut, Susan told herself. And after Thanksgiving would be just right. Being there for the holiday would be too sad if they knew she was leaving again. But seeing the farm and attending church services would no doubt remove some of the nostalgia that seemed to be hanging around lately. And another good thing about a trip home: Thomas would see her again and realize what he'd missed out on by switching his affections to Eunice. Yah, *now* that *would be a sight to see!*

Math! Susan sighed and turned back to the problems, scribbling the answers on her paper in pencil and then checking them when she was done. Most of them were correct. English she was good at, but these math equations were a little complicated. Amish math lessons didn't reach into the realm of symbols. It stayed with plain adding, subtracting, dividing, and multiplying. Like much of Amish life, even in education they stuck with the basics.

Perhaps Duane would help me with math. Do I dare ask him? Maybe. I'll see how it goes. Exposing one's ignorance to a man was a little scary—especially to such a handsome man. *Is he getting serious about me? Likely not. He hasn't even kissed me. And don't* Englisha *men kiss women fairly quickly and often?* Yah, *they did.*

Thomas had never kissed her in all the time they'd known each other—except once. It had happened when she agreed to marry him. He had kissed her then, a slight touch on the lips, almost like he was afraid of her. His hands had brushed her shoulders, leaving without a hug. She had wanted a hug. Shouldn't a woman at least get a hug on her engagement evening? And here he had gone kissing Eunice the first chance he got.

She knew Thomas found her attractive. At least his eyes said so… and his words. But what were his words worth? Not much, from how things had turned out.

Math! she reminded herself. Susan turned back to the paper. She must study math. A thump came from the street below. Had Duane arrived? She walked to the top of the stairs to listen. She heard nothing else, so she walked over to the window and looked out. Everything was normal, the flow of traffic on the street ebbing after the evening rush hour.

It must have been street noise, Susan thought, glancing back toward her work on the kitchen table. Sighing, she stayed at the window. If she thought life was confusing, how must Teresa feel? Teresa was expecting a child. Now that would be confusion—with no husband around and her mother not wanting her to keep the child. How did the young woman find the strength to do what she did? To believe at all? To hope there could be a better life for her child? What bravery Teresa had.

Perhaps that was why Teresa had latched on to the image of the Amish. It was something she could see—the buggies on TV, the bearded men with their women beside them. They were together, secure, and at home on their farms. The wash flapping in the wind, the children underfoot, people loved and protected. No wonder the girl grabbed for straws! And she had no idea how hopeless her idea of finding an Amish family for her son might ultimately be.

Would I have that kind of courage in a similar situation? Going Englisha *had been more about running away than believing in anything. But yah, I came looking for love—still believing it can be found even after my heart was stomped on. Isn't that courage? A little at least! But compared to Teresa's, it doesn't seem like much.*

Now here she was, standing at the window and staring out and Duane just pulled up to the curb. He would think she'd been waiting for him, longing for his presence. Susan laughed. The one time she moved to the window, Duane showed up. Great. She grabbed her purse and was halfway down the stairs when the knock came.

She opened the door. "Good evening, Duane."

Duane nodded. "Good evening, Susan." He took in her dress.

"You don't mind the Amishness, do you?" she asked.

"No. You look great. In fact, you are one of the only girls I know who looks good in an Amish dress!"

"I doubt you know any other girls who wear Amish dresses."

"True," he said as they walked to his car. "But it was supposed to be a compliment anyway."

As they secured their seat belts, Duane spoke. "How did your day go?"

"The usual. Robby came by this evening for another driving lesson. They aren't quite as scary anymore. For me or for Robby."

"He gives you driving lessons?"

"Yes. Well, sort of. The first one was mostly a lesson. The rest of the time it's just me driving and him telling me which way to turn."

"You know you could go to a driving school."

"Laura and Robby didn't mention that. I suppose it's expensive."

"Safe though." He raised his eyebrows. "You haven't wrecked Robby's car, have you?"

"Not yet! Don't tease me."

"Sorry. I was kidding, of course."

"Okay." Susan took a deep breath.

"I'm glad you could come," he said.

"It's nice of you to invite me out again so soon. And I think I figured out what I can shop for tonight."

"What is it?"

"Something for Teresa's baby. Wouldn't that be just the thing? The poor girl is in so much trouble. My heart really goes out to her."

"So you've been caught up in one of Laura's charity projects?" he said.

"Is that what they are? Remember, the young woman came to *me* at the bakery for help."

"You and Laura have soft hearts," he said. "That is good. Laura is a great woman—and so are you for caring."

"Maybe I'm Laura's charity project," Susan said.

He laughed. "Then she picked a good one. Although, believe me, you are no charity project. I'm sure Laura finds you a great help."

"I hope so."

"And the Amish don't have sordid pasts. Not like Teresa does anyway, right?"

"No." Susan felt warmth pushing up her neck. What if he knew about the suspicions that she might be arousing at home? That was enough to make anyone feel dirty all the way through.

"I didn't expect so," he said. "I guess that's one of the good points."

"Rumors can also be hurtful," she said. "And Amish aren't exempt from them."

"Do have you some floating around? That's hard to imagine," he said, smiling.

"It's not funny," Susan said.

"I know," he said. "I'm sorry I gave you that impression."

"I suppose I'm just touchy on the subject. See, if you go into the *Englisha* world, folks back home start talking about you pretty easily."

"That *Englisha* thing is funny," he said. "The *Englisha*. It sounds like the invasion of 1812."

"Now that is funny!" she said. "We studied the war in eighth grade social studies. We use the word *Englisha* to describe outsiders. I don't know how someone would change that. Even if it doesn't make sense to you, it makes sense to us."

"I see," he said. "That's interesting."

"Speaking of studies, would you be willing to help me with math?" she asked.

"You're doing math? Why?"

"I'm studying for my GED. I think I told you about it. But you must think that's silly. You've been through college and everything."

"No, not silly at all, Susan," he said. "I think it's gutsy of you. Really, it is. You don't have to be ashamed. If you pass your GED, you can go on to college if you want to."

"Me? Go to college?"

"Sure! Why not?"

"*Should* I go to college?"

He shrugged. "It's a personal decision, of course, along with whatever financial considerations there are."

"Would you go to college if you were me?"

"Sure. But I'm *not* you. It has to be *your* choice."

"I'm not used to having so many choices," she said.

"There's more around here than on the farm, that's for sure."

"It comes from being Amish," she said. "So will you consider looking over the test sample I did? And give me some advice on the math problems?"

"Sure. When would it suit you?"

"I think the question is when would it suit you?"

"How about Sunday afternoon?"

"At my place?" Belatedly she thought, *Is there anything wrong with having him come to my apartment? We would be alone…*

"Sunday then," he said. "Later on in the afternoon, perhaps. Can you last that long without my wisdom?"

"I'll try," she said.

Duane pulled into the parking lot of the Monmouth Mall and found a spot close to the entrance.

"I'm starved!" he said, as they got out of the car. "Shall it be shopping or eating first?"

"We'd better eat," she said. "I don't want you passing out on the floor."

"Pizza?"

"Sounds good to me."

Inside the mall, he led the way toward the Pizza Hut sign halfway down the first corridor.

"What will it be?" he asked when they arrived and glanced up at the menu board.

"Whatever you order, I'll take a few pieces."

"I'll be ordering a meat lover's. Does that sound okay?"

"*Yah*," she said. "That sounds good. I'm not hard to satisfy when it comes to pizza."

He ordered and paid the cashier. Susan filled her drink cup, and they chose a booth to wait in until their number was called.

When it was announced a few minutes later, Duane said, "That was fast! They must have the popular pizzas made up ahead of time."

Duane returned with the pizza on an aluminum tray and set it on the table.

"It sure smells *gut*," Susan said.

"Do you have pizza on the farm?" Duane asked.

"Yes, but we make our own."

"I bet that would taste even better," he said. "Let's pray and then find out how good this one is."

He bowed his head, and she followed suit.

When he pronounced "Amen," Susan looked up and motioned at the pizza with her hand. "You go first."

He removed a piece, sliding it onto a small plate. He waited for her. She picked up a smaller piece and took a bite, and he did the same.

"It's good!" she said. "It has the same good taste as *Mamm's* does."

"Then to the good name of mother…er, *Mamm*, and Pizza Hut." He lifted his piece of pizza as if in a toast.

He is more laid back tonight, Susan decided. That made her relax a bit. She realized that in the *Englisha* world she was more of a Pizza Hut person than a fancy Italian restaurant type. She imagined she could get used to fancy restaurants if she had to. *What would it be like to marry Duane? Stop! Quit imagining a future that might include such a thing,* she ordered. *Duane is simply a friend and nothing more, is he not? And that is gut. I need friends.*

They ate in companionable silence occasionally broken by small talk.

"Done?" he asked, finishing his third piece.

"Yes, I think so," she said. "Let's go to Penney's."

"I'll follow you," he said. "I don't come here much."

"You can do something else while I shop if you want to," she said. "I won't be long."

He shook his head. "Baby shopping it will be. I'll tag along."

She found the infant department easily and looked for something for a boy. She held up a blue jumper, looked at it, and asked, "What do you think?"

"Looks fine. Just my color," he said with a smile.

"Okay then. Now a bag of disposable diapers and we're done."

She found the right size, and they made their way to the nearest checkout counter.

Duane pulled out his wallet and pulled out a credit card. "I'm paying half."

"You don't need to do that."

"I want in on the charity project," he insisted.

They made their way to the car, and he stowed the purchases in the backseat.

"That was awfully nice of you," Susan said when they were both in the car and buckled in. "Thank you."

"It's your project, so the thanks belongs to you and Laura. In my business I don't often get a chance to help out on things like this. It's a pleasure."

From the mall, he drove back downtown and parked on the street. He got out, opened Susan's door, retrieved the packages, and walked her to the apartment door.

"I'll carry these up the stairs for you," he offered.

"Thank you. I appreciate that."

When they got to the top of the stairs, he set the packages down on the table. "Sunday then," he said, smiling. "I enjoyed the evening."

"*Yah,*" she said. "Sunday. Thank you for the pizza—and your part in our 'project.'"

She walked with him down the stairs and watched as he reached the car. She quickly ducked back inside and locked the door. It wouldn't be good if Duane saw her watching him leave. Seeing her watching him arrive had been bad enough.

CHAPTER THIRTY

T he traffic coming home from church was light, and Susan was glad
  for the extra time to relax before Duane would show up later that
afternoon.

"Thanks for the ride, Laura." Susan gathered her things. "It was a
nice sermon today."

"I suppose it's different than what you're used to," Laura said.

"Well, it's not in German. But I like it."

"If we could just get Robby to come," Laura said, sadness in her
voice.

"He's a nice man. He'll come around. Look at all the help he's giving me. The driving lessons even though I've scared him half to death!"

"Robby does have a soft heart."

"Yes, he does." Susan paused. "Laura, would you call Duane for me?"

"Why?"

"Well…" Susan felt a blush coming on. "He's coming over to help
me with my GED math studies, and I've made him supper. We didn't
talk about supper, but I'd like to invite him."

"That's nice!" Laura opened her cell phone. "He'll love it, I'm sure.
Why don't you call?" She punched in the numbers and handed the
phone to Susan.

Taking the phone, Susan listened for a moment and then said,
"Hello, Duane. This is Susan. I wondered if you'd like to have supper
when you come over this afternoon." After a brief pause, Susan flipped
the phone closed and handed it to Laura. "He says he'll be glad to come
for dinner."

"You have a good time now. The man is a good catch," Laura said as Susan got out and shut the car door.

In shock, Susan watched Laura's car disappear. *Is that what I'm doing? Catching a man? I thought I was just being friendly, but is that the case?* Duane had taken her out twice for a meal, and fixing him an Amish supper seemed appropriate. At least in her book. But did it mean more in the *Englisha* book? *Well, it's too late to worry about that now. Two pies are made and a roast is in the oven.*

Susan climbed the stairs, hearing the squeak at each step. The comfort of being reminded of home could soak deep inside if she let it. And the aroma of the roast coming from the top of the stairs was also a blessed reminder of home.

Entering the apartment, she went directly to the oven and checked the meat. It seemed fine. Cooking with electricity—especially in her own apartment—was still a novelty. Later she would toss a small salad, finish the mashed potatoes, and prepare gravy. While she had time, she wanted to walk over to Teresa's to see how she was doing.

Susan pulled out two large paper bags. In one she put the disposable diapers and the blue jumper. In the other, she tucked in a peach pie. She was saving the pecan pie for Duane. The men at home loved pecan pie, and she hoped the same was true of *Englisha* men.

With everything in order, she left the apartment. Crossing the railroad tracks, she located Teresa's street. The neighborhood made her uneasy. She glanced around for any unsavory characters before heading down the row of crumbling structures.

Finding the house, she knocked on the rickety door. When there was no response, she opened the door. Teresa had said to just come on in if no one answered. Before she started up the stairs she heard Teresa call out, "Susan, is that you?" from somewhere upstairs.

"Yes, it's me!" Susan hollered back.

"I hoped so," Teresa said, appearing at the top of the staircase. "I couldn't imagine who else would be visiting on a Sunday afternoon."

"Is your mom in?" Susan asked as she arrived at the top of the steps.

"No." Teresa gave Susan a long hug. "I'm so glad to see you. Likely Mom won't be back till late. She's working at McDonald's this afternoon.

I've been listening to TV preachers this morning. How I wish I could find some Amish preaching, but there isn't any I could find."

"No, Amish ministers wouldn't be on TV," Susan said with a laugh as they entered the small apartment.

"I brought you some things," Susan said, setting the bags on the table.

"Really? You didn't have to. You've already done so much. I was going to visit the bakery shop this week, but my legs are giving out on me," Teresa said. "It comes from carrying this big boy around," she said with a smile.

"I hear everything went well with the doctor," Susan said. "And that it *is* a boy!" She took the blue jumper out of the bag and handed it to Teresa. "Do you think he'll like this?"

"A blue sleeper! Oh, Susan, it's perfect!" Teresa looked away and wiped her eyes. She ran her fingers over the soft cloth. "I'm sorry about the tears. I've never had anything like this before. Baby clothing—and soon a baby! And then someone who can really take care of him. If Charlie would only be the father he should be, we could make a go of it. But he refuses."

"Are you thinking of keeping the child?" Susan asked. "I think you'd love that."

"I'd love to," Teresa said amid more tears. "The closer I get to my due date, the harder it is to *not* be thinking about keeping him. I find myself thinking of what he's going to look like and how his little cheeks and hands will feel. I think about what it would be like if I nursed him. But that won't happen if I let him go. And I do have to let him go. That's the best thing for him. I can't raise him in this place."

Susan left the diapers on the table, and the two women moved to the couch.

"I don't know how to thank you," Teresa said again.

"And I wish there were more I could do."

"Have you written to your parents?"

Susan nodded.

"That's more than enough. I just know it will work out. Someone in the Amish community will say yes. I just know it!"

"Teresa, don't get your hopes too high. Adoption isn't something Amish people commonly do. I don't want you to be disappointed."

Teresa laughed but it sounded hollow. "I'm afraid I've got myself painted in a corner on that one. I guess it goes to show what happens when a person shoots for the stars. Mom always told me, don't shoot for the best, you'll be shooting too high, and you'll end up with nothing. But me? I went ahead and shot anyway."

"You could always put the child up for adoption with a local couple. Surely the clinic knows of nice Christian people who would love to give your boy a good home."

"No. I'm praying real hard, Susan. I'm praying like I've never prayed before."

Susan decided to mention something that had been on her mind the past couple of days. "Teresa, you know you could come to live with me at the apartment until the baby is born. That way your mother couldn't pressure you with the adoption."

"I don't think so," Teresa said. "Despite our differences on this, Mom has stood by me for so long. I can't just walk out on her. The only reason Mom is agreeing to me pursuing the Amish adoption is because she wants something nice for me. I haven't had a lot of nice things. Life hasn't always been easy for us. And because I want this so badly, she's allowing it. But if this Amish thing doesn't work out, that will likely be the end of it. She knows I would want to keep him, and she's not going to allow that."

Susan got up to pace the floor, stopping to look out the window at the debris-strewn sidewalks. "Well then, what about coming home to the community with me? That would get you away from here. I've been thinking of visiting home anyway." There, she said it. Susan was grasping for straws now, and she knew it. But Teresa's face spoke volumes of hope. Susan just couldn't see her let down.

"Go home...with you?" Teresa asked, almost laughing at the idea.

"Why not?"

"Because it wouldn't do any good if the Amish don't take my child. And if the Amish do take my child, then I shouldn't be there."

Susan sighed. "I just wish there was more I could do for you."

"You've done plenty." Teresa patted Susan on the arm. "Look at the presents you brought. Mom will be really surprised. I think she's surprised almost every day by what keeps happening. At least she's not laughing at me anymore."

"I've also brought you a pie." Susan slid the pan out of the bag. "A peach pie. I know it's not much with all that you have to face, but I hope you'll like it."

"Oh dear." Teresa wrapped her arms around Susan. "It's a home-baked pie, isn't it?"

"Yes," Susan confirmed.

"It is an Amish pie." Teresa leaned over the table, taking in a long breath. "That must be what the air of heaven smells like."

"I doubt that." Susan laughed. "It's just a peach pie."

"To you it might be only a peach pie, but to me it's the smell of home. Oh, I so want God to allow my son to grow up in a place where they make things like this!"

"I know, Teresa," Susan said, hugging her friend with both arms.

"And I think He will!" Teresa said. "I really think He will because He's a good God. He might not do it for me, but he'll do it for my baby, who has never done anything wrong."

Chapter Thirty-one

✦

Susan hurried down the sidewalk, her purse strap wrapped around her arm. She waited for long moments at the traffic signal, pushing herself to walk faster when the light turned green. The time at Teresa's place had gone longer than planned, and now she was late. Still, the visit with Teresa had been wonderful. Susan marveled at the young woman's bravery. How Teresa kept her faith up under the pressure was amazing. Would God answer her prayers with a yes or would a no send Teresa crashing into despair?

What would it be like to have so many fears and doubts about the world you lived in that you didn't want your own child to live there? In comparison, being raised Amish was like the green pastures of heaven. Which was exactly how Teresa saw Amish life. *But the Amish aren't saints,* Susan reminded herself. *Teresa has never met Thomas.*

Susan sighed, jiggling on her feet as another light took its good time turning green. There were more people out now, mostly couples, a few with baby carriages. The women were window shopping while the men followed along. Susan smiled at the thought. What would Thomas do out on a city sidewalk on a Sunday afternoon? It was impossible to imagine. He would be like a duck without water or a cow without pasture. He would feel like a barn with no horses. No, Thomas definitely didn't fit in here.

So why am I here, drifting so far from my people? Is it just a whim? No, she told herself, *God has a purpose, even in my bumbling foolishness.* And she'd had a reason: She'd needed to get away. *Well, I've done that! There's no question about that.*

Finally, here was the last light. She would soon be at her apartment, plunging elbow deep into preparing supper for Duane. That ought to take her mind off troubling thoughts. She was not going to be a *boppli*, mourning for what could never be. Yet somewhere deep inside she had to admit that it would be nice to be back home tonight, preparing supper for *Mamm* and *Daett* instead of an *Englisha* man.

This street was not as crowded as the one she had just left. In fact, she found it eerily quiet. There were no shops here—and thus no strolling shoppers. Susan quickened her pace. Seconds later she felt a wrench of pain on her arm, spinning her around, burning. Her purse was being pulled off her arm! Susan struggled to keep her balance, her fingers still grasping the strap. With a great upward jerk of his hands, a young man threw her off balance. She went crashing to the sidewalk, sliding on both hands. Her purse had been stolen! And in broad daylight on Main Street!

Struggling to stand and eyeing her bleeding hands, she turned toward the running thief. "Stop! Give me back my purse!"

She couldn't afford to lose the purse. There was the little money she had in it, and her learner's permit, and, more importantly, the key to her apartment.

The man was already half a block away, glancing over his shoulder and even laughing at her. Where had the strolling couples gone now that she needed them? Likely an empty street was what the rascal had waited for to inflict this indignity on her.

Now what am I supposed to do? She couldn't go running after him like an *Englisha* girl might. But wasn't she now trying to be an *Englisha* girl? Her Amish ways must be left behind. Surely *Englisha* girls didn't allow their purses to be stolen without protest.

Well, she would see then. He was still running, just turning a corner. She made the decision. *Yah.* She hadn't grown up running across hay fields for nothing. She took off after him at a fast clip. Once she turned the corner, he turned to look back at her, and she almost laughed at the startled look on his face. *Perhaps* Englisha *girls don't pursue their muggers after all,* she thought.

He dashed across an intersection, defying the red light, maneuvering around moving cars. Susan did likewise. Even as a car squealed its brakes, she kept going. And *gut,* it looked like the man was panting hard.

Up ahead there were a few scattered pedestrians. Again Susan hollered, "Stop him! He stole my purse!"

Two nearby men reached for the thief as he passed their way, but he dodged them at the last moment. Susan ran on, hollering, "Drop it!"

The man met her eyes, and she saw fear in them. He quickly swerved down an alley. *The rascal,* she thought. Well, he still wasn't going to get away with this. She followed him into the alley and out onto the next street. By now she had gained on him. She was only yards away. *What do I do when I catch him?* She wasn't about to tackle him. Even Amish girls had their limits.

The thief slowed down and so did she. She wanted her purse, but how close could she get to the man and not be in danger? He was now panting so hard he could hardly breathe. This time there was no alley at hand.

"Give me the purse!" she yelled again.

"Give the lady her purse," a voice behind her said.

Susan turned, surprised. She hadn't heard someone walk up.

"I said give the purse back." The man glared over Susan's shoulder. "You heard me."

His voice was deep and gruff. He was tall, sturdy, and obviously knew how to handle this situation. It was *gut* to have him here.

The young thief glanced both ways, unable to make up his mind. *Mr. Gruff* walked around her and grabbed the thief by his shirt collar. He retrieved Susan's purse.

"Now, young lady, do you want me to haul him into the police station for you? Or can I beat him up right here?" Mr. Gruff asked.

"No, I can't let you do that," Susan said draping the purse over her shoulder. "Maybe he's learned his lesson. Just let him go."

"You sure, ma'am?"

"Yes," Susan said.

Mr. Gruff released the thief, who took off running again.

"He might steal from someone else," Mr. Gruff said. "You're not afraid to testify against him are you? Or do you know him perhaps?"

"No, I don't know him," Susan said. "I don't want him to go to jail though."

How did she explain something like this to a stranger? She wasn't supposed to chase the thief, let alone send him to prison. That was the Amish way, and though she was no longer Amish, old beliefs die hard.

"Bennett," the gruff voice said, offering his hand.

She shook it. "I'm Susan. Thanks so much for your help. I couldn't have gotten my purse back without you."

"Someone would have helped you, Susan." He motioned toward two men just approaching. "Most people are nice around here. Sorry you had to experience this."

"I'm still thankful," she said. "It was nice of you."

"You live around here?" he asked.

"I live over on Main Street. I have to head back or I'm going to be very late. Thanks again."

"You were putting on quite a sprint there," he said with a smile. "Are you a long-distance runner?"

"No," she said with a laugh. "I just wanted my purse back."

"You got it back. I hope you enjoy the rest of your evening, Susan," Bennett said, turning to leave.

"I will. I hope you do too. God bless you!" Susan said as she too turned to leave.

Susan turned the key to the apartment door and rushed up the steps. Now she really was late, but at least she had her purse back. Running water into the sink, she washed the blood off her hands. Thankfully, there were only small scratches. She checked the time. Supper would be late, but that couldn't be helped. Opening the oven, she jabbed a fork into the roast. Just right. She turned the dial to off, removed the roast, and set it on the counter. She continued with the rest of the preparations.

Minutes later, Duane knocked on the door. Susan rushed down to greet him.

As she led him up the stairs, he said, "Wow, something sure smells good!"

"It's a roast. I hope you're hungry!"

"Of course," he said. "I can't wait."

"I have just a bit more to do. I'm afraid I got delayed."

"Did you burn something and have to start over?" he teased.

Susan burst out laughing. "Do you think Amish women burn their meals?"

"No, but my mother often did. She wasn't Amish though. Late dinners at our house usually meant Mom burned something."

"Why don't you have a seat while I finish?"

"So what happened?" he asked, pulling up a chair.

Susan turned to the stove and drained the potatoes. "Well, a thief stole my purse, and I chased him down," she said with a grin, glancing over her shoulder.

"What?" he said, standing up.

"You don't believe me?" she asked, turning toward him. "I know it wasn't very Amish of me, but I couldn't afford to lose that purse. Besides, I'm trying to not be Amish."

"I guess I believe you," he said scratching his head. "I would have loved to be there to help out."

"Well, thanks," she said as she mashed the potatoes. "But someone else did the honors." She told him the whole story, including her visit to Teresa's and concluded with, "Ta-da! Supper is ready!"

"Wow, everything looks good—really good," he said.

Susan shrugged. "What can I say? Amish women know how to cook!"

They sat at the table and bowed their heads for prayer. Afterward, Susan passed him the potatoes, waiting until he had taken a large scoop before handing him the gravy bowl.

"Will you please slice the roast?" she asked.

"I'd be honored," he said with a slight bow and smile.

He placed a slice of roast on her plate and then on his own.

She watched him eat out of the corner of her eye. Curious, she finally asked, "Is the food okay?"

"Oh, it's excellent!" he said as he helped himself to more roast.

Susan continued to watch as Duane focused on enjoying the meal. When he finally pushed his plate a few inches toward the middle of the table and let out a contented sigh, Susan said, "Pecan pie? With ice cream?"

"Dessert too?" he asked with wide eyes.

Duane with wide eyes over food? He's never looked that excited about food. Not at fancy restaurants, not at the bakery. But he is about my cooking! She was grinning from ear to ear.

Suddenly and to Susan's surprise, Duane said, "I'm just too full. It must be the wholesomeness of your cooking. I really need to go. I don't want to keep you up late when you have to get up early for work at the bakery."

"It's not late. You don't have to rush off," she said.

"Thanks, Susan," he said as he got up. "It's been a great evening. Maybe we can do this again sometime."

"O—okay," she said, still in shock. She followed him down the stairs.

He opened the door. "Goodnight" was all he said before he turned and disappeared under the dim light of the street lamps.

Susan locked the door and climbed the stairs again. She sat down at the kitchen table and buried her head in her hands. *What went wrong? Duane even forgot to help me with math—and that was the reason for his coming over in the first place. First Thomas and now Duane...*

Chapter Thirty-two

M enno Hostetler walked in from the barn, the evening sky already darkening behind him. Low thunderclouds were rolling in from the northeast. He paused to smell the air, remembering that his *Englisha* neighbor had said rain was coming. *This could just as easily be snow,* he decided. *Winter isn't far away.* Miriam and Joe were coming for Thanksgiving dinner today—a *gut* thing. He was pleased though tired. He shouldn't have been plowing all day yesterday, but someone had to do the work. Renting the place might be an option come spring, but what he really wanted for the farm was new blood and a fresh pair of hands. Someone who would own the place, not a renter whose heart came and left when his lease was up.

Menno let the screen door slam behind him, the report echoing in the washroom. He ran water into the sink. His hands were soaped by the time the hot water arrived. With a sigh, he rinsed them and wiped them dry. He looked at them. They were old hands now. The skin was wrinkled, showing the years of hard work. Did not the Holy Scripture say that a man's days were few and full of trouble? They had seemed few, and they were still full of trouble. Susan was seeing to that. But he shouldn't blame her, he supposed. He hadn't always lived his life the best way either.

"Are you coming in?" Anna called from the kitchen.

"*Yah!*" he hollered back, pushing open the kitchen door.

"I want you to read Susan's letter again," Anna said.

"You told me what's in it," he said.

Anna bustled about, putting the last touches on their Thanksgiving fare spread out on the table. "A fresh set of eyes might see something I haven't. And Joe and Miriam are coming any minute. Perhaps they would have some advice. We can't just bury this problem in the sand any longer, Menno. You know that."

"Okay." He got up. "Where's the letter?"

"On the desk," she said.

He took the letter to his old rocker and lowered his weary body down. Pulling the single piece of paper out of the envelope, he unfolded it.

Susan's handwriting was still beautiful, a graceful cursive that lifted off the lines to descend again in perfect harmony. He shook his head, rubbing his eyes with the back of his hand.

> *Dear* Mamm *and* Daett,
>
> *Greetings in the name of the Lord.*
>
> *I hope this finds you well, and that little Jonas fully recovered from his hog bites. That was quite a terrible thing to have happen. I called Edna's phone shack afterward using a cell phone I borrowed. Since I haven't heard anything more by now, I assume his recovery is coming along well.*
>
> *Life here at the bakery goes on as usual. I get up at four each morning—conditioned from the years on the farm I suppose—to help with the baking. Laura seems satisfied with my help, and I am able to save a little money. Not much, but some.*
>
> *I am writing this letter with a strange request, but I promised Teresa that I would ask. She is a young, unwed woman I met in the shop. She came up to me the other day and asked if I would adopt her child. Yes, Teresa is with child. She has apparently become very enamored with the Amish life, which she has seen on TV.*
>
> *Please understand, I did not encourage her in any way. I told her I couldn't take the child. I mean, how could I? She told me about her life and how desperate she is to have her son have a better life than she has. When I told her I couldn't take her child, Teresa begged me to ask if there are any Amish couples who would consider adopting him.*

I brought Laura into the conversation, and she suggested that the local Crisis Pregnancy Center could find an Englisha *couple who would be willing to adopt the baby. Teresa, though, is quite determined that her child go to an Amish home.*

Would you consider asking around to see if anyone is willing to adopt the child? I'm not sure exactly how such things are done, but let me assure you that Teresa is sound of mind. It's her living condition that is bad. I know because I visited the apartment where she and her mom live.

I am adding my own plea to this request, especially since I have the story from both Teresa and her mother. Anyone who would be interested in the child can write to me for more details. I suppose the baby would have to be picked up here, as this is where the adoption would have to be done.

Thanks so much for your consideration, and much love.

Your daughter, Susan

Menno folded the letter and slid it back into the envelope. He rocked slowly, stroking his chest-length beard.

"Well, what do you think?" Anna asked, coming in from the kitchen to take a seat on the couch.

"I don't know," he said. "It doesn't make much sense. Susan would still have to sign the adoption papers if she's the mother. And our people would learn of this thing then."

"It wouldn't be as bad as admitting it up front." She watched his face. "I'm afraid it makes way too much sense."

"No, I don't think so," he said.

"So what is Susan up to then?"

He shrugged. "I'm not sure I agree with your conclusion."

"Well, it's true we can't tell just from reading her letter. But you have to admit this would explain an awful lot of things. Like why an Amish girl would just up and rush off to the *Englisha* world like Susan did."

"You shouldn't jump to conclusions, Anna," he insisted.

"I don't think I am, Menno," she said. "I try not to think ill of her, but when something makes too much sense, I just have to believe it.

Look at us. We never picked up on any problems she was having with Thomas. Everything between them was going fine, and the wedding was planned for next year. Then *boom!* it flies apart."

"But Susan wouldn't do anything like that," he said.

"You're forgetting that people can fall, Menno. Any of us can. This is the only way it makes any sense."

"Everything might make sense—but Susan wouldn't do something like this. She doesn't lie," he said.

"Then what should we do? Do you think we should do what she asks and see if anyone wants to adopt this baby?"

"Can you think of anyone who might want a child?" he asked.

"No. And you know what they will think. It doesn't take much to arrive at the same conclusion I did. And that would drag Thomas into this. He might never be able to clear his name, even if Susan comes home without the child. People might think she let the child go to *Englisha* parents. No, once we ask around as she asks, we're going to open her—and Thomas—up to gossip and rumors."

"You don't think Susan has thought of this?" he asked.

"She can be a little rattlebrained sometimes. You know that, Menno. Even if she's your favorite daughter."

"I never tried to have favorites," he said.

"I know. And I hate to accuse her, Menno. Oh, how I wish we would have placed more pressure on her to stay home after her *kafuffle* with Thomas. *Da Hah,* forgive us. I thought a little time away might do her good. Who would have thought it would lead to this? If Susan had stayed here, we could have borne the shame together. Or married them off this year before she showed."

"You did the best you knew." He stood. "And I did too. We have to pray about this."

"Then you're not going to ask Miriam and Joe about it?" she asked as they heard a buggy rattle in the lane.

"I don't know," he said.

"It might help if they knew." Her eyes pleaded. "The load is almost more than I can bear."

Menno nodded and went out to greet his daughter and son-in-law.

"Howdy!" he said to young Jonas, lifting the boy's hat and ruffling his hair as he jumped out of the buggy. "Have you got that hog-bit hand all better by now?"

"Pretty much!" Jonas rotated his hand for Menno to see.

"Nice scars," Menno said with another pat on the head of his grandson.

"Now, don't encourage him," Miriam said, climbing down from the buggy and turning to take the baby from Joe. "He'll be wanting more scars if you praise him," she said, facing her *daett* again.

"No more scars!" Jonas said. "It hurts too much to get them."

"See, he's learning fast," Menno said, holding the buggy shafts as Joe got off the buggy, undid the tugs, and led the horse forward.

Menno walked ahead of Joe to the barn, dropped the buggy shafts, and then walked to the door and pushed it open. A sudden wind blast made Menno grab his hat.

"You think snow's coming?" Joe asked as he led his horse inside.

"They said there would be rain, but it smells like snow to me," Menno said, waiting by the barn door while Joe secured the horse. As they walked toward the house, they leaned into the wind, holding on to their hats.

"Kind of sudden, those storm clouds," Menno said, when they arrived at the shelter of the porch. "It'll probably blow through quick enough."

"I hope so. I have to get back in the fields tomorrow," Joe said, washing his hands at the sink and then drying them. "Are you caught up with your plowing?"

"No," Menno said.

Joe opened the door into the kitchen and entered, Menno close behind him. They took their seats at the table, Menno at the head. Jonas and the other children were already waiting at the table, the younger ones wiggling in their seats.

When the two women had the last hot dish on the table, they pulled chairs out and sat down. Menno led the prayer in German. When he was finished, Anna and Miriam passed the food around, keeping an eye on the children. Two-year-old Mandy banged her spoon, scooping the mashed potatoes straight into her mouth without waiting for the gravy.

"She's hungry!" Jonas said, laughing at his sister. "She doesn't know any better."

"I guess she likes her mashed potatoes without gravy," Miriam said. "Babies are that way sometimes."

"She's not a baby," Jonas said. "Nancy's the baby."

"Just eat!" Joe ordered.

Jonas nodded and stopped his flow of words with food.

When they finished, Anna brought out pumpkin pie from the cupboard, sliding two round pans on the table. "Freshly made yesterday," she said. "Jonas, would you like a piece?"

"A *big* piece!" he said, grinning from ear to ear.

Anna cut one for him and slid it onto his plate. He wolfed it down but savored each bite, his face aglow with pleasure.

Miriam beamed at Jonas. "Now all we need is a rub on the stomach, and we'll have a big boy."

"They grow up fast enough." Anna's voice was tinged with sadness.

"I know." Miriam glanced at her mother. Both of them fell silent as Menno and Joe took the conversation toward farm work and the expected nasty weather.

When everyone was done with their pie, Menno led in prayer again. The chairs scraped the hardwood floor as they got up. Joe and Menno headed for the living room, taking the children with them. Miriam and Anna began cleaning the kitchen.

"Miriam, we have something we need to talk about," Anna whispered above the soft clink of dishes.

"Just us two?"

"No, with the menfolk too."

"Then it must be serious, *Mamm*."

"I'm afraid so," Anna answered, her washcloth busy.

"Does it have to do with Susan?"

Anna nodded.

Miriam fell silent.

When they finished, Anna led Miriam into the living room, picking up the letter on the desk before taking a seat on the couch.

"Here." She handed the letter to Miriam.

Miriam read the letter and passed it on to Joe.

Menno rocked, his eyes on the blast of the storm outside the window. It had begun snowing, little spits driving against the panes.

"Is this what I think it is?" Miriam asked. "I can't think that Susan and Thomas would do such a thing."

Anna kept her eyes on the floor. "I wish we didn't even have to speak of this."

"You certainly can't ask around like she wants you to," Miriam said. "It would always stick in people's minds, even if Susan should prove to be innocent."

"So what *can* we do?" Anna asked.

"I think we should trust Susan," Menno said.

"What do you think?" Anna asked Joe, who had just finished reading the letter.

"I agree with Menno," Joe said. "It's not *gut* to think bad of people, even if they have done wrong. In this case, we don't know."

"You are both being soft on her," Miriam said. "You forget that any of us can fall."

"We must not blame Susan and Thomas for this," Menno said. "I forbid it, no matter how things might appear."

Joe scratched his head, "Well, I think I know what we could do. It would solve this without offending anyone."

"Really?" Anna said. "Please tell us."

"You could write her back and tell her you don't think anyone would be interested in adoption, but that she is welcome to bring this Teresa girl here. The girl could be away from her old life for a time and eventually find an *Englisha* family—a good solid Christian family—who would take the child."

After a pause to think, Anna asked, "Would you do that, Menno? Would you allow the girl into our home—if there is such a girl?"

"If she's Susan's friend, then she's our friend," he said. "I think Joe has spoken great wisdom. I would have done well to think of anything better."

"But she comes from the city...if there really is this girl," Anna said.

"We must believe that *Da Hah* has His reasons for everything,"

Menno said. "Are you thinking this solution also is a way to bring our Susan home again? If she has not told us the truth, I know of no better place than home to make confessions and begin over again."

"I will write her tomorrow then," Anna said. "Susan can let the girl know she is welcome to come. Perhaps there *is* a reason for all of this after all."

They nodded and turned to watch the storm blow and listen to the sound of the children playing upstairs.

Chapter Thirty-three

𝔖 usan eyed the space between the two vehicles, straining to look over her shoulder. She had Robby's car stopped at an angle on the empty side street.

Who on earth had ever invented parallel parking!

What had started as a wonderful Thanksgiving celebration earlier in the day was quickly turning to frustration.

After the sumptuous turkey feast, Robby had insisted today would be a great day for another lesson.

"Everyone's home either eating or watching football," he had said. "The streets should be empty."

He hadn't told her he wanted her to practice parallel parking. Now her nerves were more than a little raw. All week long she had managed to hide from Laura her disappointment with Duane on Sunday night. Now her emotions were finally bubbling over.

"I can't do this." She threw her hands in the air and brought them down to pound the steering wheel. "There is no way. No way. *No way!*"

"Well, well," Robby said. "Have you been out on your broomstick?"

"I've been on my broomstick since Sunday night," Susan said. "And don't ask why."

"Not that it would be any of my business." Robby clucked his tongue. "Me? Why, I'm just the innocent, sweet fellow who offers to give the poor Amish girl driving lessons. A fellow, mind you, who risked his life. And now, on the last leg of the long journey, just when victory is within sight, she goes bonkers on me. All because she had a bad night with her boyfriend."

"He's *not* my boyfriend," she asserted.

"Oh," Robby said. "You could have fooled me. Now would you please get my car off the street before we get run over? There's a car coming."

Susan gave up on the parking attempt and slammed the car into drive. She mashed the gas pedal. With a squeal of tires, she jerked the steering wheel to the left and out into the lane, bringing the car to a sliding halt at the light.

"The light's red," she said, staring up through the windshield.

"It must have been a very, very bad night," Robby said. "Do you want to tell me about it?"

"No, I do *not*."

"I'll listen to you and not say a word. Now, how many handsome young men would do that?"

"Ha! You didn't take me out to the ocean—even when you promised."

"Now, now," Robby said. "This is about him, not me. I don't need razor blades run across my back."

"What do razor blades have to do with anything?" Susan glared at him and then stomped the accelerator when the light turned green.

He hung on to the door handle. "Sweet heaven, get me out of this alive, and I'll pay my tithe faithfully every Sunday! This woman has turned into an Amish Frankenstein."

"Who is Frankenstein?"

"Don't worry about that! Just take it easy. There are cars parked all along this street."

"And you don't think I can see that?" she snapped.

"Yes, *sweetie*, I know you can see them. Just don't hit them."

"Don't *sweetie* me," she said, turning right onto another side street. "Now there are two empty spots. More room. I'll try this again."

Robby placed both hands on the dash as Susan pulled alongside a car. She put the car into reverse. She swung the vehicle backward into the parking spaces, rubbing the tires against the curb. She then straightened the car and drove into the first space.

"See, that wasn't all bad," she said. "All I needed was two spaces to get my courage up."

"Take three, or five, or six," he said. "Just calm down."

"I *am* calmed down."

"And you have parallel parking mastered," he said. "Now you're ready for the test tomorrow."

"No," she said. "I have to back into a single space, don't I?"

"Yes," he said. "But you'll do fine. I think you'll pass with flying colors."

"I hope so! I've studied and I've practiced. I can't do anything more."

"True," he said. "I'll pick you up tomorrow morning early, and we'll get all this taken care of in no time."

"Maybe you should drive back to the bakery," she said. "My nerves are kind of shot."

"Sure," he said, getting out of the car. She did the same.

"I have just one more, teeny tiny little request, Robby," she said when he had climbed behind the wheel and she was in the passenger seat. "Then I'll let you go."

"Really?" he said. "And from where would you remove the pound of flesh?"

"Pound of flesh?" she asked, snapping her seat belt in place.

"Forget it," he said. "It's just an expression."

"Robby, I need help with my math. I thought that…well…maybe you could tell me just a little bit about it. And then I can do the rest. It's the last thing I haven't figured out on the GED sample test. Will you help me?"

"I guess if it doesn't take too long. But why are you taking the test tomorrow, the same day as your driving test? Isn't one test a day enough for you?"

"It won't take long…and I'm taking both tests so I get this over with. I'm so tired of studying! If I don't know it now…" She settled back into her seat.

"I'd probably do the same," Robby agreed. He quickly navigated the streets, pulling up to park near the bakery door.

Silently they got out and she led him up the stairs, showing him to a chair at the kitchen table. She retrieved the printed test papers, slapping them down on the table.

"This!" She pointed with her finger. "What is a number line? And what are these symbols?"

"You've never seen a number line before?" he asked.

"Robby, please don't tease me. I just need answers. The Amish don't teach stuff like this."

He bent over the sample booklet, muttering under his breath.

"So do you know?" she asked.

"Yes. And don't beat me over the head. I was thinking, refreshing my mind about these math symbols."

Moments later he smiled up at her. "Ready?" When she glared at him he continued, "A number line is the same thing as what you're used to, the difference is that this goes both ways from zero. That way you have negative and positive numbers. For example, you have two here, and you have minus two here on the left. Does that make sense?"

"I guess so. Isn't it more complicated than that?"

"Nope! Now for the symbols," he said. "You have to think in terms of the number line. The problems will usually compare left and right sets of numbers with a symbol in between."

"I knew that number line was the key," she said, glaring at the paper.

"It's not that hard." Robby scribbled with the pencil as he talked. "There is the equal sign between the two sets. That means they are the same."

"Yes, they equal each other."

He nodded. "Then there's the minus sign, the plus sign, the sub-tract sign, and the multiplying sign, all the usual math symbols. A y or an x stands in for the missing number."

"Is that all there is to it?"

Robby laughed. "No, but that should get you by. I doubt if they go too deep for the GED."

"So…" Susan did the calculations out loud. "Two times three equals seven minus x. The answer would be one."

"See!" He tilted his head. "It's easy. Just follow the logic."

"Thanks, Robby!" she said. "It's nice of you to take the time. I really needed the help."

"That's because I *am* nice," he said. "Now, if some decent female in this town would agree with your assessment of me, that would be helpful."

She patted his arm. "They will in time. Remember: All good things take time."

He snorted and got up to go. Susan followed him downstairs. Stepping outside, she watched as he got into his car, started it, and pulled away from the curb. Turning back inside, she made her way back up the stairs and sat down at the kitchen table. With pencil in hand, she stared at the practice problems based on the number line.

Moments later she was scribbling away. The problems were still hard, regardless of what Robby had said. Deep into the numbers, she jumped when what sounded like a rap or bang came from the door below. Walking over to the window, Susan looked out but didn't see anything unusual.

I'm just jumpy, that's all, she thought. The purse scare from Sunday afternoon had rattled her, but she didn't want to allow one man to affect her this way. She decided she should be sure no one was at the door. She walked slowly downstairs to investigate. She opened the door far enough to see out and was relieved to find Duane standing outside.

"Hi," he said.

"Hi," she said warily.

"I saw Robby's car pass me. Was he helping you with something?" he asked.

"Just the math problems you were going to help me with Sunday."

"I'm sorry, Susan. I really am. That's why I stopped by. I'd like to explain the reason I left so suddenly. Can I come up?"

Susan paused, thinking. *Should I let him in?* She decided and opened the door wider. "Okay."

He walked past her and started up the stairs, not waiting as she closed the door. She followed him.

"May I sit down?" he asked.

"Of course."

He squirmed a moment before speaking. "I can't tell you how foolish and stupid I feel. You are a wonderful woman, Susan. Beautiful, talented—especially considering your background. I had no reason to treat you like I did."

"Really?" she said, still standing. "I thought you were here to explain the reason you left so abruptly."

He looked out of the window for a moment. "Well, it caught me

by surprise, I guess. How you fixed supper for me. I mean, that was a
gigantic, delicious, full meal. When Laura said supper, I was thinking
soup or sandwiches or something."

"You didn't think I could cook a real meal good enough for you?"
she asked. "Is that what was wrong? Well, I'll have you know that no
one at home on the farm, from the greatest to the least, would have
found anything wrong with my supper."

"Oh, I know! That's not what it was, Susan. The supper was delicious."

"Then what was the problem?"

Duane looked Susan in the eye. "It was the seriousness of it. That's
what suddenly hit me. I didn't know our relationship had gotten that
far along in your mind."

"What?" she said. "This is what we do in Amish country. We eat
good meals!"

"So that's all that was, then? This wasn't you moving us on to the
next level in our relationship?"

"I don't even know what that means."

"Well, dating seriously," he said. "I thought…well, that you might
be thinking…um…marriage."

Susan laughed. "Marriage! Sorry, Duane. No! It was only supper.
An Amish supper."

He took a deep breath. "Then we're okay like we are?"

"Duane, I really don't think so. I'm sorry," she said.

"We're not?"

"No, we're not," she said. "In the first place, I have a few problems
to work through. I won't bore you with them other than to say that I
have a trip home coming up, which could lead in any one of several
directions."

"I don't want you to be angry with me."

"Okay," she said. "I won't be angry. But let's let it end with that."

"Well, we've had some good times together," he said, getting to his feet.

When she was silent, he said, "Are you sure you're not angry?"

"No, Duane, I'm not angry."

"Then goodnight, Susan. Perhaps we'll see each other sometime
again," he said, turning to go.

She followed him down the stairs and stood on the street by the open door.

"Goodnight," he said again and waved before he turned to go.

When she was back upstairs, Susan felt the tears. She washed her face and cried some more.

They are skunks, all of them! Men are nothing but barnyard skunks.

CHAPTER THIRTY-FOUR

✦

Susan threw the covers off at the sound of the alarm. She dressed quickly in the bright glare of the bedroom lamp. One of these days she would use the kerosene lamp again, simply for a calmer awakening. She poured a bowl of cereal for breakfast, and then finally took the time to look out the front window. Seeing the normal gray haze that always seemed to hang over the city, she looked forward to enjoying the early morning stars again when she was home for her visit. Susan turned on the coffee machine and listened to the crackle of the water flowing. At home the water would be hissing in the kettle for *Mamm's* coffee. *Daett* would want his after breakfast, a quick cup to gulp down before he left for his day working in the fields. Here so much was different—the coffee made by electric machines against the backdrop of car engines revving outside.

But it's still the same coffee, Susan told herself. *Just as I have learned to do things differently, but I'm still the same person.*

Am I really going home? Thanksgiving had come and gone. Now it was time to decide. The question raced through her head. *Do I want to go home?* The answer was *yah* and *nee.* It was difficult to explain. Laura said she could have time off whenever she needed it, so that part of the problem was solved. The other issue was Teresa, who was still waiting for an answer about the adoption. Yesterday she had questioned Laura again during their trip to the doctor.

Susan rinsed the dishes under the sink nozzle and rushed downstairs to the bakery. Slipping into an apron, she joined Laura in the kitchen.

"Good morning," Laura said, looking up. "I heard about your problem with Duane. I'm so sorry."

Laura certainly doesn't beat around the bush, Susan thought.

"Yesterday I stopped by his office, and he told me. He said he was really sorry for so completely misunderstanding you. He blames himself totally."

"So he really thought I was going after him?" Susan asked.

"I guess men around here aren't used to big suppers prepared for them," Laura said, laughing. "I certainly don't think you did anything wrong."

"I didn't think so either," Susan said.

"Of course you didn't," Laura agreed. "The two of you are miles apart with your cultures. I still think you'd make a great couple, despite the differences."

"I don't know," Susan said. "Sometimes I lie in my bed at night and wonder what I'm doing out here in the great big wide world. The differences sometimes scare me. I often wonder if it's worth it. Maybe I should just make *Mamm* and *Daett* happy and go home."

"I understand. I wouldn't want to persuade you one way or the other, but you know you have a job here as long as you wish—and the apartment."

"Thanks," Susan said, rolling out dough.

"The paper was on the stoop when I got here this morning. They finally caught the guy they think was kidnapping and killing the young women."

"That's wonderful! We can all breathe a sigh of relief."

"He was in the middle of another abduction when he was caught. The woman screamed and fought hard enough to prompt someone to call 9-1-1. He had all but given up on her and was trying to get away when the police arrived."

"What did he do with the other girls?" Susan asked. "No one has ever told me."

"What those kind of men always do," Laura said. "I'm sure the police hope he'll confess, but it's a long shot. They don't always cooperate."

"I'm glad he was caught," Susan said. "I guess that ends that."

"I sure feel much better about you staying in the apartment," Laura said. "But you are still welcome anytime at the house."

"Thanks," Susan said. She had never told Laura about the purse snatcher. There was no sense in that. She would only worry.

"Have you had word from your parents?" Laura asked. "Teresa seems desperate for news."

"No, not yet. When I visited her Sunday, I tried to persuade her again to give the child up for adoption here, but she has her heart set, I'm afraid. What will happen when it doesn't work out, I don't know."

"I don't either," Laura agreed.

"Do you think Maurice might change her mind and let her keep the child?"

"You know the answer better than I do," Laura said. "Teresa seems to confide in you more than she does in me. Maybe Maurice will come to her senses, but don't count on it."

"I hope *something* happens because I'm pretty sure my parents won't be sending the news Teresa wants."

"No, I don't think so either. I can't see the Amish people taking in a strange child."

The two women turned their energy fully on their work. Just before the bakery opened, Susan made the coffee and unlocked the doors. The morning rush began soon afterward, with Susan and Laura working side by side.

"I'll sure miss you if you go," Laura whispered in the middle of getting a roll for a customer. "Having Sherry help will be fine, but it's not going to be the same."

"I'll miss you, too," Susan said. "Sherry will work hard I'm sure."

"Then you *are* going?" Laura asked.

"Probably," Susan said with a sigh, and the two fell silent.

Just before nine o'clock, Sherry walked in and Susan took off her apron.

"Hi!" Sherry said. "I'm here."

Sherry was good at serving the customers, but she didn't like getting up at four o'clock in the morning to be at the bakery by five. That was the problem with Susan leaving, but Laura would manage somehow. Robby would help if it came to that.

Robby pulled up outside, and Susan grabbed her purse and went out to his car, waving a quick goodbye to Laura, who was waiting on a customer.

Susan slid into the passenger side seat.

"Are we ready for the day's adventure?" Robby asked.

"This is really nice of you," Susan said. "I'll never be able to thank you enough for all you've done for me."

"Whoa, whoa, *whoa!*" he said. "It sounds as if we were at the end of some road somewhere."

"I know. It feels like it," she said, as he pulled out into the traffic.

"So where are you going?"

"I've decided to go home sometime before Christmas. Maybe in the first part of December."

"Mom was talking about the possibility. Are you coming back?"

"I don't know," she said. "It's hard to tell. But thanks for all you've done for me."

"So you're going to pass today? Both tests?" he teased.

"I hope so!"

"That's a lot of confidence there."

"If I don't," she said, "at least I tried."

"And what will an Amish girl do with a driver's license?"

"Probably hide it under my pillow."

"You're not serious, of course."

"No, but I'll keep it until I decide to be baptized. Until then it will be my escape ticket."

"That is, *if* you pass."

"*Yah,* that is," she agreed.

"If you kill the instructor, they'll never give you a driver's license," Robby teased.

"You are so funny," she said.

He pulled into a parking lot at the college minutes later. "Here we are for our first stop. I think I'll come in and read up on my romance life while you check the boxes on your test."

"That's a good idea. You need all the help you can get!"

Susan went to the information desk and was directed to a room in the back. Two other women were already there, along with a scrawny man who looked like he was in his twenties.

"Are you nervous?" one girl asked when Susan sat beside her.

"Yes," Susan whispered back.

"Charlotte's my name," the girl said.

"Susan. I hope we all get good grades."

"I hope so too," Charlotte said, crossing her fingers.

A stern-looking lady entered the room and gave instructions to the four. She passed out the tests, face down. When she was done, she said, "You may start now." She sat down on a chair behind the desk that was in the front of the room.

Susan took a deep breath and began. The questions on the first page looked easy enough…and on the next. She took longer on the math section and rushed to finish.

The instructor said, "Time's up!" She gathered up the test papers and said, "You will receive the results through the mail in a week or so. You can also look for your results online, if you'd like."

Susan and the others got up to leave.

"How did you do?" Charlotte asked on the way out.

"I hope okay," Susan said. "How about you?"

"Can't tell. This was my second time. So hopefully a little better than last time."

"You did fine, I'm sure," Susan said. She turned and searched for Robby.

"Is the great conqueror of the GED exam finished?" Robby asked from behind her, coming out from an aisle of books. "I think I have my love life all figured out."

"Let's go!" Susan said, ignoring his comment. "I think the worst still lies ahead of me."

"The slayer of Robby's car goes forth to ravage the countryside," he announced while holding the door for her. They walked outside.

"I haven't put so much as a scratch on your car," she said going down the stairs toward the parking lot. "Not one."

"No, but you've scared about five years off my life," he said. "And made me lose five pounds."

"Well…" She climbed into the car. "I admit you've been a very patient man. So keep practicing, and your girl problems will soon be over."

He gave her a glare and drove to the DMV.

"Now the real fun begins!" he said as they got out.

"Don't rub it in," Susan said, steadying herself by putting her hands on the side of the car.

"I think the instructor is over there," Robby said, pointing.

Susan walked over to the marked car. The instructor was standing by the building and holding a clipboard. He was dressed warmly with a sweater under his suit coat. Susan guessed he was in his mid-forties. He looked calm and patient.

"Eleven o'clock appointment?" he asked.

Susan nodded.

He introduced himself as Bob and asked, "May I see your learner's permit, please?"

Susan handed it to him. He looked it over and gave it back.

"You're ready then?" he asked.

"Yes," Susan said. "The car I'll be driving is over there." She pointed toward Robby's vehicle.

The instructor walked over to the car, circled it, checking to make sure everything outside was legal. He climbed into the passenger's side.

Robby said, "Good luck, Susan! I'll wait for you inside the building."

Susan nodded and opened the driver's side door and slid in behind the wheel. She glanced back. Robby was watching.

After the instructor went through his "everything is in good operating order in the car" list, he nodded to Susan. "You may start whenever you're ready. I want you to pull out at the marked exit and then turn left," he said. "I'll give you directions as we go along."

Susan placed the car into drive, repeating silently to herself, *Think farm. Think farm. Think horses. Think driving buggies. Left, right. Left, right. Pull lines.* She turned left at the entrance, finally relaxing a bit when they came to the the first light. *What is there to worry about anyway? I've done this many times with Robby. And if I fail, so what? Amish people don't need driver's licenses.*

"You're doing fine," the man said minutes later. "Let's try this street. A left, please."

Susan turned on the blinker, waited for two cars to go by, and then pulled across the traffic lanes.

"There's an empty parking spot up ahead on the right. Can you parallel park?"

"I think so," Susan said barely above a whisper.

Susan turned on her blinker and pulled up next to a parked car. Repeating under her breath, "I can do it. I can do it," her gaze jumped back and forth between the rearview mirror and her side mirror. She craned her neck over her shoulder and swung the car into the spot on the first try.

"Not bad!" the examiner said. "Now pull out, and let's go around a few more blocks. Then we're done."

Susan took a deep breath, glanced into the mirror, flipped the turn signal, looked over her shoulder, and pulled out. She followed the man's direction as they moved through town, eventually returning to the DMV lot, parking where they'd started.

"Come inside with me," Bob said, climbing out.

Susan followed him. "Let me pass, please let me pass," she whispered to Bob's back.

"What was that?" he asked over his shoulder.

Susan felt blood rushing to her face.

"I hope I passed," she said. "I was just talking to myself."

"You did pass," he said. "Wait a minute here, and I'll have your license ready for you shortly."

Susan found Robby and briefly waved. He walked toward her as she lowered herself into the chair, wondering why her body suddenly felt so weak.

"Is the picture we used on your permit okay to use on your license?" Bob asked, interrupting her thoughts. "Or do you want a new one taken?"

Susan jumped at the question, deciding quickly, "The first one is fine, *yah.*"

Bob nodded. He was soon back, handing her a piece of plastic.

"Thank you! Thank you so much."

"Congratulations! You have fun now," he said. "And drive safely."

"Robby!" she exclaimed as soon as Bob had turned away. She held up her license. "My driver's license! Can you believe it?"

"You are amazing!" he said as they walked outside and moved to his car. He opened the passenger door for her. "Absolutely amazing!"

Chapter Thirty-five

Susan slid the last doughnut into the large box and closed the lid. "That will be eleven dollars and twenty cents," she said to the two well-dressed ladies.

"We have a little office surprise this morning," one of them said with a giggle. "It's the boss's birthday, and he loves your doughnuts!"

"I'm glad to hear that," Susan said as she took their money and handed back the change. "I hope he enjoys the surprise."

"Oh, he will," one of the ladies assured Susan, taking the box, and following the other woman outside.

Susan looked outside and saw Laura's car go by, heading toward her usual parking spot. On the way in, Laura and the postman almost collided. After a hasty "Sorry," he handed Laura the day's mail.

Approaching the bakery counter, Laura held up an envelope and said, "Susan, I think the letter from your parents has arrived."

"My parents?" Susan grabbed the envelope.

"Looks like it to me," Laura said.

Susan studied the familiar handwriting and slid into a chair at a table. "I think I'd better sit down to read this."

"I'll take care of this customer," Laura said moving behind the counter just as someone walked in.

Susan opened the envelope and forced herself to pull the paper out. She unfolded it and read.

Dear Susan,

Greetings in the name of Da Hah.

The weather here has turned a little nippy. It snowed last night, although not much stuck to the ground. Joe and Miriam were over, and Jonas is coming along okay. The doctor said the infection might flare up again, but we hope not. Jonas showed Daett his scars. I hope some of those will go away or at least become less noticeable. A little boy might think they are good to have, but they might bother him as he grows older.

I know we have taken longer to answer your question about the baby than you might have hoped. But it was such an unusual request. Your daett and I spoke at length about the matter last night with Joe and Miriam. We think, first of all, that no one in the community would be interested in adopting the child. Second, it might not be a wise thing to even ask the community. I don't want to say more, but I'm sure you can imagine how things might appear. Joe and Miriam have agreed with us that the best solution would be to invite your friend Teresa to come here to visit. Has she ever considered joining the faith since she so admires our way of life?

I know that's not quite what you asked, but we would be more than willing to have her come. This would remove her from her present surroundings, which from what you say is not the best. After the birth of the child, perhaps Teresa would be better able to decide whether to return or place the child up for adoption with an Englisha couple.

There is always the possibility that someone from the community would wish to adopt the child once they know Teresa. But we can make no promises. I trust you've been straightforward with her so she won't have false hopes.

I wish there was an easy answer to all of this, but I'm sure you know there isn't. Life is hard, Susan, for us as well as for others. We can only seek to obey Da Hah and follow His will.

Our hearts and home are open to you and to your friend, should she desire to come.

Sincerely, your mamm, Anna

Susan stared out of the window.

"Not good news, it appears," Laura said, coming to stand beside her.

"No," Susan said. "But not unexpected. They've offered to let Teresa come and stay with them for a visit, but they won't ask the community about the adoption."

"Do you want me to break the news to Teresa?"

"No," Susan said. "I'd better do it. Perhaps after work I'll go."

"Why don't you go now and get it over with? You can make it back in time for the lunch hour rush."

"Are you sure?" Susan looked up at Laura.

"Yes. Go now and you'll be back sooner."

"I'll rush as fast as I can," Susan said, taking the letter with her. "It might be best if Teresa read the letter herself."

"Please help me, Lord," she prayed as she crossed the street with the flow of people at the light and hurried down the side streets. "Help us find a way out of this mess."

Susan paused when she arrived at the apartment. The street was empty and seemed a little cleaner today. The yard, though, had been untouched, debris still thrown everywhere.

Crossing the uncut grass, Susan knocked and then pushed the door open and went up the rough steps. No one hollered a greeting.

"Hellooo!" Susan called from the top of the stairs. Silence greeted her.

"Hello!" she said again, this time a little louder.

The door was open, so Susan went in. She heard a rustle from the bedroom.

"Teresa?" Susan called.

"I'm in here," came a voice from behind the closed curtain.

"Shall I come in?" Susan asked.

"Yes," Teresa said.

Susan stepped inside. Teresa lay on the bed dressed in a worn, dark-brown nightgown, the edges frayed, the front bulging over her swollen abdomen.

"Are you okay?" Susan asked as she sat down on the bed.

"I don't think it will be as long as the doctor says." Teresa looked up, her face pained.

"The baby isn't due until December, right?"

"I think the doctor was wrong!" Teresa grimaced.

"Are you having pains now?"

"Sort of."

"Maybe it's false labor," Susan said, stroking her arm. "*Mamm* had nine of us. And my sisters—all eight have babies. Sometimes it seems like the baby's coming, but it really isn't."

"Did you hear from your parents?"

Susan was silent, not meeting her eyes.

"You have a letter from them?" Teresa's face lit up.

Susan nodded.

"It's not good news, though. I can tell from your face."

Susan's words tumbled out. "They've invited you to come and have the baby there, Teresa. Here is the letter if you want to read it yourself."

Teresa didn't move her hand when Susan held out the pages. She shook her head. "I'll only go if it says someone will take my boy. And it doesn't say that, does it?"

"No, it doesn't," Susan said quietly.

Teresa stared at the wall. "Why would God do this to me? Doesn't He care? I know I don't have much to offer Him. In fact, I have nothing to offer Him. But He's God! He can do anything. Does He only give things to good people?"

"He cares about you!" Susan took Teresa's hand. "He cares even more than Laura and I do, and we care a lot. That's why we want to help you. Why won't you even consider their suggestion?"

"You mean go to the Amish myself?" Teresa said. "But they won't want me there. If they would just take my baby, that would be enough."

"Teresa, they've invited you. If you want there to be a chance for your baby in the Amish community, you're going to have to go about it the way *Mamm* and *Daett* are suggesting."

Teresa climbed out of bed and moved to the kitchen. She leaned against the table and lowered herself into a chair.

"Would they?" Teresa asked. "Really?"

"Would they what?"

"Would the Amish take me into their community?"

"That's what the letter says," Susan said, fumbling for the paper in her pocket.

"No." Teresa shook her head. "You don't understand. Can I become Amish?"

"Why yes, Teresa," Susan said. "Of course you can. *Mamm* also mentioned that option. But it would be very hard."

A light played in Teresa's eyes before she looked away. "You know I'm not pure. I've done so much wrong in my life. I have faith that holy people would take my child, but I'm not sure they would take me." Teresa reached for Susan's hands. "Would they love me?"

"Teresa!" Susan gathered her into a hug. "I love you, don't I?"

The two held each other for long moments until Teresa said, "I'll go if you'll come with me."

Susan hesitated. "You really want to go home with me?" She held Teresa at arm's length and looked into her eyes.

"If you come with me," Teresa repeated, her face beaming. "Maybe it's something I've always wanted and just didn't know I did."

"It would be lovely," Susan said. "You could meet my parents. You could have the baby there. And you could watch your son grow up in the community."

"Oh, Susan!" Teresa exclaimed. "Can that really happen? Then I wouldn't have to give the baby up, would I? It would be the best of both worlds."

Susan took a deep breath. Was this going to set poor Teresa up for even more disappointment? Becoming Amish was very difficult. Teresa might not be able to adjust. Susan sighed and realized that was something neither she nor Teresa could know until she tried.

"Looks like we'd better start planning our trip," Susan said, sitting down beside Teresa.

"It will be like going to heaven before I die," Teresa said, her eyes shining.

Chapter Thirty-six

✛

Susan rushed back to the bakery, even running at times, catching her breath while she waited at the red lights. It had taken longer than usual, but Laura would understand. Who would have thought things would turn out this way? She opened the bakery door and let out a deep breath. "Whew!" she said to Laura, who had turned to see who had come in.

Susan slipped on her apron, washed up, and then joined Laura behind the counter, offering a quick, "Sorry, it took longer than I thought." Laura nodded and the two worked steadily as the lunch crowd surged in for the next forty-five minutes.

When there was finally a let-up, Laura said, "Let's get something to eat ourselves before someone else comes in. You can fill me in on the news. I hope you could talk some sense into Teresa's head."

"I'm still trying to absorb what happened," Susan said, following Laura to the kitchen.

"I take it there's good news?" Laura pulled meat and cheese from the refrigerator.

"I guess so. Teresa wants to go Amish."

"She wants to 'go Amish'? Do you think that's even possible?"

Susan shrugged. "*Mamm* made the suggestion in her letter, but it will be very hard. Not impossible though. People have done it before."

"Now that's a strange twist of events," Laura declared. "Did you suggest it?"

"No," Susan replied. "That would have been the last thing I would have thought of. Like I said, even though *Mamm* mentioned it, I didn't

249

take the suggestion seriously. I don't think *Mamm* did either. Teresa came up with the idea on her own. Which is *gut*. Teresa will need all the resolution she can find in the days ahead. If I had talked her into the plan, it might have made things worse."

"Amish!" Laura mused. "I guess it might work. You never know. Do you think Teresa will be welcomed into the community? She doesn't exactly fit the Amish profile."

"That seemed to be Teresa's biggest concern, but I don't think it's a problem. The Amish judge a person's current actions as much as their past. What concerns me more than anything is Teresa's high ideals. She thinks being Amish is almost heavenly. She doesn't seem to realize the Amish aren't perfect either."

"That could be a problem," Laura agreed. "There's no heaven on this earth, anywhere we go."

"Laura, there's one more thing…"

"What's that?"

"She won't go unless I go with her."

Laura was silent for a minute. "You already planned on going sometime, so you will go with her, won't you?"

"I think I have to. I keep telling her how I'd do just about anything to help her. So how can I say no?"

"When are you leaving?"

"I don't know. Maybe next week," Susan said as she followed Laura out to the front with their sandwiches.

"That soon?"

"The sooner the better, I think. We have good midwives in the community. And this way the clinic doesn't have to be burdened with the hospital costs."

"How is she feeling?" Laura asked. "She's not due until December, so you don't have to worry about her going into labor on the train."

"It was Teresa's idea as much as mine," Susan said. "She can't wait now that's it's decided. I know my head is still spinning from the suddenness of it. Any advice you have is welcome."

"I don't have any, really," Laura said. "You seem to be doing well enough by yourself. You will have your hands full, that's for sure. You probably never thought your adventure to the *Englisha* world would end up like this."

"I didn't," Susan agreed. "I guess it will be worth it if I can really help Teresa."

"Will you be coming back?" Laura asked.

Susan hesitated. Finally she said, "I don't know. I've been delaying a decision about going for a visit. But going for and with Teresa, I may have to stay. At least until she's settled, that is."

"It may be difficult, you know. You could be asked to stay for her. That might be a big sacrifice."

"Yes. But maybe that's why God brought me here in the first place," Susan replied. She then grinned and added, "But, hey! I have my driver's license now. If I decide I want to come back, I'll just buy a car and be on my way!"

"That's hard to imagine!" Laura laughed.

"I think so too," Susan said. "It's hard to believe I even have a license! But then I look and it's right here in my purse as sure as the sun is shining!"

They ate their sandwiches then, each wrapped in her own thoughts.

"Well, I'm relieved about Teresa's situation, that's all I can say," Laura finally said. "This could have turned out quite differently."

After another few moments of silence, Laura spoke again.

"Susan, I've been meaning to ask you something…and feel free to say no if it's too much."

Susan tilted her head. "What is it?"

"Well, the holidays are such an important time of year for the bakery…and I was wondering if you'd consider baking some Amish items for the shop before you leave. And perhaps suggesting some decorations. Amish ones. That would be so neat—and different. I think the customers would like it."

Susan's face shone. "Of course I will! Even if it means staying longer. It would be fun."

Laura was smiling now. "Oh, that's so good of you. Do you have any suggestions?"

Susan shrugged. "There are several good possibilities. Russian tea cakes are an Amish specialty. And buckeyes of course. Peanut brittle. Rocky road cookies. Party mix and turtles. How do those sound?"

Laura laughed. "Wonderful! You're an angel. That's more than enough, and will draw in crowds of people I'm sure. This is so good of you."

"I'll be more than glad to help," Susan said. "And for decorations I can color angels and trumpets. Maybe shepherds. Hang them around on the ceiling. That's what Amish school children do."

Laura beamed over the possibilities.

The door opened behind them, and Susan jumped up to serve the customer.

"I'll take a dozen assorted doughnuts," the man said. "You can just mix them up."

Susan grabbed a box and filled it with an assortment.

He paid with cash and left with the box under his arm.

"Did you know that man?" Laura asked.

Susan shook her head. "Should I have?"

"I don't know. He looked familiar, that's all."

"After a while, I think they all look familiar," Susan said. "Laura, are you sure you can find someone to take my place when I leave?"

"Oh, I'll find help. Whoever it is won't be as good a worker as you are, but I'll be all right. I've so enjoyed having you here."

"And I've enjoyed working for you, Laura. You didn't have to hire me even though your sister asked. But you did, and I'm glad."

"That reminds me. Bonnie called yesterday. She asked about you."

"That was nice."

"She thinks the world of you, Susan. And her children love you. Not always an easy thing to accomplish—with other people's children."

"He's the sweetest boy, Enos is," Susan said. "I couldn't help but love him."

"Robby, on the other hand…" Laura started.

"Oh, don't be so hard on Robby," Susan said. "He'll come around. You've done a good job with him. God will reach Robby. Your son has a good heart. I don't know what I would have done without him!"

"He's told me how much he enjoys and appreciates you, Susan."

Both women were tearing up. Laura finally said, "This is silly. You're not leaving yet. It's too soon for goodbye."

Susan nodded and wiped her eyes with a dishtowel. "Shall I start washing up in back?

"Yes, that's a good idea. That is, until another customer comes in. I'll help you maybe get at the Christmas decorations?"

They walked back together. Susan turned on the hot water in the sink, while Laura scraped dishes. The front door opened minutes later, and Laura left to wait on the customer. "I'll call if I need help," she said over her shoulder.

Susan followed the routine of a hundred washings before, scrubbing hard where the pastry dough had hardened on the metal bowls.

Laura returned and worked on the counters. The bell over the door signaled another customer, and she went to take her order.

By closing time Susan had the last dish and mixing bowl clean. She had found the recipes she needed, filling in the rest from memory.

"Sorry I couldn't help you clean up more," Laura said when Susan walked out to the counter. "I had just enough customers to keep me from coming back."

"Don't worry," Susan assured her. "I was okay, and now things are clean so we can both go home happy."

"I'll see you tomorrow then," Laura said.

Susan slipped out of her apron, taking one last look around before heading upstairs. *I'm going home soon. There is no question about it now.* She had mixed emotions about it, but one thing was certain: *Mamm* and *Daett* could see for themselves that she had not been defiled. As she sat down to eat her supper of leftovers, thoughts of home kept running through her head. Soon she would be eating with *Daett* at the head of the table and *Mamm* sitting across from her. How *gut* it would be to hear *Daett's* prayers again. The German words she'd heard from childhood and could almost repeat by heart. She swallowed hard.

Darkness had fallen outside, but the streets glowed as the streetlights came on. Soon she would see darkness again—*real* darkness. The sky would be sprinkled with stars that actually twinkled. And the moon, so glorious over the woods, rising to proclaim that even the night belonged to *Da Hah*.

A loud pounding came from the stairwell. She sat bolt upright in her chair with alarm. It continued, and she hurried to the window to look out. A girl was at the door, wrapped in a thick black coat. Her face was hidden from view.

Susan ran down the steps and jerked open the door.

"Oh, thank you!" Teresa said, plunging inside with relief.

"Teresa!" Susan exclaimed.

"I'm sorry to disturb you so late!" Teresa gasped, sitting down on the steps.

"Is someone after you?" Susan asked.

"No."

"Are you okay?"

"Can we go upstairs?" Teresa asked as she wrapped her arms around herself. "I need to sit down and get warm."

"Do you want a blanket?" Susan asked, leading the way, her hand holding Teresa's arm. "You're shivering."

Teresa nodded.

Susan took her to the couch and then went into the bedroom for a quilt. She wrapped it around Teresa's shoulders. "Is that better?"

"Yes, thank you," Teresa said, her teeth chattering.

"So what happened?"

"I got scared thinking about what I planned to do," Teresa said.

"Why?" Susan asked. "Are you changing your mind?"

"No, but I was afraid it was all a dream. I wanted to be close to you. Mom came home early tonight, and I told her about my plans. It nearly broke her heart. You know, the idea that I would be leaving."

"I wondered what your mom was going to say. I knew she'd miss you. But I was hoping she'd give you her blessing."

"Well, that's partly it," Teresa said, her eyes on Susan's face. "Mom cried. She hugged and kissed me, and then she told me to run over here at once. She said she didn't want to think too long about this or she might not be able to let me go. Can I stay with you until we leave? If I stay with Mom, I'm afraid she won't let me go or I'll be too scared to go."

"Of course," Susan assured her. "We can talk to Laura about it tomorrow. I don't think she will object. Are you hungry? Surely you have to be after that long walk."

"Starved!" Teresa said, looking around. "You have it so beautiful up here, Susan."

"Well, it's Laura's apartment," Susan said. "We need to get you some food. I was just having leftovers. Does that sound okay to you?"

"Of course!" Teresa said, looking at the food on the table. "Meat and potatoes, gravy, and pecan pie? I don't think I've ever eaten so well."

"I guess I'm used to good cooking." Susan smiled and prepared a plate for Teresa. *Already Teresa looks a little better. There is color in her cheeks,* Susan thought. *She's not shaking so much under the blanket. To come here in that cold and being so pregnant, it must have taken a lot of effort. Teresa must have been really determined.*

Susan set the hot plate in front of Teresa and sat down. They both hesitated a moment, and then Susan bowed her head to pray, and Teresa bowed her head too.

When Susan said, "Amen," Teresa looked up. "Will we pray over meals like this in Amish country?"

"A lot more than that," Susan said. "*Daett* will pray before and after meals and sometimes before we go to bed."

"I've never heard a man pray except on TV."

"Not even in church?" Susan asked.

"I've never been to church," Teresa said. "Except for what I've seen on TV, and that's not really church."

"Then you have plenty of new experiences in front of you," Susan said.

Teresa ate quietly, seeming lost in her thoughts.

"Can we leave tomorrow?" Teresa asked when Susan looked her way.

"I don't think so," Susan said. "I have to help out in the bakery for a few days yet. But we'll go as soon as possible. I'll tell you what. We'll talk with Laura about that tomorrow."

Teresa nodded. "How will you let your parents know we're coming?"

"I'll write," Susan told her. "Or better yet, I'll call my sister Edna's place if there isn't time for a letter to arrive. There's a public telephone near their mailbox."

Teresa finished her plate of food, and Susan cleared the table.

"Thank you so much!" Teresa said, pushing away from the table.

"Do you want to go to bed now?" Susan asked. "I only have one bed, but it's big enough for both of us."

"Even with me...like this—so huge?"

Susan laughed. "I think so. Help yourself to what you need. The bathroom is over there," she said, pointing.

Teresa left, and Susan finished kitchen chores.

Finally Teresa came out of the bathroom. "I'm really tired, Susan. Do you mind if I go to bed now?"

"I don't mind one bit," Susan told her. "I hope you sleep soundly. I'll try not to wake you when I come to bed."

The rustling in the bedroom soon ceased, and Susan finished washing the dishes, drying them, and putting them in the cupboards. She walked over to the front window and looked out on the street. All seemed the same, the traffic in the usual quiet roar and a few people out walking.

It's gut *that I'm leaving this place,* she decided. *The time spent with Laura and Robby has been a blessed season, but Teresa's situation and needs are definitely* Da Hah's *doings. Teresa's like a shining torch leading the way back home.*

"Keep us safe, Lord," Susan whispered to the sky as she wiped her eyes. "For Teresa and the baby's sake, and for the sake of her faith. She may not want much out of life, but already she has moved mighty mountains."

Chapter Thirty-seven

✦

Susan dreamed she was at home, lying on her bed late at night, listening to a vicious autumn thunderstorm. The window went white with blinding sheets of lightning, filling the air with crackling hisses. She held her hands over her ears as the booms of thunder rolled over the house. Rain drenched the old window panes, the water running down in rivers. The wind heaved against the wooden siding with each gust. The bed was even shaking. *How can that be?* she wondered. *This is only a thunderstorm. No…wait…*

Susan screamed and sat bolt upright in bed.

"It's me, Susan!" Teresa said, her voice hoarse. "Remember? I'm staying here for the night. Are you okay?"

"Oh!" Susan inhaled deeply. "Did I just scream?"

"Yes! I suppose I frightened you. I was shaking you, trying to get you to wake up!"

"I was dreaming," Susan said. "Are you okay? Did you hear something on the street?"

Teresa groaned. "I think the baby is coming!"

"The baby!" Susan exclaimed and jumped out of bed. She turned on the light and looked at Teresa. "But it's not time yet!"

"I know, but he's coming!" Teresa shielded her eyes with one hand while the other clutched her stomach.

"Are you sure it's not a false alarm?" Susan asked.

"I don't know, but the pains are coming right regular. Just like they told me they would," Teresa said.

"I have to go down to the bakery and call Laura!" Susan grabbed her coat. "I'll be right back. You'll be okay until I get back, won't you?"

Teresa nodded and laid back down.

Susan hurriedly took the steps one at a time and made her way into the bakery office where the phone was. She switched on the light and quickly dialed Laura's number. After five rings, the answering machine came on. She hung up and dialed again.

"Hello," a sleepy sounding Laura answered.

"Laura, it's Susan! Teresa came over this evening. I was going to wait to tell you the whole story in the morning, but she thinks she's in labor. And I think it's the real thing."

"How far apart are her contractions?" Laura asked.

"She said they're regular, but I didn't time them. Should I call an ambulance?"

"You could, but I live so close. Wait until I get there. I'll come as fast as I can. Keep her calm until I arrive. Okay?"

"Okay. Thank you!" Susan hung up the phone, turned off the office light, and hurried back upstairs. Teresa was still lying on the bed, her breath coming in gasps.

"That was a big one!" Teresa said. "I don't think it will be long now."

"Laura's on her way." Susan ran her hand over Teresa's forehead. "I think babies take a while to come. I sure hope we get to the hospital in time. I've never delivered a baby."

"You have eight sisters," Teresa reminded. "And don't the Amish have their babies at home?"

"*Yah,*" Susan said. "But I've never been at a baby's birth. *Mamm* takes care of that, and a midwife comes..."

"Then this might be your first time! Mine too!" Teresa's face contorted again and she moaned.

Babies do take a while, don't they? Yah... *most of the time, but we never know what's going to happen.* Susan directed her thoughts heavenward. *Lord, please help Teresa!*

"Are you praying?" Teresa asked.

Susan nodded.

A big smile covered Teresa's face. "Someone is praying for me while my baby is being born. Now I know for sure that God is good! And He will help me in my new life ahead. You are still taking me to Amish country, aren't you? Even if my son is born here?"

"Of course!" Susan said. "If that's what you want."

"Yes, more than ever," Teresa said.

"Then let's get you ready to go to the hospital, okay?"

"I think I'd better go like this—just putting my coat over the nightgown you loaned me."

"Okay," Susan agreed. "Do you want to sit out in the kitchen until Laura arrives?"

"It might be better," Teresa said. "Walking around is supposed to help."

Susan helped her out of bed, guiding her to the kitchen. They heard a door open below them, followed by hurried steps coming up.

"Laura's coming!" Susan said. "Let me help with your shoes."

Susan was on one knee when Laura rushed in.

"How regular and often are the contractions?" Laura asked.

"I don't know," Teresa said. "I know they hurt a lot."

"I'd judge about every three minutes," Susan said, standing up. "That's about how long between the ones she's had since I've been awake."

"Let's go then." Laura helped Teresa up, and Susan followed them downstairs. Together they helped Teresa into the backseat. Susan slid in beside her. Laura got in and took off down the empty streets, going as fast as she dared.

"I'm sorry about getting everybody up at this time of the night," Teresa said and gasped as another contraction came.

"Babies have their own timing," Laura said, watching Teresa in the rearview mirror. "It's nothing you can help or should feel badly about."

Five minutes later Susan saw a blue hospital sign. Laura turned down a long driveway.

"Almost there!" she said. "How are you doing back there?"

"About the same," Teresa answered.

Parking near the emergency doors, Laura went inside while Susan helped Teresa out of the car.

"You don't know how much this means to me," Teresa whispered. "The two of you taking care of me in the middle of the night."

"We're glad to help," Susan said. "Just think about your son right now, okay?"

Laura reappeared at the hospital entrance. The automatic doors into the emergency room opened moments later, revealing a wheelchair being pushed by a white-clad attendant.

The attendant parked the chair next to the car and reached out to help Teresa into the wheelchair. "Are you doing okay, ma'am?" the attendant asked.

Teresa nodded and lowered herself with the attendant's help.

"Will you stay with me?" Teresa asked Susan, clutching her hand.

"If they let me," Susan said.

"That's a great idea," Laura said.

The attendant and Teresa disappeared through the ER doors.

"Let's talk with the front office," Laura said, holding open the door. Susan entered, and followed her over to the desk.

"Excuse me," Laura said. "The young lady in labor who was just admitted has requested that one of us be with her."

"That shouldn't be any problem," the girl said. "I'll take you back now."

"Just give us a minute." Laura took Susan aside. "Do you want me to stay with you? Or I can wait out here. Or we can take turns if you get sleepy."

Susan shook her head, "There can't be much to do, and you have responsibilities at the bakery. Go back home and get some sleep."

"If you have any qualms, I can stay. I can even go back and try to get Teresa's mother if you think that's wise."

Susan shook her head, "Birthing babies comes most every day in the community. I think we should wait until after the baby is born before we contact Teresa's mother. They had kind of a rough parting tonight."

"Then you'll call me when the baby's born?" Laura said. "You have my cell number."

"I'll let you know," Susan assured her.

"Oh," Laura said. "Why didn't Teresa call me from the pay phone close to her place? She had my cell number. I can't imagine why the girl walked all the way over to your apartment at this time of the night while starting labor."

"She didn't," Susan said. "She came last night before the labor started. Teresa's mom is taking her leaving pretty hard. I guess her mother thought Teresa should get out of the house before she changed her mind and tried to get Teresa to stay."

"Then Teresa shouldn't go back there before she leaves with you. But don't worry, she can stay with us at the house for a few weeks at least."

"Perhaps that might be the best decision," Susan said.

"First, we have to get this baby safely into the world. I'll be praying for Teresa, the baby, and you."

Susan tried to smile. She waved one last time as Laura went through the doors, then turned to the receptionist who was standing behind her, waiting.

After a brief walk down a hall, the girl said, "Here we are."

"Do I just go in?" Susan hesitated.

The girl nodded, "I called back and told them you were coming."

Susan pushed open the door and stepped inside. Teresa lay on the bed breathing hard and draped in white sheets. A weak smile spread across her face.

Susan went over to Teresa's side and took her hand. The nurse on the other side of the bed gave her a quick nod.

"It's almost time," Teresa said, her brow sweaty. "I told you the baby was coming!" She tried to laugh.

The door opened and the white-clad doctor came in, his face cheerful for this time of the night. Then Susan realized he was obviously on duty and this was like day to him.

"Well, well," he said, "so are we ready to deliver, young lady?"

"I don't know," Teresa moaned. "I think so."

"I think so too," the doctor said a moment later. "In fact, you're quite ready. When the next contraction comes, you push hard. Okay?"

"Okay," Teresa said, her voice quavering.

Susan held Teresa's hand as the doctor and nurse worked, wiping

Teresa's brow as another contraction began. Teresa pushed and cried out at the same time.

After the second attempt, the doctor said, "We're almost there! Do you know the gender of your baby? "

"A boy," Teresa gasped as another contraction hit and she pushed as hard as she could.

Susan watched in awe. She had been close by with several deliveries at home, but this was the first time she'd actually seen a baby being born.

Before she or Teresa could speak, the doctor took the baby as it left the birth canal and handed it to the nurse for cleaning. "Well, you were right. A boy it is!"

"Oh, Susan!" Teresa whispered, as the baby's cries filled the room. "My son has been born."

Susan nodded, not trusting her voice.

"And he's going to be Amish," Teresa said.

"You are also, don't forget," Susan said, squeezing Teresa's hand.

Teresa nodded.

"Would you like to hold him?" The nurse brought over the newborn boy.

Teresa's face glowed and her arms reached out. "Yes, I would!"

"What's his name?" the doctor asked.

"He's going to be Amish," Teresa said. "He'll need an Amish boy's name."

"Amish, eh?" the doctor said with a small laugh. "Well, let's see. You could call him Harrison Ford. But that's not really Amish, is it? What about Samuel? That sounds like a good Amish name."

"Is it?" Teresa looked at Susan.

"It's a very *gut* Amish name," Susan said.

"Then his name is *Samuel*," Teresa said, her face beaming. "My little Amish Samuel."

Chapter Thirty-eight

The motorboat rocked in the slight waves, the shoreline far behind them. Susan clutched the sides of the boat and made the effort to relax.

"I'm not going to drown you!" Robby promised with a laugh. "You can be thankful I didn't take you out on a sailboat."

Susan looked up at the sweep of the stars, more visible here than in the city. "You still have memories of me driving on your mind," she said. "I don't trust you not to pay me back."

"A sweet fellow like me?" Robby said. "Why would I have killing you on my mind?" He grinned.

"You know why. All those scares I gave you," she said. "You could capsize the boat, dump my body into the sea, save yourself, and no one would ever know."

Robby laughed as he took in the open water.

Susan pointed at a low cluster of lights in the distance. "What is that?"

"A ship. Probably a freighter," he said.

"I can't see anything but lights," Susan said. "How can you tell?"

"Because I've seen them many times before," he said. He was smiling in the dim light while standing at the wheel of the boat.

Tears suddenly sprang to Susan's eyes, and she turned away.

"Are you really leaving?" Robby asked as he guided the boat into a wake between large waves.

Susan ignored the question, trying to think of something else to talk about. Leaving was a subject that brought tears. Baby Samuel was doing well, but Laura still wanted them to wait until Teresa had grown stronger before making the long trip. As much as Susan was looking forward to going home again, leaving Robby and his mother would create a sizable hole in her heart.

"Why are the waves picking up?" Susan finally asked, looking at him again.

"They're coming from the freighter," he said. "She's a big one."

Susan stood up and braced herself against the increased rocking.

"Have you ever wanted to go far away—like to China or maybe to the South Sea islands?" she asked. "Spend time sitting under coconut trees, or walking sandy beaches, or looking at the coral that goes all the way to the bottom of the ocean? They say the waters are bluish-colored, and clear as crystal."

"You're such a romantic!" he said. "Have you nothing better to do than dream?"

"I work in a bakery, and I'm about to head back to the Amish community I've always known. Wouldn't you dream too if you were me?"

"I suppose so," he said. "I do plenty of dreaming myself, believe me. I keep thinking you will change your mind at the last minute and stay."

"I have my reasons for going back," she said. "And don't think they are all noble, either. Teresa—she's the noble one, with her head filled with thoughts of how wonderful it will be to be among the Amish."

"Will it be?" he asked.

"All my life I was told it was, and I believed it. Then Thomas popped the bubble. It hasn't been the same since."

"So you might come back here?" he asked.

"Maybe…but I really don't know. It might be hard to go back and settle down there knowing I left all this behind. What do you think? Will I come back?"

"How would I know? I've never been Amish." He paused to turn the wheel. "Honestly, though, I'd say you have a high chance of staying and working it out with that boyfriend of yours. You see the negative things about the Amish world you grew up in. I see the downside of life here. It's not all it's cracked up to be either."

"Robby, do you really believe that?"

"Life here is not all motorboats and car drives," he said, gazing at the sea.

"Or watching the moon rise over the ocean?"

"So you haven't forgotten that?" He took the boat through another wave.

"How could I forget that, Robby?" she said. "That was the first wonderful thing you did for me."

"Well," he said with a smile, "you've sure been nice to have around."

"You puzzle me, Robby. You can be so nice sometimes, but then so were Thomas and then Duane. Thomas betrayed me and Duane went into hives just because I fixed him supper. You men are so hard to figure out!"

He laughed again. "You never really loved Duane. Admit it, Susan."

"Okay," she agreed. "He was nice, and I wanted to see what love would be like out here in the *Englisha* world. But I wasn't trying to play him, Robby."

"Did he ever kiss you?"

"That's none of your business," she said with sly smile.

"Come on now, 'fess up."

"Robby, quit it! This is not like you at all. I'd almost think you're jealous."

"Maybe I am," he said. "It's not hard to be jealous over someone like you, Susan. You're quite a woman."

"Now you're making me turn red, and it's not even warm out here."

"Well, you are," he insisted. "And you don't have to be embarrassed about it. Didn't that Thomas fellow ever tell you so?"

Susan nodded as she looked out over the waves. They were calmer now, and the lights of the freighter were nearly lost in the distance.

"Yes, he did. Lots of times. And look where that got me."

"He'll be seeing his mistake before long, mark my words."

"I don't think so," she said.

"Ah," he said, "there's hope in your voice. I can hear it."

"Come on, Robby! Do we have to talk about this? This is our last night together for a long time…maybe forever."

"I'm sorry." He stared off into the distance for a long time. Then a smile crept across his face. "I didn't bring you out here to have a fight, Susan. The Lord knows I have enough of those already."

"So why did you bring me out?" she asked.

"To keep my promise. And to say goodbye, I guess…to show you what you've meant to me."

"Robby, I've had a grand time with you, and you've been ever so nice. But we will always be just friends. You do know that, don't you?"

"Yes," he said. "Even when I've wished it could be more, I knew it wouldn't be. For more reasons than one. But that didn't stop me from wanting to help you. And this is my attempt to do something nice for you."

"Well, you've succeeded, Robby!" she said. "I didn't do much for you though. You're the one who gave me driving lessons and drove me around when I needed to go somewhere."

"And you are the one who helped me find faith. Isn't that a little better than driving lessons?"

"Yes, it is. But I don't see what I did to give you faith. Does this mean you're going to church again?"

"I went last Sunday. Don't discount the part you played. You inspired me, Susan, with your devotion to God, your fun-loving ways, and your sincerity. Granted, I might have gone back to church eventually, but you helped make it sooner than later."

"I'm glad," Susan said. "And thank you for the boat ride tonight. It's beautiful out here—almost as beautiful as the sky at home but in a different sort of way."

"I'll have to come visit you sometime," he said. "I'd like to see what Amish is all about."

Susan laughed. "You're welcome anytime. And your aunt lives close by, so you'd have a place to stay."

"It would be nice to see my nephews again," he said. "I haven't seen them in ages."

Robby cut the motor and let the boat drift, the silence broken only by the lap of waves against the sides of the boat. The stars stretched all the way to the horizon, their glory broken only when light and water came together.

"You deserve a kiss for this," she said. "I've never had a brother to kiss."

"Ah, so the princess would kiss the frog under the moonless starry sky? I promise you, I won't turn into a prince."

"Robby, hush." She walked up to him, trying to keep her balance on the boat.

He smiled and turned his cheek toward her. She drew him close, giving him a playful smack.

"There!" She let him go. "You have now been properly thanked."

"More than properly thanked!" he said. He restarted the motor and pointed the boat to shore.

"Look at the city lights and how they mix in with the Christmas lights," she said. "They're beautiful against the night sky."

"They are," he agreed. "But not as beautiful as where the water and stars meet."

"But the city has its own glory," she insisted. "Look at the blend of nature and man, that bubble of colorful light against the night sky. It brings to mind a savage wrestling of man against the darkness, warring against it, fighting to keep it at bay."

"You are a poet tonight." He laughed. "I sure will miss having you around."

"Hey, by the way, how are your girl problems coming along?"

"I wasn't sure you were interested."

"You know I am, Robby! Tell me. Is there someone special?"

He smiled. "There is this woman at church. I saw her on Sunday. I've known her since grade school, but we lost touch."

"There you go!" she said. "Treat her like a princess, and that's all she'll need."

"Look! There's another ship," Robby pointed out.

"It's come to bid me farewell."

"You sure have a wild imagination," Robby said, as they watched the ship pass by.

"It's so beautiful," she whispered when the lights had faded away.

"Susan, when are you leaving?" he asked moments later.

"As soon after Christmas as Teresa and the baby are strong enough. Your mom brought Teresa's mother over yesterday for a few hours. So I think goodbye has been said. We'll make our minds up this week sometime, and I'll go down to the station and buy two train tickets to the farmlands of Indiana."

"And here we are," he said, bringing the boat into the marina and up to the dock. He cut the engine, jumped out, and tied the boat up. He turned and helped Susan climb out. They walked up to the office to return the boat and then made their way to Robby's car.

"I want to thank you again," she said. "I'll remember this evening for a long time."

"You're welcome," he said as they drove out of the parking lot. "I'll remember it too."

Robby drove to his mother's house and parked in the driveway. When they got out and went inside, they found Laura sitting in the living room.

"Did you two have a good time?" she asked.

"Excellent!" Robby said.

"Is Teresa asleep?" Susan asked.

"She's in the bedroom," Laura told her. "I think she's still awake, but I'm not sure."

"Okay," Susan said. "And how has the baby been?"

"He's been quiet for an hour now."

"I think I'll take a peek," Susan said. "Then I'd better write my parents about our plans. I can call my sister Edna's place once we're on the way and know when we'll arrive."

"Speaking of writing, you have a letter on the kitchen table. From the looks of it, it might be the results of your GED test."

"Oh! I'm not sure I want to open it. What if I didn't pass? That would spoil this wonderful evening I've had with Robby."

"Oh, go ahead! You know you want to open it!" Robby encouraged.

Susan took small steps toward the kitchen table and reached for the letter. She opened it, read a few lines, and then handed it to Laura.

Glancing over the paper, Laura smiled. "You passed! And with a really good grade."

"Yes!" Susan shrieked. "I passed!" She grabbed Robby and gave him a hug. "I passed! I can't believe it."

"Well, you deserved to pass. You studied hard, Susan. Congratulations!" Laura said.

"Yes, way to go!" Robby said.

After a brief pause, Susan said, "It's been a wonderful but long day. I think I'll turn in after I check on Teresa and Samuel. Goodnight!"

"Goodnight, dear!" Laura said.

"Happy dreams of home!" Robby said.

Susan slipped into the living room and stood for a moment in front of the lighted Christmas tree. It was so beautiful and so not Amish. She would always cherish this memory of an *Englisha* Christmas with Laura and her family.

Susan moved up the stairs clutching her test results. She knocked quietly then opened the door to the bedroom. Teresa was asleep. Susan tiptoed up to the crib. Samuel was also fast asleep, lying on his back, his arms spread wide.

"Goodnight, Samuel!" she whispered. "Sweet dreams little boy."

Later, back in her apartment, she pulled out paper and pen to write a letter home.

Dear Mamm *and* Daett,

Christian greetings.

We are all doing well here in Asbury Park and will soon be heading home after Christmas. Thanks so much for your invitation to Teresa. She accepted the offer even before her son arrived, and now baby Samuel is with us. The doctor thinks baby and mother can travel before long.

I plan to buy tickets for all of us soon. I expect it will be by train for most of the way and then by Greyhound. That's how I came to Asbury, and I see no reason to change. Our travel time will be after Christmas, so I hope we can still find tickets even with all the holiday travelers.

Just to warn you, Teresa has gotten it into her head that she wants to become Amish. I told her that would be okay, and that you would approve because you mentioned that in your letter. I hope to see you soon. I will let Edna know by phone once I have our exact arrival time.

My best to you. I love you.

Your daughter, Susan

CHAPTER THIRTY-NINE

Thomas drove his buggy south from his parents' place, taking his time. *Surely Susan will come home over Christmas,* he thought. "When is Susan coming back?" several of his aunts had asked again yesterday during dinner at his grandparents' place. He'd just shaken his head. There was no sense in letting them know he didn't know. They knew he had broken up with Susan, but thankfully not about the reason why or the Sunday evening he'd spent with Eunice. That still appeared to be a secret. Likely the aunts expected his quarrel with Susan to be on the mend. Well, it wasn't. And since he wouldn't see Eunice again, it was time for a talk with Susan.

Even if Susan were home already, he wondered if she'd speak with him. He could wait until Sunday, and see if she paid him any attention at the hymn singing, but that had its own risk. How could one be certain about such matters? And how much time might be wasted trying to figure things out in advance?

A troubling thought raced through his mind. Had Eunice been right about Susan? Had she been living wild while spending her time in the *Englisha* world? Surely she had not. Susan wasn't like that.

He slapped the reins and pushed the fear away. The time had come to be a man and face things. He would apologize and see if amends could be made. He could have asked his *mamm* to obtain Susan's address from her *mamm* so he could write but that wasn't the right way to approach this. Besides, he wasn't a letter writer. He needed to speak to Susan in person.

Up ahead he saw the Hostetler farm surrounded by open fields. He was south of the buildings. He'd brought Susan to this vantage point so many times on Sunday afternoons and evenings. He paused. Susan's bedroom was on the second floor, on the other side of the house. She wouldn't be able to see him approach…if she was even home. The kitchen windows were on this side of the house, so anyone there would see him coming. He moved on. He would have to suffer the indignity of being rejected if that was what awaited him. Susan was worth the effort. He'd been a fool to let her slip away.

Thomas turned into the driveway. He tied Freddy to the hitching post by the barn. He pulled out the buggy blanket and draped it over the horse's back to protect him against the morning chill. He looked around on the short walk to the front door. Menno kept the farm up well for his age, but that would end soon enough. The man was getting old. Thomas reminded himself that instead of having these troubles with Susan, he should have been spending these past weeks making wedding plans and even building Menno and Anna's *dawdy haus*. He noticed there were still the same cracks in the concrete walkway. The green strings of grass that had managed to poke through in summer were now gone. Broken brown stems lay sideways, the roots still clinging to the sparse soil. Stepping over them, he knocked on the front door.

It was opened almost at once by Anna, her white apron tied to her waist.

"Yes, Thomas?" she asked with a smile.

He cleared his throat. "Would Susan be home yet?"

Anna shook her head. "No, she's not home yet."

He let disappointment show. "Won't she be home over Christmas this year?"

"We don't know," Anna said. "I hope to receive a letter from Susan any day now."

"Is there some way I can reach her?" he asked. *I might as well do what can be done,* he figured.

Anna shrugged. "You could write, I suppose. I can give you her address."

Thomas ran the tip of his shoe over the steps, chasing two broken leaves around in circles.

"I'm not much of a letter writer," he admitted.

"I can let Susan know you stopped by when I write to her next," Anna said.

"I really need to speak with her," he persisted. "Does she ever call? Or can I call her from the phone shack?"

Anna's eyes brightened at Thomas's interest. "*Nee,* she has only called Edna once. She writes occasionally, Thomas. It's been awhile since you've talked of Susan. We thought perhaps the relationship was over. But I'm glad to see you're still interested."

"I know I haven't done the best by her lately," he said. "And I'm sorry."

"We all make mistakes," Anna said. "Menno and I would love it if you had a chance to speak with her, but I don't know how it can be done unless you wish to visit her."

He thought for a moment. "Maybe that would be an idea. Can I have her address just in case? I'm not saying I'll go, but I'll consider it."

"Certainly," Anna said. "If you'll step inside, I'll get the address for you."

Thomas followed her inside and closed the door. He stood quietly while Anna went into the living room. Moments later she returned with a piece of paper.

"Here's the address."

"I see," Thomas said, taking the paper and glancing at it. "Thanks. I'll see what I can do."

"Thank you for stopping by," Anna said. "I hope things work out."

Thomas turned to leave, and Anna stood at the door for a moment. When he glanced back after pulling the blanket off Freddy, Anna was gone. Climbing in the buggy, he slapped the reins and drove out.

Is this idea wise? he wondered. *Do I have time to drive all the way into Salem for details on bus fares?* Yah, *I do,* he decided. *Susan is worth the effort.* He turned his horse north toward Salem, pushing Freddy hard.

I will go to see Susan in Asbury Park. The trip will be worth every minute.

Susan should be deeply impressed with his devotion. If he waited until she returned—whenever that might be—the effect wouldn't be the same. She would likely greet him the same as before, with closed doors and snubbed visits.

Thomas drove through the edge of town and parked at the gas

station with a little Greyhound sign hanging in the window. With a firm step he approached the lady at the front desk.

"I'd like to inquire on the bus schedule to Asbury Park, New Jersey," he said.

"Asbury Park, New Jersey," the lady repeated. "Let's see. I can put you on a bus early tomorrow morning that would get you into Asbury Park two days later. How will that work?"

He thought for a moment. "How soon can I leave after Christmas?"

She ran her fingers over the schedule page before answering. "The day after, if you want. So will it be a ticket to and from Asbury Park?"

"Yes," he said, pulling out his billfold. "And I can board the bus in Livonia? Our people do that all the time."

She nodded and printed the ticket.

✦

The slow whine of the Greyhound engine rang in his ears, monotonous and irritating. Thomas slouched lower in his seat, the early morning sun glaring through the window. More sleep was out of the question, which didn't matter anyway. Asbury Park was the next stop.

What a name for a town, he thought. *Is there even a park?* He sighed as he looked out the window. Businesses were visible here and there with residential homes in between. *What a dreary place to live, brightened up,* he supposed, *by the many Christmas lights flickering through the windows of the houses.* Off in the distance a faint sheen of water glimmered. *At least the ocean is close by. That might be interesting.*

Up ahead Thomas saw a large Greyhound sign painted on a building. He reached for his hat in the overhead compartment. He might look strange wearing his Amish-style hat in the big city, but there was nowhere else to put it.

"Asbury Park!" the driver announced over the intercom as he pulled up to the curb. "We only have time to drop off and pick up passengers. No break time, please. If this is not your final destination, please keep your seats."

Thomas grabbed his carry-on bag. Two other men were already in the aisle, and he followed them outside. Several passengers walked out of the station and came toward the bus. Thomas stopped on the street and watched them board. Then he looked around. Traffic was roaring past, and the buildings rose tightly along the street.

So this is where Susan went to get away from me. It certainly looks worse than the idea I had of her perhaps joining the Mennonites. Thomas started walking. Every once in awhile he slowed and stared at the buildings. Suddenly he stopped. Why hadn't he asked for directions to Main Street instead of just setting off? There had to be a better way, and the bus station people would have known about it. He also needed to be able to find his way back. Pulling out a pencil and paper from his bag, he turned and walked back until he could see the bus station. He wrote "10th & Filbert." That should do for directions back.

Thomas stepped to the curb and looked up and down the street. He didn't see anything in traffic that looked like a taxi. Returning to the bus station, he approached the attendant.

"Sir, are there taxis around here?" he asked.

"I can call one for you," the man said. "Where do you want to go?"

"Downtown, on Main Street."

"Then the city bus would be better, son," the man told him. "The bus stop is two blocks north of here. It will take you right downtown for a lot less money."

"Can I come back the same way?" Thomas asked.

"Yes, unless you stay too late. They don't run all night."

"I won't be staying late," Thomas said. "I have to catch the Greyhound bus back home later today."

He left and walked the two blocks. He climbed onto the next bus that arrived. "Will this bus take me to Main Street?" he asked, looking at the paper Anna had given him.

"Yes, we'll come pretty close. You'll have to walk a block. I'll signal you when to get off."

"Thank you," Thomas said. He moved down the aisle and took a seat by the window. He took his hat off and set it in his lap. Leaning back, he watched as they passed building after building. One section of town did look like a large park, he decided. And a beautiful one at that. Wide-open lawns carried a light dusting of snow. Benches were set up under the trees, but no people strolled about. A few Christmas decorations hung on the lamp posts. Did Susan come out here to walk and relax when the weather was nice? Well, he would have to ask her that question—and several others once he found her.

"This is your stop, young man," the driver announced as he pulled up to the curb. "Main Street is a block that way," he said, pointing.

Thomas thanked the man and stepped off the bus.

"Well, Susan!" he muttered out loud. "Here I come."

Walking up the street, he looked for the address. When he found the building, he was surprised to see there were two doors. One appeared to open into a bakery, the other onto a stairway. He knocked on the stairway door, but there was no response. *Maybe Susan works someplace and won't return until evening,* he thought. *If that's the case, I might miss her. The Greyhound bus leaves at nine. I guess I could stay another day, if worse comes to worse. Susan is worth that much effort, and they'd probably let me change my ticket.*

Uncertainly, he walked toward the bakery. Maybe someone there would know about Susan. A cheerful holiday wreath hung on the door and a small Christmas tree was in the window. On the ceiling were strung paper angels and shepherds, not unlike what the Amish school children made. He entered and saw an attractive, middle-aged woman behind the counter. A younger woman was clearing a table. "May I help you?" the woman behind the counter asked.

"Perhaps," he replied. "I'm looking for a Susan Hostetler who apparently lives upstairs. Do you know her?"

"Susan?" the woman repeated. Then noticing the young man's clothes and straw hat, she said, "You wouldn't be Thomas, would you?"

"I am," he said. "Do you know Susan?"

"I'm Laura." She offered her hand. "Susan worked here. We became quite close. She…um…happened to mention you."

"Oh!" he said, plunging right ahead with his next question. "Do you know if she'll be back before this evening? I'd like to speak with her."

"I'm afraid not," Laura said. "She left for home on the train yesterday, taking a friend and her baby with her."

"I see." Thomas said, his disappointment obvious. "Then I missed her."

"Yes, I'm so sorry," Laura said. "How long are you staying?"

"I leave tonight on the nine o'clock bus."

"You're welcome to stay around here if you want. My son, Robby, will be in later. I'm sure he'd like to meet you."

"Robby?" he asked.

"Yes. He and Susan are friends. We love Susan. We're going to miss her if she decides not to come back."

"So Robby was with Susan often?"

"They did seem to hit it off quite well. Susan is a wonderful young woman."

"Thanks," Thomas said, turning to go. "I think I'll look around town until my bus leaves."

"There are nice restaurants on Main Street," Laura said. "And the ocean lies a few blocks east."

"I appreciate the information," Thomas said over his shoulder, already halfway across the room.

"We have some Amish buckeye party mix left," Laura said. "Susan made it. Would you like to have some?"

Thomas paused a moment before saying, "No thanks. I think I should be going."

The young woman standing beside the tables smiled at him.

"Susan is a real nice girl," she told him. "I enjoyed getting to know her."

Thomas nodded, put on his hat, and moved toward the door. It opened before he arrived, and a man came in. A customer, Thomas assumed. He waited until the man passed before stepping out to the street. He turned and walked back the way he came.

His mind was whirling. *What happened to the Susan I knew? She must have really changed to be friends with these people. And she had been making Amish food for them? Maybe I shouldn't have come. I have more questions than before!* "I can't believe this," Thomas said out loud, stopping to look around. "Susan not only lived here, but she has been seeing an *Englisha* man!"

Chapter Forty

✦

Susan sat on the soft seat of the Amtrak train watching the steep grades and valleys of West Virginia's Appalachian Mountains go by. The train climbed the ridges, seeming to cling to the side of the mountain for long stretches before dropping downward again. Baby Samuel was sleeping in Susan's lap, nestling up against her shoulder. Teresa, her face weary, had her seat all the way back in a reclining position.

Christmas was behind them and now their long-planned trip had finally come to pass.

It had been interesting to experience a real *Englisha* Christmas at Laura's.

Susan smiled to imagine if *Mamm* and *Daett* could have seen her standing around Laura's Christmas tree, opening presents, they would have thought for sure they had lost her forever.

She could never tell them how much fun it had been. She had even enjoyed the last minute shopping at the mall, bursting with other last-minutes shoppers.

Back home, *Mamm* and *Daett* would have been gathered around the table having one or two of the older girls and their families over for the big meal. She had missed that, and if she stayed in the *Englisha* world, she would always miss it. Both worlds—the Amish and the *Englisha*—had their own particular delights. If only she could have both.

Jostling the baby only slightly to not awaken him, Susan reclined her seat. Perhaps she could catch a few minutes of sleep before Samuel stirred again. He had been restless all night, but then what could be expected from an infant taken on a long overland trip by two inexperienced girls?

Samuel moved against Susan's chest, and she held still. He rubbed at his closed eyes with his hand, wrinkling his face as if ready to cry. Susan reached for the seat position button but stopped when Samuel settled down. Minutes later he was sleeping again.

Susan closed her eyes and drifted off. She dreamed of open fields, of snow blown in great drifts against a barn door, of struggles to clear a path from the house to the barn, of cows lowing in agony from swollen udders.

She saw her *daett* in front of her, shoveling fast, throwing snow off to the side until the bank was higher than he was. Offering to take her turn, her face wrapped in shawls and mufflers, she felt her fingers becoming colder and colder as she hurled snow. No matter how hard they worked, the wind drove the snow back faster than they could remove it.

"We'll have to get back to the house," her *daett* said. "It's useless trying to reach the barn."

Susan turned to look toward the house, and the way back was as bad as the way forward.

"What shall we do?" she gasped.

Her *daett,* the one who knew all the answers, who never hesitated regardless of the circumstances, sat down in the snow and threw up his hands in despair. She was the one who would have to decide.

"The wind will let up in a bit," she hollered at him. "We can make it then."

He got to his feet, staggering forward, and fell face down in the snow. She took his hand, pulling him upward, but he didn't move. Kneeling beside him, she tried to listen to his breathing, but she couldn't hear anything in the roar of the wind. Great blinding sheets of snow came over the drifts and already covered her *daett's* legs and hands.

"*Mamm!*" she screamed. She sat bolt upright.

Samuel jumped in her arms and bawled at the top of his voice. Beside her, Teresa too had jolted awake.

"What's wrong? Why did you scream?" Teresa asked, frightened.

"I was dreaming," Susan said, rocking Samuel gently as his little voice filled the train car.

Irritated faces turned in their direction, and one younger couple whispered to each other.

We must look like a bedraggled traveling party, Susan thought. *Two young women on the train with a small child, with no husband in sight. And one of us dressed like an Amish girl. Well, that is how it will have to stay.*

Susan's *Englisha* dresses were in the bottom of her suitcase where her *mamm* would never see them. And if she did, Susan hoped she would assume they belonged to Teresa.

Teresa had wanted an Amish type dress for the trip, but Susan didn't think that was the best. It would be *gut* for her *mamm* and *daett* to see Teresa as an *Englisha* girl first. Changes could come later.

"Where are we?" Teresa asked, interrupting her thoughts.

Susan looked at Samuel. He was nestled against her, quiet again. "I'm not sure," Susan said. "The last I knew we were somewhere in the mountains of West Virginia."

"I think we still are," Teresa said, looking out to the window. "How long until we get to Indiana?"

"We'll be getting there late tonight on the bus, which we get on in Cincinnati," Susan said. "The train doesn't go close enough to Salem."

"Susan, do you really think they will want me?" Teresa asked, not for the first time.

Susan reached out and touched Teresa's arm. "Of course they do, Teresa. They invited you."

Teresa still looked worried. "Have you called them?"

"I called from Laura's place. Everything will be fine. I hope *you* like it there. It's quite a change from the city."

"I know I will!" Teresa said. "And I'm sure everyone will like Samuel. He's such a wonderful baby!"

"And you'll love *Mamm* and *Daett*," Susan said. "And the farmhouse we live in is warm, even in the winter. It's old and creaky but cozy."

"I know I'll love the place—and your parents too, of course. They must be wonderful people to have a daughter like you."

"I want you to write your mother as soon as we arrive," Susan said, touching Teresa's arm. "I know she's worried about you."

As silence settled over them, Teresa dropped off to sleep again. Eventually Susan did likewise, having quieted Samuel.

She awoke to see flat land rolling past the window. Teresa was already awake, with Samuel on her lap. He was waving his arms around.

"I fed Samuel," Teresa said.

"Are you hungry?" Susan asked.

Teresa nodded. "Can we go to the diner?"

"It's kind of expensive," Susan said. "But I guess we have no choice. We should have brought more food from the bakery."

They stepped out of their seats, and Susan led the way through the car. Teresa covered the baby's head when they carefully crossed between the cars and were accosted by blowing wind. Susan held the swaying train car doors open until Teresa had passed, laughing above the wild racket of the wheels clanging on the metal tracks.

"I'm surprised Samuel didn't cry," Susan said, once they were seated in the dining car.

"He's a sweet baby," Teresa cooed, gazing at Samuel's face.

"May I help you?" the waiter asked.

"You go first," Teresa whispered.

"Okay," Susan said. "A ham sandwich for me and a glass of water."

"The same thing for me," Teresa said. "Anything will taste good right now," she said to Susan.

A few minutes later the waiter returned with their order.

"Anything else?" he asked.

"No thank you," Susan answered.

They ate slowly, enjoying the view and the food. Afterward, they returned to their seats. They entertained Samuel and talked about their hopes for the days ahead.

By early afternoon the train pulled into the Cincinnati station. Susan led the way through the large depot to the correct baggage belt and collected their luggage. She waved down a taxi on the sidewalk, and with little time to spare they arrived at the bus depot and boarded.

"Wow, this is a different ride," Teresa said, settling into her seat.

"You kind of get spoiled on trains," Susan said. "But we don't have far to go."

Moments later, the bus pulled out of the station, the whine of its engine filling the air. Baby Samuel wrinkled up his face and cried. Teresa rocked him, but he wouldn't quiet down. Susan offered to take him, but she didn't have any better success.

"He doesn't like the bus," Teresa said. "That's got to be what's bothering him. He can't be hungry again. I just nursed him in the cab."

Lifting the baby up to the window didn't help either, so Teresa took him back.

"People are starting to stare at us," Teresa said, desperation in her voice.

"I think the bus is stopping soon," Susan said. "I see a town coming up."

Teresa got up and walked to the back of the bus, and Samuel quieted down. She stayed in the back while a passenger boarded the bus. When they continued on, Teresa walked up and down the aisle with the baby. Susan was ready to offer to take a turn when Teresa slipped back into the seat. Samuel was sleeping. He slept through the next hour until the driver announced over the speaker, "A thirty-minute layover here, ladies and gentlemen. If you wish to get off, you can."

Hungry, the two girls made their way to the small diner by the station where other passengers were also eating. While Teresa held Samuel, Susan ordered sandwiches and chose a seat near an outside window.

"I don't trust bus drivers," she muttered to Teresa. "I like to see the bus while I wait. It would be awful to get stranded this close to home."

A lady Susan recognized from the bus walked up to their table. "You might try rubbing his ears for the baby's crying," she suggested. "That always worked for mine when we traveled on the bus."

"Thank you, ma'am," Teresa said. "I'll try anything!"

"How far are you going?" the lady asked.

"A little beyond Salem," Susan said.

"Ah, Amish country," the lady said. "I should have guessed. Are you both Amish?"

"I am," Susan said. "I'm going back home. Teresa is my friend."

"Visiting?" the lady asked in Teresa's direction.

"I'm planning to join," Teresa said, smiling.

"Oh my!" the lady exclaimed. "Joining…Yes, that will be an adventure indeed."

"I suppose so," Teresa agreed. "But a good one, I hope."

"Well, the best to you," the lady said, patting her arm and moving on.

Teresa watched the lady leave. "Susan, I really want an Amish dress and one of those white head coverings tomorrow. I want to be recognized as Amish."

Susan laughed. "That shouldn't be any problem once we're home."

"Boarding in five minutes!" the bus driver called from outside.

Susan jumped. "Those bus drivers always make me nervous!" Susan said again as she stood up. She reached out and Teresa put Samuel in her arms. "I always think they'll leave without me."

"I doubt if they would," Teresa said, leading the way outside. "You worry too much."

They neared the bus, and Susan paused to speak to the bus driver standing beside the steps.

"Sir," Susan said, "can we be dropped off at Livonia on the other side of Salem? I know it's not a regular stop, but we have folks waiting for us there."

"No problem," he said.

Susan and Teresa boarded the bus and returned to the seats they'd been in. She handed Samuel to Teresa after she settled in her chair. As the bus drove out, Teresa rubbed Samuel's ears. To her amazement he settled down right away.

"It's working!" Teresa whispered. "He's not crying."

"I wonder if it would have worked on the train?" Susan asked. "Our bus stop is coming up in about fifteen minutes, judging from what I see outside."

Teresa rose half out of her seat to look out the window and then sat back.

"I'm so worried," she said.

"They'll like you!" Susan assured her.

The whine of the bus rose and fell around them. Outside the houses moved closer together, and when Susan saw the Livonia town sign go by, she nudged Teresa.

"We're almost there!"

Teresa said nothing, unmoving except for the slight tremble in the hand draped over Samuel.

The bus pulled up to the curb and stopped.

"There they are, standing by the buggy waiting for us!" Susan exclaimed. "See, Teresa? That's *Mamm* and *Daett*."

"He has such a long beard," Teresa replied. "Just like in the movies."

Susan laughed. "This isn't the movies, Teresa. It's the real thing!"

"That's what I'm afraid of." Teresa got to her feet.

"We are only stopping to unload passengers," the bus driver announced. "If this isn't your destination, please stay in your seats."

"Go!" Susan encouraged when Teresa faltered in the aisle.

"I don't know them."

"They'll love you, believe me. It's too late to back out now!"

Teresa moved forward when Susan touched her on the shoulder. She stopped on top of the bus steps, and Susan urged her on again.

Over by the buggy, Susan's *mamm* walked toward them. Then she ran. Susan's *daett*, moving slower, followed.

"*Mamm!*" Susan cried as she was smothered in her *mamm's* arms.

"Susan, you're back!" Anna gushed, stroking her daughter's face.

"*Mamm*, I'm not a *bobli* anymore," Susan said with a smile. "This is Teresa and Samuel."

"Teresa." Anna turned to give her a hug, gently squeezing Samuel between them. "I'm so glad you could come. Susan had such nice things to say about you. And this is little Samuel, *yah?*"

"Yes, my baby!"

Anna reached for Samuel.

Teresa wiped her eyes after she handed Samuel to Anna.

"What have we here?" Menno asked, his voice booming in the evening air. "If it is not my long-lost daughter and her friend!"

"*Daett!*" Susan shook his hand. He clasped her hand in both of his and then turned to do the same with Teresa.

"Come!" Anna said. "We have heating blocks in the buggy, what with the baby and all. We wanted to give you as warm a welcome as possible."

"How thoughtful!" Susan said. "The drive isn't that long for you to go to all the trouble."

"It's nothing," Menno said, still booming. "And it makes the ride more comfortable."

With Anna leading the way and holding Samuel, they walked to the buggy. Handing the baby to Teresa, Anna climbed in and then reached for Samuel again. After Teresa handed him to her, Susan gave her friend a hand at the buggy step, making sure she didn't slip on the climb up. Menno brought their luggage over and loaded it into the back. He climbed in and slapped the lines.

"Get-up, horse," he hollered. "We've got to get these girls home now."

"Make sure your feet are on the bricks," Susan whispered to Teresa, who was sitting snuggly beside her.

"I don't think I'll ever stop crying," Teresa whispered back, her voice choking. "I'm so happy we're here!"

Susan said nothing, squeezing Teresa's hand under the warm buggy blanket. The lights of the small town could be seen through the buggy's storm front. Christmas lights still twinkled in many of the windows. The familiar beat of horse's hooves on the pavement filled Susan's ears as Teresa snuggled up beside her.

"I've really come home. I know I have," Teresa whispered.

Susan smiled, pressing back the tears.

Discussions Questions

1. As Menno and Anna Hostetler struggle with the pain of Susan's leaving, is Menno correct in insisting that Susan be allowed to find her own way home?

2. Do you think Anna would have gained anything by a trip to Asbury Park to plead with Susan that she return?

3. Do you think Robby secretly desires a deeper relationship with Susan beyond their friendship?

4. Is Susan wise in making cautious choices of *Englisha* clothing and accessories, or should she have taken bold steps into her new lifestyle?

5. Did Menno's troubled state of mind over Susan's absence contribute to the barn fire he started and the hog injury to his grandchild, Jonas? If so, to what degree?

6. Should Menno have allowed Anna to write Susan, advising her to make a visit home due to Jonas's injuries?

7. Do you think Teresa had reasons for the request that her baby be adopted by an Amish person beyond the ones she stated?

8. Did Susan make a wise decision in pursing the purse snatcher?

9. What are your expectations for Teresa as she plans to travel home to the community with Susan? Beyond Susan's *mamm* and *daett*, will she be as welcomed as a newcomer or will the community be suspicious of Teresa?

10. Is Thomas's trip to Asbury Park in pursuit of Susan evidence that he has changed his ways? Will he seek reconciliation with Susan when he returns?

If you enjoyed *Missing Your Smile,* be sure and pick up
the second book in the Fields of Home Series...

FIELDS OF HOME

FOLLOWING
Your
HEART

Jerry
Eicher

Will Susan's return home turn out to be just a visit...or
something more permanent? How will the Amish receive
Teresa...and her son, Samuel? Will Teresa accept the hardships
of the Amish life...or yearn for a return to the big city?

ABOUT JERRY EICHER...

✛

Jerry Eicher's bestselling Amish fiction (more than 350,000 in combined sales) includes The Adams County Trilogy, the Hannah's Heart books, and the Little Valley Series. After a traditional Amish childhood, Jerry taught for two terms in Amish and Mennonite schools in Ohio and Illinois. Since then he's been involved in church renewal, preaching, and teaching Bible studies. Jerry lives with his wife, Tina, and their four children in Virginia.

Visit Jerry's website!
http://www.eicherjerry.com/

Also check out Harvest House Publishers'
Amish Readers' page!
www.amishreader.com